Counterfeit Commoner

KELLE Z. RILEY

Counterfeit Commoner

Copyright © 2022 by E. H. Kelle Zeiher (Riley)

ISBN 978-1-7367811-3-5

Cover Artist (Illustrated Cover): Books Fluent
Cover Arist (Photographic Cover): Ronald J. Rice,
Novel Cover Designs by RJRice Photography

To Thomas Patrick Riley, husband, lover, soulmate, and light of my life.

ACKNOWLEDGMENTS

Writing a novel is hard work. Publishing a novel is even harder work. Without my team of dedicated experts and tribe of writer friends, this work would not have been possible. Special thanks go to:

- Tina Winograd, editor extraordinaire. Your input always makes my work better!
- Connie Leap and Theresa Huber, proofreaders. Thank you for catching errors and providing feedback. Your comments challenged and inspired me.
- Katie Salidas, formatter. Thank you for taking on this task and turning my manuscript into a real book.
- Ron J. Rice, Novel Cover Designs by RJRice Photography, cover designer. Your clear eye and ability to turn my words into evocative images is second to none.
- Laurie White, PA. Thank you for helping me manage the social media aspects of the writer's life and countless other details. I'd be lost without you.
- Special thanks to my beta readers and writer friends, Susan Gibberman, Dyanne Davis, Denise Swanson, Frederica Meiners, and Cheryl Woodson. You are my writer tribe. You inspire, motivate, and help me find my way out of plot corners I've backed into. Thank you for the many helpful discussions and great plot twist ideas!
- Thanks to the rest of my writer tribe, members of CARA; Windy City RWA, GRW, TGN, CWG, KOD, and the Crazy Buffet Club Writers. You are a constant source of inspiration, prodding, and laughter.
- Thanks to my family, for standing by me and supporting me as I pursue my dreams.
- Finally, thanks again to Tom Riley, for knowing when to guard my writing time and energy, and knowing when to pull me away from the process. This one's for you.

All errors and omissions are mine alone.

TABLE OF CONTENTS

Chapter 1

June, the royal wedding of Constantine Phillippe Ramon D'Malia

Married.

Sophia sank into a brocade covered chair in the empty palace reception room, not caring that she crushed the hand embroidered skirts of her formal gown. Her fiancé, the man she'd planned to marry for her whole life, had finally tied the knot.

With someone else.

Relief surged through her in a giddy rush.

She bounced up and paced the wide room, flicking back a sheer, white curtain here, peeking around an open door there, reassuring herself that no one with a telephoto lens lurked nearby recording her uncontrolled exuberance. The swish and rustle of her skirts echoed off the high arched ceilings and frieze covered walls, accentuating her every step.

Sophia grinned. She could picture her scheming uncle—may he rot in prison—turning purple with rage. She'd slipped from his control. His shattered plans for her held no more menace than a thimbleful of salt in the sea.

She was free—for the first time in her twenty years. No politically obsessed uncle directing every tiny detail of her life. No formidable, distant fiancé looming over her future. No one.

She stopped abruptly, the whisper of her skirts fading into silence. If only she could avoid becoming a dancing marionette in someone else's schemes.

A faint cheer floated through the open French doors on a waft of sea-scented air. The island kingdom of Melesia, with its reputation for romance and fairy tale charm, teemed with visitors celebrating the new royal couple.

Sophia pivoted toward the sound, imagining the happy bride and groom stepping onto the presentation balcony, surrounded by lush island greenery, waving at the adoring crowds. Today everyone—tourists and natives, press and paparazzi—loved them. Tomorrow, who knew?

The people, as fickle as honeybees in a flower field, had buzzed around Sophia and her cousin Helena for years seeking vicarious thrills. But no more.

Now, King Constantine and his bride—formerly Jill Bradley of the United States, now Queen Jillian of Melesia—could deal with the crowds. Sophia was free.

At least until someone posted a blog or started a Facebook page dedicated to poor Lady Sophia de Lyons, the modern princess jilted by her one true love.

What— "bullshit." The word burst out, uncensored and wonderful. She giggled, liking the feel of the forbidden sounds on her tongue. She tried a handful of other swear words, each more tantalizing than the last. No one chastised her for behavior unfitting for a Melesian noble. No one—Sophia stopped at the sound of footsteps in the hall.

She raced back to her seat, smoothed her skirts and donned her mask of indifferent perfection just as the door opened. The bride's sister, Grace, entered, shoes dangling from her fingers with a casual carelessness that Sophia envied. If Sophia mussed her hair and slouched, could she become just another average blonde like Grace?

And if she could, what would it be like to not care how the public viewed you? Not to wonder if today's innocent gesture would turn into tomorrow's front page?

"Someone else seeking refuge from the crowds," she said softly. Sophia suppressed a smile as Grace snapped her head around, startled eyes widening. Grace's grip tightened on the shoes, turning her knuckles white as she edged away, gaze darting to the door. "I envy you," Sophia added quietly.

Grace hesitated, slowly facing Sophia again. "Why? You belong here. I'm just the bride's sister, dressed up and trying not to embarrass her."

"Exactly. Soon the press will forget you. They'll hound me for weeks, prying to see if my wounded heart is mended." Sophia sighed. Grace had been almost invisible since her arrival in Melesia. Sophia wished she knew the trick to being invisible. She wished she knew about life outside the palace walls.

Grace crept closer and perched near the carved arm of the brocade covered sofa, questions dancing in her eyes. "Was your heart really broken? Were you in love with Constantine?"

The blunt, intrusive question shocked Sophia. Until she remembered what freedom felt like. *Bullshit*, she repeated silently, enjoying at her new, blunt, reckless streak. *Bullshit, bullshit, bullshit.*

"Love was never part of the picture for us," she said out loud in her normal, boring voice. She rose and walked to the French doors—in her normal, sedate, *boring* steps—beckoning Grace to follow. "I envy him too. He broke the rules and found love. Alex and Helena are also in love," she said, referring to the ailing King Emeritus who'd recently abdicated in favor of his half-brother. "I'm just the spare bride who's now out of a job."

"I don't understand."

"How could you?" How could anyone who hadn't grown up a pawn to be married off for the sake of her family's political ambitions? She pointed to the new bride and groom. "Look. A royal wedding is a fairy tale come true. If I'd been on the balcony instead of your sister, the fairy tale would have unfolded in exactly the same way. Except the looks in their eyes are real. They love each other. He and I would have been pretending.

"I'm very good at pretending," she continued, voicing feelings she'd not dared to express until now. How easily a small taste of freedom unraveled a lifetime of control. "From the moment I came to live with the Duke de Lyons, he's prepared me to be the spare bride. He fed the press with enough romantic nonsense to fuel the illusion. I played along."

"What do you mean—the spare bride?"

"Royal sons are *the heir and the spare.* Alex was the heir. Helena was raised to be his bride. Constantine was the spare. I was the spare bride. At least that's what the duke planned."

"It must have been awful."

Sophia shrugged. "It makes a great story. *Lady Sophia, Foster Daughter of The Disgraced Duke, Jilted by the Prince Who Broke Her Heart.* The tabloids will adore it."

"If your tabloids are anything like ours, they'll have you engaged to someone else within a week."

She shuddered, recognizing—and hating—the truth in Grace's words. "Of course. When Alex abdicated in favor of Constantine, I suppose Stephan became the next spare. One brother should be as good as another. But I don't wish to be bounced from prince to prince until the public gets its next big romance."

Sophia glanced at Grace. Years of decorous protocol, pounded into her by everyone from her uncle down to the castle cook, warned against speaking openly to this near stranger.

Bullshit.

The rebellious voice won. "I'm tired of being controlled by the papers. And by my family. And even by the king. I want a life of my own."

The American didn't flinch at her shocking words. Sophia envied her all the more. What would it feel like to be so unfettered by propriety?

The glint of sun off a camera lens made Sophia stiffen and move back inside, quickly this time. "Photographers," she explained to the wide-eyed Grace. "Tabloids. We're this week's entertainment."

If she were truly free, she'd march into the offices of the *Weekly World Stir* and give the reporter "Mack the Pen" a piece of her mind. And an imprint of her royal slipper on his backside. Or she'd live incognito right under his nose, invisible but happy, daring him to peel away her disguise. But no Melesian blue blood was that free. Not even the king.

"I see why you envy me," Grace said. "No one cares about the bride's brainy half-sister." Grace chewed her lip. A pensive gleam lit her eyes. "Do you ever want to just disappear?"

"All the time," Sophia replied, wondering if Grace had somehow read her mind. "I've made plans to spend a year abroad with Princess Lydia at her home in Europe. After that, I'll join a Melesian goodwill tour scheduled to visit Europe and the Americas."

It wasn't the escape she wanted, but it was better than nothing. "The press will speculate I'm nursing my broken heart. If I'm lucky, I can stay away until the next heir to the throne is born. When your sister becomes pregnant, I'll have a measure of peace. I will never have the freedom that you do."

"What if you could be someone other than Lady Sophia for a few days?" Grace paused, staring off in the distance. Sophia nearly squirmed with impatience. "Someone like me?"

Sophia stared at her, impossible fantasies swirling in her head, begging for the chance to become real. What if this brainy young American could come up with a better plan than a scripted, goodwill tour where her every move would be choreographed with brutal precision? Sophia would gladly give the de Lyons wealth—now under her sole control—for the chance to walk barefoot in the grass or eat a double scoop of ice cream from a dripping cone or swear in public without censure. She'd trade her designer gowns, Hermes clutches, and ancestral jewels if she could be invisible for a single day.

"You said the goodwill tour is scheduled to visit the Americas eventually," Grace continued. "If you could get away from the entourage while you're in the U.S., I could buy you a few days of freedom."

Sophia's heart slowed, its thud, thud, thud stretching between beats as if it were afraid of drowning out a single word that Grace said. Sophia held her breath. If Grace truly had a plan…

Sophia asked a carefully worded question. Then another. Skillfully she pulled information from Grace and planted suggestions in Grace's head as she'd done so many times in ballrooms and political receptions around the world. Then she listened, hiding a smile of triumph, while Grace created a perfect escape plan for her.

Later that day, Sophia sat in Grace's room staring at the United States driver's license in her hand, the triple-fast pounding of her heart making up for lost time.

She glanced in the mirror. The similarities between them were close enough to be believable. The plan Grace had outlined just might work. She clutched the pages filled with Grace's cramped script, detailing precise instructions for Sophia's escape from the tour and her return home. With nearly a year to refine and modify the specifics, what could go wrong?

For a few glorious, free days, she would become Grace Bradley, free to roam the United States at will. Free to sample all life had to offer.

"Hot damn." Freedom had never tasted so good.

Chapter 2

September, one year later. Chicago, Illinois.

Sophia edged toward the back of the Willis Tower observation deck, away from the floor-to-ceiling windows with their panoramic view of Chicago. While the other dignitaries listened to the guide, she motioned to her aide.

"I need a few moments alone in the ladies' room," she whispered. She passed the woman a sealed envelope. "Please hold this for me until I return."

She slipped out of the room, her heart racing. This was the moment. Nine long months of planning and dreaming all came down to this. She mentally reviewed her escape plan.

No one turned as she edged out of the room. Instead of heading to the ladies' room, she found the elevator and hurried inside. Luckily the attendant on duty was still on the observation deck with the tour. She pushed the button and held her breath.

Nonchalantly, she reached up and massaged her scalp, loosening the pins that held her elegant upsweep in place as the doors slid closed. The moment they shut, the elevator lurched to life.

One minute till she reached the ground floor.

She shimmied out of her skirt, pulling her hidden leggings down at the same time. She grabbed the belt from the skirt and refastened it over her oversized, silky blouse, then shrugged out of the jacket.

Thirty seconds left. She shook her hair, pins flying and pinging against the elevator walls as she balled the vibrant red suit up, inside out so only the black lining showed.

The elevator slowed. She tugged at the rest of the hairpins, pulled a black beret out of her bag and slipped it on over her long, loose hair just as the elevator stopped moving.

The doors slid open. She covered her eyes with sunglasses and peeped out.

Empty. *Thank Zeus and the rest of the Olympians*, she thought, invoking the gods of her Greek ancestors. She headed toward what she hoped was the building's entrance and made it half-way down the hall.

"Miss. Stop." A guard hurried in her direction.

She froze, her heartbeat so loud, she was sure he could hear it. *Please. Not when I'm so close.*

"The observation deck is closed to tourists. You'll have to wait until tomorrow." The guard took her by the elbow and led her down a different hallway.

She breathed a sigh of relief as he showed her to the door. A quick dash landed her in the rush hour crowd where, pressed and jostled between bodies heading to the nearby commuter trains, Lady Sophia melted away, invisible for the first time in her life.

The rush of people surged into Union Station where commuter trains ran between the city of Chicago and the western suburbs. Sophia paused to check the directions Grace had given her. *Train to Aurora, IL.* A passerby directed her to track eight, and she hopped on the train just before it pulled away.

She looked cautiously around and behind her. No one but other passengers. She checked her watch. Only ten minutes had passed since she left the observation deck.

Success. Freedom. She'd done it.

A giddy rush filled her senses as she rested her forehead against the cool glass window and watched the world zoom past. Could it really be this easy? By now Melesian security teams would be swarming the observation deck and the surrounding city blocks, searching for her.

She only hoped her aide would open the letter Sophia had given her explaining that she'd slipped away of her own free will. Otherwise these moments on the train would be the beginning, and the end, of her freedom.

Sophia pulled a list of instructions from her purse and scanned it, memorizing her next steps until the train pulled into the last station. She exited and took a taxi to a pawn broker where she sold some of the lesser de Lyons jewels.

Then she headed to a shopping complex to purchase her first, and only, pair of jeans. She added a couple of shirts in vibrant red and sunshine yellow, and a handful of other supplies before catching a taxi to a hotel, her nerves still zinging with nervous excitement.

After a fitful night, she made her way to the suburban Naperville train station where she eventually collapsed, exhausted, onto the westbound California Zephyr to Reno. To everyone who saw her, she was just another tourist dressed in jeans toting a backpack.

Three days of freedom stretched ahead of her like a golden promise, filled with everything she'd ever wanted.

Reno, Nevada

Three days weren't enough.

Her journey had been everything she'd planned, but not everything she needed. Sophia longed for one big, memorable, unplanned adventure.

An adventure that ended with a kiss.

A *passionate* kiss.

With a handsome stranger.

She'd never been kissed before, except for the dry pecks from the few boys who'd slipped past the duke's army of tutors, bodyguards and chaperones. That didn't count as far as she was concerned.

Unfortunately, the duke had clamped down on her few freedoms after that, fearing someone, or something, could interfere with his plans for her. He'd overseen her every move so carefully that she'd never been alone with another young man, unless it was one of the royal brothers. And they'd never stirred her interest.

Surely, a real kiss wasn't too much to ask. To Sophia's mind, the world owed her a good kiss—and a whole lot more.

After all, she'd spent her entire life saving herself for a royal marriage that never materialized. Yes, the world owed her at least one good, romantic, soul-stirring kiss in return for all she'd sacrificed.

But it wasn't just the simple press of lips against hers that she craved. It went deeper than that. She longed for a taste of what might have been if she'd been born with a normal birth certificate instead of a mile-long royal pedigree.

Sophia dug in her pocket, leaned over the rail of the pedestrian bridge as far as she dared, and tossed a handful of coins into the Truckee River below. The afternoon sun glinted off the coins as they spun through the air. The plop of silver in the water carried Sophia's wishes to The Fates, but didn't disturb the newlywed couples locked in loving embrace along the riverbanks.

She hadn't come to find love.

She'd hoped to find excitement. Stolen kisses. The giddy rush that supposedly made people reckless. Too bad the giddiness and excitement seemed reserved for the couples below.

If The Fates granted her wish, she'd have one last memory to carry her through the years of lonely perfection that her country demanded. If not, so be it. Either way, tomorrow she'd return home, marry, live, and die at her king's command.

Sophia drew in a breath of desert air. The sun baked her unprotected skin and a dry breeze fluttered through her newly cropped hair, ruffling it about her face.

She ran her hand through the soft, springy curls, so different from the sleek, smooth coif she'd worn her whole life. Cutting it snipped the ties to her past, just as pawning her jewels had unlocked the diamond handcuffs shackling her to tradition.

She'd treasure those small acts of rebellion for a lifetime. Freedom suited her. She'd crammed a lifetime of dreams into the few days of freedom she'd had since leaving the goodwill tour.

Amazingly, no one had commented on her absence. Not the Royal Press Corps. Not the swarm of legitimate reporters buzzing around the fringes of the tour. No one. It could only mean someone was covering for her, giving her the freedom she'd begged for in the letter she left behind. She sent up a silent prayer of gratitude.

Not even the *Weekly World Stir* had gotten a whiff of her absence. She pulled a copy of the tabloid from her backpack and glanced at the headline. *Marilyn Monroe Cloned at an Undisclosed Cryogenics Lab.*

Reality chilled her as effectively as any cryogenics lab. Today she was an unknown. Tomorrow, she'd surrender herself to the Melesian consulate in San Francisco and step back into the public eye for the rest of her life. Icy fingers of regret clawed at her gut, causing a painful spasm—the kind she'd learned to bear in smiling silence during her years of training.

A lifetime of loyalty and patriotism nagged her, chanting the motto *Duty, King and Country* until she stiffened her spine in a response as automatic as breathing.

Sophia hauled her canvas backpack onto one shoulder and headed to the curb, enjoying the comfortable bump of the bag against her hip. A gentleman slipped out of a cab and held the door for her. She settled into the seat, tossing the crumpled tabloid—and her dreams—aside. Loyalty and patriotism won.

En route to her hotel, she gazed idly about the cab, trying to memorize the details. The slight whiff of smoke, the worn vinyl seats, the crackling radio, the dusty carpet-

A wallet lay at her feet. A tingle—the kind Melesian legends ascribed to the touch of The Fates—ran down her spine as she picked it up and flipped it open. A card fell into her lap. *Compliments of the Three Fates. Admit one for a night where dreams can come true. Three Fates Lounge, Reno.* She froze.

"Driver, can you take me to the Three Fates Lounge?"

"Three Fates? Never heard of it. You got an address?"

Sophia flipped the card over. Nothing. "No." She suppressed a sigh. "Just continue on to the hotel."

If the card wasn't directing her to the lounge, then what? She turned and studied the wallet. A badge from a food show—ending two days ago—indicated it belonged to the owner of Maguire's Irish Pub and Grill, Morgan's Outpost, Colorado. Another chill tickled her spine.

Sophia dug through her backpack and pulled out the rumpled train schedule. She scanned the list of stops. She'd passed through Morgan's Outpost on her way west. Not far from Reno by train, but not on the way to the consulate, either.

Sophia considered her options.

Duty pulled at her. *King and Country.*

She could turn the wallet in at the consulate. Someone else would find the owner. It was the way of her world.

Someone else always handled everything. Her past. Her future. Even her days of freedom had been choreographed by someone else.

Duty tugged again.

Another force—Rebellion? Responsibility? Fate?—pushed back.

She stared at the wallet in her hands, acid churning through her stomach. She fought the cold, unwelcome cramp. Uncle Julian's voice, as sharp and clear in her imagination as in life, scolded her. *Stop wasting time with daydreams. The servants will handle it. You are destined to be a princess.*

But her uncle was in prison, and she'd left the world of servants behind. She didn't want to be a princess.

She slid the driver's license out of the wallet and studied it. Return it? Or return home? *Do a good deed yourself, for once. Don't let someone else do it on your behalf.* The new voice in her head offered a tantalizing alternative. An alternative that eased the twisting pain in her gut.

Her uncle prized political and social power, placing his faith in the failed marriage plan he had constructed to make her queen of Melesia.

What's important to you? The question whispered through her mind, begging for an answer.

Sophia focused on the voice that argued against duty, straining to recognize it, until the pieces fell into place. It was her own voice. Her own, rarely used, voice.

Returning the wallet was a link in a chain—albeit a small one—forged by her own decisions. A chain that led away from the Lady Sophia de Lyons the world expected to the Sophia she was only now discovering that she wanted to be.

And if it gave her an extra day or two of freedom, all the better. Sophia glanced over at the *Weekly World Stir*. How ironic that she would pass undetected—once again—within the shadow of their Denver, Colorado headquarters. The long ago fantasy of living in freedom beneath their eyes merged with present day reality.

She checked her watch. Checked the train schedule.

"Driver, I have changed my mind. Take me to the train station."

Calm—tinged with the pleasant flutter of excitement—replaced the discomfort in her gut, and she smiled again.

Freedom agreed with her.

Chapter 3

reedom, Sophia decided as she stood in the dark outside Maguire's Irish Pub and Grill clutching the lost wallet, was a lot more fun in the daytime. And when you had money. Budgeting, it turned out, wasn't one of her skills.

A damp night chill numbed her fingers. Her stomach rumbled, as empty as her coin purse. Hunger and anxiety twisted into an unpleasant lump. She ignored both the chill and the hunger-laced anxiety.

In the slivers of light from the flickering green and orange neon sign, Sophia checked her watch. Nearly eleven. Too long since she'd slept or eaten, but her dwindling cash reserve and the thrill of adventure had prevented her from doing either.

She took a deep breath, trying to clear her head and push back the waves of exhaustion that had her swaying on her feet. All she had to do was return the wallet. In half an hour, she could be tucked up in a cheap hotel. Then she'd be on her way home to a hot meal and a warm bath with the early morning train.

Fear and excitement chased down her spine fighting for dominance as she crossed the threshold of the pub. *Head up. Hide your fear. Maintain your poise.* Those words had guided her through a lifetime of uncertainty. Now, she clung to them with each step into the dim interior of Maguire's.

Blaring rock and roll assaulted her ears, broken only by the crack of balls and muted voices from a pool table in some hidden corner. A waitress, shoulders slumped against the heavy weight of her tray, cleared tables in the dining room to her left. To her right a few customers lingered over mugs of beer at the long, polished bar.

Sophia headed to the bar, not quite sure what to do next.

"What can I do for you, miss?"

The deep, rich timbre of a man's voice washed over her, and she looked up, peering, trying to make out his face in the shadows. "I'm looking for James Michael Maguire. I found something that belongs to him." She held the wallet up for his inspection.

He moved from behind the bar and leaned against it, bringing him closer to her level. In the light of the wall sconce, she could see more clearly. His hair—an undecipherable shade of dark that might have been reddish brown—was cut short in a style that didn't quite hide its unruly curl. A smile softened his strong jaw, showing a dimple. Friendly hazel eyes assessed her, a hint of a twinkle visible in their depths.

"Which James Michael Maguire?"

"Excuse me?"

"I'm James Michael Maguire—Mike to my friends. Since that isn't mine, it must belong to my dad. Besides, I'd remember someone as pretty as you if we'd met before." His gaze slid over her, lingering on her lips, her throat, her breasts, touching everything from head to toe and back again, sizing up her curves with thoroughness of a connoisseur. "I'd definitely remember you."

Sophia's lips tingled, and her breath caught as if he'd caressed her instead of just looked at her. Her pulse thudded in her throat, sending blood coursing through her veins in a rush.

The men in her life didn't make her feel this way. This tingling, hyper-sensitive awareness didn't exist in Melesia. It was foreign, exciting. It was…the very thing she'd been searching for.

A small silver coin—probably dropped by someone she couldn't see—rolled off the bar and spun to a stop at her feet. Two others followed, winking at her in the dim light. A shiver of awareness snaked up her spine. She'd thrown her coins and wishes to The Fates. Now The Fates dropped both back in her lap.

A stolen kiss, she thought, remembering exactly what she wished for. What did the legends say about The Fates? That they toyed with humans, granting their favors to the bold rather than the deserving. She caught a shallow breath, painful against the hammering of her heart, and gathered her courage. *Be bold. Daring.*

"James *Michael* Maguire," she whispered, her voice a breathless sigh. She dropped her backpack to the floor with a soft *thunk*. The wallet followed, tumbling out of her slack fingers. She took a step toward him and wrapped her arms around his neck, leaning every inch of her trembling body against this solid, warm man with the twinkling eyes.

"Junior," she added, her words filling the space between his surprised lips and her own. Then she plastered her lips to his and kissed him with an enthusiasm born of a lifetime of longing.

It was an awkward start, her lips simply pressing against his, her head twisting, trying unsuccessfully to deepen the kiss. But only for a second. He widened his stance, cradling her body with his and raised a hand to thread through her wind-tossed hair, stilling her motions. Then he claimed the kiss, his lips caressing hers, nibbling them, exploring them.

She forgot to worry about the mechanics of kissing, instead concentrated on the soft, but firm, feel of him, the way each nip brought a prickle of awareness to her lips and each lick—

Heavens! He licked her lips, and she almost sighed with pleasure until his tongue stroked the inside of her mouth and the sigh turned to a moan. She wiggled closer, urged on by the sweep of his broad palm down her back.

When he cupped her behind, she melted into him, overcome by the heat of his hands and his mouth. He tasted of moist, smoky musk, a manly, earthy taste and scent that filled her senses. She mimicked his explorations, thrusting into his mouth to seek pleasure at her own pace.

Her lips and mouth pulsed and burned, little fiery sparks of desire igniting at his touch. Her breasts swelled, nipples hard and straining through layers of clothing, toward the flannel of his shirt. And lower…

Heavens, again! She throbbed and rubbed along the hard ridges of the man, her stomach pressed to his rock-like abs, the junction of her thighs snugged up against another hardness as she pulsed, and strained, and tried to surround him with her own aching want.

One more minute of this and she might burn up, glad to incinerate at his touch. Another taste. Then—

Her lips tingled, the throbs of desire fading into a restless itch. She pressed her tongue against his, awkward again, trying to ease the agony. Her throat tightened. A rush of fear hit her, unpleasant and unwanted.

Sophia pushed away from him, gulping air and swallowing the dizziness that threatened. But she couldn't stop it. It pressed in, sweeping away her resolve. Weakening her legs. "Please excuse me," she murmured as her body softened against his arms and the darkness claimed her.

Mike closed the ledger and pushed it into a shadowed corner of his scarred desk, not needing to see the numbers he'd long since memorized. The stack of overdue bills his father had shoved at him, along with the keys to the pub and instructions to take care of the family, weighed on him like a backpack full of granite. One punishing, heavy rock for each blarney-filled lie he'd told in a decade of fast and easy living.

He rubbed his temples, trying to ease the ache that throbbed like an executioner's drumbeat. Overdue. Last notice. Foreclosure. Bankruptcy. All leading to—drum roll, please— failure. With a capital F.

He'd paid off the worst of the creditors, begged for more time from the rest, cut the menu, and raised the price of drinks, but they were still operating in the red. The future of his staff and his family depended on him turning the red into black.

Memories taunted him. *You had it all*, they whispered. *Girls. Cars. Hollywood. New York. The rich and glamorous.* Their stories netted him plenty of cash. Cash he'd squandered.

If he'd known Dad was in trouble, or that his sister Katie's life had snarled into an expensive tangle, he could have helped. If he'd known. Or cared enough to find out.

But he hadn't, and while he played, life at home quietly unraveled. His mother died. His father sank into depression—followed by gambling and recklessness—leaving the pub in the hands of his former brother-in-law. The one who emptied the cash drawer and left, stranding Katie and her three girls without a visible means of support. When they hit rock bottom a year ago, they'd called him home.

He'd come, already bored with his lucrative life. Or maybe it was disillusionment. Instead of changing the world with his words, he'd ended up selling tawdry tales for easy money.

Whatever. He'd come. And he'd been scraping along ever since, trying to piece his tattered family back together.

What was it they said about the luck of the Irish? Without bad luck they'd have no luck a'tall.

A groan dragged his attention to the blonde stretched out on his threadbare office couch. Another innocent counting on him for something—although in this case he wasn't quite sure what he was supposed to do with her.

It wasn't everyday a luscious woman walked into his bar, threw herself in his arms, and kissed him like her life depended on it. That part had been good—until she fainted and sprouted red splotches all over her pale skin in a matter of seconds.

Just his Irish luck to find a willing woman who was allergic to his kisses.

Thank God his friend Jaycee, a local paramedic who'd stopped by for a drink, knew what to do. While Mike cleared the customers out of the bar, Jaycee had managed to get the girl awake. She mumbled something about a food allergy and swallowed some medicine she pulled from her backpack.

After declining to see a doctor or go to a hospital, she'd asked for a few moments alone then promptly fell asleep. Jaycee had told Mike to watch her for a couple of hours. Fortunately, the swelling and red spots subsided, and she breathed easily. At least a trip to the emergency room wasn't looming in his immediate future.

Mike moved past a dented filing cabinet and squatted down next to her. "How are you feeling?" he asked softly.

She mumbled in response, lifting her hand. "Kind of you to ask. Your hospitality is most gracious. So pleased to meet you." Her sleep-slurred words held the hint of an accent. It seemed familiar, but he couldn't quite place it.

"Pleased to meet you too," he replied, awkwardly squeezing her limp fingers. He shook his head as he watched her drift back into sleep. "You are one odd woman."

Odd, but apparently honest. As soon as he'd taken care of her, he'd checked out the missing wallet story. Typically, Dad didn't even know his wallet was lost. Since both his money clip and his bed were full at the moment—neither of which boded well for the family's future or finances—he'd thrown the responsibility to Mike. As usual. A few quick calls revealed that none of the cards had been used. So the lovely lady wasn't a thief.

Who was she? Mike pulled her backpack over to the desk and rifled through the contents. Clothes, a toothbrush, what looked like a jewelry case. A tiny purse contained only a comb, a tube of lipstick, and a cell phone. He dug deeper.

Bingo. A little cash—far too little for someone traveling on her own–and a driver's license.

Grace. The name suited her, summing up her long willowy legs and slight, but perfectly proportioned curves. She moved like a dancer. Fainted with a deliberate delicacy. Even asleep on his couch, she exuded poise. So, Grace it was. Grace S. Bradley of Ohio.

He squinted at the tiny photo. It didn't do her justice, but the stats on the license were about right. His Colorado pub was a long way from her home.

He looked back at her and yawned, tamping down on the instincts that screamed something wasn't quite right. He wasn't a hotshot celebrity reporter anymore. He was the down-and-out owner of the debt-ridden Maguire's Irish Pub and Grill. And he was too tired to unravel mysteries tonight.

Mike ambled over and covered the blonde—Grace—with a blanket. "Tomorrow, when you're awake, we'll see about getting you home, sweetheart. For tonight, sleep." He snagged her backpack and silently left the room, hoping that her missing belongings would be enough to hold her in place until they could talk.

Chapter 4

Sophia jolted at the unearthly howl, tangling herself further in the soft blanket. She cracked an eye open and quickly closed it again, but the image of huge jowls and slathering yellow teeth set in a grotesque chocolate brown head still burned in her memory.

"Cerberus!" she mumbled, trying to ignore the warm breath on her cheek and the rapid-fire thud of her heart. The mythical three-headed dog—the monstrous guardian of hell—had haunted her nightmares and shadowed her days while the duke broke and reformed his orphaned niece into the woman he wanted.

But now? Had her determination to be independent unleashed the fiend? Or had her reckless kiss summoned him to punish her for behavior unbefitting a future princess? She squeezed her eyes more tightly shut, willing herself back into dreamless oblivion.

An answering growl reverberated through the room. Followed by a whine.

Sophia risked another peek, barely opening her eyes. This time all three heads came into focus. The huge brown one seemed less menacing when flanked by two pale, little girl faces framed in bright red hair. Her panic faded into confusion as she stared at the unfamiliar children.

Was this a hotel? The train? Surely not the consulate. She searched her memory, struggling against the grip of sleep. There had been a wallet, and a stranger and—

Zeus! She groaned, covering her face with her hands. She'd actually kissed the stranger. And now she was in the-gods-knew-where instead of on her way home.

"Now you've done it," said a voice from across the room. "Uncle Mike told you not to wake her."

Sophia peered through her fingers, looking past the dog and girls at the gunmetal gray filing cabinets and mismatched tables piled with papers.

"We didn't do it. Max did."

"Yeah, Max did it. He didn't mean to." One little girl gave Sophia a gap-toothed grin before throwing her arms around the dog's neck.

"You're still going to be in trouble."

"Did someone," Sophia cleared her throat and lowered her hands, "did you say Mike?" The two girls flanking the dog nodded.

"Uncle Mike." Sophia followed the voice to a third girl, standing by the door, hands thrust onto her tiny hips. Though barely older than the other two, she looked prim in her white blouse and crisp jeans, her mahogany hair neatly brushed and tamed by a headband.

"He told them not to come in here."

"Did not." One of the girls by Max shook her head vigorously, messy red curls flying about her face.

"Did too." The Prim One tapped her foot impatiently.

"Anyway, Max is sorry. Aren't you, Max?" Gap-Tooth gave the dog a big, smacking kiss on the ear.

Max growled.

"Time to go."

"No. You're not the boss of me." Miss Flying Curls didn't look away from Sophia as she dismissed the Prim One's order.

"Me either," said Gap-Tooth. "You're not the boss of me. Or Max."

Sophia ignored the squabbling voices. *Uncle Mike.* The name penetrated her foggy memory until the image of Mike Maguire swam before her eyes. Somewhere, buried in her memory between *That Kiss* and *This Couch* were likely dozens of newsworthy mistakes that spelled trouble. She had to get out of here.

"Backpack," she muttered, looking about the room, "where did I leave my backpack?" No canvas bag slouched against the filing cabinets near her feet or hid under the table-turned-desk next to her. Panic jolted her heart into high gear. Her train ticket, Grace's ID and what was left of the family jewels were in the missing bag.

Sophia pushed against the rough weave of the couch, trying to sit, only to be trapped in place when Max dropped to the floor, heaved a sigh and rested his massive head on her stomach.

Even lying down the gigantic brute trapped her. But something in his liquid brown eyes, as mournful and longsuffering in reality as they had been terrifying in her hazy, early morning dream, also calmed her. If she took a minute to gather her scattered wits, she could find the backpack, put last night behind her, and leave with dignity.

She took a deep breath and patted Max, gently rubbing behind his ears until a low, deep-throated growl stopped her.

"That means he likes you," said Miss Flying Curls.

"Yeah. He's purring. He learned it from Minx. That's our cat. He's all black," added Gap-Tooth.

Two little girls clamored for her attention while the third tried to rush them out the door. "We should leave. Uncle Mike said—"

"Hey! What's all the commotion in here?" A gruff masculine voice cut through the noise. "Just because school's closed for the day doesn't mean you can run wild. I thought I told you girls to leave her alone."

"It wasn't me—"

"Max wanted—"

"I told them—"

Mike Maguire leaned against the door frame, laughter dancing in his eyes as his gaze darted from girl to girl. His tee shirt stretched tight across his shoulders and down to the waistband of his jeans, outlining his body in hard perfection. Long legs—clad in denim with intriguing worn spots—crossed casually at the ankle.

Too late to run away now. Instead, Sophia studied him from head to toe. Her heartbeat went into overdrive again, the direction of her thoughts decidedly wicked—and surely capable of rousing the hound of hell. Max shifted against her hand and growled in pleasure while she rubbed his ears.

Mike flashed her a quick grin, then smothered it and turned back to business. "Enough, girls. You know the rules. Max isn't allowed in the restaurant or the office."

"He didn't mean to—"

"Pipsqueak, Squirt, just get him back outside where he belongs. You, too, Miss Manners," he said turning to the older girl. "Give me a couple of minutes before we take Max over to Grandpa's yard. Then you can come back here and help me. Okay?"

Sophia watched the group file out while digesting the new information. She was still in his restaurant. In his private office. Alone with him.

The room suddenly felt smaller. She sat, inwardly wincing at the sticky pool of dog drool on her shirt and the gritty taste in her mouth. A lifetime of training pushed the discomforts and uncertainties out of her mind as she smiled at Mike and accepted the mug of coffee he handed her.

"Thank you for your hospitality."

"Such as it is," he replied. Mike pulled the desk chair close and straddled it, trapping her as effectively as Max had earlier. He crossed his arms and rested them on the ladder back while he studied her. "I hope plain black coffee is all right."

"Of course." She took a sip, wondering what topic to broach first. *Where are my belongings? How did I come to be sleeping on your couch? What happened after we kissed?* Nothing in her training prepared her for this.

A nervous giggle burned in the back of her throat, begging for release. She swallowed the bubble of hysteria along with the scalding coffee.

A glance at Mike showed his good humor had faded. His wrinkled brow and the flat, hard line of his mouth spelled trouble. Even so, she couldn't stop staring at his lips.

The last thing she remembered was his lips. Specifically, kissing them. A flush warmed her body as the memory sparked to life. His touch. The ticklish stroke of his tongue. The dizzy, heady rush of following her heart instead of her training. The deep, sucking heat—

"That was some reaction last night."

His words stopped the pleasant surge of memories, leaving her chilled. Somehow her instincts, her reactions, had been wrong. But wrong how? Too forward? Too eager? Too innocent and awkward? Or perhaps just too much to handle for someone who wasn't interested.

"My reaction—uh—surprised you?" Good grief! She—who'd soothed over faux pas between warring heads of state with a smile—was reduced to stammering nonsense because of a kiss. Thank the gods the press wasn't here.

"It's just," he made a helpless gesture with his hands. "I'm sorry. I didn't mean to embarrass you. But I've never had anyone pass out like that before. I was half afraid to even bring you the coffee this morning. You aren't allergic to coffee, are you?"

"Allergic? No, I," she stopped and looked at him. "Exactly what did happen last night?"

"You, uh…" He raked a hand through his hair and looked away. "That is we, well, after we… After we met, you kind of passed out on me. Turned all puffy and red for a while."

Her hand flew to her face, searching for evidence.

"Oh, no. I'm sorry," he said. "Again. You're fine. Now. Actually, you're more than fine. You're beautiful. Even with, um, all of that." He gestured at her, swirling a finger from her head to her stomach.

"You mean even with uncombed hair and dog spit on my shirt?" She flashed him an easy smile, her confidence returning at his obvious discomfort. "Thank you. I don't believe I have ever received a compliment quite like that."

"Yeah, well, I'm usually a little smoother at giving them. My Irish gift of gab seems to have left me for the moment." He assessed her again, a little half grin playing on his face. "I was really worried about you last night. Thought I might have to call your family or something. You're a long way from home."

"Call the family?" The hysterical giggle threatened again. She rubbed a sweaty palm on her jeans, breathing slowly while trying to calm her racing heart.

The Family. The Royal Family. Surely, he couldn't know who she was. Besides, the royal family wasn't really her family. Except for Helena. And he wouldn't know that.

"Sure. Your family in Ohio. Under the circumstances, I hope you'll forgive me for snooping, Miss Bradley. Or can I call you Grace?"

"G-Grace? Oh, Grace. You found my driver's license. Grace Bradley."

"Is something wrong?"

"No. Nothing. I just—" She grabbed the first lie that came to mind. "My mother's name was Grace. I have been going by my middle name for a long time now."

He chuckled. "I understand. My mom was Mary. All my sisters wanted to honor her when they named their girls. So in good Catholic tradition, we have Mary Theresa, Mary Grace, and Katie's three that you met today. Mary Margaret, Mary Frances and Mary Katherine. Shout *Mary* at a Maguire family reunion and you'll be mobbed by about twenty women from ages five to fifty."

"It must be fun, having all of that family." A de Lyons family gathering would have been nothing but a reason to scrutinize her behavior.

"It's crazy at times, but that's what family's about. So, if I can't call you Grace, what shall I call you?"

"My friends call me Sophie." She liked the casual way the word rolled off her tongue, not stiff and formal like Sophia. "Sophie Bradley. From Ohio," she added.

Mike stood, easily swinging his leg over the chair seat and moving away from the couch. "Well, Miss Sophie Bradley, it seems the coffee didn't do any harm. Anything else I can get you? Breakfast? Just tell me what you want. Or at least tell me what you can't eat."

"I am fine, thank you. More coffee would be nice. Maybe toast. I do not want to put you out."

"In case you forgot to notice, we're in a restaurant. I think I can rustle up breakfast. What about an omelet? We've got ham, bacon, onions, mushrooms—"

"No mushrooms." She tossed him a smile and a shrug. "Normal people are allergic to shellfish or peanuts, but with me it's mushrooms. I was sensitized as a child. Now, even a mushroom garnish on a dinner plate can trigger a reaction. Although that doesn't explain last night. I never eat anything with mushrooms."

He reddened. "No, but I did. When we kissed you must have—" He broke off, turning to the doorway. "Why don't I see about that coffee and toast? And I'll stay away from the mushrooms and…" He glanced over his shoulder. "Anything else I should avoid?"

"Nothing." She smiled at him, hoping to ease his discomfort.

"Okay, then. Toast and coffee." He moved back toward her and held out his hand. She passed him the mug. "All set?"

"I seem to have misplaced my backpack. If I could find it and freshen up a bit before I head out, I would appreciate it." Though heaven knew what she'd do between now and the morning train to Reno tomorrow.

"Oh. God, yes. I should have thought of it earlier." He sized her up with his eyes then sent her a grin that sizzled all the way to her toes. "There's an apartment above the bar. I took your things there for safekeeping last night. I'll show you the way, and you can make yourself at home.

"It's got a shower. Washer. Dryer. TV. Whatever you need. And as much privacy as you'd like. I'll be busy down here until opening anyway. The three Marys are going to help me with the quarterly inventory." He rolled his eyes, but she could see the affection in his face.

Sophia hesitated, the longing for a hot shower and something solid in her queasy stomach at war with her desire not to impose. She could head off and find a hotel. Or…

A tingle skittered up her spine, and the hairs on her neck stood, reminding her of her reckless wishes in Reno. The Fates had granted her another day. Another day with Mike. "To Embrace Fate is Folly; to Ignore her, Disaster," she murmured, citing an old Melesian proverb.

"Pardon me?" Mike's brow furrowed as he looked at her.

"Sorry, I was talking to myself. I really should not impose on you."

"Come on," he said a teasing note warming his voice. "You deserve a reward for returning Dad's wallet. And sleeping on my couch isn't it. Besides, I've got to find some way to make up for your rude awakening this morning. Kids. Dog. General mayhem. Not to mention the mushroom business. And that kiss."

She nodded and followed him out of the office. He was wrong to try to make amends with her. None of this was his fault. And while she might regret the dog and the mushrooms, nothing on earth would ever make her regret the kiss.

Chapter 5

Mike surveyed the upheaval in his usually orderly kitchen and wondered, not for the first time, how he'd come to this phase of his life.

His entire staff—four full-time servers, two part-time student workers, and three talented, underpaid, overworked cooks—swarmed about the space, cleaning the walk-in refrigerator, checking the condition and quantity of the supplies, and counting every dish and pan in the place. Instead of grumbling, laughter and teasing camaraderie filled the air.

Nine people, all of whom depended on him for their livelihood, blissfully unaware of how close they were to losing their jobs if the pub closed.

Not to mention his nieces. After extracting Katie from a legal nightmare and supporting her desire to go back to school, he'd volunteered to help with the girls, giving them the desperately needed stability of a real family. He didn't mind the cost. Didn't mind the sacrifice. But he shuddered at the thought of failure.

Everything could disappear if Maguire's closed its doors.

A crash broke through the general clamor in the kitchen and snapped him back to reality. Instinctively he zeroed in on five-year-old Mary Katherine standing amid broken china. His heart raced as he crossed the room and scooped her up.

"Hey, Pipsqueak, you okay?" He sat her on the counter and ran his hands over her arms and legs, scanning for injury.

She sniffed and nodded. "I was just counting plates, like you said. I didn't mean to break anything. It slipped."

"I know it did." He breathed a sigh of relief when he didn't find any cuts or worse. "I didn't like that plate anyway."

Her chin stopped wobbling, and she giggled a little. Good. He didn't think he could handle tears today. He picked her up and wrapped her in a bear hug. "I'll tell you what, though. I've got a better job for you. I need someone to sort through all the forks and spoons. You need to pull out all the bent ones and count the rest. It's a pretty big job. Would you be in charge of that for me?"

Within minutes, he had her settled in the dining room, a pile of spoons in front of her. Seven-year-old Mary Frances sat nearby, her own table filled with forks.

If only assuring the future of Maguire's and the rest of his staff was as easy as settling the girls. He headed to the office, determined to tackle the latest stack of invoices and loan applications.

Forty minutes and five phone calls later, nothing had changed except that his headache was back. He could keep the pub afloat through the end of the year by cautiously infusing some of his personal funds, but after that, who knew?

When Katie finished school…if Dad stopped gambling and took an interest in the business again…if he could parlay an English degree and a career in yellow journalism into a meaningful source of income… Too many ifs. Too few answers.

The phone rang and Mike picked up, not bothering to hide the weariness in his voice.

"Hey, Mack, how's my favorite reporter? Ready to get back to work? You gotta be tired of that pub by now."

"Frank Kincaid." Mike tried to fake enthusiasm with his former editor at the *Weekly World Stir.* "The pub's doing great. Not a care in the world."

He cringed as a loud crash sounded from the kitchen. Phone clamped tightly to his ear, he headed toward the sound, keeping up a stream of blarney with Kincaid. One of the cooks waved him away from the scene. No injuries. Just a rack of china that would have to be replaced. On credit. Mike sighed.

"So, what do you think?" Kincaid's question caught him unaware.

"I, uh,"

"Mack, listen up. I need you. Circulation's dropped since you retired last year. The new guy doesn't have your nose. I'm not asking for full time. Just one simple job. A couple of 'Mack the Pen' features.

"Your famous *all the truth—and a little bit more* spin on the lives of the idle rich. The public's hungry for it. Your stories help them weather the tough times. No matter what you say, that's a noble calling."

"I'm tired of digging through people's lives looking for scandal."

"At least consider it. The Melesian royal family sent a bunch of blue bloods on tour. They're making whistle stops all over the American heartland. A no-brainer. Take a couple of days and nose around."

"Get someone else."

"No one knows these guys like you, Mack. You practically put their country on the map. No one's busted a good story on them since the king snubbed tradition and married that American woman last year. What was her name? Bailey? Brady? Whatever.

"Right after the wedding the jilted fiancée secluded herself in a castle in Europe. Not a single reporter could get a story on her. Word is she's back in circulation and on the tour."

"Look, Kincaid," another crash resounded from the kitchen and Mike winced. "I don't do sensationalism anymore."

"Sure, sure. But here's the kicker. We were following the tour until last week, then, bam! Something changed. Now no one can get close to that tour. Not even the so-called legit press." Kincaid paused and Mike's interest picked up in spite of himself.

"They got their own press corps and access to the tour—or tours, no one's sure how it's organized—anyway as of four days ago, access is tighter than the lock on a virgin's chastity belt. Something's up. You could break it, Mack.

"Write two stories. Give me a jazzy exclusive with all your trademark innuendo and then sell the watered-down version to the AP. I'll make it worth your while." Kincaid cut the call off before Mike could say another word.

But the idea wouldn't let him go. Kincaid knew his stuff—something wasn't right. Mike's brain itched to know the reasons behind the change in the tour's security. The lure of a real news story tempted him. And the money wouldn't hurt. Besides, what was one more story on a spoiled aristocrat crying because she didn't get to be a princess?

Details of his years reporting on the antics of the Melesian royal family flooded back. He hadn't minded messing with the playboy princes or the royal intrigues. It wasn't until he'd covered the transformation of a young American into a queen that he'd balked.

Somehow watching Jill Bradley learn to shoulder the responsibilities of her adopted country, often at great personal cost, had transformed him too. He'd quit the business shortly after a tasteful, professional coverage of her wedding.

But now?

His gaze lingered on his nieces, happily sorting silverware at the tables. He surveyed the group of people working in the kitchen. Surely, their futures were worth a single sensational story on the former royal fiancée.

He could live with the guilt of burnishing the truth more easily than he could live with the guilt of nine out-of-work employees and bankruptcy for the rest of the family. Just one last story.

What was her name? Lady de Lyons, that was it. Lady Sophia de Lyons.

Sophia de Lyons.

Jill Bradley.

Sophie…Bradley.

Mike froze in his tracks, hardly daring to believe he could merit good luck for a change. She had the right height, the right coloring. Her hair was different—short and curly instead of long and sleek—but hair was easy to change.

He reviewed what he'd learned of her so far. The hint of an accent he hadn't quite placed. The funny, stilted way she talked. Her slight evasiveness.

Improbable as it sounded, it all fit. His gaze slowly wandered to the ceiling and something shifted in his gut.

He didn't have to lie. Or even burnish the truth.

The story of the century was, even now, sitting in his apartment.

Sophia flopped on the couch and huddled into the oversized bathrobe drawing her bare feet into the warmth of its terry cloth folds. The spicy smell of masculine soap drifted up, teasing her nose. Being wrapped in Mike Maguire's robe reminded her of being wrapped in his arms last night, making her skin tingle from the warm intimacy.

Her rigid shoulders relaxed. For the first time in days, no one had looked askance at her. No hotel clerk stammered in surprise when she handed him cash instead of a credit card. No bellhop noted her lack of luggage with a suspicious twist to his lips.

She didn't fear the knock on her door that would end in scandal and exposure. The note she'd left with her aide and the second one—addressed to Prince Stephan—must have been found. Against all odds they'd kept her disappearance secret and granted her the freedom she'd longed for.

Instead of worry, her mind filled with unanswered questions about her host. She glanced about the room. A duffel bag in the corner near a collection of athletic shoes, a softball bat, and a jumble of racquets hinted at a sports enthusiast, but no photos or personal touches softened the room.

She grabbed a TV remote off a dog-eared copy of *Sports Illustrated* and surfed the channels until a story about Melesia flashed onscreen. Sophia twisted her fingers through the belt of her robe as the anchorwoman highlighted the goodwill tour and showed a photo of Sophia with school children in the southern United States.

Then she moved on to recap last year's royal wedding and to speculate whether a half-American heir to the kingdom could be expected soon.

Sophia loosened her grip on the belt, her tension giving way to puzzlement. No mention of her disappearance. And the photo—contrary to the anchor's pronouncement—had been taken in Chicago the day she left the tour. Was escaping her life really that easy?

An unexpected knock brought the tension back in a rush. Maybe not so easy, after all.

Sophia headed to the door on leaden feet. A look through the peephole revealed only little Mary-, Mary something. Miss

Manners balanced a tray almost as big as she was on her skinny arms. Sophia relaxed and opened the door.

"Uncle Mike sent me with breakfast." Mary placed the tray amid the heap of sports magazines and uncovered fruit, pastries, toast, eggs, and coffee. "He said to help you with anything you needed. Unless you don't want me." Mary studied Sophia, her dark eyes wide and unblinking. She edged to the door. "I can wait in the hall."

Her serious, yearning expression caught Sophia. She knew what it was like to be unwanted. "Of course, I'd like your company, Mary—"

"Mary Margaret."

Sophia nodded "I'm doing laundry. Would you help me fold it?"

While Mary Margaret headed toward the dryer, Sophia turned back to the TV, alert for breaking developments. Nothing. She flipped it off and watched as the static faded from the screen.

"Miss Bradley?" She looked down at Mary Margaret, immediately sizing up the disappointment etched onto her small face. "It's okay. You don't have to pretend. Not everybody likes little kids getting in their way."

"Actually," Sophia stooped down to the girl's level, "I was thinking about my family and feeling sad. I could use a friend if you want to stay."

"Do you miss them?"

"Sometimes." A wave of loneliness pinched her heart. How could she tell a child that her uncle cared more about power than about her? Those closest to her—her cousin the Emeritus Queen Helena, her former fiancé, and the rest of the royal brothers—didn't care enough to alert the world to her disappearance.

She'd failed her family when the king slipped through her fingers. He didn't want a tailor-made bride. Her family couldn't use her anymore for political gain. Melesia hadn't missed her. Even the press had moved on.

In short, no one needed Sophia. She swallowed the unexpected lump in her throat.

"Why don't you tell me about your family?" she asked, striving for a light tone and steering Mary Margaret to the laundry niche. Maybe she'd learn more about Mike. "So far, I know you have two sisters, one uncle, a black cat, and a four-footed monster you call a dog."

"Max isn't a monster. He's a Mastiff. Sort of. Uncle Mike says he's part Mastiff, part Saint Bernard, and all baby."

"Some baby."

"He's supposed to be a watch dog 'cause he looks scary. Uncle Mike says Max is a worthless eating and sleeping machine. He says Max couldn't even lick a thief to death."

"Your uncle has a lot of opinions."

"He's used to being the boss. Mom says we have to be nice to him."

Alarm bells clamored in Sophia's head and her muscles tensed in an involuntary reaction. The duke—publicly praised for taking in his orphaned niece—tyrannized his family in private.

She laid a gentle hand on Mary Margaret's shoulder and sat on a kitchen chair to bring herself eye-to-eye with the child. "Is Uncle Mike the one who told you he didn't like children? That you were in the way?"

"No." Mary Margaret's hair slid forward and hid her face as she focused on one pristine tennis shoe twisting and squeaking on the shiny linoleum.

Sophia waited.

"Daddy..." Mary Margaret drew in a shaky breath. "Daddy didn't like us. That's why he left. Before Uncle Mike came home." She looked up, blinking and somehow managing to keep the tears from spilling over.

"So I guess you spend a lot of time with your Uncle Mike."

Mary Margaret nodded, her face brightening as she chattered about Mike. Sophia gathered the information like a squirrel harvesting nuts. He'd left a lucrative job to run the family pub.

He'd helped his sister go back to school. He spent his days shuttling the girls to community classes, neighborhood parks, or the quiet of his office where he helped them with homework. He spent his nights working at the pub.

A picture of a warm, loving family etched itself into Sophia's mind—a stark contrast to the cold, demanding home where she had grown up. She pulled the Mike Maguire-scented robe more tightly around her and inhaled, trying to draw the warmth, the scent, the essence of this man, this family into her soul.

Had she lived her whole life without knowing she was lonely? Or had she simply learned to bury her feelings beneath duty to king and country?

Mary Margaret's gasp turned her attention back to the girl. "Did you want to do this?" The girl pulled a shirt from the dryer. Followed by a pair of panties, and a lone sock. All pink.

Her red pullover had faded to a dusky rose. Everything that used to be white was pink. The things that used to be yellow—well, she didn't have a word for the color they were now. At least her jeans were still blue, sort of.

So much for thinking she'd mastered the mysteries of the washing machine and dryer. *Damn.* The first two things she'd done on her own—truly on her own—had ended in a muddled mess. Finding and kissing Mike Maguire left her helpless and stranded in Morgan's Outpost. Washing a load of laundry…well, even Mary Margaret knew more about life than Sophia did.

No wonder the king preferred the headstrong American to her. She wasn't an asset to her country; she was a laughable liability. Correction. She had been a laughable liability. Past tense.

Sophia grabbed a handful of clothes and strode to the bathroom, determined to change her life. She yanked on her jeans, then dragged the pullover over her head. It hugged her curves in a way it hadn't an hour ago. The bare strip of midriff showing between its hem and the waistband of her jeans hadn't been visible before either. So what? In America no one cared about an exposed navel. In America, she could even pierce her navel and no one would berate her.

She glanced at her reflection. She'd survived the duke's brutal training. Learned to navigate political intrigue without flinching. She'd balanced for years on a shaky public pedestal, not quite a princess but far from a commoner.

She could learn to stand on the ground, invisible and independent.

Starting now.

Or at least as soon as she was dressed in something that wasn't skintight and pink.

Chapter 6

Like paused outside of his apartment door, his half-formed strategy to keep Lady Sophia in Morgan's Outpost interrupted by an unexpected sound. He cocked his head, straining to hear better. Laughter. Feminine laughter and girlish giggles.

He hadn't heard Mary Margaret laugh in all the months since he'd returned home. His nickname for her—Miss Manners—matched the perfect, unflappable little shell she'd retreated into. He'd tried everything to break through. Teasing her only netted him a sad little smile and a haunted, melancholy stare.

Sports didn't help, either. Instead of burning her unhappiness out on a soccer or softball field, she'd approached the games with grim determination, memorizing the rule book rather than railing against the unfairness of life.

Yet in a matter of hours, Lady Sophia de Lyons had done what he couldn't in months of trying. She'd made Mary Margaret behave like a little girl.

He knocked softly—too softly for anything other than to ease his conscience—and edged the door open. Mary Margaret stood at the kitchen table clutching a mixing bowl and dragging a wooden spoon through it.

"It's definitely too thick," she said between giggles.

Sophia moved into view, a baggy chef's apron knotted about her neck and waist, hiding everything but the perplexed look on her face. She held a page up to Mary Margaret and pointed. "It says right here to use one, one quarter cup of water."

"Maybe they mean one *and* one quarter cup." She lifted the flour covered spoon out of the bowl. "They were never this thick when Mom used to make them."

The hint of sadness in her voice sounded more like the child he'd come to know. Just as quickly, her giggles returned. Mike stood frozen in place, watching as Sophia poured more water into the bowl, doling it out only when Mary Margaret urged her on.

"Your mom is going to love these cookies. When she does her studies late at night, she will be nibbling them and thinking of you."

"Thanks for helping me, Miss Sophie. I'm not allowed to use the oven without a grown up around."

"Want to know a secret?" Sophia leaned closer to Mary Margaret, but her whisper carried to where Mike stood, just inside the door. "I have never baked cookies before. Or used an oven."

"Or a washing machine," added the girl. The giggles started again.

For an instant Mike wanted to back out the door and forget his plans. Kincaid's offer of fast cash paled in comparison to his niece's laughter. Yet the children's future security hinged on him keeping the pub doors open. He'd learn the tricks to making them laugh later, after he'd earned enough to keep a roof over their heads.

It was just one story.

Mike caught another glimpse of Sophia, bending to put the cookies in the oven, a smooth denim-clad curve slipping free of the baggy apron. His hands itched for his camera. He could turn that one photo into a full-fledged story—damning her with the truth. *And a little bit more.*

In the old days, he would have done it without a qualm, adding innuendo to make her appear silly or self-serving.

He couldn't do it now. Not when Mary Margaret flung her arms around Sophia's waist and thanked her with the childlike exuberance he hadn't been able to summon from his niece. Not when Sophia's cheeks flushed with pleasure. Not when the icon he'd reported on for years transformed into a living, breathing human being.

Just one story. To save his family. Maybe a few photos. Nice ones. Tasteful. He'd stash a tiny digital camera in his pocket to have handy from now on.

He promised himself he'd craft a story that showed her grace and courage. One that made her into a hero. Even if he had to lie to create it.

Mike stepped forward, noble intentions firmly in place. "Hello, ladies. What are you two up to?"

"We're baking cookies." Mary Margaret dipped her spoon into the batter and plopped a bit of cookie dough onto a baking sheet, lining it up precisely with the others in the row.

"Once again, it looks like I'm in your debt," Mike said softly to Sophia as he looked at her over the girl's head.

"Not at all." Sophia smiled. "We are having fun, are we not?"

"Miss Sophie's never baked cookies before." Mary Margaret grinned up at Mike. "She says it's harder than it looks."

Mike grabbed a mound of dough off the sheet and bit into it. "She's never baked before? Now that, I find hard to believe." He winked at Sophia. "These taste about as good as any I've ever had."

"You're supposed to wait until they're baked and cooled," Miss Manners said, rolling her eyes. "Everyone knows that."

"Everyone?" Mike chuckled. He moved around the table closer to Sophia. "What do you think? Should we be proper and follow the rules?" He scooped a finger-full of dough out of the bowl and held it near her lips. "Or do you want to live a little?"

She took the bait. Sort of.

She pinched the cookie dough off his finger with her own hand, nails lightly scraping from knuckle to fingertip. The move put her a fraction of an inch further from him, a tiny bit more in control. But it left him off balance like a rookie reporter in a roomful of Pulitzer Prize winners.

He watched her slip the morsel between her lips, savoring the Toll House batter as if it were a fine gourmet concoction instead of an everyday treat. She swallowed, drawing his gaze to her perfect throat. "I want to live. A lot."

Mike scooped up more dough and offered it to her. "How about a walk on the wild side of life?"

The pulse in her throat quickened. "I—"

"Eew." Eight-year-old disgust cooled the moment like a dash of ice water. "You guys had better stop eating raw cookie dough or you're going to get salmon-vanilla poisoning." Mary Margaret glared at them, hands on hips.

A grin tugged at Mike's lips. "You're right, Miss Manners. We don't want anyone getting hurt."

A buzzer sounded, sending both Mary Margaret and Sophia into an excited frenzy. As he watched them pull one batch of cookies from the oven and slide another in, he took stock of the situation.

His goal was to write a story on Lady Sophia, not to seduce her. He needed her to be eating out of his hand in a metaphorical sense, not a literal one.

He had to keep his charm—which had convinced more than one palace insider to reveal secrets—under control. This time he wasn't working the angles with the harried, under-ap-preciated assistants. He wasn't ferreting out quirky habits of the upper crust by flattering the maids. This time he was per-sonally involved. And everyone could get hurt if he let himself forget it was just a story.

Sophia's newfound confidence evaporated as she watched Mary Margaret leave the apartment, a plate of cookies in hand for her sisters and a package of them wrapped for her mother.

Alone with Mike Maguire, the kitchen seemed smaller, boxing her in like a rat in an experimental lab. His easy, prob-ing banter—What were your favorite cookies when you were a girl? Did you play sports in school? What was your favorite subject?—unnerved her. A normal person would have had the right answers. She didn't. And now she wasn't able to deflect the attention back to Mary Margaret. She was alone with him. And her secrets.

Why hadn't she quizzed Grace on the details of her life? She'd had a year to prepare for this adventure. But then, end-ing up at Maguire's Pub in Morgan's Outpost hadn't been part of the original plan.

Striking out on her own after Reno hadn't been part of the plan, either, but it was now. At least until someone missed her and gave her a reason other than duty to return home.

"You look like you're ready to bolt at any minute. Did I do something to upset you?"

Sophia shifted her gaze from the door to Mike, giving her-self a mental shake for letting her concentration slip. How many times had the duke—curse him—subjected her to blis-tering lectures and sleepless, supper-less nights before break-ing her of that habit?

"Sophie?"

She'd done it again. "Sorry. I was lost in thought."

"Thinking about how you're going to get back to Reno? Or were you headed home?"

"What?"

"You rearranged your plans to bring my dad's wallet back. I'm sure Morgan's Outpost wasn't on your list of places to visit. You know, not many people would go out of their way to do something like that. I'd like to make it up to you."

"There is no need. Really. It was my pleasure. I enjoyed meeting your nieces. And baking cookies."

Mike smiled, sending a shot of warmth to her toes. He snagged a cookie off the plate between them and downed it in three bites. "The cookies are good. And Mary Margaret had fun. But that's not the point."

"Every little girl needs some fun in her life."

"What about grown-up girls? Is that what you were doing in Reno? Having fun?" He sat at the table and gestured for her to join him. "Wait. Let me guess. You were taking advantage of Reno's checkered history of providing quick marriages and even quicker divorces."

"Nothing like that," Sophia answered with a smile. She was ninety percent sure he was teasing and one hundred percent sure that her response would derail that thought even if he wasn't. "I was on vacation." Which was more or less the truth.

"Alone? Or with friends? Or family?"

"Oh no. I was alone. For the first time. I enjoyed every minute of it. Have you ever taken a train ride across the United States? It is breathtaking."

"Tell me about it." Mike cocked his head, ready to listen.

For some reason, as much as he unnerved her in other ways, talking to him was easy. Details of the trip spilled out as Sophia let herself relive the experience. His responses fueled her enthusiasm, and she didn't tamp down her excitement. She didn't have to.

"So," she said, finally wrapping up her journey, "what about you? What is your life story?"

His eyes twinkled and a slow grin lit his face. "My life story? You didn't tell me a life story, you just told me a vacation story. It's not fair to ask for a life story in exchange."

"I will owe you. Tell me something about yourself." She leaned in and rested her elbows on the table like she'd seen people do in her travels.

"Believe it or not, some of the important points are a lot like your vacation story. It was pretty much assumed that I would go to college, graduate, and come home to run the family business. So going to Denver for school was my one chance to get out on my own."

"Denver is not all that far away, is it?"

"No. Just down the road, in fact. But times were good and I'd gotten some scholarship money, so my folks were willing to let me live on campus if I found a job to foot some of the bills. It may only be a few miles from Morgan's Outpost, but it's a different world. A big city with lots of opportunity.

"So there I was, surrounded by kids who'd come halfway across the country to study at the university. Not more than a handful of them knew what they wanted to do with life."

He paused and took another cookie from the plate, breaking it in half but not biting into it. "Can you imagine what it's like to have your life mapped out for you? Get your business degree. Come home. Run the pub. I was like a kid who brought a sack lunch to a smorgasbord."

"It is not fun to watch everyone else make choices and feel powerless over your own future."

"It sounds like you understand." He paused, his gaze suddenly sharp and perceptive. "Do you have a family business to go home to, also?"

"Nothing as grand as Maguire's," she said with an airy wave. His eyes followed her gesture and she relaxed. "But, yes, my family basically decided what I should do with my life before I was old enough to have any say in the matter."

"Are you going to do it? Follow their plan?"

"I do not know." Sophia pushed away from the table and turned to the sink, focusing on the pile of dishes rather than Mike's gaze. His questions might be innocent, but her responses weren't.

"One thing I learned is that you don't have to decide right away." Mike's voice sounded near her ear. She felt him next to her but didn't turn.

He grabbed a couple of cookie pans and opened a device under the counter. "Let me toss this stuff into the dishwasher and get it started. Maguire's runs a clean kitchen, you know."

She followed his lead, stacking bowls and spoons where he told her—avoiding his eyes, but listening to his voice as he talked while working.

"I didn't want to run the pub when I was younger. You might say I rebelled against everything that had been planned for me."

"But you came back."

"Eventually." He closed the dishwasher and leaned on the counter, arms crossed, his eyes taking on a smoky brown hue as he regarded her. "But first I had a long taste of life on the outside. When I came back, it was my choice."

"I like the sound of that."

"Yeah, well you know what they say about adventure. It's long periods of boredom interspersed with brief moments of panic." He laughed, lightening the moment. "I kept my needs simple and bounced around for a few years. When I found good jobs, I splurged a little; when jobs were scarce, I dipped into the rainy-day fund. I wouldn't trade those years for anything."

"Where did you go?"

"Anywhere I wanted to." He flashed his cocky grin. "And before you ask, I took any job that paid the bills."

"What made you come back?" Her fingers tangled in the knot at the front of her apron, hiding her nervousness as she waited. She hoped, prayed, that his words would have a bearing on her own situation. How would she survive until she decided to return home? And how would she know when it was time to do so?

He laid his hand over hers, stilling her motion. "You'll know. When you've experienced everything you need to, you'll know. Something will change and then, just like the autumn sliding into winter, you'll head home."

"Is that what going home is like? A desolate winter of duty and expectations?" Her winters consisted of ski trips to the Alps. She couldn't imagine living in the cold forever. But wasn't that the emotional landscape she envisioned when she thought of home?

Mike turned her, his hands warm on her hips. His mouth quirked into a smile as he worked the apron knot loose. "No, Sophie, coming home wasn't desolate for me. It was right. Take my advice. Follow your heart for a while. When home ceases to be a place to avoid and starts to be a fond memory, then it will be time to go back."

He whisked the apron over her head but kept one hand firmly on her hip. The warmth of his palm seeped through her jeans and the touch of his slightly roughened thumb on her bare midriff stole her breath.

Until he moved his thumb in a tiny sweep of flesh on flesh. Her breath whooshed out in a sigh.

"Don't complicate things, Sophie. Don't try to control them. Just go with the flow."

She nodded, caught in the warmth of his breath on her cheek and his other hand, strong and capable, supporting her back. Caught in the brush of his lips across hers.

"So, live in the moment?" she whispered against his lips.

She felt him nod; gave in to the urge to kiss him again. Living an unscripted life both satisfied her and left her longing for more. She leaned into Mike, the touch of his body on hers fueling her need to get closer.

She craved this. Simple human contact. Hugs and tender touches. She'd missed them in the sea of sweaty palms and clammy kisses pressed against her knuckles over the years. Missed them in the marble stillness of her uncle's home where his touch demanded or reprimanded, but never cherished.

When Mike broke the kiss and pulled away, a sweep of loneliness engulfed her, as tangible as the wash of cool air on her skin. His hands still rested on her hips, giving a taste of closeness. Not quite what she needed, but more than she'd ever had.

"I don't want to make this difficult for you," he said softly. "But I know a little of what you're going through. I'll help you in any way I can."

He released her completely and stepped back. His gaze traveled down her body, lingering over the tight shirt and practically bursting into flame as it swept across her bare navel. Heat simmered between them, warming her in places that had been cold forever.

She savored it for as long as she dared. "Mike?"

At her quiet question, his gaze snapped back to her face. "Yes?"

"What happens next?"

His eyes darkened again, the smoky brown burning away the flecks of green and gold. "Next, I'm going to make you an offer. One you won't want to refuse."

Chapter 7

ike followed Sophia down the stairs, admiring the stretch and shift of her jeans as she moved. Too bad they weren't going up so he could get a closer look at those curves. Instead, he imagined running his fingers through her soft, bouncy curls.

This Sophie was as far removed from the Lady Sophia of Melesia as a flesh and blood woman was from a statue. This one tempted him in a way the other never had.

He slowed his steps and gripped the handrail in a choke hold, steeling himself to resist the temptation—on all levels. Exploiting her was as wrong as it was easy. He might as well stoop to stealing pennies from Pipsqueak's piggy bank.

Sophia had fallen for his lines exactly as he'd planned, practically jumping at the chance to live in his world for a few weeks.

He promised himself again he'd write a tasteful story, even though the *Weekly World Stir* didn't print tasteful. He had to try.

A faint giggle snaked its way up the stairs, followed by a cheer coming from the direction of the kitchen. He had to try for the sake of his family and the nine—make that ten, counting Sophia—employees depending on him. What a muddle already.

He caught up with Sophia at the bottom step and walked beside her down the short hall to the pub's main room. "Thanks again for agreeing to help out at the pub. Otherwise I'd be shorthanded with Ashley and Eric leaving for school next week. It's not vacation, but—"

"Nonsense. It sounds like fun. Are you sure I am not putting you out by staying in the apartment?"

"Absolutely not," he cut in before she could offer any alternatives. "Bunking at Dad's will give me a chance to discuss the business with him. Plus, it's closer to Katie's in case she or the girls need me."

"Tell me about your sister."

Mike hesitated. He was used to running the interviews, not answering anyone else's questions. Still, a little openness couldn't hurt. "Katie's had a rough time lately. So when she wanted to go back to school, I encouraged her." When Sophia didn't fill the silence, he continued. "She's studying culinary arts because she thinks it will help the pub."

"Will it?"

He shrugged. Katie had burned through half a dozen majors before dropping out of school to marry years ago. So far, she'd handled her heavy workload and long hours with a maturity that surprised him, but he'd learned not to depend on his family.

"We'll see. Somehow, I can't imagine replacing burgers and cheese fries with Chateaubriand and asparagus in hollandaise sauce."

Mike led Sophia to the kitchen where the crew traded stories over plates of sandwiches. Sophia blended in almost immediately, easing everyone into conversations, smiling, as comfortable in the kitchen as he imagined she'd be at a royal ball.

By the time he convinced her to spend the afternoon shopping with Ashley, she'd won the loyalty of everyone in the room. Including his nieces.

"Here." Mike intercepted her at the door as she and Ashley were leaving. "You'll need some cash."

She drew back. "I cannot accept your money. I am indebted to you for far too much already."

"It's an advance on your salary. You'll need something more than what you packed for vacation once you start working. Pay me back later." He heaved a sigh of relief when she took the money and headed out.

When Ashley's car rounded the corner, Mike sprinted upstairs to pack his bags. He shoved his laptop and files into a gym bag, rifling through the drawers looking for anything that tied him to his journalistic past.

Notebooks full of scribblings, some battered press passes and a research book on Melesian culture all landed in the bag. He scoured the room for any other clues to his identity then, satisfied, carried the lot to the downstairs office and locked it in the filing cabinet. One more trip upstairs and he had enough clothes for his extended stay at Dad's place.

He glanced at his watch as he hauled the duffel bag to the car. Two hours had passed. He still had time. Sophia may—or may not—be able to while away hours shopping, but he was sure Ashley would stay away as long as possible.

Mike checked the kitchen. The cooks were busy with dinner prep while out in the dining room, Eric taught the girls how to roll silverware into the napkins. Satisfied, Mike grabbed a beer from the cooler and slipped into the privacy of his office.

For the next hour, he mapped out his plan, only dialing the number for the *Weekly World Stir* when he had his facts in order. His gut churned with each ring. Visions of Sophia, her green eyes brimming with trust, clamored for his attention as he asked to speak with Frank Kincaid. He shoved the visions away, popped open the beer, took a swig and promptly gagged. God, he hated warm beer.

"So, Mack, I take it you called to reconsider my offer." Frank's booming voice had Mike reaching for the beer again.

"Depends on what's in it for me, Kincaid." He waited, forcing himself to relax so that the tension wouldn't seep into his voice. He propped his feet on the desk and leaned back while Kincaid hemmed and hawed.

"Let me get this straight," Kincaid said after a while. "This morning you told me you were out of the sensationalism business. Now you don't sound so sure. Let's cut to the chase, Mack.

"We've worked together too long to pussyfoot around. You're going to ask for an outrageous sum. I'm going to counter with a ridiculously low offer. We haggle and end up in the middle. Is that how you remember it?"

Mike took a swallow of the beer. Better warm than not at all. "Yep, that's about how I remember it. Back when you weren't asking me to come out of retirement, that is."

"That don't mean the rules have changed, kid."

"Unless you figure in the decrease in sales since I left. I believe you mentioned that earlier."

"I was just pumpin' up your ego, kid. Sales are fine."

"The financial pages don't agree. Judging from your quarterly financial reports and my stack of fan letters," *and the rumors of a corporate takeover he'd read about,* "I'd say the price for my work just went up."

Kincaid named a figure.

Mike repeated the number, keeping his voice calm even while his pulse raced. He mentally counted to ten. Kincaid interrupted him at around eight. "For one piece. I could be persuaded to go higher for a series."

"How about for an exclusive? *Reclusive Royal Reveals All.* An intimate look at the life behind the glamour."

Kincaid whistled, low and long. "You think you can get it? A personal interview with the girl? That's big, even for you."

"What's it worth to you if I deliver?"

"Look, cards on the table, kid. If you deliver on your promise, it'll be worth more than you ever made here before." He named another figure. "I can have an advance in your account by morning."

"Give me another couple of grand up front for research and travel expenses and you've got a deal." Mike drained the beer and tossed the empty in the trash.

Silence stretched over the phone line. Finally, Kincaid sighed. "Done. But I'm sending a contract by courier in the morning, and it had better be on my desk, signed and official by afternoon, or I stop payment on the advance."

"Sure thing, Frank. Don't forget to send it in an unmarked parcel. I don't need to have the staff and family wondering what I'm up to. That kind of interest could blow my cover and risk the story."

"Trust me. Your confidentiality is as important to the paper as it is to you. We own your moniker. Spill the beans about your identity as Mack the Pen and you're in legal shit up to your neck for the next decade. Read your old contracts if you don't believe me."

"You may own the byline, but you don't have anyone else capable of delivering the goods or you wouldn't have called me in." He tried to sound smug, but his gut twisted uneasily as he remembered the clauses that had kept him lying to his family about his job for years.

Still, for the sake of Dad, Katie, and the girls, he'd swallow his pride—and whatever else it took—to buy them a few more months of security.

"You'd better deliver, Mack." Kincaid's voice was edged with flint. "If you fall through on this, I'll make damn sure you never work in journalism again. You won't even be hired to write an obit for the local news rag."

"Understood."

Two minutes later, Mike smiled with satisfaction. The easiest contract he'd ever negotiated. His haze of contentment burst when he heard the jangle of the pub's front door followed by Sophia's and Ashley's voices.

He'd studied the classics long enough to know that when you sold your soul to the devil, the devil always collected. And God knew he'd rented his soul to Kincaid often enough to know that, in that respect, Kincaid and the devil were very much alike.

"I would like to request one Portobello burger with cheddar, two hamburger specials, one medium and one well done, and a Lucky Chicken Nuggets meal, please."

The clatter in the kitchen continued unabated.

She tried again. "Excuse me. I would like to place an order."

"Sophie, honey, this is no place to be soft spoken. Listen." Ashley grabbed the ticket from her and turned to the window separating the kitchen from the dining area. She shouted in a staccato burst. "Order in. Porto burger, cheddar. Burger special, medium. Burger special, well. One lucky chick. Got it?"

Joe looked up from the stove where he juggled half a dozen pans and repeated the order in a shout. "Got it, Ash."

Ashley flashed Sophia a smile. "Save the *please* and *thank you* for later. Hearing the order over the noise in the kitchen is more important. Shout it clearly and listen to make sure they repeat it right. Then put the ticket here."

She shoved the slip of paper containing the order into a clip on a rotating wheel and turned it toward the kitchen. "Listen for your table number and *order up* or check the window for your plates. Keep your eyes and ears open. We'll help you. You'll catch on."

Sophia looked from server to cook, dazed. One never shouted at servants. She never shouted at anyone. Did she even know how to shout?

Ashley waved a hand in front of her face. "Earth to Sophie. We've got tables to wait. Follow me." For the next hour, she trailed behind Ashley, learning the duties of her new job.

"Now try one on your own," Ashley whispered to her. "Smile. And remember, the customer is king."

She headed to the table, confidence lightening her step. What could be easier than smiling and keeping the guests happy?

A scant two minutes later, Ashley grabbed her arm and hauled her away from the table. "Sophie," she hissed, "you're not a hostess at a society party. Just go up to the table. Smile. Get their drinks. Take their orders. And leave. Don't hover."

"I am sorry. I only wanted to make them comfortable."

Ashley sighed. "I know. But comfortable to them means getting their meals on time. Let's just fill the drink orders."

Sophia felt a flush creep up her neck.

"You did get their drink orders, didn't you?"

Sophia shook her head and followed Ashley back to the table. She glanced at the clock. The long night was just beginning.

And so it went. First, she hovered too much. Then she didn't check back often enough. She served the food too quickly. Or let it get cold while a guest lingered over salad. Her throat burned from bellowing orders, and her fingers blistered from grabbing searing hot plates. In short, everything she did was wrong.

When Ashley suggested they take a break, Sophia steeled herself for a lecture. Slumped against the wall in a tiny break room off the kitchen, she nearly dissolved into tears when Ashley gave her sympathy and understanding instead.

"For someone who's never waited tables before, you're picking it up really fast."

"Fast? You don't even trust me to handle the money."

"Sophie, you've got enough to learn without having to fight with the cash register tonight. Don't worry, I'll share the tips with you at the end of our shift." Ashley gave her a smile.

"Tips?"

"Sure, you know, the extra money for doing a good job."

"Oh, tips." Sophia nodded vaguely, not wanting to appear stupid. Ashley must be talking about some kind of bonus Mike paid them based on the number of tables they served and how he perceived the customer's satisfaction. She'd ask Mike about it later.

In any case Ashley deserved—and needed—the extra money. Sophia didn't. Once she was home in Melesia someone else would handle the money, just as they'd always done in the past.

She pushed the thought of her return aside and smiled at Ashley. "That's nice of you," Sophia said, "but you don't have to share your bonus money, I mean tips, with me. After all, I messed up every table you sent me to tonight. You had to jump in with excuses for my incompetence."

"Excuses? Honey, I just told everyone it was your first night on the job. They understand. Besides, we all start somewhere. Right? My first night I mixed up every single drink order at all my tables. You—Sophie you don't even need to write down the orders. I had to beg you to do it for the cooks' sakes. You memorize everything, without a single mistake."

"I suppose it's something."

"Remember the teens at table sixteen? They're tricksters, putting in convoluted orders then switching places when the server has her back turned. Most servers mix up the orders and get flustered. You didn't even blink. And you didn't mess up a single order. No one's ever done that before."

Sophia chuckled softly, remembering the teens and their antics. "I thought maybe it was a test of some kind. The twins almost had me. Unfortunately for them, they didn't have twin mustard stains on their shirts."

"So that's how you worked it out." Ashley flashed her a thumbs up. "You'll be everyone's favorite server in no time. Don't sweat the details, Sophie. It gets easier."

As they stood, an unexpected pain shot up her leg. She couldn't hide her grimace in time. Ashley glanced at Sophia's feet. "Oh my god. Sophie, you aren't wearing the new shoes we bought today, are you?"

"You said they were the right kind to work in." Sophia stared down at her shoes, her stomach sinking even as the muscles stopped their protests. "Did I do something else wrong?"

"Only if you want to save your feet. Even sneakers take time to break in. Didn't you have an old pair? Your feet must be aching tonight."

"My feet are fine. These shoes are amazingly comfortable." Besides, she didn't have any other shoes, unless she counted the sandals she'd worn when she arrived or her dress pumps. And if she focused on the springy cushion of the sneaker's soles, she didn't mind that they pinched and rubbed in other places.

She'd danced in shoes that pinched far more than this and kept her smile intact. Complaints had only earned her a sure, and even more painful, attitude adjustment. The duke—curse his hide—had taught her that a royal daughter never let the world see her pain.

She brightened her smile with each uncomfortable, pinching step as she made her way back into the dining room. Funny, she'd always assumed only the royal family smiled through their pain. She'd never wondered if the servants did the same. In fact, beyond a cordial politeness, she'd never wondered about the servants at all. But now, now she was the servant.

Something clicked in her mind, and she paused at the door to the dining room, concentrating on the last state dinner she'd attended. Someone had always been beside her, offering drinks or hors d'oeuvres, before melting magically away, only to materialize again long enough to take her empty glass or plate.

Later, they'd served her dinner—soup, salad, entrée, dessert—efficiently, slipping the plate in from the left, whisking it away from the right. Efficient. Invisible. Attentive.

She'd work the rest of her shift trying to imitate those nameless servants. The ones she'd thanked a thousand times but never appreciated. She shook off the stab of guilt, vowing to do better when she returned home.

But for now, she had customers to serve. And by the gods, she'd learn to serve them as well as she'd once been served. She owed her nameless mentors at least that much.

Chapter 8

Sophia eyed her new sneakers warily. After a relaxing day of reading, getting used to the apartment—and the obligatory text home to let Grace know she was fine—it was time to get ready for work.

She perched on the edge of the couch and eased a thin pair of socks over the raw blisters on her heels, gasping as the socks disturbed the bandages. The discomfort diminished after a minute and she steeled herself for the next chore.

Loosening the laces as far as she could, she forced her foot back into the offending sneaker, clamping her teeth tightly against the gasp of pain. Instead, she curved her lips into a semblance of a smile. *Like a good, little princess.*

"Bullshit," she muttered, lacing the shoe with more force than necessary. When had her uncle's words started sounding like her own?

She wasn't Lady Sophia anymore. She was the independent new Sophie. Her own woman. She squeezed into the other shoe, uttering an oath when the unyielding leather scraped against her raw skin. But the oath didn't make her feet burn less or quell the throbbing pain in her heel.

Either way—privately hiding her pain or publicly complaining about it—she still had work to do. Tonight she determined she'd prove she was as good at waiting on tables as she was at working a royal reception room.

Although she'd refused to take Ashley's tip money, the girl's parting compliments—*great first night, Soph*—buoyed her. If she could corner Mike before opening tonight, maybe she could convince him to let her work alone.

Once downstairs, she peeked into the pub. Dust motes swam in the shafts of late afternoon light that streamed through the windows. Smells of braised meats and simmering sauces hung in the air, making her stomach rumble in appreciation.

The kitchen hummed as the sharp cadence of a knife chopping vegetables blended with the sizzle of oil and the splash of water creating a special kind of music. As she listened, a descant of tinkling glass wove into the melody from another direction.

She followed the sound and peered behind the bar to find Mike, crouched in front of a bank of shelves, unloading a box of liquor. Empty boxes littered the floor behind him.

"Need help?"

His head snapped up, and he flashed her a grin that sent a jolt of heat—the good kind this time—down to her toes. "I could use some company." He motioned for her to join him.

"That looks like quite a bit of unpacking you're doing."

He nodded. "We were low on supplies, so I picked up a few orders." He grabbed a bottle of whiskey and lined it up in front of a row, six deep, of identical bottles. "This should keep us from running dry."

Mike stood and dusted his hands. "Sorry I wasn't around to help you settle in today. Besides picking up the orders, I had some banking to handle and Dad was due in from Reno." A frown crossed his face. "You'll get a chance to meet him Monday."

"Does your dad work at the pub?"

Mike shrugged. "Dad does whatever he wants to these days. But, yeah, most days that involves working at the pub."

"Sounds like you are disappointed in him."

"It's just," he braced his hands on the bar, "I thought sending him to the food show in Reno would make him interested in the place again. You know, as more than just a legacy. Turns out, that trip may have been more trouble than it was worth."

"Because of me?"

"Because he spent too much, gambled too much, and came home with crazy ideas about a woman he just—" Mike slashed the air with his hand, the irritated gesture turning defeated when he rested his head in his palm a moment later. "Like I said, Dad does what Dad wants these days."

He scrubbed his hand over his face, erasing the tension before he turned to her, cocky grin and twinkling eyes firmly back in place. He leaned, one elbow propped on the bar in exaggerated casualness while he inspected her from head to toe.

"His trip wasn't all bad. You coming to Morgan's Outpost is the bright spot in an otherwise murky turn of events. Anything that starts with you throwing yourself in my arms and ends with you sleeping in my bed, can't be all bad."

"It may be your bed, but I am sleeping in it alone. You are sleeping elsewhere."

"I didn't say things couldn't get better." He flashed her a devil-may-care grin full of promise.

"You are incorrigible."

"Incorrigible? As in uncontrollable, unruly, uncooperative, and hopeless? That's quite a judgment to make on a man who's done so little to earn it. Yet."

Sophia giggled. "You sound like a dictionary."

"Actually, I sound like a thesaurus. A dictionary would say, incorrigible: unable to be corrected or reformed. Set in bad habits." He moved closer and tucked a curl behind her ear. "Feel free to try to reform any of my bad habits you want."

Her breath hitched at the whisper of his fingers on her ear. The nearness of his lips, no longer quirking with humor, threatened to send her heartbeat out of control.

The memory of their first kiss slammed into her, its heat and intensity waking her own restless, unruly side. But this was bright daylight, not the magical dark of the witching hour. And Mike wasn't just a handsome, available stranger anymore. He was…something more. No longer a toy for her amusement.

Still, she'd been weak enough to share a second kiss with him, and the sweetness of it had awakened more powerful, less easily satisfied cravings. It had shown she was all too vulnerable to his charms, too willing to be pulled into his world for longer than she ought to be. She dared not risk a third kiss.

Sophia stepped away. "I had best not try to reform you now."

"Maybe later?"

She smiled, leaving him no clue to her inner thoughts. "I would like to try to work on my own tonight. Without Ashley's help."

"Good thing, since Ash is off tonight." Mike winked at her as he started wiping down the bar. "She's got some packing to do before she heads off to Princeton next week. It's hard to believe a daughter of Morgan's Outpost is turning Ivy Leaguer on us. I wonder if she'll come back talking like you."

"What is wrong with the way I speak?"

"Let's just say it doesn't sound like you spent much time in a small town in Ohio. Sweet Saint Patrick! You don't even use contractions like a normal person. Did your folks ship you off to some fancy finishing school? Level with me, Sophie."

He turned back to her, the laughter in his eyes making it clear he didn't know how close to the truth he was. "Are you some rich kid trying to see what the other side of life is like?"

"No. I am, I mean, I'm just like you. Trying to see the world before I settle into the family business."

"And what business would that be?"

"It is—it's—complicated. Just like dinner service is going to be if I don't study the menu and get the tables set." She turned to leave.

"Sophie. Before you get to work, ask the guys to set you up with something to eat. And have them send me a burger—regular, no 'shrooms this time."

"No mushrooms?" She quirked an eyebrow at him from the safety of several steps away.

He winked in response. "I'm incorrigible, remember? Things can always get better."

Even from several steps away, her restless, unruly side responded.

Sophia counted the change again, carefully, while the cash drawer stood open. She checked to be sure the twenty-dollar bills her customer had given her rested in their compartment, not hidden among the fives or tens. So far, so good. Fumbling over waiting tables could easily be chalked up to inexperience but fumbling over currency could end her charade as quickly as it had begun.

Not that she had much experience with Melesian money, either. Like everything, the brightly colored notes engraved with the faces of the past generation of royalty were things that others—servants, shopkeepers, accountants—handled for her. Except once.

"This," Uncle Julian said as he held the crisp, seashell pink note in front of her eyes, "is an engraving of our queen—a half-American upstart unworthy of the title. One day, your cousin Helena will replace her and Melesia will be great again." He crumpled the note and tossed it toward the trash can. It hit the side and rolled down in a crack between the can and the desk.

"Yes, sir," she said, tearing her gaze from the pretty pink note and locking her eyes on his. She gave him a slight nod to show she understood. Sophia waited in front of his desk, shoulders square and spine straight, the way he had taught her to stand, knowing that the lesson wasn't over yet.

"Now this," he said extracting another, larger note from his desk drawer, "is worth studying. Do you recognize the engraving?"

Sophia studied the small portrait on the yellowish green note. The color reminded her of the mashed, overcooked vegetables the cook sometimes served for dinner. Both made her stomach lurch, although she knew from experience to hide her reaction from the duke. "It is a portrait of you, sir, like the one in the reception gallery."

"Very good." Uncle Julian favored her with a cold smile. "Do as I say, and one day you may have your portrait gracing our currency. Do you understand?"

"Yes, sir."

"Excellent." He handed her the mashed vegetable colored note. "You may keep this as a reminder of all you are to aspire to."

Sophia held the note, her every outward appearance showing respect even as she recoiled inside, until he dismissed her.

Later, while the duke was away, she crept back and retrieved the rumpled pink note. The creases in the paper didn't dim the queen's gentle smile. Instead, she radiated a calm_happiness that even the duke's anger didn't destroy.

Sophia imagined that her mother's smile would look like that if she were engraved on the currency. So she smoothed out the wrinkles and hid the paper away.

She'd carried the pink note for years, sometimes folded small and stashed in a corner of her handbag, sometimes tucked into the toe of a dancing slipper, or—when she was older—slipped inside the curve of undergarments her uncle dared not inspect. The queen had given her courage during a time when few others noticed, or cared, about her.

Now...

"Sophie, are you almost done there? I'm in a rush." Betsy Malone paused to push a strand of graying hair back into the clip that held it away from her face. "I'm trying to turn the tables as fast as I can. The kids need new shoes for school."

"Done." Sophia pushed the drawer shut and moved aside. So Betsy was working fast to earn extra money. Sophia remembered Ashley's comments yesterday. Turning the tables fast must be one of the ways servers earned the extra tip money from Mike. Which meant she'd better hustle herself or she'd owe him for room and board by the end of the week.

She hurried back to table eleven, cash in hand, only to find it empty. *Damn.* She'd kept her customers waiting so long, that they'd left without a word. And without their change.

Fear hit her body in a rush that turned her stomach to acid and her knees to jelly. If they were angry enough to leave without their change, would they be angry enough to deny the pub their future patronage?

Memories of the duke plagued her. He'd taken his seal of approval from merchants for any number of perceived slights in the past, usually sending them one of the yellow-green notes engraved with the ducal image along with a letter stating that this was the last patronage they could expect from him.

Sometimes, according to the hushed whispers she'd heard, the merchants never recovered from the loss of his business. Surely, no one here in Morgan's Outpost wielded the same power. But she couldn't be sure.

She looked at the notes in her hand. Dark green, without the sickly yellow cast of her uncle's money. A five and several one-dollar notes, with assorted coins. She had no idea how it equated to her home currency, but either way, if the residents of Morgan's Outpost were anything like her uncle, it spelled trouble. She steadied herself with a hand to the back of one of the chairs.

She'd heard other whispers too. Recently. Ones that hinted the pub might be having its own financial troubles. She'd never forgive herself if her actions put Mike's livelihood in jeopardy. Especially after his kindness to her.

"Hey, Sophie, you okay?" Eric's voice broke into her thoughts. "Don't worry about this table. I'll bus it for you. You go sit for a minute. You look pale, like you're going to pass out or something." He started clearing the plates at an amazing speed.

She nodded, barely aware of anything but the worry in her gut. She wandered to the break room, grabbed a slip of paper and wrote down everything she could remember about the customer. Then she wrapped the money in the note and put it in her apron pocket. She'd find a way to return the cash and apologize for the misunderstanding—whatever it was.

Back on the dining room floor, she threw herself into providing excellent service for the rest of her tables. Efficient, but quiet. Serve from the left. Clear from the right. Keep the water and drink glasses full. Anticipate needs. And this time, drawing on her hostess skills, she managed to get the names of all her customers.

Her eyes ached from squinting across the room to check her tables without hovering. Her mind raced with dozens of orders and names. The mnemonic skills she'd used in the past for remembering diplomats, their countries, political concerns and personality quirks didn't work as well in the dining room as in the state room. She'd kept up—barely. Still, there had been no complaints, and everything seemed to be going well.

Tables five, eleven and sixteen had just finished their meals and paid. She moved first to table sixteen—Mrs. Steinbrenner—who'd paid by credit card.

"Your receipt, Mrs. Steinbrenner."

"Thank you, my dear. Your service was excellent." She smiled as she signed the credit slip and put the card away.

"My pleasure," murmured Sophia. "I hope you will come back again soon." She melted into the background, knowing better than to linger as Mrs. Steinbrenner finished her coffee and left with the young man accompanying her.

Sophia hugged the compliment to herself as she moved to the other tables, only to have her hopes come crashing down again. More cash, flagrantly thrown down, at each of the other tables. Fives, tens, ones, coins, all mocking her.

This is the last business you'll get from me. Her hands shook as she gathered the money, added names to her growing list of disappointed patrons and bundled the cash into her apron to return later.

She eyed table sixteen, remembering that at least Mrs. Steinbrenner had been pleased. Whatever she'd done for her, she could do for the others. Sophia headed toward the table and stopped, her heart plummeting. A twenty-dollar bill lay prominently placed on the table.

Even Mrs. Steinbrenner, despite her smiles, had been displeased with her service.

Mike stole glance across the room, watching Sophia, wondering if her royal pride would get her into trouble or if she really could handle the dining room alone. Almost before her shift began, Eric was bussing her tables while she headed to the break room. Disappointment hit him like a sledgehammer.

Three days ago, if he'd dared to imagine a Lady of the Realm in his dining room, this was exactly what he'd have predicted of her.

"Maguire, hurry up with that drink."

"Coming." He sloshed scotch into a glass, topped it off with water, and slammed it in front of the customer, eyes still on the break room door.

"Don't know what's buggin' you, Mac, but whatever it is, I like it." The customer swigged from his glass and heaved a sigh. "Last week you were so tight-fisted with the scotch I thought you was gonna slap a cherry and one of them little umbrellas in my drink. Fit for a girl. Whatever's eatin' you, at least it's got you pourin' man-sized drinks."

"Shout if you need another," Mike answered, not caring what he thought of the drinks. *Damn it.* He'd wanted to be wrong about her. Yesterday she'd seemed more...more something. More than just a royal slacker. He'd staked his reputation and slaked his conscience on the hunch she was more than the world believed her to be. *Sweet Saint Patrick! If she let him down he'd—*

Thank God. His full-steam-ahead rant fizzled into a sigh of relief when she exited the break room in record time. He refilled a bowl of bar mix and went back to pouring drinks, one eye on her. Hours later, she'd turned tables like a pro, never breaking stride or taking another break.

Mike slipped a tiny digital camera from his pocket and snapped a couple of photos while she wasn't looking. His conscience nagged, but he stilled it. Just because he had the photos didn't mean he was going to use them.

He caught her eye as he was stashing the camera and flashed her a thumbs up. She answered with a smile and a little nod. But then she wiped her eyes as she turned away, making him wonder if she'd misunderstood his compliment.

Before he could move in her direction, she summoned her smile for a table full of customers. His mistake. It was nothing—smoke or fresh cut onions, or, who knew, maybe she teared up from the smell of mushrooms. Whatever. The moment passed.

"Mike, how 'bout I spell you for a while?" Betsy Malone slipped behind the bar. "That new girl is catching on fast. I don't think you need me in the dining room now that the dinner rush is over."

"So you think she and the others can handle it?"

Betsy chuckled. "She's up to it, all right. I about had a heart attack when Mrs. Steinbrenner ended up at her table."

"Olivia Steinbrenner? Food critic for the *Denver Post?*"

"That's the one. Her son took an internship at the local hospital. She's out here visiting him. But word around town says she's researching a book on the best diners in America."

Mike whistled. "That's big, even for a rumor."

"Yeah, well, like I said, I nearly had a heart attack when she sat at table sixteen. But Sophie had the woman eating out of her hand from the get-go. Mrs. Steinbrenner left full of smiles and she left *cash* on the table. Not something she's known for."

"Great. Thanks for keeping an eye on Sophie."

"Only problem she's had so far is making change. She counts it out half a dozen times. Typical of young people these days. They don't teach 'em math. Other than that, she's okay. So how about it? Why don't you let me handle the bar for the rest of the night? I could use the tips."

Mike untied his bar apron and flung it aside. "Thanks. It's all yours tonight. The tip jar's already half full. Keep it and anything else you earn." He headed off to make a quick round of the dining room and kitchen before locking himself away in the office.

For the first time in months, his step was light.

# Chapter 9

Olivia Steinbrenner was fast. Her email to Mike, along with a review of the pub to run on the *Post's* website and feature in her book hit his in-box before closing time. He read it again, savoring the praise.

… beyond the old-fashioned comfort foods and obligatory coziness, Maguire's Pub boasts something truly unique. Five-star restaurant service. From the moment I was seated, my server behaved with cool professionalism and uncommon elegance.

Fresh lemon slices delivered at the same time as my chilled water. Warm-from-the-oven rolls presented to me "compliments of the chef" rather than dumped unceremoniously in the middle of the table. Never obtrusive. Always attentive.

And serving—heaven forbid!—according to old world manners rarely observed outside of formal settings with a formally trained waitstaff.

This magical blend of best-in-class service, warm, inviting ambiance, and nicely prepared food makes Maguire's one of my top picks for enjoyable dining.

The rap on the door broke his concentration. "Come in."

Sophia slipped inside the office and closed the door softly behind her.

"Just the person I wanted to see." He jumped up and took a step forward, slowing when her ramrod straight body tensed as their gazes locked. His gut registered a problem a fraction of a second before his other senses clamored in agreement.

Her stillness, the tiny twitch of a cheek muscle hinting at a clenched jaw and the slight widening of her eyes froze him in place.

"What happened? Is it your family?" He'd been scanning recent Melesian news stories when Steinbrenner's email came in. Had he missed something? "Come in and sit down." He led her to the couch and waited while she perched on the edge.

"I am sorry to have failed you." Her carefully enunciated words contrasted sharply with the banter of the woman who'd laughingly called him incorrigible only a few hours ago.

Failed him? He hadn't asked anything of her, unless you counted his private hope she'd give him a story. Unless—

His gut churned with foreboding.

She knew.

God knew how, but she'd discovered his past. How else could he explain her cool, remote demeanor? He peered into her eyes, searching for a hint of the innocent rebel who'd sauntered into his bar and plastered a kiss on him. Or the plucky woman who'd jumped at a chance to work in his pub.

Her icy green gaze slid past him in a trick as old as royal hauteur itself, focusing not on him, but on a point just behind his shoulder. Giving the appearance of attention without the bother of really seeing him.

Her stillness mocked the blood pounding through his veins. Lady Sophia of Melesia, legendary for her ability to waft, untouchable, beyond the reach of the press and the people, didn't sully herself with the likes of him.

"I don't—"

"You have been so kind." She laid her hand on his arm, shattering his illusions as she met his eyes at last. A shadow lurked beneath the cool gaze. Pain—frozen in place by the icy aloofness that held the world at bay. Not shutting him out. Shutting herself in.

"Tell me what's wrong, Sophie." He covered her hand with his own, willing his warmth to penetrate her self-imposed prison.

"You gave me shelter." Her eyes stayed dry, but the barest hint of a wobble colored her voice, letting him know he'd gotten through. "You gave me a job. I thought I could handle the work, but I let you down."

"You're kidding, right?" Relief at not having been found out warred with his concern for her. He squeezed her unresponsive fingers.

"Everything is a mess. I have all of this money." Her voice cracked and she jerked away, an avalanche of movement replacing her former stillness. She pulled wads of cash out of her pockets, dumping it in his hands. "They were so angry they walked out without waiting for their change. I don't know what I did wrong."

She shoved more bills into his hands. Coins bounced onto the floor. Finally she pulled a paper from her pocket. "I kept a list. Maybe if I write an apology, I can convince them to give the pub another chance."

He pushed the money back into her lap. "Sophie, honey, what are you talking about? Who was angry with you?"

"The customers. They left this. Every one of them left money."

"Of course, they did. They were thanking you, not— Listen, I don't know how things are done—" *in Melesia,* "in Ohio, but around here, when someone leaves a tip—money on the table—it means they are thanking you for good service. That's your money."

She looked at him, her brows slightly flattened, concentrating. "Why thank me for doing my job?" She frowned at the money as if it were poisonous.

Maybe to her it was. She'd probably handled more money in the past week than in her entire life. Mike sighed inwardly.

"Sophie, this isn't going to work," he said softly.

"Of course, it is. I just made a silly mistake. My family is a little eccentric. We never leave tips. And I—"

"Sophie, stop. We both know you're not the small-town girl from Ohio that you're pretending to be."

Silence stretched between them. Sophia's fingers tightened on the dollar bills she clutched in her lap, but she didn't speak.

All the truth and a little bit more. His old tag line flashed through his head. Mack the Pen was an expert at spinning stories any way he wanted to take them. He'd once prided himself on that ability. Maybe tonight he could use it for a better purpose. What spin could he put on tonight's situation to salvage both her false identity and his real story?

"Listen, Sophie, I don't care if your father is a senator, the CEO of an international conglomerate, or some philanthropist the world hasn't heard of. It doesn't matter to me. All I know is you're a young woman who wants to make her own way for a while. I respect that. Admire it, even. And I'll help you find what you're looking for. Just come to me whenever you're in over your head."

She looked at him for a moment, a glimmer of life returning to her face. Trust—that he didn't deserve—shone in her eyes. "Do you mean it? You won't tell the rest of the staff?"

"Not a word to them." *At least until they read his series.* He pushed the thought aside.

She nodded, slowly, as if still considering her situation. When she spoke, he leaned in to catch the soft whisper of words. "You were close to the mark this afternoon—when you asked if I had been sent to a finishing school. My parents were..." her voice trailed off.

"That part does not matter. They died in an accident when I was a child. I was sent to live with my uncle. Uncle—" She paused, stopping short of saying a name. "Uncle traveled outside of the country quite frequently. Tutors always traveled with us to take care of my education."

"I imagine it must have been fun, seeing the world that way."

Sophia absently smoothed the bills in her lap, stacking them randomly. "It was my life."

Mike waited, his gaze fixed on her slender fingers as she toyed with the money. The icy precision in her voice and her restless fiddling told him there was more she wanted to say.

"Uncle," her voice hitched again in the odd stutter as she avoided naming him, "didn't approve of frivolity. He expected perfection. When one failed, he expressed his displeasure in memorable ways."

As she detailed the callous way he dismissed his creditors, Mike made a mental notes of people to interview regarding the duke's behavior. No wonder Sophia buried her pain in ice. He dredged up a smile for her and eased the conversation back toward everyday issues.

"I don't know much about the rest of the world, but here in Colorado a displeased customer won't leave any tip. Or he might leave a penny. No one who's unhappy with the service leaves folding money. Especially not something that size." He gestured to the twenty on top of her cash stack.

"So I did a good job?"

"Sophie, you did a wonderful job. Let me share this with you." He handed her a printout of the restaurant review and filled her in on the Steinbrenner visit.

When her eyes widened and her smile turned from feigned to real, a warm pressure built inside Mike. Pride, maybe. Or joy. Something that made him want to cheer—like when the girls kicked a soccer goal or solved a difficult homework problem. He'd given Sophia a chance to be proud of herself.

The glow in her eyes and the blush tinting her cheeks told him she hadn't experienced many such chances before. What else could he give her that she hadn't experienced before?

"Let's celebrate your achievement tomorrow."

"You hired me to work, not to play."

"Tomorrow's Sunday. Pub's closed. So how about it? I know you've probably seen Paris in the spring and all that high-brow stuff, but nothing beats Morgan's Outpost in the autumn."

He winked at her. "Have you ever picked apples for a homemade pie? Or driven through a canopy of autumn leaves? Or visited the fairgrounds for a pumpkin festival?"

"Pumpkin festival? What is that?"

"It's an American tradition, that's what. No self-respecting Ohio girl should have to ask that question. You, Miss Sophie Bradley, spent so much time traveling the world that you don't know your own culture. I would be privileged to help you make up for lost time."

"Since you put it that way, how can I refuse?"

"Just the answer I was hoping for." Mike grinned at her and scooted his chair closer to the couch. "Now lean back and relax. Put your feet in my lap. After two days of waiting tables, your legs probably feel like lead."

The tension in her shoulders eased slightly, and she settled back onto the couch, but her feet remained firmly planted on the floor. "It is not that bad."

He cocked a brow at her.

"I mean it isn't bad."

"At least that sounds more like a typical American woman. But you've got a way to go before you learn to relax. You make lounging on the couch look like work."

He rose and stacked a couple of pillows in the corner of the couch, then eased her back onto them. "Lean back and relax. Prop your feet up here and stretch out."

As she closed her eyes and lifted her legs to the couch, he settled down at the other end. "That's right. Take it easy for a while. You've been working almost nonstop all night."

Mike stroked his palm along her denim-covered shins then gently lifted her feet to his lap. As he moved to massage the tense muscles in her calves, she sighed in pleasure.

"If it wasn't too bad before, does that mean it's better now?" He slipped his hands under her wide cuff and touched bare skin as he continued to soothe the tightness in her muscles.

"It's definitely better, now," she murmured.

"And to think, a minute ago you didn't trust me." He kept up the firm strokes, easing her deeper into relaxation. "You probably think you've got ticklish feet, too, but it's all in the pressure. Let me show you."

He loosened her laces and tugged a shoe off. Instantly she stiffened, her lips and eyes squeezing tight, but not quite tight enough to contain the tiny gasp of pain.

"It's okay, Sophie." He soothed her calf while cradling her heel in his other hand. A wet stickiness covered his fingers and he looked down to see pink tinged dampness seeping through her thin socks.

"Sweet Saint Patrick!" Mike rested her calf on his knee and eased the sock off her blistered heel as gently as possible. A useless, crumpled bandage—too small for a wound this size—dropped to the ground. The mangled flesh beneath his hands, hot and red, didn't come from an hour too long in her shoes. A glance at her pale, composed face told him even more. If not for the slight tightening of her lips, he'd have never known she was in pain.

"How long have you been working like this?" His voice was rough, but his fingers gentle as he removed her other shoe and sock. "You should have told someone. We could have helped."

"I had a job to do. Complaining changes nothing."

Her calm acceptance irritated him. Mike rubbed her instep gently, trying to draw her attention to something pleasurable, not painful. "Believe it or not, I take the health of my employees—and my friends—seriously. At the very least, I could have gotten you a better bandage and a more comfortable pair of shoes. Or found you a job that didn't involve as much standing."

"I don't expect favoritism."

"And I don't expect you to hide something like this from me ever again. Understood?"

"Yes."

"Good." His voice softened. "Now, lie still while I get something to take care of this."

Mike propped another pillow under her legs to keep her comfortable and left the office in search of bandages and supplies.

Memories of his days as a reporter in Melesia swirled in his head. How many functions had he attended where she was present? How many times had he snapped a photo of her practiced smiles and watched the seemingly effortless way she worked a room?

How many of those times had he missed the almost imperceptible clench of her jaw or tightening of her lips? If he dug into his photo files would he be able to see how many of her smiles were fake and which—if any—of them reflected real pleasure or happiness?

You're an idiot, Maguire. What else explained his glib assumption that her life consisted of kowtowing servants and endless pampering? The Sophia he'd seen so far might not know how to handle money or load a dishwasher, but she knew how to make a little girl laugh and a grumpy reviewer smile. And she exhibited more grit than many of the people he'd worked with over the years.

He filled a bowl with warm water, then rummaged through the break room supply cabinet for a soft cloth, antiseptic cream and gauze bandages.

She was his responsibility—temporarily—until she chose to go back to her former life. Once there, he couldn't protect her from public opinion or the ravages of the press. Even his own story—which he swore again would show the world her substance instead of a stereotype—might cause her pain.

But for the time being, he could protect her from herself. And maybe, if the blessed saints continued to grant him a little good luck, he could show her that her worth ran much deeper than a pretty face and a practiced smile.

Sophia sagged against the couch, embarrassment running hot through her veins. Mistaking a common American courtesy for an insult was bad enough, but having Mike see her injuries was a dozen times worse. He must think her a pampered idiot.

Of course, so did the rest of the world. Tabloids thrived on the exploits of Lady Sophia, or at least, they had until she disappeared. Now speculations on the queen's health and possible pregnancy eclipsed even her disappearance.

Isn't that what you wanted?

The reality of her wish paled in comparison to her dreams. How long could she realistically survive in this life she'd wished for? Not long enough, if the mistakes of the last twenty-four hours were any indication. Thank the gods Mike accepted the twisted version of her life story.

At the sound of his footsteps, she closed her eyes and forced her thoughts away from her deception.

"How are you holding up?" A hint of concern warmed his voice as he settled on the couch once again.

"I'm fine." His unjustified concern did strange things to her. Exciting, unfamiliar, wonderful things. She jumped slightly when he drew her feet back into his lap, but quickly waved away his apology.

His touch, tender in a way the servants and doctors had never been, melted her resistance as he bathed her wounds. His voice, soothing and resonate, thawed other barriers as it soothed the ragged edges of her spirit.

"A year ago, I might not have known what to do for you. You can thank my sister Katie and the three Marys for bringing my skills up to par. I've bandaged more scrapes and cuts in the last year than in my entire life." He dabbed ointment onto the clean skin with such gentleness that she barely felt his touch.

"Thank you. But it wasn't necessary. I could have done that myself."

"It never hurts to let someone else take care of you for a while." He covered the area with gauze and taped it down. The warmth of his hand seeped through the thin gauze. "Besides, I wanted to give you something more than simple first aid."

He covered her instep with his palm, heating more than just her flesh. With slow, deliberate strokes, he pulled his thumb across the ball of her foot, massaging circles in the tired muscle.

"I don't offer this service to just anyone, mind you. But since you are sleeping in my bed," he winked, "and since I'm incorrigible, it seemed appropriate."

The wink, and the timbre of his voice, sent shocks of pleasure tumbling across her skin and making her stomach churn and dip as if she were standing on the deck of a ship during a storm. Floundering emotions battered her defenses until only the strong, sure press of his fingers anchored her to the present. Fingers that worked magic on her foot.

And her calf.

And… Heavens!

His touch never strayed above her knee, but heat burned a path from his hands to the juncture of her thighs, setting off a firestorm of reaction.

She squirmed against the couch, consumed by memories of the last time she'd felt this way. When they kissed. Before she'd, well, just *before*. She closed her eyes and savored his touch.

"You okay?" Mike slowly swept his thumb across her arch.

"This is the most wonderful thing I've ever experienced."

"If you say so." His voice held its familiar teasing note. "But I have a sneaking suspicion you're lying."

Memories of the kiss and her reaction heated her cheeks. "All right. This is the second most wonderful thing I've ever experienced."

"And the first is?"

"The first is a story for another time."

His laughter warmed her as effectively as his hands.

"You know," he mused after a while, "you remind me of a bedtime story I sometimes tell the girls." He massaged the ball of her foot, carefully keeping away from the injured heel. "Once upon a time, far, far away, a young girl lived with her stepmother and two stepsisters. Although she was beautiful and kind, they were mean to her and made her work in the kitchen."

"Everyone knows this story," Sophia interrupted. "A magical fairy godmother sends her to a royal ball. The prince falls in love with her, and when she disappears, he searches until he finds her and marries her. The end." She shuddered. The prince searching for her wasn't driven by love. And marriage to Stephan or some other political husband wouldn't end in a happily-ever-after.

"That's not quite the way I tell it, but the facts are essentially the same."

"Why does it remind you of me?" Heaven help her, she should get up and walk away before he started thinking of her as a princess-in-training. But his hands melted her resistance even before she could summon it.

"If you remember, the prince had one clue to her identity. The glass slipper." Mike moved from her foot back to her calf, long languid strokes keeping pace with the mesmerizing cadence of his voice.

"In the children's story, Cinderella easily fits into the slipper after her stepsisters try and fail. The original version is far more gruesome. You see, the stepsisters were so desperate to marry the prince that they went to extraordinary lengths.

One," he cradled her foot in his hand and drew his fingers across the base of her toes as he spoke, "cut off her toes to try to fit the slipper. The other, cut off her heel."

Sophia cringed as he carefully traced her bandaged heel. "That's horrible. Why would someone do that?"

"I don't know the point the Brothers Grimm were trying to make, but when the girls are older, I know the point I'll make. Don't be pressured to fit into someone else's shoes. Be proud to be yourself. If the stepsisters had filled their hearts with kindness instead of envy, they might have found their own happiness."

One hand swept the length of her calf, absently stroking it. "Try on anyone's shoes you want while you're with me, Sophie. But don't force them to fit. I'll never ask you to be anyone but yourself."

"Thank you," she whispered, giving him a smile.

"On that note," he rose and scooped her up, "it's time to tuck you into bed and head home for some shut-eye myself."

Instead of protesting, she looped her arms around his neck and buried her face in his shoulder. Beneath the lingering scents of the bar and grill a whiff of spicy soap and warm male tickled her nose. With each tread of the stairs she shifted and rolled against him, the jostling both comforting and exciting.

When he settled her on her bed, she pulled him down into a kiss, but rather than the deep searching hunger that they'd shared initially, this kiss tasted of hope and new beginnings, lingering only long enough to leave her longing for more.

"Save that thought," he murmured, "and sleep well. Tomorrow I'll give you a day you'll never forget."

Like today, and yesterday, and every day since we met, she thought as he slipped away, and she dressed for bed in a drowsy haze. The fairy tales had it all wrong. She slid under the covers and closed her eyes. Happily-ever-after wasn't about fitting in a glass slipper. It was about tossing it away, letting the shards fall where they may, and dancing, barefoot, in the grass.

Chapter 10

Mike stared in the mirror, humming to himself as he rinsed his razor and reached for a comb. His gaze traced a crack in the plaster above the mirror. When had the bathroom he'd once shared with his sisters shrunk? For that matter, the whole house seemed smaller than when he'd left it a little more than a decade ago.

He tossed his comb back in the toiletry bag and shrugged the memories aside. Today was about the future, not the past. He dubiously eyed his unbuttoned plaid flannel shirt with solid tee underneath. Too Paul Bunyan? He buttoned it halfway and inspected the result. Maybe Sophia preferred the collegiate sweatshirt look. Or he could…

Enough. He wasn't some obsessed teen on a first date. Nothing he wore could compete with the tailored suits and tuxedos of the crowd Sophia routinely mingled with. That was exactly the point. She hadn't escaped her world to find more of the same in Morgan's Outpost. She'd escaped to find something else.

Mike grabbed his gym bag from the bed and shoved a few items into it. Sophia would need the sweatshirt, extra socks and other gear he'd accumulated. He threw it over his shoulder and headed downstairs, lured by the promise of coffee.

Once in the kitchen, it didn't take long to brew the coffee and down a first mug. He'd just poured the second cup and stretched his legs out under the kitchen table when his dad walked in. Even clad in old sweatpants with the night's stubble—showing hints of gray that hadn't yet reached his head—James Michael Maguire Sr. exuded the enthusiasm of a much younger man.

Which was part of why they were in their current mess. "You're up early." Mike took another slug of his coffee. "I thought you might be jet lagged today. Or something."

"One hour isn't enough to jet lag me." His dad filled a cup of coffee and joined him at the table. "So that means you must be referring to the *or something*. Her name is Destiny. Destiny Fairchild."

"It wasn't bad enough with your internet dating. Now you're picking up—what?—showgirls from Reno? I sent you there for the restaurant show, Dad, not to find some hot, new diversion."

"I picked up plenty of ideas for the pub. I cared a damn sight more about it during my two weeks in Reno than you did while you were dating wanna-be models and actresses." James glared at him over the coffee mug.

"Look, Dad, I didn't plan to argue with you over coffee. It's just—" Mike rubbed at the ache in his temples. "Things are complicated. It's a lot harder than I thought it would be."

"Running the business? Hell, yes. If it's not headaches over produce deliveries, it's nightmares about the staff taking a five-finger discount with the liquor. It's always something. Believe me, I've seen it all over the years."

"Including Sam robbing us blind."

"That bastard." James slammed his fist into the table with enough force to slosh Mike's coffee over the rim. "Stealing from the pub was low, but divorcing Katie was criminal. My little girl was an innocent till he came along and broke her heart. He threw her and the girls aside like they were yester-day's coffee grounds."

Mike moved to the sink, letting the air between them cool while he grabbed a cloth to wipe up the spill. Convenient as it was to blame Sam for their problems, dwelling on the past didn't change the future.

"So, how's she doing these days?"

Mike tightened his grip on the cloth at the sound of his dad's quiet voice.

"She? Katie's doing fine, Dad. School keeps her busy, but—"

"Not Katie, you numbskull. I know how my own daughter's doing. I meant the pub. How's she doing?"

"Maguire's is fine. Still a little in the red, but better." Mike sopped up the spilled coffee and tossed the cloth in the sink. "Last night was especially good. Olivia Steinbrenner paid us a visit."

"Who?"

"Don't tell me you've been out of the business so long that you don't know Olivia Steinbrenner is the food critic for the *Denver Post*. The one who just posted a rave review about Maguire's Irish Pub and Grill."

"Really?" Dad's eyes lit up, and he leaned toward Mike. "A fancy food critic liked our pub? Tell me more."

As Mike filled him in on news, a hint of the man he'd once known peeked out from behind the whiskers and mussed hair. For the first time since Mike had come back to Morgan's Out-post, his dad showed interest in the business. An interest that, according to Katie, had waned years ago.

Half an hour later after hashing through the business and a hastily cobbled together breakfast they fell into a companion-able silence.

"At the risk of spoiling our domestic tranquility," Dad said as he put the dishes in the sink and refilled the coffee cups, "do you want to tell me why you're sleeping in my house instead of your apartment?"

Mike shrugged.

"Woman trouble?"

"How'd you guess?"

"Give me some credit. I may not have a college degree, but even I can put two and two together. You hired a down-on-her-luck waitress, and now you're living here. You let her move into the apartment, didn't you?"

"It's temporary. As soon as she gets on her feet—" *she'll leave* he finished silently as he let his voice trail off.

"As soon as she gets on her feet, she'll find her own place and you'll move out of here. Taking in strays is a bad Maguire habit, Mike. Look where it got Katie. Besides, having a grown son living here cramps my style."

"Your style?" Warning bells sounded in Mike's head. "Is this about the showgirl in Reno?"

"I already told you, her name is Destiny. And yes, I've invited her to come for a visit. I don't need my son playing chaperone while she's here."

"When?"

"She'll be free when her current singing gig is up in a few weeks." A happy grin crossed his dad's face. "I promised to let her pass out goodies to the trick-or-treaters if she comes for Halloween."

"Are you sure she shouldn't be going door-to-door collecting candy instead?" Mike grabbed his gym bag and headed to the door. "Maybe you should listen to your own advice about taking in strays, Dad."

His dad's lips tightened and Mike braced himself for the return of hostilities. Instead, his dad's eyes landed on the bag.

"Planning on going for a run before we take Katie and the girls to Mass this morning?" he asked.

"You guys are on your own today. I'm spending the day with Sophie—the new waitress. After showing her the sights and taking her to lunch, I've got a meeting with the mayor and some council members about the fundraiser at our Fall Pumpkin Festival."

His dad grunted. "Sorry about saddling you with the mayor and that group of curmudgeons he calls a city council. He and his cronies have been hounding me for years. Ever since I stole his girl in high school, in fact."

A mischievous grin flitted across his dad's face. "I figured you had enough of the blarney in you to handle him. Maybe helping this year will get them off our backs."

"Yeah, well, the funds are going to rebuild the youth center. The three Marys don't say much, but I saw how they reacted when it burned down. I can put up with anything for the sake of the girls."

"They're good kids. I don't want to see them suffer any more."

"Keep that in mind while you're interviewing candidates for their new grandmother."

"Give me some credit, son. I'm not as helpless as you think I am. I did a lot of soul searching in Reno. It was my wake-up call. My head's on straighter than it's been in a long time."

"I wish I could believe that."

"Believe what you want. Time will tell. And Mike?"

"Yes?"

"Don't forget about Mass."

"You're awfully concerned about Mass for a man determined to throw his life to Destiny."

"Seems to me you're too nonchalant about Mass, considering the gleam in your eyes when you mention Sophie."

"I'll catch an early Mass." Mike flashed him a grin and stepped outside. "Or I'll add skipping it to the list of sins for my next confession. Meanwhile, say a prayer for me."

"I'll do that," he heard his dad mutter into his coffee cup. "I'll pray your sins result in giving me a grandson."

At the knock on the door, Sophia jumped from the table, scattering toast crumbs and licking her sticky fingers. It was too early. She wasn't ready. She— Mike rapped again. Ready or not, he was here. She fluffed her still damp hair, ran to the door on bare feet and opened it.

The sight of him leaning there, grinning down at her, sent a jolt of adrenaline through her veins. "Hi," she managed. The breathy whoosh of her words, so unlike her normal polished speech, mocked her attempt at nonchalance. "I just finished breakfast."

"So I see." His smile turned warmer, and he cupped her cheek in one hand, his thumb gently brushing a crumb from her lips.

She licked the spot he'd touched and felt his fingers tighten as they slid around to weave into her hair.

"Keep reacting like that and I may give in to my baser instincts." He moved closer until she could feel the warmth of his body and smell the scent of his soap.

Unable to stop herself, she licked her lips again. "What baser instinct?"

"This one." In the space of a heartbeat, he closed the distance between them and sealed his lips to hers. Warmth surrounded and penetrated her. The touch of his tongue on hers drew her closer and ignited sparks of pleasure, but the heat of his body seduced and ensnared her.

The press of his arm when he snaked it around her waist and the feel of his hand cradling her head awakened a hunger—a craving—she couldn't fight.

She wanted more. Sophia slid her hands around his waist, burrowing beneath the layer of soft flannel to touch even softer cotton. She wiggled closer to him like the puppy she'd once had as a child.

The one who snuggled next to her in her bed and fell asleep with his nose buried in her shoulder. The one her uncle had left behind when he'd taken her into his home.

She broke the kiss and rested her cheek on Mike's shoulder, fighting the tears hovering beneath the surface, surprised she could still mourn a piece of her life that had disappeared so many years ago.

She squeezed tightly, using him as a buffer against the memories, not resisting when he stroked her back and cupped her hips, drawing her closer. As she pressed the soft planes of her body into the hard muscles and ridges of his, childhood memories fled, swamped by the rush of newer, urgent memories.

Memories of the night when her body first nestled against his and she learned the power of a kiss. When the taste of him intoxicated her more than the finest champagne, more than her uncle's potent cognac.

Then, her body had betrayed her and cut the lesson short. Not so today. Sophia shifted her grasp, leaving the warmth of his back and looping her arms around his neck. She urged him down into another kiss. One he entered into without resistance. One she took without hesitation.

If nothing else, Sophia learned quickly. She kissed him as thoroughly as he'd kissed her the first night, nearly sighing in satisfaction when she felt his response. She ground her hips into his, excited by her own power to arouse him.

In her training as a royal fiancée, she'd learned—how could she not?—the importance and mechanics of providing a royal heir. Uncle Julian and his army of acting, modeling and dancing coaches drilled her endlessly, crafting an alluring, attractive creature, just seductive enough to secure her prince.

Her gynecologist had explained the details of copulation in cold, clinical detail. But no one had told her anything about passion—neither the intoxicating rush of it through her veins nor the heady power of arousing it in another.

She shifted the pressure and angle of her hips, thrusting her tongue into Mike's warm, pliant mouth as he groaned in response. This was power. Passion.

He broke the kiss, his breathing heavy. "Sophie, honey, if we're going to continue like this, at least you could invite me inside."

Without waiting for her answer, he maneuvered them inside and kicked the door shut. And as quickly as the latch clicking into place, he whirled her between him and the door, surrounding her with his kisses and heat that singed rather than warmed. His lips devoured. His body demanded. And hers responded, still in the flush of passion but without even the illusion of control.

He shifted again, wedging his knee between her legs, lifting her to rub his hard thigh against her soft, intimate flesh. No matter that layers of denim separated them, she felt him sear her, each movement a brand. Tender, untouched places on her body throbbed. Her knees threatened to give out. Still he pressed her against him. Liquid weakness washed her from head to toe.

Sophia tore her mouth from his, gasping. She sagged in his arms, sliding down his thigh till her trembling feet rested on the ground. Gulping air and shuddering with each heartbeat she clung to him, while the world righted itself and her strength returned. All the while, he held her securely.

"So," she managed, her still ragged breaths making talk difficult, "now that you're inside, is there anything else that I can offer you?"

Mike laughed, his ribs and back shaking beneath her fingers. He planted a kiss on her forehead then, hands on her shoulders, stepped away. "There are a million things you could offer me, and I'd be tempted by every one of them. But let's take the safe road. Got any coffee?"

She felt herself blush. "Actually, no. I started to make some but the first batch was too strong. The second was too weak."

"Let me guess. Coffee making is another thing your sheltered life kept you from learning." He brushed a stray curl behind her ear and gave her a tender smile. "Mind if I give you a lesson?"

Sophia followed him to the kitchen, savoring his baritone rumble as he talked about coffee. She tracked his movements, her eyes feasting on his hands as he went through the motions. Broad, capable hands that had, minutes ago, lifted her as effortlessly as he now lifted the steaming carafe.

Come morning, she still wouldn't be able to make coffee, but until the day she died, she'd remember the sound of his voice and the shape and texture of his hands. And even with her last breath, the memory of those hands sweeping along her awakened body would be as vivid as it was today.

Mike busied himself in the kitchen, making coffee he didn't want, whisking away crumbs that weren't his, wiping down already clean counters—anything to keep him from reaching for her again. But his eyes, as if they had a will of their own, darted to her, catching her every gesture and expression.

Especially the smug cat-with-cream smile that hovered on her lips. If he didn't know better, he'd have sworn she deliberately aroused him by wiggling her soft, lush body against his.

But he—and dozens of political and entertainment reporters—knew she'd been all but promised to a Melesian prince for most of her life. He doubted the strict confines of her life had allowed for dating.

Unless… A dark thought crossed his mind. He glanced at Sophia. Tight jeans and a skimpy pullover sweater hugged her curves. Mentally he peeled them away, imaging those curves sunning in a scrap of a bikini on a private beach. Or splashing in the waves until the material outlined her nipples in near transparent glory.

The rules governing Melesian royals didn't belong to the normal world. They mimicked an era when women were bartered and sold in marriage to buy peace between warring nations. When the right of kings—and their whims—superseded morality or decency. If her alleged fiancé, now King of Melesia, had wanted her in his bed, nothing would have stopped him.

Even now if the younger prince—Stephan—wanted her, nothing would stop him from having her. Hadn't Mike and the other tabloid reporters speculated about a relationship between Stephan and Sophia when the king announced his engagement to his American fiancée? Any man would be a fool not to want a woman like Sophia in his bed. Whatever else they were, the royal princes of Melesia weren't fools.

Mike's hand tightened as he imagined gripping a royal throat instead of the spoon he'd used to measure the coffee grounds. Tighter. He moved his hand out of sight so Sophia wouldn't notice his silent struggle. A little more. The metal bent under his steady pressure, the smooth flex of steel releasing the tension from his body in a trick he'd learned long ago.

As he tossed the bent spoon away, Mike silently thanked the coach who'd shown him the technique for channeling his anger when he wasn't on the playing field.

Behind him, Sophia cleared her throat. "May I offer you some coffee?" Her voice held both the hint of formality and an underlying thread of laughter.

Mike turned and accepted the mug she held out. His spirit lifted at the sight of her sparkling eyes and pink tinged cheeks. From the top of her tousled hair to her bare feet, she radiated energy, nearly quivering with excitement.

Excitement that washed away the bulk of his fears. Surely someone this vibrant couldn't have been wounded by love or battered by unfeeling lust. Besides, he reminded himself, only a handful of days ago she'd wandered into his bar, and his life, without the faintest idea of how to kiss.

"So, are you ready to see the sights in Morgan's Outpost?"

"Do I look ready?" She twirled revealing a view that made him add to the list of sins he'd like to commit with her. Maybe he should have actually attended Mass this morning instead of lurking in the back of the church for ten minutes and hoping God would give him full credit for his half effort.

He gulped the coffee to ease his dry throat. "You look good enough to eat."

"As soon as I put on my shoes—" she grimaced "—I'll be ready to go."

"Hold it. I said you looked *good*, not that you looked ready for the day I have planned. Do you even know how to dress for cool weather?"

"I've been skiing. Does that count?"

"Not unless you have a ski jacket stashed away in the closet." He winked at her. "I brought you a sweatshirt, some heavy socks and other stuff. How are your feet today?"

Sophia made a face. "If I could go barefoot, I would."

"What I have is almost as good. Let's get you some fresh bandages then get you bundled up."

Half an hour later, outfitted in a Denver Broncos blue and orange hoodie, two pairs of thick socks and his mother's old gardening clogs, she followed him to his jeep. The sun glinted off her curls as a crisp fall breeze mussed her hair. She pushed it off her forehead, rooted in her bag for sunglasses, and slid into the passenger seat as naturally as if she belonged in Morgan's Outpost.

It was a fantasy. One he dared not buy into. The most he could offer her was a few days of harmless flirtation in exchange for milking her for a story that justified the sum Kincaid had paid him.

Mike headed out of town and onto a back road. Brilliant orange, bright yellow, and crisp reds burst into view as the road wound through a copse of scrub oak and bigtooth maple trees. He glanced at Sophia. Her mouth was slack, her attention riveted on the scenery. Behind her dark glasses, he'd bet her eyes were wide.

"This much color is unusual for the Colorado plains," he said. "Most of the land is used for farming. But someone, a couple of generations ago, decided to sacrifice a little farmland for the sake of beauty. The local trees and some of the surrounding parkland are the pride of Morgan's Outpost."

He eased the jeep off the road and pulled to a stop. "You picked a perfect time to visit. For today's lesson on what it's like to be a real American, we're going for a walk in the fall leaves." He pulled her from the passenger seat and laced his fingers through hers.

The crunch of the leaves beneath their feet, the cool freshness of the air, and the sparkle of the sunlight slanting through the canopy of color, created the perfect fall day. Mike shuffled through the leaves, kicking up little puffs of curling, dried leaves.

"When I was a boy, we used to rake the leaves in our yard and take turns jumping into the piles. My two older sisters—Angel and Maggie—dared me to jump off the roof into an especially big pile. Thank goodness Dad got wind of it and stopped me before I broke my neck."

"He must have been very angry."

"Angry? Not really. By the time I came along, he'd dealt with his share of pranks. Of course, I didn't learn that until much later. He gave us a lecture and so many extra chores that we didn't have time to get into any other trouble for a while." He grinned. "Those were good days."

"I'm surprised you remember your punishment with such fondness."

"What I remember is that he spent a lot of time working with me on projects he dreamed up to keep us out of trouble. The point was to channel our energies into something constructive instead of foolish.

"I'll bet if you dig deep enough, you'll find that your parents did the same." He stopped, waiting for her response, wondering if she'd elaborate on the half-truths she'd told him earlier. Would she risk sharing true memories of her childhood—the kind he'd tried to ferret out as a reporter—with him? Or make up another story to try to keep him in the dark?

Seconds passed as they crunched through the leaves. Beside him she shuddered, and he wrapped an arm around her shoulder, pulling her closer. "Cold?"

"A little." Shyly she returned his one arm embrace, working her hand between his flannel shirt and tee shirt as she'd done earlier.

Mike enjoyed the warm feel of her pressed close as he guided them through the trees. Eventually, she spoke—as he'd hoped she would—breaking the silence.

"I remember my fifth birthday. My parents gave me a puppy. I named him Plato and insisted he was the smartest dog in the world. He followed me everywhere. I used to sneak him into my bedroom at night, even though I wasn't supposed to."

"Typical kid stuff. Your parents probably laughed to themselves and took a dozen pictures of you sleeping with the puppy."

She smiled, a wistful upturn of her lips. "I suppose so. They scolded, but he was allowed to stay."

"So you do have happy memories. Tell me more. What other mischief did you and Plato get in to?"

"Not much. I—" The smile disappeared. "They died before my next birthday. When I went to live with my uncle, Plato had to stay behind. Uncle didn't like animals unless they had a pedigree. He said Plato served no useful purpose."

Mike waited, hearing the hesitation in her voice and knowing there was more.

"Everyone and everything in Uncle's world served a purpose or they didn't stay in his world." Her voice was as dry as a student chanting Latin verb conjugations by rote.

"Even you?" A cloud drifted across the sun, turning the day from bright to chill and Mike drew Sophia closer, trying to protect her from her memories as much as from the weather.

"Especially me," she whispered, her voice unsteady. "I was supposed to give him a kingdom."

Chapter 11

Sophia broke out of Mike's grasp and crunched her way through the leaves to a tree on the other side of the path. How could she have been so stupid? A kingdom? Not even wealthy, well-traveled American girls—the kind she'd pretended to be—aspired to marry into royalty.

Only a handful of people aspired to that goal. A handful of people who made the news, lived in glass houses, and pretended not to feel pain or rejection or any of a myriad of emotions normal people experienced. A handful of people like her.

She glanced over her shoulder at Mike. He leaned carelessly against a tree, hands in his pockets, looking at the trees and the sky until he saw her. Then he grinned—not the smirk of a man who knew a juicy secret about her, just the kind of smile that made her toes tingle.

Her toes were just the beginning. A flush of heat warmed her despite the wind as she remembered their kiss. The hours hadn't dimmed her body's response. Her breath quickened, and her nipples tightened as the lines between memory and reality blurred. Fire pooled low in her belly, burning a path to the juncture at her thighs.

Mike's lips tipped farther up, his grin taking on a knowing edge.

She tore her gaze from his, fighting to keep her body under control. Her slip hadn't changed the dynamics between them. But the memory of that kiss had incinerated any lingering innocence she'd gathered since the morning.

Sophia tilted her head, staring up into the colored, leafy canopy, admiring the tree next to her. She drew in a breath of the cool, fresh air and felt the heat in her cheeks subside. Intent on the tree, she traced its bark with her fingers. Rough, patterned with scars and blemishes, its life force pulsed beneath her touch. A rustle in the branches above drew her attention just as a shower of orange-gold leaves floated down around her.

The maples were as unlike the gangly, pretentious palms of her home as she was unlike the mold the damn duke had tried to force her into. The palms towered, looming over the landscape, growing taller and more unreachable each year. Each alike without individuality, without soul.

They hid signs of age—tattered brown fronds of years past—under new green shoots, a perpetual illusion of youth even as they decayed and died. As unchanging as the Kingdom of Melesia.

Not so for the maples and oaks. Each tree twisted, bent, and branched out in its own unique statement of independence. Even in the face of winter—death—they blazed with color and vitality. She spread her palm across the rough bark, vowing to spend her days in Mike's world like the maple—stretching to the sky and the world around her, blazing with life until the last moment.

As if summoned by her thoughts, Mike came close and put his hands on her shoulders. She relaxed into the familiar warmth of his body. "They're beautiful," she whispered.

"Did you know the leaf colors are the tree's way of reacting to stress? The cool, dry autumn nights make it hard for the tree to turn sunlight into food. So it sacrifices the dormant energy in the leaves and turns it into color before shedding them and living off of stored energy in the sap. It prepares the tree to survive the winter." He wrapped his arms around her middle.

"Wise people also shed the vulnerable parts of their past so they can prepare for the future," he continued, his voice a soft rumble in her ear. "You don't have to be defined by your uncle or any other people in your past. Only you can choose your future."

Sophia rested her hands on top of his, soaking up his words and feeling the comforting thump of his heart. Too bad his advice wouldn't work in her world. She might choose a day or a week of freedom, but her soul, her destiny, was too rooted in duty to allow her a lifetime of it.

"Did you choose your future? Running the pub?"

"I chose to help my family. Right now, they need me to run the pub and, for all my grumbling, I enjoy it. Dad's starting to take an interest again. Katie's determined to help out and support the girls. Everybody's pulling together for the first time since Mom died. And I'm a part of it. I don't know if I'll stay forever, but I'll stay for now."

"If I had your family, I'd want to stay forever." She thought back on the girls and the way Mike spoke lovingly of his sisters and his dad—even when he was frustrated with him. If she loved someone that way, she'd never leave. And if they loved her in return…

"So, are you ready to move on?" Mike unwound his arms and clasped her hand again. "I thought we'd grab some lunch then I can show you the fairgrounds. In a few weeks, they'll be setting up for the Morgan's Outpost Pumpkin Festival."

"I thought we were going to see a Pumpkin Festival today." She smiled up at him. "Did you bring me out here on false pretenses?"

"Not at all. I said I'd help you learn about your own American culture. I didn't promise we'd see the festival today. If you're still here at the end of October, I promise I'll take you to it."

"Deal." She savored the thought of being in Morgan's Outpost for another couple of weeks. But how?

Mike steered them back toward his vehicle while Sophia's mind raced. The bare outline of a plan began to form. The news channels and papers had paid lip service to her visit to the U.S. during the past days, peppering in the occasional photo that she knew to be a fabrication. Which meant that someone in power at home—either King Constantine or Prince Stephan—was working with the Melesian Press Corps to keep her flight a secret.

Before she'd left the tour, she'd penned a note to Stephan, informing him that she'd slipped away for a day or two alone. Every morning she laid the envelope out with her belongings. And each night when she came back to the hotel, she'd packed it away.

Shortly after her disappearance was discovered, she'd been sure the note would be opened and read. She'd hardly dared to hope they would allow her the freedom she craved, but it seemed they did.

Grace's daily text updates assured her that no one in the kingdom, except a few palace insiders, knew of her disappearance. Stephan had been charged with finding her, but, to date, had kept his investigations low key. If she could somehow get him another note without alerting him to her whereabouts, maybe he would continue the ruse.

Another week, another month—what difference did it make to Melesia? She'd have still been on the tour, posing for photos and entertaining the foreign media during that time anyway. If they could be entertained by manipulated photos, why shouldn't she enjoy her freedom for a while longer? It was little enough to ask in return for the years of service she'd given her country.

"Mike? Did you say Ashley is leaving for school in the east this week?"

"Yep. She's starting a little late, but she's a smart girl. She'll make up for lost time."

"Do you think she'd do me a favor?"

"Probably. What do you need?"

"My," she paused running the explanations over in her mind. "That is, while I was traveling, I developed a friendship with a student in a Caribbean country. He collects foreign postmarks. I used to send him letters from all over the world. If I gave Ashley a letter for him, do you think she'd mail it from school? He doesn't have many east coast postmarks."

"I'm sure she'd be glad to help." Mike looked sideways at her, his brow slightly wrinkled. "Does he have a letter from Morgan's Outpost yet?"

"Of course. I sent it the first day." This time the lie rolled easily off her tongue. It wouldn't do to have Mike helping her mail letters from her actual location.

"Well, then, write your letter and we'll have Ashley mail it for you. I'm sure I can find some other friends who'll do the same. We even get occasional truckers stopping by the pub who travel the entire country. We should be able to keep your friend happy."

"Thanks." Sophia grinned, glad to have Mike's unwitting help. With his army of contacts, she should be able to keep Stephan's eyes trained anywhere but on Morgan's Outpost for a long time to come.

Mike focused on the road, keeping up a light banter with Sophia and pointing out what few sights there were. He bit back a smile. Her ploy to keep the Melesian Royal Family—at least that's who he thought she was contacting—appraised of her safety while hiding her location was a subterfuge he could admire.

One that promised to keep her by his side for a while longer. The thought of spending more time with her—for the sake of the interview, of course—made it impossible to hide the smile any longer.

Later, alone, he'd sort through the information she'd given him and plan to ferret out new details of her life. And he'd look through the photos he'd snapped on the sly while she enjoyed the fall foliage. For now, he'd follow his gut and enjoy her company.

His gut reminded him that it was nearly lunchtime.

"What kind of food are you in the mood for, Sophie? We have a couple of fast food places and local diners to pick from."

"Anything you choose would be fine."

"Ever had roadkill?"

"What's that?" Wariness flashed across her features, hidden as quickly as it came.

"Mostly it's a joke. You know—the rural folk made supper out of whatever was killed on the road by passing vehicles. Like that squirrel over there." He pointed.

True horror crossed Sophia's face as she struggled to keep impassive. "Is it a traditional food?"

"It's not all that bad if you smother it with onions and peppers." He pulled into the gravel parking lot of a roadside café and slowed to a stop.

Sweet Saint Patrick! She was too busy steeling herself against his suggestion to catch the teasing in his voice or see his smile. Her jaw tightened, and she swallowed, eyes closed for a mere second, before she adopted her normal, placid expression. He would have missed it entirely if he hadn't been intent on watching her every movement.

"Please assure that mine does not contain mushrooms." Her voice, cultured and calm with a hint of hauteur, belonged to the Lady Sophia of Melesia. The one he thought he'd known so well.

He didn't like the cool tone or the aloof resignation in her posture. He wanted the laughing, trusting woman who'd started the day with him.

"Sophie, honey, I was teasing you." He reached for her hand and gave it a reassuring squeeze. "The onions and peppers are real, but underneath it's ground beef mixed with spices and served over a bed of fried potatoes."

"Thank the gods," she murmured. The relief that washed over her transformed her before his eyes. "I really wasn't looking forward to eating something scraped off the pavement."

"But you would have?"

She shrugged. A smile teased her lips. "You'll never know for sure, will you?"

Mike ushered her into the small diner and placed their orders, settling back to watch as she enjoyed her meal. Despite her light comments, he suspected that she would, indeed, have eaten anything he put in front of her.

Picky Princess Snubs Staff. An old headline flashed across his memory as he watched her take a dainty bite of the roadkill special. The story filed years ago detailed her behavior at a diplomatic party held in honor of Julian, Duke de Lyons and his niece, Lady Sophia. His words came back as sharp and clear as if he'd written them yesterday.

The spoiled socialite, seemingly unaware of the chef's efforts on her behalf, waved away dish after dish of delicacies, demanding instead that the overworked staff find something to her liking.

According to a teary-eyed kitchen maid, a letter—detailing the royal lady's likes and dislikes—had gone astray, precipitating the royal temper tantrum.

The rest of the article continued in the same vein.

His sketchy research revealed a three-page letter had been issued to the host's staff. At the time, he'd thought it the height of arrogance, but now, watching Sophia polish off her roadkill and gamely order shoo-fly and grub cobbler (actually made with apples and raisins), he knew he'd been wrong.

Whatever other information the lost letter had contained, its primary purpose, undoubtedly, was to alert the staff to her mushroom allergy. He'd bet every dish she refused posed a health threat she didn't dare risk.

How many other details had he misinterpreted in his rush to make a press deadline? Worse, how often had he ignored the facts for the sake of painting her in a negative light?

It was just entertainment, he'd told himself time after time. And every reported detail was the literal truth. She did wave away food, hurting and embarrassing the staff. They did scramble to offer her alternatives. All literally true. But the image he'd created with his words twisted the misunderstanding, transforming it into an example of royal callousness, all for the entertainment of his readers.

He gagged on the last bite of roadkill, tasting nothing but guilt despite the years that had passed.

"Are you all right?" Sophia's voice broke through his self-imposed castigation. "You look a little like I feel when I eat mushrooms. Are you going to pass out on me?"

Mike laughed, his humor restored as she treated him like a friend rather than with the contempt he deserved. No doubt even if she knew about his past, she'd offer him forgiveness instead of anger. The humor faded, replaced by a rush of tenderness and a resolve to make it up to her.

"I think I overdid it with the double helping," he said, pushing his plate aside. "Next time I'll slow down. What about you?"

"It was the finest roadkill I've ever tasted."

"Great." He signaled for the check. "Listen, if you're planning to stick around for a few weeks, I could use your help on a project. No pressure and no strings attached, of course, but—"

"I'd enjoy helping you with a project, but I'm not sure what I'm qualified to do."

"You underestimate yourself. Look how quickly you learned to wait tables like a pro. In your travels across the world, did you ever have the opportunity to plan events? Parties?"

She nodded, just as he'd known she would. He chose his next words carefully. "Maguire's Pub committed to helping the mayor and city council with a fundraiser. It's a little out of my element, and I could use some help."

"You have come to the right place. What sort of event are you interested in planning? How many people? You mentioned it's a fundraiser—what cause are you supporting?"

He held up a hand. "Whoa. You're going too fast for me." He checked his watch. "Why don't I fill you in on the way to the fairgrounds? I'm supposed to meet with the mayor and a couple of others in about an hour."

As he paid the bill and walked with her to the car, Mike caught the sparkle in Sophia's eyes and felt the excitement in her step. His own step lightened. She was his—at least until the fundraiser was over next month.

Chapter 12

Sophia smiled at Mayor Aimsley, hoping to put him at ease. It didn't work. He bustled about finding her a seat, apologizing for not having refreshments, and generally falling at her feet.

"This old building's seen better days. Of course, everything at the fairgrounds has seen better days. Not that it matters much when the festivals are going on. Decorations spruce it up quite a bit."

"Don't trouble yourself, Mayor. I prefer seeing the room empty so I can assess the possibilities. Let's start by discussing the purpose of the fundraiser and what you have in mind."

"Yes, yes. Of course." The mayor threw Mike a resentful glance and Sophia felt the tension in the room intensify. "Maguire, you could have warned me about what you had up your sleeve. How was I supposed to be prepared for someone who'd served in diplomatic corps, for crying out loud?

"People like that don't just drop into Morgan's Outpost out of the blue. I never put much stock into your dad's bragging about you till now. Guess he had it right on one score. You sure get around."

"Trust me, Mayor, Sophie's full of surprises. For the record, she didn't tell me about her past experience either. Seems we both got lucky today."

Sophia cleared her throat, drawing the eyes in the room back to her. "My background was not relevant until now. I simply wanted to assure you that I've planned large events before." She smiled at the mayor and the council members who flanked him then addressed them. "Mr. Johanson, I understand parks and recreation are your field of interest."

"Well, Miss Sophie," Lars Johanson said as he straightened his shirt, fiddling with the cuffs, "when I grew up, mothers stayed home with their children, and the kids played in the backyard. A lot's changed since then. Everybody works and the kids have too much time on their hands. They used to rot their brains on TV, now it's the internet. But in the end, a video screen is a poor substitute for real life."

She listened as he chatted on about his grandchildren and the state of the world in general. One by one, she led each council member into discussions of why the festival was important to them. And one by one, bent old men and pudgy middle-aged businessmen sat taller and took more interest in the proceedings.

Mike had settled into a corner, arms crossed, chair tipped back on two legs. She was grateful he'd retreated into silence. He and the mayor had bristled like two dogs fighting over the same bone from the minute they'd walked into the room.

She glanced at him, trying to judge his mood. One angry man in a roomful of agreeable ones could jeopardize the most mundane negotiations. His quick half grin and sly wink settled her worries on that score.

She turned back to the council members. "Thank you so much for helping me understand the situation. Let me see if I have everything straight. When your children's recreation center burned down last year, you all decided that the proceeds from the festival should go to rebuilding it."

A handful of heads nodded. "The high school gym isn't big enough to hold all the classes the center sponsored," replied

Councilman Spritz. "My daughter volunteered to teach dance and they turned her down flat, because the room was already bein' used for volleyball."

"Mrs. Aimsley wanted to offer sewing and craft classes for the girls, but she was turned down too," added the mayor.

Sophia nodded. "I see. Although the schools sponsor lots of sports for the children, it is important that they have a balance of activities—especially for the girls."

She made a few notes on the pad of paper Mike had given her. Zeus! She wished she understood more about American culture. The events seemed to center on Halloween celebrations. Well, when in doubt, act with confidence.

"The main money-making events—other than paying for entrance to the fair—are your corn maze and the haunted schoolroom. Is that correct?"

"Yes." The mayor nodded his approval. "The high school drama club does a bang-up job on the haunted schoolroom. Just enough to scare the kids without giving them nightmares. And the local grange sets up the corn maze."

"Beggin' your pardon, Miss Sophie," added Mr. Johanson, "but we've been doin' those events for years. Not that we couldn't use your help to make 'em better, you understand, but that's not what we're worried about. It's this chili cook-off that Maguire suggested that's got us in knots. We've never done something like that before. That's what we need your help with."

"All right. Let's focus on the cook-off. Mike told me that the idea is to charge contestants an entry fee and give a prize to the best tasting chili. Correct?"

Again the councilmen nodded.

"Okay, what about this? The festival runs for a full week. Let's kick off the beginning of the festival with the entrants bringing in a batch of their chili for the judges—that would be you gentlemen—to taste. You'll vote by secret ballot for the best entry. Then, each day of the festival, we'll supply pots of chili from two or three of the recipes.

"We'll invite the crowd in to taste and vote for their favorites. At the end of the week, we'll reveal the judges' favorites. Everyone who casts a vote for the winning recipe will be entered into a drawing for a grand prize."

"Prize?" Mr. Spritz frowned. "I'm not in favor of taking money from the profits to buy prizes."

"I understand." Sophia turned her attention to him. "We all want to raise the most money possible for the center. But by asking people to vote on their favorites and giving prizes, we'll convince them to attend each day of the festival so they can taste all of the recipes."

"Which means they'll pay a fee to enter the fairgrounds each night." The mayor rubbed his hands together. "Should we make them pay to taste the chili and vote too?"

"I have two suggestions." Sophia smiled at him. "First, in addition to your usual admission fee, why not offer a slightly more expensive fee that allows people to come for several nights? Most people will pay a little more if they think they're saving in the long run—and it won't matter if they come back or not, you'll have the extra money.

"Second, everyone should get a free taste of each chili. That will lure people to the tent, and once they've had a taste, they'll be willing to pay for a full bowl."

"I like it," said Mr. Johanson. The others nodded in agreement.

"We can also have a variety of games and raffles in the tent. I'm sure that you gentlemen will be able to convince local businesses to donate the prizes."

"The health department isn't going to let people bring in their own batches of chili for sale. So who's going to cook for the crowds?" The mayor looked at Mike. "You?"

The legs of Mike's chair hit the ground with a crash. He ambled over to the rest of the group and fixed the mayor with a stare. "Maguire's will be happy to do the cooking if you can get the grocery store to donate some of the ingredients. What do you say?

"You've got connections in the grocery business. Maguire's will split the cost of ingredients with them *and* do the cooking. As long as we get credit for sponsoring the event."

The mayor's brow puckered, then cleared. He thrust his hand at Mike. "You got a deal, Maguire. I'll talk to the in-laws. But don't be surprised if they offer to foot the bill for everything—and take the credit for sponsoring the event."

Sophia forced herself to laugh as she stepped up to the two men. The air between them crackled with the kind of posturing she'd seen all her life—in one form or another.

"Mayor Aimsley, Mike, this is delightful. It's so exciting to see you trying to out-do one another for the sake of the children's recreation center." She smiled at each and placed her hand over theirs—still clasped in a death grip. "The event is fortunate to have two such dedicated co-sponsors. Now," she briskly changed the subject while disentangling the opponents, "shall we discuss advertising for the event?"

As the afternoon progressed, Sophia surveyed the peeling paint and the grimy windows of the fairground's administration building, contrasting it to the marble and gilt halls where she'd organized royal receptions and international dinners.

In her mind's eye, she saw the faces of the three Marys— serious, sad Mary Margaret and her two boisterous sisters. She thought of what the youth center could mean to them, and for the first time in her life, she knew what she was doing mattered.

Chapter 13

Two weeks later, Mike dragged a box from the store-room and hefted it onto the bar. Dust tickled his nose when he opened it. Inside, coils of black and orange lights tangled together with plastic skulls and other ghoulish items. "Girls, want to help me put up the lights?"

"Yes!"

"I do!" Pipsqueak and Squirt rushed to him—two bundles of red-orange hair and black smudges, perfectly in keeping with the season. He lifted them to the barstools and started them on the task of untangling the strands.

"Miss Manners, are you going to give us a hand?" Mike looked across the room, searching for his third niece.

"I'm helping Miss Sophie with the cobwebs," she answered from her perch atop a ladder near the cashier station.

Sophia hovered beside the girl, hands lightly on Mary Margaret's waist while she called out directions. "I think we need a little more in the corner. Then we'll try to anchor some of it onto the cash register."

"While you're up there, toss a few of these into the web." Mike's dad handed Mary Margaret a handful of black plastic spiders. She giggled while throwing them into the sticky threads, aiming for the far corners.

Mike's gaze lingered on Sophia's profile, drinking in the smile that curved on her lips and the way the afternoon sun turned her golden hair into a halo. His heart kicked into an unfamiliar rhythm, part lust and part something stronger. Longing. Tenderness. Emotions that could ruin his plans and rip his heart out if he didn't control them.

"Uncle Mike? We're ready."

He turned back to the two other girls, plastering a devil-may-care grin on his face for their sakes. "Guess that leaves the three of us to decide where to put these lights. What do you think?" He pulled a strand loose from the tangle.

"Along the bar," said Squirt.

"Yeah. Like last year," added her sister. "And look! We can put these into a bottle of that icky-licky the grownups like so much." She tugged at a dilapidated skeleton, pulling its bones loose and handed Mike a leg bone.

"I don't know about putting this in the liquor bottles," he began.

"Please."

"Yes, please. Let's do it."

The two girls started tearing apart more skeletons, passing him pieces of plastic bone between giggles.

"All right, you two. Stop." He collected the assorted bones from the bar top and grabbed two empty whiskey bottles from under the bar. "We'll put the bones in here—one bottle for each end of the bar—and later we'll see if Dr. Wizard can teach us how to make them float. Okay?"

"And we'll make the water green, and glowing and…" Squirt rambled on, full of gruesome ideas that might require a team of special effects technicians rather than a visit to the drwizard.com website.

"Can we put the skulls in one of those?" Pipsqueak pointed to a martini glass.

"We'll see. Let's get the lights up first." Mike ran the strands along the edge of the bar, anchoring them in place while the girls helped.

A shriek from the direction of the cash registers had him halfway across the room before he realized there wasn't trouble. His dad dangled a giant black and red furry spider with pipe cleaner legs in front of Sophia and Mary Margaret, daring them to add it to the intricate webbing they'd created.

Mike grabbed his camera and snapped a couple of quick pictures while everyone's attention was on his dad.

"I'm not touching that," Miss Manners said, her refusal prim and unmoving. Then she squealed and ducked away when Mike's dad teased her with the oversized arachnid. Mike smiled. It was good to see the children acting like children.

Across the room, Sophia reached for the spider, muttering about her bravery in between giggles. Before she could snatch it from his dad, Katie popped out of the kitchen.

"Sophie, can I borrow you for a minute? I want your opinion on one of the chili recipes entered in the contest."

Mike gazed around, warmed by the laughter and love filling the old dining room. With Katie trying new recipes in the kitchen, dad laughing and doing odd jobs around the bar, and the girls underfoot, things seemed just about perfect. The family was together, doing what families did: enjoying each other.

Having Sophia as a part of the rag-tag group added to the appeal. He finished hanging the lights around the bar and stepped back to admire the handiwork.

Styrofoam pumpkins rolled around on the bar top, waiting to be placed on tables and in windows. Assorted witches, soon to decorate the shelves and hang from the ceiling, lay in a pile nearby. Still a long way to go but looking good so far. Mike reached for a witch, only to be interrupted by the phone ringing in his office.

He answered it to find the mayor on the other end, asking for Sophie. Mike glared at the receiver then set it down and headed to the kitchen.

"Hey, Sophie, you've got a call. It's your fan club president."

She looked up from the simmering pot of chili. "What? Oh, you mean the mayor. I'll slip out and take his call then be right back."

Mike watched her leave, enjoying the view, if not the reason for her departure. Still, he had to admire her. At their first meeting with the mayor she'd charmed the old coot into becoming her most devoted fan. Then she'd single-handedly transformed their half-baked idea into a spectacular fund raiser.

She'd walked from the meeting, a perfect example of diplomatic composure, until they reached the privacy of his car. Once on the road, like an icicle melting in the sun, she'd morphed from the confident Lady Sophia to the slightly befuddled and utterly irresistible Sophie. He chuckled at the memory of her question. *Mike, what exactly is chili?*

"A penny for your thoughts, bro." Katie's voice sounded at his shoulder. "Heck, I'll even give you a dime if they're as spicy as I think they are."

He smiled down at her. "You'd better save your money, and I'd better—"

"—keep your thoughts to yourself? It doesn't matter. I can guess. You like her, don't you?"

"What's not to like? Do you realize what she's accomplished? In less than two weeks, she convinced the grocery store to foot the bill for all the cook-off ingredients, the newspaper to run full page ads for the fundraiser, a local printer to print up thousands of flyers, and someone else—I don't even know who—to pay for postage to mail them. She's also recruited dozens of high school athletes to work the fair during the fundraiser. Amazing."

Katie shook her head. "Mike, she's talented, I'll give you that. But it isn't her talent that has you watching her every move. It's the way she fills out her jeans and sweaters."

"It's not like that, Katie."

"Not like what? Not like you're attracted to her?"

"Not like I want to jump—" He glared at Katie. "There's a lot more to Sophie than just her looks. She's a hard worker. Doesn't complain. Has a sense of daring. A quick smile. She can charm the girls into just about anything. She—"

"She's got you tied in knots. And you love it. Admit it, bro. You've fallen—and fallen hard—for the first time in your life."

"Nope." He crossed his arms and adopted a cocky stance, ignoring the inner voice that agreed with Katie. "I'm not admitting to anything. Except, maybe, to the possibility that you've finally learned your way around a kitchen. Let's have a taste of that new chili recipe and see if it's any good."

He steered Katie into talk of the culinary school, recipes, kitchen management, and anything else he could think of to keep her from interrogating him further.

"So, what do you think, Mike?"

He blinked. What was it Katie had been talking about? Something about the pub and her studies. "Uh, could you repeat—"

"You haven't heard a word I said, did you?" Katie pinned him with a look. "I want to take the pool table and juke box out and set up a few tables in the back room. Dad already agreed to it but told me to ask you."

"Tables? For what?"

"For my final school project. I'm going to add some gourmet fare to the menu and set up my own pop-up restaurant within the pub. Just for the winter semester."

"Oh, I guess," he looked out the pass window and saw Sophia returning. "As long as Dad's okay with it, Katie, I'm sure it will be fine." He gave her a peck on the cheek then waved Sophia back into the kitchen.

When she and the rest of the family joined Mike and Katie in the kitchen, he supervised carving pumpkins, as delighted at the sight of Sophia carving her first one as he was at the girls drawing faces on them with unsteady hands and indelible black markers.

He wished it was as easy to carve or paint a silly smile on his face as it was to etch one into a pumpkin. But though he tried to keep his expression superficial, one look at Katie—and another at his dad—confirmed that they weren't buying it.

And, God help him, neither was he.

Sophia walked into the town library, unwinding her scarf at the blast of warm air on her wind-stung cheeks.

"Good morning, Sophie." The motherly librarian at the desk waved to her. "I've got your usual selection of newspapers already waiting for you at the reading table by the window. Or you could access the online versions."

Sophia suppressed a shudder at the thought of leaving an online trail that Stephan's security teams might follow and smiled at the woman. "Thanks, Ellen." Facts and figures clicked in place in her memory. Ellen Whittenhouse, head librarian, had worked in the same job for thirty years. She had two grown sons and one daughter, a senior in high school. "How is Allison?" she asked, referring to Ellen's daughter.

Ellen beamed. "She's doing well in school. And so excited about helping with your fundraiser. Believe it or not, she convinced the woman's volleyball squad, the Future Homemakers of America, and the drama club to team up to work on the haunted house. Talk about groups with different interests! I don't know how she did it."

"She's got her mother's talent for influencing people." Sophia enjoyed the blush that crept along Ellen's cheeks. Like everyone else who'd reached out to her in Morgan's Outpost, Ellen radiated a homey warmth—the kind that accepted lost puppies and lonely out-of-town-newcomers with equal ease. Sophia doubted that her title would have gained her any more respect in Ellen Whittenhouse's eyes than her work on the charity fundraiser.

"Why don't you go sit and get comfy?" Ellen held out her hand. "I'll put your coat in the back room and smuggle out a fresh cup of coffee for you."

"You're bending the rules for me again," Sophia said, knowing that food wasn't permitted in the reading rooms.

Ellen leaned close and patted her on the arm. "We'll just let that be our secret."

Sophia smiled to herself. It was the same exchange every day, and it warmed her in ways that knitted scarves and thick socks couldn't. It warmed parts of her soul that only Mike had touched. She headed to her favorite table by the window, burrowing her hands into the pockets of the hoodie he'd given her.

Cool, bright mornings had given way to clear, sunny days and crisp, cold nights as her time in Morgan's Outpost slipped past. She treasured each day, knowing that whatever happiness she found here wouldn't last.

When Ellen came over with the coffee, Sophia had already scanned the headlines of the papers in the stack. She thanked the librarian and settled in to read in more detail.

An hour and a half later, she'd caught up on major news events, tracked the locations and dealings of half a dozen world leaders, and satisfied herself that events in Melesia—especially news of her disappearance—were still unnoticed in the major media outlets.

She leaned back, secure in her anonymity, and let her thoughts turn to the fundraiser. What started out as a good deed morphed into much more when she visited homes with a local social worker.

Children, often in single parent homes, greeted her with looks she instantly recognized: older children whose bravado covered up a fear of abandonment; younger ones who still flinched at loud voices while trying to shrink into invisibility.

Each revived a memory from her early days in the duke's household, where the threat and fear of punishment gradually overshadowed her need for independence. Where she learned that duty, not love, defined her place in the world.

Still other children had loving, but overburdened, families where mothers struggled with multiple jobs or fathers tried in vain to understand what made little girls tick. A few—like Mike's nieces—had extended families who worked to fill the gaps in their lives with positive influences.

The recreation center was a start—but it wasn't enough. Children needed more than a checklist of events and classes to occupy them while their parents worked. They needed parents, extended family and loving adults to spend time with them. She knew, better than anyone, how lonely a life of being shuttled from lesson to lesson could be.

Parents, she'd learned, struggled with their own needs. Chores sapped enthusiasm, financial and other pressures drained resources. Mike, his sister Katie, and her coworkers at the pub had opened her eyes to the real world. Being a modern parent made the mythical labors of Hercules look easy by comparison.

Yet Mike's family had also given her hope. He'd told her that his father had spent time dreaming up projects to keep

Mike out of trouble. Projects to channel his energy into something positive. Projects they'd done together.

Together. That was the missing piece.

Sophia grabbed her empty coffee mug and headed to the main desk, following a hunch. "Ellen?"

The librarian looked up from her work. "More coffee, dear?"

Sophia shook her head. "Do you know what sorts of organizations help children, especially those from single parent families?"

"Off the top of my head, I'd say Head Start and other preschool programs, Big Brothers and Sisters, and I'm sure there are more. If you give me some time, I can find out for you."

"You'd do that?"

"Of course, dear. That's what librarians do. We research things for our clients." Ellen gave her a sharp, but compassionate, look. "I assume your interest is academic, but if you need help on a personal level…" she let the words hang in the air, neither question nor statement. "Just remember you have friends here in Morgan's Outpost."

"Thank you," Sophia said after the tightness at the back of her throat relaxed. She leaned on the counter and gave Ellen a smile. "I appreciate your friendship. What I'd really like to know is what needs the available programs are meeting and which needs are left unmet. I'd also like any information you have on how to set up a charitable foundation."

"Aren't you the ambitious one?" Ellen remarked as she scribbled some notes to herself. "Setting up a foundation is likely to be more work than organizing a fundraiser, but I'll see what I can learn."

"Anything you find will be helpful." Sophia thanked her again, then gathered her coat and scarf and left the library. She might not be able to do much as Sophie the waitress, but soon—too soon—she'd be Lady Sophia of Melesia again.

Then she'd have a staff at her disposal and the power of the aristocracy behind her. Her influence could make a difference. Doing so might make sacrificing her personal happiness for the sake of king and country bearable.

Chapter 14

A few dry brown leaves scuttled across her path as Sophia headed to the corner market to buy the latest installment of the *Weekly World Stir* and other tabloids and entertainment news magazines that the library didn't keep in stock. One block later, she reached the small diner where she appropriated a booth and settled in. One of the servers hustled over.

"Morning, Miss Sophie," she said as she poured a cup of black coffee. "Are you here for breakfast or lunch today? You can have either."

"I think today I would like to try," she scanned the menu quickly, "a Belgian waffle with pecans."

"Still working your way through the whole menu, I see. Do you want your usual side of bacon with that?"

"No, just the waffle. We're cooking up batches of chili recipes this afternoon."

"You sure are getting the town fired up about this chili cook-off and fundraiser. At this pace, we'll have the funds to start groundbreaking as soon as the weather cooperates." She smiled and moved off to put the order in.

Sophia sipped her coffee and scanned the tabloid, a habit born of years of being one of their favorite targets. Knowing the source of slander helped one prepare to ignore it. Following last week's official announcement of Queen Jillian's pregnancy, the magazine had devoted an entire issue to the topic.

This week's reporting included speculations about the baby's gender, coverage of the queen's daily habits, and purported interviews with select members of the royal family. No mention was made of the tour Sophia was supposed to be on.

She breathed a sigh of relief and set the tabloid aside when her breakfast arrived. The sweet, tantalizing aroma of syrup mixed with the rich, dark scent of coffee making her stomach rumble. After a lifetime of eating whatever was put in front of her, she reveled in the pleasure of discovering her own likes and dislikes.

Waffles, it turned out, ranked near the top of the list. Right up there after Mike's kisses and the heady intoxication of being her own woman. At least the waffles were a pleasure she could continue to enjoy after her return to Melesia.

The smell of chili permeated the pub, tickling Mike's nose with a sweet, spicy aroma. Laughter drifted from the kitchen into his small office, tempting him to leave the stack of grocery receipts and other paperwork for tomorrow.

His cook, Joe, had come in around noon, eager to chop onions and sweat behind the stove as long as Sophia showered him with attention. Hell, Mike couldn't blame Joe—until an hour ago he'd been letting her run him ragged too.

But someone had to handle the paperwork and keep the pub moving out of the red and into the black. Mike reluctantly closed the door to the office, shutting out the laughter, and focused again on the receipts. He almost welcomed the phone call that interrupted him.

"Maguire's."

"Mack." Frank Kincaid's voice boomed over the line. "How's my story coming along?"

Mike winced at the ice-pick sharp pains pounding his temples in time to the rhythm of Kincaid's voice. "I've been a little busy lately."

"Yeah. I left half a dozen messages you've been too busy to answer." The editor sighed. "Level with me, Mack. Have you lost your edge?"

"Look, I've got my ear to the ground. I'm getting bits and pieces, just not enough to fill in a whole picture yet."

"Time was, when you'd create two stories for every piece of information you ran to ground. You're expecting me to believe you can't get me a story with what you have now?"

Mike felt a second throb attack the spot between his eyes. He yanked open a drawer and pulled out a spoon, taking deep breaths and focusing his anger on it rather than on Kincaid.

"I haven't lost my edge, Frank. But this piece isn't just fluff. The more I learn, the deeper the story gets." That much, at least, was true. The bowl of the spoon bent under the steady pressure of his fingers until it was at a right angle to the handle by the time he finished his speech. He flipped it in his hand and began bending it back.

"I've got a lot riding on you, Mack. Don't make me regret it."

"I'll get you a story, I swear. It'll be the first of several. The *Royal Tells All* angle will be the end of a series. I'm still working on getting that opportunity."

Silence filled the line. Mike clamped his mouth shut letting the tension seep from his body into the warm metal of the spoon. His headache eased.

"Fine." Kincaid broke the silence. "I'll wait another week. Your sources should pan out by then. If not, I've got a junior reporter here anxious for his big break. He'd jump at the chance to help you do some legwork."

The spoon snapped, bowl skidding underneath the desk while the jagged metal rasped along Mike's thumb. He bit back a curse. "Sure thing, Frank. Next week."

He sucked the raw skin of his thumb to keep from saying more. Kincaid's offer of an assistant meant one thing: Mike's time was up.

Afternoon faded to evening in a blur as Mike went through the motions of opening the pub and doing his job. The conversation with Kincaid gnawed at him, pushing its way back to the front of his mind every time he tried to shove it aside.

He looked around the dining room, watching the early regulars begin to fill the tables. The pub hummed with energy. He felt a spurt of pride strong enough to block out his worries for a moment. He said a word of encouragement to Joe, dredged up a smile and a wink for Betsy Malone, then gave his dad a thumbs up as he headed past the bar toward his office.

Seeing the old man pouring drinks and chatting with customers like in the old days gave him hope. Maybe this time dad wouldn't throw it all away on a woman.

Katie, too, seemed more settled. She remained as committed to her education today as she had a year ago, and the new menu items she'd convinced him to try were a hit with the customers. Even the girls seemed happier than he'd seen them in a year. His struggling family just might be finding its feet.

He slipped into the office and closed the door, letting the sounds of the pub fade into the background. In the last weeks, between spending time with the girls, his dad, and Sophia, and working on the fundraiser—now only a week away—he'd been able to put off the inevitable and bury himself in work.

Now, with Dad taking over some of the day-to-day running of the pub and Kincaid's veiled threat, his reprieve was over.

He unlocked the filing cabinet, wishing he could stuff his conscience inside and lock it away as easily as he'd stashed the laptop and incriminating files.

But, conscience or not, his deal with the devil demanded payment. Frank Kincaid's calls—probing for updates on the *Stir* exposé he'd promised—came almost daily. And he wouldn't be satisfied with tidbits of information. Kincaid's offer to send a junior reporter to help with the research told him as much.

Too late, Mike realized he couldn't pull the story without bringing a slathering pack of cub reporters to his door. He could protect his sources—and Sophia—only as long as he could keep her away from Kincaid's snitches. He needed a story, and soon.

Mike pulled a yellow legal pad from the desk drawer and started a list, organizing what he knew about Sophia and what he had yet to learn.

Hard worker. Doesn't complain. Able to bring grumpy, quarreling old men together for the sake of charity. Could make his niece laugh. Was learning to laugh at herself. Great smile. Long legs. Killer curves. He sighed and tore off the page.

When had his professional interest become something more? Or had it always been something more? Since the day she'd passed out on his couch, he'd felt something for her. Protectiveness, that had to be it. At times, she seemed as vulnerable as the girls and as much in need of his help as they were.

Underneath her capable exterior hid a shy child. One who longed for connection and cried out for affection. His gut told him as much, even though she'd tried to hide it. And his gut never led him astray. He started a new page, thinking in head-lines now, to keep his personal thoughts at bay.

Lonely Child—Useless Except for Her Pedigree. She'd given him the facts. Watching her with his family filled in so much more. This was the story of her life. The one he wanted to show the world. But it wasn't a story for the *Stir.*

The Domineering Duke's Demands. He'd dug into the Duke de Lyons, researching everything he could about the man who'd raised Sophia. True to her accounts, de Lyons often took his royal seal of approval from merchants, twisting the knife by sending a five hundred damia bank note engraved with his image—worth about fifty U.S. dollars—to the unfortunate merchant.

But if avarice characterized de Lyons, an insatiable lust for power drove him. Mike's research uncovered a centuries-old feud between the de Lyons family and the ruling D'Malia clan. One that drove the duke to commit treason.

Unfortunately, the duke's arrest and imprisonment gar-nered little media attention, coming as it did on the heels of a new king's coronation. Yet a few carefully worded questions to the merchants who'd suffered the duke's wrath unearthed a treasure of information.

Excitement sizzled in his veins as he organized his notes. Not once in his years of celebrity reporting had a story with this potential come along. This wasn't entertainment—it was news. It was the thing he'd been hoping for when he majored in journalism. His Woodward-and-Bernstein moment, albeit a small one.

Murder, subterfuge, betrayal, and so many other things the press had glossed over in their initial coverage were the seeds from which he could grow a newsworthy story. If he broke it, it could lead to the career he'd always hoped for.

And if he spun it into tawdry half-truths, it could get Kin-caid off his back. It could keep Sophia safe for a little longer.

His gut—the one that never led him astray before—and maybe a piece of his heart, told him what to do.

Mike scrawled a few notes, outlining a story on the "Disgraced Duke." If he stuck to the facts concerning the duke's treasonous attempt to invalidate King Constantine's coronation and the rumors that de Lyons had tried to poison King Emeritus Alexander, he could lead the public away from Sophia. At least for a while.

He owed her that much. Actually, he owed her far more than what one article could give. But he had to start somewhere to redeem himself. He thumbed through the file, pulling out various headlines he'd crafted over the years, repulsed at his calloused treatment of her—and all of them.

Reclusive Royal Rebukes Reporters. It had been at a press conference shortly after the announcement of the king's engagement. Someone had asked Lady Sophia if the king had warned her of the impending announcement.

Cool as ice, she'd replied that the king's confidences were not hers to report. Her response—and a little pumping of her palace staff—had given him weeks of stories. Articles like *Lady Locked Lips* and *Sophia the Silent* drew scores of new readers who gobbled up his tales.

He pulled a photo of her from the file. The glossy eight by ten showed her shaking hands with a reporter from the *New York Times*. Mike looked closer. The tightness of her lips and the slight unfocused quality of her gaze hit him like a sucker punch to the gut.

This was Sophia fighting exhaustion. The same look she wore when she shut down the pub after a long shift. Except that in the pub, she didn't radiate the desolation that he now saw in the photo.

Damn. He couldn't write a story to expose her to more scrutiny. Not now. Not a few weeks from now when the duke's story would no longer be enough for Kincaid. Never.

But if he didn't eventually write the promised story, Frank Kincaid would give it to someone else. Someone who didn't care about Sophia. Someone who would ruthlessly slander her without a second thought. Someone like the man he'd once been.

There had to be a way out of the quagmire. Mike rubbed his forehead, feeling the impending headache take hold despite the aspirin he'd downed earlier. He dug in his desk drawer for a spoon but came up empty handed. Instead, he grabbed a packet of pencils, snapping half a dozen of them before he felt calm enough to face his dilemma again.

He stared at the photo, searching for answers in her face, but finding none until a knock pulled him from his reflections.

"Come in."

Sophia opened the door. "Hi, Mike. Got a minute?"

"Yes, sure." His fingers were clumsy as he fumbled with the folders, trying to push photos and story clips inside in a random order. He gave up and shoved the whole mess in a drawer as she walked toward him.

God above! How he wanted to come clean with this woman. Maybe if he let her dictate the story, or he offered to give her final editing rights, or… Who was he kidding?

The confidentiality clause in his contract with Kincaid was a gag order. Break the confidence and the *Stir* would demand repayment of monies he'd received for every story he'd filed since day one. And likely rerun the stories out of spite.

Besides, Sophia would be out the door in a minute—and rightfully so—if he so much as hinted at his former profession.

And whatever else he wanted, he didn't want her to leave. Not when there was the possibility of-

"Mike, are you sure this isn't a bad time? You look like you're in pain."

Her voice washed over him like warm rum-laced molasses—thick, sweet, and intoxicating. When she rested her hand

on his shoulder, he flinched, knowing he didn't deserve her gracious touch.

"I'll come back later," she said, her rum sweet voice sinking deeper into his soul. "I'll just get you some aspirin and a glass of water then tell everyone to leave you alone until closing."

"No." His own voice came out as rough as day-old beard stubble. He grabbed her hand. "I'll be all right. Just sit with me for a while."

She pulled up a folding chair and sat, angled more toward him than the desk. When she took his hands in hers, he didn't resist.

"Are you worried about your dad and his new girlfriend?" she asked after a few moments. "I've seen how you react every time he talks about her."

Destiny. Shit. He'd forgotten about that in his preoccupation with Sophia. Now it hit him full force. He looked up, captivated by the compassion in her clear green gaze.

"I—" He cleared his throat. "I don't want to see Dad hurt. He was lost after Mom died. When he started living the high life, trying to impress the ladies, everything got out of control. A couple of them thought they'd snagged a rich businessman and broke his heart when they found out we were barely holding on. Of course, they'd done a good job of emptying his bank account before the end."

"Was his heart really broken or just battered?"

Mike looked at their clasped hands. He spoke slowly. "I don't know. I was too preoccupied with having fun in my own life. Katie says he took it hard. Since I've been back, he's gone through an internet dating phase, and now he's fallen for some casino showgirl. It can't be good."

"Don't be so quick to judge her, Mike." Sophia squeezed his hands and took a deep breath. "I've lived in a few glass houses in my lifetime, and I can tell you it's never fun being misjudged."

Misjudged. The word rolled around in his gut, far too tame a word for what he'd done to her. He'd caused her so much pain. Was he repeating the same mistake with Destiny? He shook his head. It couldn't be. "Sophie, what am I supposed to think? Her name is Destiny Fairchild, for crying out loud. That reeks of showgirl. And she sings at the *Three Fates Lounge* in Reno."

"The Three Fates?" Sophia's voice sounded strangled.

Mike looked up in concern. "What is it?"

"It's nothing. I—" She shivered. "I think you should meet her. In my cul—"

She turned red and tried to pull her hands away. Mike registered the slip. *In my culture.* The Melesians—descended from exiled Greeks who'd crossed the ocean to settle in the Caribbean—mixed the cultures of both their native and adopted lands.

"Fate has nothing to do with her dating my dad," he said firmly. "Everything about Vegas and Reno conjures the image of fate and luck. That's how they convince the tourists to drop good money on bad gambling. And this Destiny Fairchild is wagering that Dad's a likely candidate for her Sugar Daddy."

"*To Embrace Fate is Folly; to Ignore her, Disaster,*" Sophia murmured. "It's a proverb I picked up in my travels. You might be right, Mike, but at least meet her before you decide."

He nodded. "Okay, I'll meet her first." For Sophia's sake, he'd do it her way. But if Destiny was taking his dad for a ride, she'd find the price higher than she'd bargained for.

"Now that my dad's love life is settled, what can I do for you? You said you wanted something." He smiled at her.

"I need your help for the chili cook-off. We have an odd number of recipes and since we're cooking two per day for the customers, I'd like to even that up. It wouldn't be an official entry, of course, just something to round out the menu."

"You want me to make up a recipe? Why not ask my dad for Mom's recipe?"

"No, although that would be a good idea. I was thinking of a spicy fish stew that I came across in my travels. It's tomato based, so it should fit with the theme. I remember it has corn, white fish, tomatoes, and spices, but I don't think I could reproduce it without a recipe."

"Let's see if we can find it." Mike fired up the laptop, glad he'd locked his Melesian research away in a password secure area. "Where in your travels did you encounter this fish stew? It must have been in an ocean side location."

"It was in a Caribbean archipelago called Melesia. My uncle spent a lot of time there." She spelled it for him as he typed. "It's actually quite a tourist hot spot. You've probably heard of it."

The trepidation in her voice told him she was fishing. Trying to find out how safe her secrets were. "Vacationing in the Caribbean isn't exactly my style," he said, glad to see the wariness drain from her face.

A link to Melesian cuisine popped up. A few more clicks and he found the recipe. While the printer set to work, he engaged her in conversation.

"You said your uncle spent a lot of time here. Do you have a favorite memory of the islands?"

"Most of the homes are only a few miles from the coast in any direction," she said as she rose and crossed to the printer to pick up the recipe. She folded it absently and put it into her apron pocket.

"My first memory is the smell of the sea after a storm. When storms came, the sky turned gray and the waters churned in a steel-colored froth. After, when everything was calm again, the ocean took on the most beautiful shade of blue. And the sunsets were brilliant."

She sat by him again and stared at the screen, a kind of wistful longing in her face. Despite her adventure, she loved her home. Mike clicked a few links, trying to find a photo of the sunsets to ease her homesickness. Click. There. Click.

A slide show began, slowly paging through stunning sunsets and gorgeous ocean views shot on various islands, the decks of ships and…

Shit. A photo of her, face bathed in the glowing light popped up. *Lady Sophia de Lyons Enjoys a Quiet Sunset.* At her strangled gasp, his eyes flew to her face.

She sat, ashen, one slim hand covering her open mouth. The slide show popped up another photo of her, standing next to a prince in military dress.

Mike's gaze shifted slowly from her face to the screen. There was no hiding from the truth. He let his eyes widen and his jaw drop, in a slack mimicry of surprise.

"My God," he said, struggling to sound natural. "That's you."

Chapter 15

"What are you going to do?" Sophia's voice, soft and controlled, filled the space between them. She rested her hands in her lap, folded, but with a tension he saw despite her attempt to hide it.

"Do?" Now his words sounded strangled.

"The pub needs money," she continued, her voice flatly reciting facts. "I am sure the Melesian government would pay a reward to have me returned safely. They are probably tired of hiding my disappearance from the world.

"A second option would be to go directly to the media. They might offer to pay you for a lead to a story on me. The tabloids would be likely to pay better, but I would prefer a legitimate news organization."

She turned to him and smiled, a professional diplomat's smile devoid of any real warmth or feeling. "Or I could offer you a reward of my own for keeping my secrets. I have some family jewelry I could give you now with more funds to follow when I return home."

"Sophie, stop." He jumped up so quickly the chair clattered to the floor behind him. "I don't want your money."

Mike paced the length of the room, dragging his hands through his hair. "Sweet Saint Patrick! You even sound like some buttoned-up diplomat again. God. A princess. Under my own roof. What're the odds?"

"Actually, I'm the niece of a duke, not a princess. My official title is Lady Sophia de Lyons. Now that the duke is stripped of his title, I'm not sure who will inherit the duchy. However, my status is unlikely to change."

"Niece of a duke. Princess. There's not really much of a distinction to a guy who pours drinks for a living."

"You will still have to decide what you are going to do." She sat as if carved in stone.

Mike's blood boiled. Sophia, lovely laughing Sophia who'd infiltrated his pub, his family, and his heart. Who'd infiltrated his pub and his family, he amended irritably. Not his heart. She sat, unmoving, waiting for him to determine her fate.

Just as she'd waited for everyone in her life to use her to fill their own needs. Her uncle. The royal fiancé. The government. A passel of de Lyons family members and sympathizers who continued to struggle against the D'Malias. The tabloids. Everyone controlled her future and not a single one gave her any choice in the matter.

Well, not him. Not anymore.

"Sophie, listen to me." He righted the chair and sat, sandwiching her cold hands between his own. "I told you once that it didn't matter to me who your parents were. I promised to help you in any way I could. I meant it then. I mean it now. I'm not rich, or powerful, or much of anything else, but if it's in my power to help you, I will. Just tell me what you want."

She blinked, her softly frozen features showing a hint of life. "Really? You'll let me stay?"

"Is that what you want?"

"More than anything."

"Then stay." He rubbed his thumb along her knuckles. "Stay for a week. Or a month. Stay forever."

"Forever is a long time. They won't allow that."

"Stay as long as you like. As long as you can."

"Thank you." All at once her icy perfection melted, and she threw herself in his arms.

Mike embraced her awkwardly until he eased her from her chair and onto his lap. She curled against his shoulder, and he tucked his arms around her. "Just don't blame me for wishing you really were Sophie Bradley from Ohio," he whispered into her hair as he planted a soft kiss there, "because she could stay forever."

And I wouldn't have to betray her confidences to protect her from the likes of Frank Kincaid and his reporters.

Sophia snuggled into his embrace, but despite the warmth of her body, a chill crept over Mike. The icy fingers of the devil clawed at his soul demanding their due. And God alone knew how much he'd have to pay before this was over.

Three days later, Sophia strode into the empty pub and dropped a canvas bag full of research notes on children's charities and her most recent tabloid purchases on a table. She sprinted up to her apartment, shedding her coat, scarf, and gloves as she lectured herself.

She'd filled the past two days with activities for the fundraiser or buried herself in the library, all the while aware she was really avoiding Mike. Avoiding uncertainty. Avoiding conflict. Even at work last night, she'd found herself pulling away, answering his innocent questions with guarded responses.

She longed for the easy camaraderie they'd shared before he'd learned her identity. Yet the tension that snaked between them wasn't his fault. Her secret tainted their relationship. Like the contents of Pandora's box, her identity—once revealed—poisoned everything.

She hung her coat in the closet, struggling for a calm she didn't feel. Who was she anymore? Sophia the royal? Or Sophie the waitress? Neither quite fit. And when Mike looked at her, knowing both, what did he see?

What did she want him to see?

A sudden cramp seized her stomach, causing her to gasp. A few short weeks ago, the pain was so much a part of her life it had been easy to ignore. The twisting in her gut always signaled a conflict between duty and desire—she'd just never realized it until now.

She took a breath and straightened, subduing the pain through sheer determination. So what if Mike knew her secret? He'd sworn not to treat her differently. But had he kept the promise? She couldn't tell, not when her own perspective on the world had altered the moment he discovered her identity.

Out of reflex—and habit—she'd allowed him to call all the shots. She hated her cowardice—then and now. Hated being everyone's idea of a good girl.

Her phone dinged, and she grabbed it, opening it to see a text message from Grace Bradley. Even Grace was trying to force her hand with frequent, urgent texts. It wouldn't work.

Sophia's perusal of the media assured her that the public didn't know of her disappearance. The royal family didn't know where to find her either, or a diplomatic and military escort would have descended on Morgan's Outpost by now. Which meant Stephan had received her letters assuring him of her safety. And that he—they—had decided to let her have this time away.

If they'd really wanted her back, nothing would have stopped them from using every media, military, and diplomatic source to see her returned.

If Grace focused on her studies and avoided the royal family, her part in this would never come to light. Sophia would claim—if necessary—that she'd forced Grace to cooperate with her. Her ethics demanded she take the blame, unless she could keep Grace quiet.

Sophia checked the message again. *Come home. Now.*

She wouldn't let someone else call the shots. Not this time. She sent a cryptic reply. *L8R.* She wasn't going to return until *she* was ready. No one would force her hand ever again. Not the specter of duty. Not Grace. No one. Not even Mike. From now on she'd decide her own destiny.

She headed to the bathroom, resolve firm. She grabbed a brush and yanked it through her tousled curls, taking her frustration out in firm, swift strokes.

I'm not a child to be pushed around.

I'll make my own decisions.

Mike won't decide my future.

I can stand up to him.

She repeated the words again and again, forcing a confidence she didn't feel into her thoughts until her scalp tingled and her fears refused to be drowned out.

Her arms dropped to her side, fingers limply gripping the brush. *Oh, Zeus. If I can't stand up to him, how can I confront the king when I return home? If I can't be strong in Morgan's Outpost, how can I hope to be my own person in Melesia?*

She stared at her hollow-eyed reflection, automatically reaching for the concealer and other makeup to transform her from an exhausted shell of a woman to someone poised and capable. *I am strong. I can do this.* She repeated the words with every practiced movement of her fingers. She knew how to hide everything from blemishes to anxiety. But she'd be damned if she hid her true self for one more day. Or even one more hour.

When Mike came in this morning, she'd put the deceptions, lies and half-truths behind them. Then she'd ask for what she wanted—everything she wanted—without begging or demanding. She was Sophie the woman, defined neither by her birth nor her occupation but only by herself.

Today she'd learn to use her voice.

She finished her makeup and scrutinized the results. Her reflection looked placid and composed, not betraying a hint of the inner turmoil that simmered under the surface. She was ready. She took a breath, squared her shoulders, and threw her future to The Fates—folly be damned.

Chapter 16

Mike opened the front door of the pub and stepped inside, taking in the dim interior as he stuffed the keys into his pocket. Faint hints of last night's cooking mingled with the tang of cleaning products and the sweet aroma of the donuts he'd purchased on the way to work. The familiar mix of scents and the early morning quiet of the place soothed his churning gut.

He planned to catch Sophia before she disappeared on some errand or other. The night he'd acknowledged her royal status, she'd melted in his arms for a few precious moments. By morning, she'd become a different person—tense and withdrawn, for the most part, but with a sharp edge. A prickly person who looked at him with suspicion and distrust in her eyes.

One day—soon, if he couldn't placate Kincaid—he'd deserve that mistrust. But for at least a little longer he wanted her smiles and laughter—the innocent trust she'd given him before her secrets came to light. *By the saints!* He missed the way she lit up with each new discovery, the excitement with which she grabbed life.

God help him. It had only been a few days, but he'd missed her exuberance enough for a lifetime. What was he going to do when she left him for good?

Mike left the donuts on a table, next to a bulging tote bag. Hers, he thought. At least she was still here. He headed to the kitchen to brew a pot of coffee, all the while keeping an ear cocked for the sound of her coming down the stairs.

When he heard her, he filled a mug and intercepted her on her way to the table. "Good morning." He held out the mug. "I thought you could use this."

"You don't have to wait on me, Mike." Her voice, stiff and remote, raised his ire and threw an invisible wall between them.

He knocked it down. "A simple 'thank you' would be appropriate, *Your Highness*."

"I told you before, I'm not a princess."

"Then stop acting like one." He slammed her mug on the table and strode to the kitchen to grab his own coffee.

"Don't tell me what to do. You don't have the right to judge me. No one does."

The shrill haughtiness of her voice held a thread of uncertainty, but for once it didn't move him. He didn't deserve her condemnation. Not yet.

He headed back to the table and slammed his mug down beside her untouched one. He faced her, invading her comfort zone until he saw her stiffen. "That's where you're wrong, Sophie. For the record, everyone judges everyone else. It's human nature. You've had a stick up your spine ever since I discovered your secret. I've had my fill of your ice princess routine."

He glared at her, watching her eyes narrow and her lips thin. She drew a breath and opened her mouth. "I'm not—"

"Don't say it. Fine. You're not a princess. How about a Diva? Prima Donna? Or just plain pain-in-the-ass?"

She held his stare, her throat reflexively swallowing in her otherwise perfectly still body. He counted the seconds, but she maintained her poise long past the ten second mark when others broke. Sweat trickled down his back and the anger drained away until he felt the pressure to speak.

Only then did she break the silence. "I'm not—intentionally—any of those things. I am simply tired of letting others direct my life." Her voice held all the warmth and emotion of an automated answering machine as she recited her speech, yet he listened, and tried to understand.

"No one is trying to direct your life right now, least of all me." Mike strove for a gentle tone, despite his frustrations. "Sheath your claws, Lady de Lyons."

Color drained from her face. *Do not irritate the lions, for our blood runs cold; our enemies cower before us.*

Her whispered words, Mike knew, came from her family creed inscribed under their crest of a lion trapping a small creature between massive paws. Right now, Sophia seemed more like the prey than the hunter. "You're not ruthless, nor cold, no matter what your family creed. But you are scratching and spitting like…" he paused searching for the right words. Not the lion of her family crest. Something else. "Like a tiny tiger cub. But there's no need to fight. You're safe here."

She nodded, her manner still too stiff for his comfort. "I have enjoyed my time here. I would like to stay, at least until the festival is over. Maybe a bit longer. When the time is right, I will decide when to return home."

"Sophie." He touched her cheek, alarmed at its coolness. He threaded his unsteady fingers through her hair and turned her face to his. "We've been through all of this. You're welcome here, for as long as you like. I want you here. What I don't want is this awkward *thing* between us. What's wrong?"

"Everything was easier before you knew who I was," she whispered. "Before, when you looked at me, you saw a woman not something else. Now I'm not sure. I miss feeling close to you."

"You don't have to." He leaned closer, near enough to catch a whiff of fresh air and shampoo that clung to her hair. Close enough to want, but not close enough to have. "I wasn't the one who moved away, Sophie. I'm right here."

"What do you see when you look at me?"

"Now?"

"Yes."

"Someone I want to kiss."

"Then kiss me." She leaned in, letting her breath tickle his lips.

He chuckled. "Not this time, Tiger. Didn't you want to take charge of your own life? If you want something, you'll have to take it."

Mike struggled to stay still, fighting the urge to draw her into the kiss that hovered, inevitable, in the space between them. The merest flick of his tongue and he could taste her lips, but still he waited.

"I want this." Her words, her breath, bridged the gap between them, and then her lips were on his, demanding, seeking, coaxing him to participate.

And he did. Mirroring her moves, he matched the press of her lips with his, wound his arms around her when she hugged him close, and answered the touch of her tongue on his with own. Matching her pace, her intimacy.

Longing for more surged through his veins, thickening his blood, making him swell with the ache to rub against her. *Sweet Saint—* She ground her hips into his and his curse ended on a groan.

Her movements broke his restraint and the hunger surged. No more Mr. Nice Guy. He plundered her mouth and gave free rein to his hands, heatedly caressing the long, lean line of her spine, the subtle swell of her hips and the firm, small but perfect roundness of her butt.

He slipped his hands lower, curling his palms around her thighs and, in a swift move, lifted her. She balanced for a moment, her thighs in his hands, her fingers clasped behind his neck, before she wrapped her legs around his waist as if she'd done it a thousand times.

"Zeus and Io," she muttered, referring to the classic Greek lovers. "I'm on fire."

"You have no idea, sweetheart." He sat her on the table, freeing his hands to slip under her sweater and caress the smooth skin of her stomach, her ribs. His calloused fingers felt rough against her satin perfection, and he almost pulled away, ashamed of his passion.

Until she arched under his touch, bracing herself on her arms and throwing her head back to expose her vulnerable neck. Thrusting her breasts forward in an invitation impossible to resist.

He wrenched her sweater higher and filled his hands with her offering, brushing his thumb over her nipple. It puckered in response and he palmed it, wishing like hell the flimsy lace of her bra didn't stand between him and what would surely be a taste of heaven.

He bent his head and nuzzled her stomach, nipping and licking the softness he found there, blazing a trail higher as she panted. He caught her garbled exclamations—Greek, maybe, or possibly her native Melesian—incomprehensible as words, but undeniably urging him on.

A warm wetness cascaded over his thighs, as real as the hot passion of sex, as unbelievable as—

She twisted beneath him. "No. Not my papers."

She rolled away and snatched up the wet bag, pulling out handfuls of paper and depositing them on a nearby dry table. Mike watched, tearing his attention from the wet, clinging denim that stretched across her bottom to stare at the spreading pool of coffee, dripping from the table, as wasted as his passion.

Her pants were soaked in rapidly cooling coffee. The rest of her still burned from the feelings Mike awakened. She'd come to associate the throbbing between her legs with Mike and his kisses.

The pleasure of it weakened her knees, yet drove her mad, like a starving person offered a single bite of food. It awakened cravings better left in the dark. But today he'd given her a second—and a third—taste of temptation.

The feel of his lips on her bare stomach imprinted itself in her memory. The sweep of his thumbs across her nipples—well they still puckered, taut and longing for his touch.

She separated the papers methodically—tabloids on the left, foundation research on the right—while her thoughts returned to the delicious pulses of desire marking her body wherever he'd touched.

She couldn't stop listing—and reliving—his actions. *His lips on her stomach, his hands on her breasts, his…* Her face flared with heat. *…his penis on her private parts through the layers of clothes.* The clinical names she'd learned didn't reflect the feelings rocketing through her psyche. Aroused and longing. Weak, yet powerful. Empty, but ready to burst.

His lips, his hands, his—

"Hey, Sophie." She turned in time catch the towel he tossed to her. His voice was tight, his features pinched as if he, too, were still in the grip of passion. *Lips, hands…*

She cut off the thoughts and busied herself with blotting the wet sheets, trying to salvage the research Ellen Whittenhouse had given her at the library early that morning. Thank the gods they'd survived, intact, but damp and stained.

"Need help?" His voice, thick and rough, rasped along her sensitized nerves like a caress. His body warmth enveloped her as he moved to her side, drawing her attention back to him. Away from the papers.

She licked her dry lips, focusing on the sprinkling of hair on the back of his hands, the way his tanned knuckles contrasted with the white dish towel. Until he stilled, his hand poised above the soaked newsprint.

"What the hell is this?" Anger replaced the soft roughness of passion as he grabbed a soggy edition of the *Weekly World Stir* off the top of the pile. He shook it. Drops of coffee splattered, hitting the table, her face.

He grabbed the next tabloid in the stack. And the next, flinging the papers to the floor and his words at her. "What are you doing? Checking up on me? Looking to see if I sold your story to the highest bidder? Don't you trust me?"

"Trust you? Mike, I'm keeping up with the news."

"News?" He gestured to the papers and magazines. "This stuff isn't news. It's gossip. Sensationalism. Lies. You can't trust anything you read in these rags."

He raked his fingers through his hair. Distaste, anger, pain, and emotions she didn't recognize flitted across his face, furrowing his brow, locking his jaw, and dulling the spark in his eyes. "I can't believe you thought I'd sell you out." He sank into a chair and slumped heavily against it.

Sophia ran her fingers through his hair, smoothing the disarray back into place. "I check the papers every day," she said, keeping her tone low and soothing. "It's a habit Uncle drilled into me for years. I need to know the players and the events on the world stage if I'm to act in my country's best interest."

He looped his arms around her waist and rested his head near her heart. His words, muffled against the sweater, still sounded pained. "That doesn't explain the tabloids."

"True enough." She caressed his hair and ran a hand down his neck to lightly knead his tense shoulders. "The royal family, like a typical American celebrity, is a common target of the tabloids. In a way, we get the worst of both worlds. Our politics are scrutinized by serious commentators and our lifestyle is picked apart for entertainment."

She sighed and stilled her hands. How likely was he to understand? Mike's world was simple. He wasn't the kind to understand political intrigue, voyeuristic intrusions of the press, or any of the other complexities unique to her life.

On the other hand, he understood courage and facing troubles. He understood sacrificing for those you loved. And, with a gut-deep certainty, she knew he understood her. His actions this morning—from anger to passion and on to this simple embrace—told her as much. She was a woman to him, not Lady Sophia and not a stepping-stone to the gods knew what.

"Knowledge is my defense. Knowing the tabloid and entertainment scandals revolving around me keeps me safe. Or as safe as I can ever be from gossip." She pulled away long enough to look him in the eye. "And for the record, I don't believe that you would betray me by selling my stories to the papers—legitimate or tabloid."

At least she wanted to believe he wouldn't. She almost believed it. Years of jaded experience insisted otherwise, reminding her that even family—damn the Duke de Lyons—could betray you. But most of her believed in Mike—all of her heart, most of her mind, and all but a tiny bit of her common sense.

It was enough.

His gaze held hers, as if searching for the truth she didn't want him to see, but after a minute, he seemed satisfied. He nodded. "I would never hurt you, Sophie."

"I know." That she believed without a single doubt.

Mike rose and rested his hands on her shoulders. "Let's start this day over, shall we? Why don't you go upstairs and trade your wet clothes for some dry ones while I brew fresh coffee? Then, we'll break into the donuts I bought, and I'll teach you why you should never believe the tabloid stories. Even the ones with photos." He gestured to a lone paper on the table with a photo. The caption read "World's Fattest Cat Weighs in at 82 Pounds."

She grinned at him and opened her eyes wide. "But Mike, the photos look so real. Did you see the one about the alien invasion?"

He rewarded her antics with a laugh. "Tiger, they can work magic with Photoshop these days. Don't believe everything you read or everything you see. Now change." He turned her toward the stairs and gave her a little push.

For the second time today, she sprinted up the stairs to the apartment, but this time her heart was lighter than her steps.

Chapter 17

The morning before the festival opened, Mike stood at the bar and watched Sophia tuck a strand of hair behind her ear as she read. She reached for a donut and took a nibble. Mike snapped a photo, not for any story, just because he liked the idea of having a picture to remember this moment by.

But the moment was ruined.

One day soon, his dilemma would come to light. Apprehension nagged in his gut. For days, he'd spent his mornings poring over the newspapers with her, discovering how her mind worked.

He'd teased her for analyzing the tabloids, but his humor was superficial. Not that she noticed. Her intensity focused solely on categorizing the stories, looking for those that featured her family or country. She zeroed in with astonishing accuracy on the kernel of truth in any story and sighed over the fabrications.

Each day he wondered how she'd react when his stories finally hit the pages. Someday, soon, he'd no longer be able to appease Kincaid with empty promises and evasions. He'd have to submit his stories on the Duke de Lyons. He'd done his best to protect Sophia and draw the public's eyes elsewhere, but even if his fabrications did her no damage, he couldn't guarantee they wouldn't sting.

The bell above the door jangled, and he tore his attention from Sophia to see his dad walking in, a spring to his step.

"Hey, kids, what's up?" Dad flashed him a grin and turned to Sophia. "Darlin', could you spare a donut for an old man?"

"Hi, James." She tossed him a saucy smile. "What's the going rate for donuts these days?"

"This." He kissed her on the cheek and snagged a donut.

"Take the rest." She passed him the box. "Share it with the staff."

Mike smiled to himself. Over the past days, he'd learned more about her. Like the donuts. She preferred maple icing over chocolate. Plain over sprinkles. Yeast versus cake donuts. After the first day, when she'd nibbled half a dozen to determine her preferences, her choices hadn't faltered. Not even when he'd included cinnamon rolls and bear claws in the mix.

He headed toward her, shaking his head. "So that's the way things are. Every morning I bring you donuts and all I get is a polite thank you. He gives you a line of blarney and a peck on the cheek and you give them all away." He put his hands on his hips and glared at her. "I'll be expecting kisses before I hand over my donuts from now on."

She abandoned the paper and stood, scanning him from head to toe while a hint of pink touched her cheeks. He'd pay more than a penny for the thoughts that put that blush on her face. "Well, then, James Michael Maguire, here's payment, with interest." She pecked him twice on the cheek.

"No, Tiger, that won't do. That won't do at all." He turned his head and captured her lips, cutting off any response she had.

She tasted of maple sugar and a sweetness that couldn't be bought. The ease with which she melted into him sent his brain spiraling off in half a dozen directions. All involving a lot more skin than she currently displayed. None of which he had the right to indulge in with her. Not when it was inevitable that she leave him for a political marriage he couldn't understand and would never accept.

"Let's run away to Vegas and get married," he whispered in her ear, surprising himself.

"What?"

He'd been kidding, of course, but…what if he hadn't been? "Why not? If we're married, your country couldn't force you to marry someone else. You'd be free. And when you got tired of me, we could dissolve the marriage, and you'd still be free."

She shook her head sadly. "Mike, you have no idea what my country is capable of. Besides, what if I didn't tire of you? You'd be stuck with me."

"Who says I'd mind?" He kissed her again, fantasizing about more than touching her intimately. Fantasizing about having the right to touch her.

"Hey, you two, knock it off." His dad stomped into the pub dining room. "Sophie, you'll have my son spending more time in confession than at work if you keep tempting him. Unless you're willing to make an honest man of him."

Dad winked at Sophia and slapped Mike on the back. "Leave the girl a few minutes of peace, Mike. I've got some things I need to discuss with you."

Mike followed him into the office, chatting about schedules and coverage during the festival and Halloween. After a few minutes, Mike perched on the desk with a nonchalance he didn't feel. "What's this really about, Dad?"

His dad rubbed his chin and stared at a framed picture of the first dollar the pub had earned, as if the dusty frame and faded matting held a secret meaning. Abruptly he turned back to Mike. "Have you given any more thought to moving back into the apartment?"

"Sophie's still living there. I assumed—with your concerns for my immortal soul and all—that you wouldn't want me moving in with her."

"I'm sure Father Cabbott has heard his share of confessions of a carnal nature. Besides, I'm more worried about your mortal life. And mine for that matter. When I was your age, I had a second child on the way. What's taking you so long? This family is overrun by girls. I don't have much time left for you to get me a grandson to round out the pack."

Mike snorted. "You're not on your last legs yet, Dad. Don't count your Social Security checks before you're eligible." He took a deep breath. "This is about Destiny, isn't it?"

His dad nodded. "I got a call from her last night. Her singing gig is up, and she's booked a flight to Denver for the middle of next week."

"That's awfully fast, isn't it?"

"We've been discussing it for weeks. Her manager kept tacking extra days on to the end of her contract. The crowds love her." His dad shrugged. "Unlike you, when I see something I want, I don't wait around for it to disappear. At my age, you learn that love doesn't come around all that often. Take it when you get it."

"Dad, are you sure it's love and not something else?" Mike shifted his position to better watch his dad's expression. "I'm not saying you shouldn't have a little fun, if that's what you want, but watch your back. I don't want anyone to take advantage of you."

Dad laced his fingers together and regarded them for a moment before leaning back in his chair. He looked at Mike, relaxed, but serious. Mike braced himself for whatever was to come.

"Listen, I know I did some dumb things after your mother died. Hell, I did some dumb things just last year. But I swear to you, son, my head is on straight this time. And Destiny is responsible for opening my eyes. Whatever image you've got of her in your mind can't come close to the real thing."

He stood, bringing himself to his full height and looking Mike in the eye. "I asked Destiny to come here so she could meet my family. I want you and Katie to get to know her. If, after you meet her, you still think she's playing me for a fool, I'll listen." He paused. "Deal?"

Mike nodded. "Okay, Dad. I'll reserve judgment until after I meet her. Just promise me you'll listen even if you don't like what I'm saying."

"Good. Now that that's settled, I think I can handle things around here for the rest of the day. Why don't you take that girl of yours out for some fun before the festival? You've both worked your tails off for the last few weeks. Live a little, Mike. Before it's too late."

Mike headed out the door, glad the confrontation was over. He'd follow his dad's advice and carve out some time to enjoy being with Sophia. Despite his lighthearted proposal earlier, he knew there was no future for them.

Which left only now.

And he wasn't going to waste another second of it.

With any other woman, on any other day, waiting outside a dressing room door for hours on end would have been torture. Today, Mike couldn't wipe the sappy grin off his face, even after visiting two other thrift stores and a Wal-Mart.

A slight click drew his attention back to the dressing room door. He struggled to look serious as Sophia exited and stood in front of him.

"What about this outfit?" She nibbled her bottom lip and waited for his response, uncertainty in her eyes.

Mike zeroed in on her lips, wanting to kiss away her insecurities. Instead, he scanned her body, taking in the soft leather jacket and scooped neck, purple sweater. His palms itched to trace the soft material that covered her curves. Snug jeans, ending in the knee-high leather boots completed the picture. His gaze lingered over every enticing inch.

"Mike? What do you think?"

His lips twitched, mocking his attempts at seriousness. It was the fourth time he'd answered the same question within the past half hour.

"You look great." He checked his watch. "But the festival begins in a couple of hours and we need to go set up. Decide on a single outfit, or take them all, but we've got to get moving."

He shrugged his shoulders. "I'm sorry to hustle you along, but that's what you get for talking me into this shopping trip."

"Hey, you were the one who told me about the wonders of the thrift stores and Goodwill outlets." She tossed him a mischievous grin. "Don't blame me for making the most of my first trip here." She flounced back into the changing room, taking the light and energy with her.

Mike fought a wave of regret. He'd introduced her to a handful of "firsts" but he had dozens of others he'd never share with her. She'd hinted at leaving after the festival. Which left him with a little over a week to entice her to stay.

Or maybe he should let her go. The sooner she returned to her real life, the less likely she was to be hurt by his machinations. Sure, Kincaid would hound him, and he'd end up creating a fluff piece for the *Stir*, but by the time it came out, Sophia would be safely in the hands of family and friends. Friends who'd help her weather the gossip rather than expose her to it.

He jammed his hands in the pockets of his jeans and wandered over to the makeshift jewelry counter. Gaudy pins—the kind his grandmother used to wear—and fake gems winked up at him from beneath the streaked glass. They looked taw-dry, misfit-colored glass masquerading as something real.

He shifted his weight from foot to foot, suddenly restless. Sophia deserved better than this. She deserved better than him. Yet the sight of sparkling jewelry grabbed his imagination and wouldn't let go. What could a man like Mike give a woman like Sophia? Surely, she had gems beyond what he could imagine, let alone afford.

But it was tradition for a man to give a woman jewelry as a token of his— Mike swallowed. A token of what? Affection. That's what he felt for Sophia. Affection. Friendliness. Fond-ness. Not the L-word.

Beyond the surface there simmered other emotions. Attrac-tion. Desire. Not the other L-word either. He couldn't let lust dominate their time together. Not when it could ruin her life.

"Okay, Mike, I'm ready to go if you are." Sophia's voice pulled him out of the morose thoughts. Her smile turned the dingy shop into something much more. He glanced at her shopping basket, heaped with purchases, feeling his heart lighten just because she stood next to him.

"Let's get moving, then. We'll drop your new clothes at the apartment and as soon as you change into something warm we can head to the fairgrounds."

On the way to the checkout lanes, something grabbed her attention and she veered toward it. Mike caught her elbow. "Slow down, Tiger. We've got to get moving. I promise, I'll bring you back later in the week."

"Oh, good. I'd love to come back."

He winked at her. "It's a date. But for the next trip, we'll have the girls along. This is where we buy the stuff to make their Halloween costumes."

"How do we do that? What kind of costumes does one make for Halloween? We don't celebrate it in Melesia. Explain your customs to me again."

For the next hour, he regaled her with tales ranging from childhood antics to local ghost stories. With every story her face lit like a child's and Mike found himself falling more deeply into attraction, affection, fondness. Definitely not the L-word.

Chapter 18

Sophia stretched under the covers, the slight stiffness of her muscles reminding her of the work she and Mike had done last night. Pleasant memories swirled in her sleep fogged brain: the spicy smell of chili filling a steamy tent; the cold, but welcome, bite of the night air; the noise of the crowds, and the absolute excitement of being part of something so down-to-earth and worthwhile.

Today, he'd promised to show her around the rest of the festival before taking the evening shift in the chili tent. With him, she didn't need to keep up the pretense of being an American, but she still longed to understand his traditions and his world. Not just the world of the pub, but the world he'd grown up in. The world she'd leave him to one day.

She hurried through her morning routine, showering with a decadent pecan and cinnamon scented soap followed by matching lotion to protect her skin from the winter dryness. It wasn't the kind of scent a duke's ward would wear, but it delighted her. She skipped most of her makeup, opting for extra moisturizer and only a coat of mascara and lip gloss. She didn't need pretense today.

By the time Mike arrived, the coffee was brewing and she was ready for the day.

"Hi," she said, greeting him as he entered the apartment. She looked at his empty hands. "Didn't you bring donuts?"

Mike shook his head in a slow admonishment. His eyes, swirled pools of gold, brown, and green lit with a touch of humor, and something else. Something mesmerizing that held her gaze for more than a glance. Something intense that made her heart squeeze and a tickling, shivery warmth slide through her body. Something hot that made her stomach do a pleasant little flip.

"No donuts today, Tiger. I wouldn't want you getting spoiled."

Tiger. A predator as ruthless as any in nature. It wasn't the kind of endearment she'd have chosen for herself. But whenever Mike said it, his voice got soft and mushy around the edges, sweet in a way that set off the tickling, shivering, stomach-flipping, heart-squeezing response that left her soft and mushy around the edges too.

"Couldn't have that," she whispered as his lips came down to claim hers.

His taste was sweet enough. The pulse of his heart between their pressed-together bodies anchored her to him, urging her closer. Without thought, she pulled his shirt free and ran her hands along the warm, solid planes of his back, pressing them into his ribs, his shoulder. Clinging to him.

His kiss remained gentle, leisurely, as if her movements didn't entice him. But the way he cupped his palm possessively around her butt, trapping her between the hot strength of his hands and the searing hardness of his groin, told her otherwise.

Still, he took his time, nibbling her lips, caressing them with his own. Urging her with a sweep of his tongue to open for him, then exploring her mouth with a tender, maddening patience.

"You smell delicious," he said, when he pulled his mouth from hers. He trailed a line of kisses along her jaw, her cheek. "Like warm sugar and spice."

He threaded his fingers through her hair and cuddled her to his chest, inhaling and exhaling on a sigh. She savored the warmth of it for a while longer until he moved his hands to her shoulders and stepped back.

Reluctantly, Sophia withdrew her palms from the warmth of his body. Fortunately, the warmth in his eyes and voice still wrapped themselves around her, keeping cold reality at bay.

"So, instead of donuts, today I'm going to introduce you to more junk food than you can imagine. Funnel cakes, pumpkin bread, cotton candy, corn dogs, corn-on-the-cob dripping in butter, caramel corn, lemon ice, hot apple cider and about a hundred other delicacies that make America great." He grinned down at her. "Are you ready for a crash course in county fair culture?"

"I'm ready for anything."

"Good. Let's start with a cup of your coffee."

She indulged in one last kiss before moving to fill giant mugs with coffee. He followed her into the kitchen and leaned in the doorframe, following her every move with his eyes.

When she offered him the mug, he took a sip and smiled. "I think you've got the hang of it, Tiger. This is good."

"It ought to be. I've been practicing for weeks to get it just right." She smiled, remembering the times he'd come in for coffee, only to find it too weak, too strong or too bitter. He'd drunk each cup without complaint, then quietly suggested ways to make it better.

This time, he just drank, watching her over the rim of his cup, his eyes shimmering with approval. She leaned on the counter, comfortable with the silence. She wanted to remember him like this, relaxed, smiling at her with a hint of humor and passion in his eyes. Her gaze traveled slowly across the width of his shoulders and the bulge of his biceps to rest on his hands.

Heat flashed through her body as she thought of the times he'd touched her, skin-to-skin, the rough texture of his fingers awakening her in the way the soft hands of a prince never would.

In her weeks at Morgan's Outpost, she'd watched those hands ruffle the hair of his nieces, bandage scraped knees, and dry tears as easily as he hefted boxes of supplies into cabinets or did any of the other tasks associated with work.

Those hands had never once been harsh or raised in anger like the hands of her uncle. Here, birth wasn't worth. She wanted to remember that, too, when she returned home.

"So," Mike began, interrupting her thoughts, "do you think you'll make coffee when you return home? Or don't Melesians drink coffee?"

His thoughts focused on her leaving too. And though he hadn't moved, though he pretended nonchalance, the light in his eyes dimmed and he focused on the coffee, not her.

Sophia smiled, trying to ease the tension. It did no good to dread tomorrow. That was a sure way to ruin today. "I doubt anyone will let me near a kitchen, let alone a coffee pot. I'll have to sneak in before they're awake if I want to keep my skills up. Even so, I'm sure I'll lose my top-notch waitress skills."

"That doesn't sound like something to mourn."

"You'd be surprised, Mike." She took her empty cup to the sink and rinsed it. "There's a great sense of freedom—accomplishment even—in doing something simple and doing it well. I like knowing that I could survive in the real world."

He quirked an eyebrow and gave her a skeptical look. "I'm not sure you're ready for that just yet. There's lots you still have to learn. For example, can you drive?"

"Drive?"

"Yeah. A car. Every normal sixteen-year-old in America has at least a learner's permit. What about you?"

She shrugged. "Okay, I haven't driven a car. How hard can it be?"

"Want to find out?"

"Today?"

He shook his head. "No, after the festival. Next week. I'll take you out on the country roads and deserted parking lots and let you try your hand at it. I dare you to try. If fact, I double-dog dare you."

"You what?"

"That's a typical American challenge. It means that you're a chicken—coward—if you don't do it."

"And how many foolish things have you done in life because of a dog dare?"

"That's double-dog dare. And I've done too many foolish things to count. On the other hand, you haven't done nearly enough, Tiger. So what's it going to be? Are you up to the challenge? Or are you chicken?"

Why not? Just a few more days... Her phone dinged, interrupting her thoughts and signaling an incoming text message. Probably Grace, demanding she return home.

Sophia didn't take her eyes off Mike. She wasn't ready to leave. And she wasn't willing to let Mike's goading go unanswered. She pulled her shoulders back and marched up to him.

"I come from a long line of noble, fierce warriors. My ancestors crossed oceans to find a land to call home. They fought warring tribes, invaders, nature, and the very gods themselves to claim the kingdoms they deserved. No one," she poked him in the chest, "no one, calls the house of de Lyons cowardly and escapes our wrath."

Mike narrowed his eyes, regarding her with amusement. "Lady de Lyons, you may come from fierce ancestors, but I'm Irish through and through. And I know a load of blarney when

I hear it." He stuck out his hand. "You're on. May the best competitor win."

She looked at his hand. "That won't do, Irish. That won't do at all." Then she rose on tiptoe and sealed the bet with a kiss.

Chapter 19

s they strolled through the fairgrounds, Mike laced his fingers through Sophia's and watched the sunlight glint off her hair. It had darkened since her arrival in Morgan's Outpost, no longer simply blonde, it gleamed with strands as yellow as just-harvested corn to those as deep as honey, with a dozen shades in between.

The complex interweave of colors mirrored the complexity of the woman herself. No longer simply cosseted Lady Sophia, out for a lark, she'd deepened into a woman of passions, contradictions, and warmth.

"Hey, Miss Sophie, how's it going?" One of the high school volunteers, laden with a tray of chili samples stopped them.

"Hi, Trevor." She turned to him with a smile. "Are things going well at the tent?"

"It's crazy busy, but we've got it under control."

"Do you need us to come and help?"

The teen wrinkled his nose. "Nope. We're good. The guys have a competition on who can sell the most raffle tickets, though. Did you buy any yet?"

Mike grabbed his wallet and handed Trevor a fifty. "Technically we aren't eligible for the raffle, but take this donation and give the tickets to someone you think could use some good luck."

"Wow. Sure thing. Thanks Mr. Mac-G." He flashed them a grin. "I gotta hustle. See you later."

Mike reached for Sophia's hand again and started walking toward the pumpkin carving tent.

"That was generous, Mike. Thank you."

He shrugged. "It's for the kids. I like to do what I can."

Sophia nodded. "I know. That's one of the things I admire about you. You're dedicated to family. And willing to go out on a limb to help others."

He felt his cheeks flush at her praise. After the years he'd spent ignoring his family while profiting off the misfortunes of those he wrote about, he didn't deserve it. Giving to the children's rec center was a pittance in comparison. Not enough to earn him forgiveness for his years of neglect. Certainly not enough to earn him praise from her. "It's nothing," he muttered.

She squeezed his hand and gave him a smile, the kind that said she didn't agree but she didn't argue. "So, Mr. Mac-G," she said, using Trevor's name for him, "what are you going to show me next? And don't take me to another food vendor. The elephant ears and funnel cakes were enough for a few hours."

"I told you not to try both. We have all week, you know. You don't have to rush anything."

"One week hardly seems long enough. Especially when I'm making up for a lifetime of missing out." She pulled him to the side of the path under the branches of a nearly bare tree and faced him. "There's so much I want to do—to experience—in life. I feel like I've barely scratched the surface."

"You make it sound like you're going to a prison, not a privileged life."

"Privilege? Is that how you see it?"

Mike propped a shoulder against the tree, considering. "For most people in Morgan's Outpost the idea of having more money than you need and a staff of people to do all the basic work of life—cooking, cleaning, laundry, mending—seems like a charmed life. That's what they see when they look at royalty."

"And you?"

He brushed his knuckles along her cheek, smoothing back the wind-blown curls. "I have the privilege of knowing you. It can't have been all roses and champagne or you would never have left."

"Did you know that before I left the goodwill tour, I'd never once in my entire life, chosen my own food? We had a cook and a dietician who prepared all the meals. At events, someone else always chose the menus."

"Is it like that for all of the royal family?"

She shook her head. "Not everyone. But Uncle Julian had firm ideas about raising children. My cousin Helena didn't grow up under quite such strict rules, but by the time I came to the house, my aunt was dead and no one could control Julian."

"Your cousin Helena who married prince—later king and finally king emeritus—Alexander?"

She nodded. "You've been doing your homework, I see."

"I wanted to understand the world you came from." He hesitated but when she made no comment, he ventured another question. Not because he was a former reporter digging for a story. Because he cared. "How did you discover your mushroom allergy, if you weren't allowed to choose your own food?"

Sophia reached for his hand again, tracing her finger along the back of it, keeping her eyes on their entwined hands rather than meeting his. "Like most children, I wasn't fond of vegetables. And like most parents, Uncle insisted I eat them. The first consequence for not eating vegetables was not having any of the rest of your supper, either."

Mike chuckled. "That leads to a hearty appetite at break-fast."

"In Uncle's house it also led to a breakfast of leftover vege-tables. Served cold. It didn't take long to learn to eat what was put in front of me."

"I imagine not."

"When it came to mushrooms, I always felt ill whenever they were served. Not anything like I am now, you under-stand, but uncomfortable. I ate them, but I complained about it to Uncle. His solution was to cure me of my complaints by serving more mushrooms."

Her eyes glazed over and though she lifted her gaze from their clasped hands, Mike suspected she was seeing scenes from her childhood. His heart twisted at the forlorn look on her face.

"One night," she continued, her voice soft with the memory of old wounds, "when I was about ten, we had fresh mushroom soup. After a few bites, I didn't feel well. I was itchy and couldn't breathe properly. Uncle accused me of making a scene. He was on the verge of taking me to his study for a dif-ferent sort of punishment when I passed out.

"Thank the gods I had broken out in hives, or he might have accused me of faking it. A doctor was called. He sus-pected a food allergy which was later confirmed. The years of force feeding me mushrooms had sensitized me. What might once have been a mild food allergy turned into something far worse."

She shrugged. "The few times someone slipped and used mushrooms in cooking after that, they were dismissed. I never ate another. Uncle made sure I was tested for a number of other foods, though. I guess he didn't want me to blame allergies for refusing any other dishes, but by then, I'd learned to eat what was put in front of me without question."

"Your uncle sounds like a brute."

"I don't like to talk about it. For all his strict measures, he made sure I had a roof over my head, food on the table, and clothes to wear. Not all children have that. I should be grateful to him rather than…"

"Rather than what?" Mike asked quietly.

"I—" Sophia looked in his eyes blinking to keep her own from misting over. "I'm not sorry he's in jail. He did horrible things. But I wish I didn't hate him."

Mike pulled her into his arms and hugged tightly. "It's okay, sweetheart," he whispered. "You're allowed to be angry at him. You're even allowed to hate him. It doesn't make you a bad person."

He rubbed her back and rocked her, listening as her breathing went from harsh to soft, wondering why she didn't cry. But she didn't. She just clung to him as if he were a life raft in a bucking storm.

"When I see you with the girls," she sucked in another breath and Mike leaned close to hear her, "I see all that I missed as a child. I didn't know until I met you how unusual my childhood was. I don't want any child to ever be without the kind of love I see in you and your family."

She pulled away and grabbed both of his hands, suddenly the happy Sophie she'd always pretended to be. "That's why I've started plans to sponsor a children's foundation when I return to Melesia. I've already started the research."

"That's amazing. Do you know how few people can take a lifetime of hardship and turn it into a passion for helping others?"

She shrugged it off. "I have the money and the resources. I can become a very public spokesperson for the cause. I'll call it the Hercules Labors of Love Foundation. Because raising healthy, happy children makes even the labors of Hercules look easy. I plan—"

Mike cut her off by pulling her back into his arms and kissing her breathless. He couldn't resist. Sophia was special in ways he'd never imagined. And he'd make sure the world knew just how special she was.

Somehow, someway, the *Stir* stories would end with a plea to support her cause. She may hate him—like she did her uncle—for exposing her, but he'd do everything in his power to make sure that something of value came from his interference.

That—and a couple of thousand Hail Marys—just might save his soul from hell. Even if it couldn't save his heart from breaking when she left.

Sophia collapsed in a chair at the back of the tent and spooned a bite of chili into her mouth. The spicy warmth chased away some of the evening chill. After a day of exploring craft tents, admiring carved pumpkins, and stomping through a twisting corn maze with Mike, she savored the break.

"A penny for your thoughts," Mike said as he pulled a chair next to hers and sat with his own bowl of chili.

"Is that the going rate these days?"

"It's an old saying. When I was in high school and my sister would use that phrase, I told her she should keep her money and I'd keep my thoughts to myself." Mike chuckled and a surge of warmth hit Sophia. How wonderful it must have been to grow up in a family like his.

Not that all families in Melesia were as cold as her uncle's family. The princes and princesses always seemed to be laughing and enjoying life—the ones close to her age that was. King Constantine and King Emeritus Alexander had always seemed serious, but Prince Stephan knew how to laugh. Or at least he had until recently. His humor seemed to have fled along with his carefree life when Constantine was crowned.

She felt a tug of regret, knowing that he was likely hiding her disappearance, shouldering yet another responsibility to allow her this precious time of freedom. But she'd done her best to keep him informed of her safety, if not her whereabouts. That counted for something didn't it?

"Sophie, you're muttering to yourself." Mike snapped his fingers in front of her face, bringing her thoughts back to the present. "Are you lost in unhappy childhood memories? Or planning something with the foundation?"

"Neither." She smiled at him. "I was thinking it's about time you made good on your promise to take me to the haunted schoolroom."

"I told Katie and the girls we'd wait for them."

Sophia nodded and focused once again on her chili until a noise from the front of the tent had the cooks, volunteers, and organizers scrambling. She threw the bowl away and moved to see the source of the commotion.

The burst of an industrial-size flash temporarily blinded her. She blinked to clear her eyes. "Sorry about that," said a slender young man in front of her. "I wanted to get a candid shot of the volunteers before announcing myself. I'm Theodore Gray, reporter for the *Telegraph*."

Out of reflex Sophia shook the hand he offered. Mike didn't.

"Theodore, I'm Mike Maguire, one of the organizers of this event. What's going on? Why is the *Telegraph*—that's the local newspaper," he said in an aside to Sophia, "photographing the food tents? Don't you guys usually cover the haunted school-room and the pumpkin carving tent?"

"Nice to meet you, Mike." Theodore grabbed Mike's hand and pumped it, not seeming to notice his lack of enthusiasm.

"The mayor told me about you. And he told me about this gem of a woman."

Theodore grinned. "You are the Miss Sophie that everyone's talking about, aren't you? The driving force behind this fundraiser?"

"I'm Sophie, but I'm not the one behind the fundraiser. I merely worked with Mike, Mayor Aimsley, Councilmen Spritz and Johanson, and the rest of the committee."

"That's not the way the mayor sees it." The reporter grinned at her. "Mike, here, is right. The *Telegraph* usually only covers the human interest and entertainment side of the festival. But this year the mayor asked us to do a piece on the chili cook-off.

"When the guys in advertising heard about it, every one of them came to me with stories of how great you were. Seems you charmed them into several full-page ads to support the cause. We didn't think you'd mind sharing a couple of your fifteen minutes of fame with us."

Sophia smiled despite the trepidation in her gut. Of course, she remembered convincing the newspaper to act as an event sponsor by donating ad space. She should have realized it might come back to haunt her.

Before she could formulate a response to the unspoken query, Mike stepped between her and the reporter. "Listen, Theodore, Sophie put a lot of work into this, and I'm sure she'd love to have you cover the event. Right, Sophie?"

She nodded weakly.

"But here's the thing," Mike continued, attention focused on the reporter. "She's a little publicity shy. It's kind of a phobia. So maybe you could just ask her about her charity work and skip the photos. Okay?"

Theodore Gray scratched his head in thought before turning to her. "No offense meant, Miss. I didn't realize it would be uncomfortable for you. I should have asked first. The mayor was so sure you wouldn't mind."

Sophia swallowed her fears and looked at the young man. "Don't worry about it, Theodore. Mike's right about my—situation. But I've been working on it. Maybe if we did just one or two photos that would be okay. If I could approve them first. And if you promise me they'll just be for the local paper."

The worried look on his face cleared a bit. "Sure thing. Heck, we won't even use your last name if you don't want. Everyone around here just knows you as Miss Sophie anyway. Between you and me, even if you wanted fame, the *Telegraph* isn't the way to get it. Outside of the county, no one knows about our small paper. I don't think the AP's ever picked up a story from us. Not even the Pumpkin Queen and her court get coverage."

She nodded. "I doubt the chili cook-off and children's recreation center fundraiser is the kind of story that will change that. It's just that, as Mike said, I'm better at organizing and staying out of the limelight."

She gave him a look that had melted diplomats before him. A look that usually—tabloids excepted—assured she would get her way. Besides, with her new hair style and new look, it was unlikely she'd be recognized even if a larger paper picked up the story.

Later, after she returned home, if the press somehow picked up the story she'd use it, with the help of the Melesian Press Corps, to publicize the Hercules Foundation.

As the reporters and cameramen from the *Telegraph* organized the setting for the photo shoot, Sophia turned to Mike. "Thank you for trying to help me."

"Don't feel obligated to do this. You can still back out."

"Mike, no matter what happens with this photo, the children will benefit. Mr. Gray seems like a nice man. I doubt he'll try to make me look foolish for the sake of a story. If he does…"

she shrugged, "I've dealt with worse." She kissed him on the cheek. "Besides, you'll be right there beside me, holding my hand. It will be okay."

Mike watched, helpless, as Sophia let herself be led away by the reporter. They sat for a while, talking. He jammed his fisted hands into his jacket pocket, bumping against his own digital camera. Well, hell. If she was going to let the yokels from the *Telegraph* take her picture, he sure as hell was going to get a couple of shots for himself.

Besides, he could possibly use them for damage control later. He'd doctored more than his share of photos to support a story when he worked for the *Stir*. He could use the same techniques of photo-manipulation and misdirection to prove the darling of Morgan's Outpost wasn't Lady Sophia of Melesia when the time came.

Or so he hoped.

Chapter 20

"What are you going to be for Halloween, Miss Sophie?" Seven-year-old Mary Frances—the one Mike called Squirt—put her hand in Sophia's as they walked into the thrift store. "I'm going to be a witch. I need a pointed hat and a wart on my nose and a big, black cauldron—is that the right word, Uncle Mike?—to put my loot in."

"You can be as ugly as you want, but I'm going to be beautiful." Five-year-old Mary Katherine—also known as Pipsqueak—squirmed in Mike's arms. "I wonder if they have Cinderella or Snow White or Sleeping Beauty or…"

The minute Mike put her down she grabbed her oldest sister's arm but Mike stopped them. "Girls, no running off alone." He squatted next to them. "We're on a hunt to find things to make your costumes, so we have to be creative. So far, we're on the lookout for one witch, one princess and," he paused, "what do you want to be, Miss Manners?"

Mary Margaret grinned. "I'm going to be a chef—like my mommy. I want an apron and a tall white hat and a big mixing bowl with a spoon to carry my candy."

"Great idea. Did you ask your mom to help with the costume idea?"

The girl shook her head. "It's a surprise!"

"Let's get busy looking." Mike offered two hands; Miss Manners and Pipsqueak grabbed them and pulled him to the back of the store.

"I want to stay with you." Mary Frances pulled Sophia in the opposite direction. Together they searched through a number of dresses for the perfect black one that could be slashed to make it look old and tattered. They also found shoes.

"Can you paint a wart on my nose? Or maybe make me one out of clay or something?"

"I don't know," Sophia answered. "But I bet if we picked up some more material, I could cut bat and spider shapes out of it to glue onto your dress." In truth, she had no idea if she could do that or not, but she figured someone—Mike, James, Katie, or one of the staff at the pub—could teach her how to do it.

"Cool!" Mary Frances jumped up and down getting tangled in the too long dress she'd insisted on carrying. She tugged and Sophia heard the fabric rip. Good thing it was going to be slashed anyway.

"Now all I need is a witch hat," Mary Frances added.

"What does a witch hat look like?"

The little girl rolled her eyes. "You don't know much about Halloween, do you, Miss Sophie? Didn't your daddy ever take you out to trick-or-treat?"

"No. This is my first trick-or-treat night ever."

"Oh my gosh. Uncle Mike!" Her voice went from an astonished whisper to an all-out scream within the space of a few words.

Sophia looked around, but no one in the nearly empty shop seemed disturbed. Except Mike, who rushed over, the two other girls in tow.

"What's wrong, honey?" He was on his knees in front of Mary Frances before the words were out of his mouth. "Are you okay?"

"Uncle Mike, Miss Sophie's never been trick-or-treating!"

Relief flooded his face, and he rocked back on his heels. He winked up at Sophia. "Wow, imagine that. We'll have to show her how it's done, won't we? Let's start by showing her the pieces of costumes we found."

Mary Frances, then Mary Margaret, took turns showing off their treasures. Mike told them he could make hats for each from some cardboard and extra material, carefully explaining to Sophia what a witch's hat looked like. When they turned to Mary Katherine, her face scrunched up and she looked ready to cry.

"They don't have princess costumes. I looked everywhere." She gave Mike a hopeful, if watery, look. "Can we go somewhere else and buy my costume? I want to be Cinderella. Or Snow White."

Mike shifted uncomfortably. "Honey, we're not buying ready-made costumes this year."

"Please!" It was close to a wail.

Sophia went down on one knee, close to Mary Katherine and took over. Somehow instinct carried her through. "I think you're going to be the most beautiful princess in the whole town. I'll help. I'll bet there are going to be twenty other Cinderella's and sixteen Snow White's all in store-bought costumes. But a real princess would never want to look like someone else."

Mary Katherine sniffed, but looked at Sophia, interested. Sophia continued in a soft voice. "Would you believe me if I told you I know a real princess?"

"Really?" Wonder infused her voice now, and her eyes were glued to Sophia.

"Cross my heart." Sophia smiled to herself. She'd grown up with enough royal princes and princesses to know a thing or two about them. More than enough to satisfy one small girl wanting to play dress up. "Why don't we look together and see if we can find something fit for a real princess? Then I'll teach you everything you need to know to become one yourself."

Two hours later, after they'd dropped the girls off at Katie's and discussed the costume situation, Mike and Sophia were alone again.

"You were wonderful with the girls," he said, giving her a warm, approving smile. "I didn't think we'd get out of the store without a fit of tears until you took over finding the princess costume."

"It feels good to make a little girl smile."

"It feels good to make a big girl smile too." Mike wondered if she'd balk at being called a girl. When she didn't, he grinned at her. "For the record, everyone gets to be a kid on Halloween. So, have you given any thought to your costume?"

"I wasn't planning on having a costume."

"Come on, get into the spirit. Even the adults wear costumes to pass out the candy. I told Katie we'd handle candy duty at her house while she took the girls door-to-door. It'll be fun. It's about as American a tradition as you can get."

"All right." She twisted in her seat to face him as he drove. "What do you suggest?"

Mike slowed for a traffic light and looked at her while he waited. "Well, you could go for funny, and dress as a clown. Or you could go for a sexy costume and be just about anything else."

He couldn't help himself. The way she leaned toward him pulled her shirt tight across her breasts, and he stared, imagining. She must have read his thoughts because her gaze grew hot, and she edged closer, licking her lips.

He moved in. Only to be stopped by the blare of a car horn. Feeling the flush creep up his neck, he looked up at the green light and gunned it. The motion caused his jeans to shift across his straining erection. Damn, even being in the same car with Sophia endangered his equilibrium.

He struggled to sound normal as he kept his eyes glued to the road. He cleared his throat. "So, let's see. Adult woman costumes. Off the top of my head I'd say you could try French Maid, Rag Doll, Princess, Witch, Harem Dancer, Cowgirl—"

"Cowgirl! That's perfect. Another American tradition." For a moment, she sounded as excited as the girls had been. "What would a cowgirl wear?"

"Hmm." Mike stole a glance at her but quickly looked back at the street. "You need some boots—"

"I already have those."

"Nope. Wrong kind." He shook his head. "Cowgirl boots are different. Then you need a leather skirt—I vote for a short one—and maybe a vest with a sheriff's badge. Cowgirl hat. Six-shooter. Maybe a lasso—that's a rope for tying up cattle—and that should about do it."

"Where do we find all that?"

He considered. He wasn't ready to go back to the thrift store. But the antique mall might be an option. At least for the vintage six-shooter cap gun he had in mind. He turned the car toward the shop.

Sure enough, a little searching turned up nearly everything they needed. In the dusty basement of the shop, he found a small pair of worn boots, and some other items. Mike helped Sophia try on a vest then he perched a red and white felt Stetson hat on her head. Her curls fanned out beneath the brim making it look like it was made for her.

"You look perfect."

"Are you sure?" She chewed her lip in a gesture of uncertainty he was coming to recognize.

He kissed the worry off her lips. "Best cowgirl I've seen in a long time. All we have to do is get you a gun belt for these six-shooters and a tin star and you'll look like the sheriff of Morgan's Outpost."

"And the lasso. You said I needed a lasso."

"Yeah, well, rope is the easy part. Dad's got some in the garage that will work."

He handed her the cap guns—a lucky find from an era before people worried themselves gray about child safety—and gathered the other purchases. Together they made their way up the narrow staircase. Always the gentleman, Mike let her go first while he enjoyed the view. At the front of the store, he directed her to a glass case.

The jewelry display featured trays and trays of items arranged on a kind of Ferris wheel that rotated them with the push of a button. He leaned on the counter and watched her face as she looked through the assorted treasures. Vintage costume pieces mingled with decades-old Cracker Jack toys and a few items Mike suspected held real value.

Sophia stopped turning the trays and pointed to something. "Look at that ring. It's beautiful."

A small silver band, with an intricate setting housing diamond chips, lay on the felt of the tray. As she looked, a vendor came up to them and opened the case.

He handed the ring to Sophia. "This is a very old piece. You young women today want the biggest possible diamond when you get engaged, but a hundred years ago, a woman would be thrilled to have a diamond this size."

She turned the ring over in her hands, studying it. She slipped it on—and off again—quickly. "The setting is exquisite—all the more lovely for its simplicity. No wise woman would turn down a gift like this. The man who bought this for his bride must have been very much in love." She handed it back to the clerk as if it were the Hope Diamond.

He blushed—who wouldn't with Sophia looking at them like she was—and stammered something. "Don't know about love, but it was expensive in its day. You interested in classic jewelry?"

"Actually, we're looking for a—what did you call it, Mike?"

"A tin star. Sheriff's badge. For a Halloween costume."

"Of course. Got just the thing in here somewhere." The vendor whirled the trays until he caught sight of what he was looking for. He handed them an old-fashioned star, with molded knobs on the five points. "This dates back to the 1940s or 50s. Don't see 'em with that kind of heft to 'em anymore."

"We'll take it." Mike checked his watch then tossed the rest of the ensemble on the counter and paid for it all. With luck, he could get Sophia to the festival and have her hard at work in the chili tent within the hour.

If he hustled, he'd have just enough time to return and buy the ring that had snagged her attention. In his heart, he doubted that she'd ever agree to marry him, stay in Morgan's Outpost, or do any of the things he longed for with each passing day. But, even so, he dreamed of these things.

Before she left, he'd share his dreams with her and give her the ring. That way, at least, she would have something more tangible than fading memories to remind her of their time together. Just as he would have his heartache to remind him of all he'd lost.

Chapter 21

The next afternoon, Mike fought to keep calm as he and Katie leaned on the bar, watching Sophia run her hands down his dad's lapels, smoothing imaginary wrinkles and tightly strung nerves. "Smile, James," she said as she fussed over his collar. "You're meeting a woman you care about, not an executioner. Everything will be fine."

James patted his pockets absently. "Easy for you to say. You're a beautiful young woman just starting out in life. I'm an old man, looking for a second chance."

"Now, Dad." Katie moved to his side and planted a kiss on his cheek. "There isn't a woman alive who can resist your charm. You're still in your prime."

"I'd have gone out with you in Reno, if you'd asked me," added Sophia.

"I didn't see you, sweetheart." His dad winked at her.

Nothing about the exchange sat well in Mike's gut. He pushed off the bar and hustled over to the group, shooing the girls away. "You look fine, Dad. You're a good catch for any woman. Just don't, that is, don't let your imagination… Aw, hell, Dad, just don't get yourself hurt this time."

Dad gripped Mike's shoulders with the strength of a much younger man. "I've learned a thing or two over the past year, Mike. You don't have to worry about me. Besides," he released his grip and gestured around the room, "that's why I want you all to meet Destiny. I've made dinner reservations at the Hitching Post Hotel. Mike, I'll pick you and Sophia up at the fairgrounds, then we'll swing by Katie's house and pick her up too."

Mike nodded. "The hotel isn't that far out of town. Why not let Destiny stay there?"

"Don't get started, Michael. She's staying at the house. And you're finding someplace else to sleep. Your sister's got extra space if you can't figure out anything else."

"I'll be fine," Mike grumbled. "I'll pack a bag and stay here at the pub. There's a shower in the locker room and a couch in the office. I practically live here anyway."

Sophia stepped closer. "James, what time does Destiny's flight get in?"

"Couple of hours from now." He patted his pockets nervously again and smoothed back his hair. "What if she's changed her mind about me?"

"Then she'd have called off the visit. Now get going."

"Traffic can be a huge snarl between here and Denver this time of day," Katie added. "Plus, you've got to park and get to baggage claim."

"James, be sure you're waiting near the first entrance she'll come through. You want her to see you right away." Sophia and Katie steered him toward the door. "The minute she sees you, everything else will fade away. Trust me."

"Bye, Dad."

"Good-bye, James"

His dad hesitated in the door and turned to Mike as if needing his blessing. Mike swallowed his fears and gave his dad a cocky grin and a thumbs up. "May all your dreams come true," he said mouthing the first part of an old Irish proverb. *May all your dreams come true but one, to give you something to strive for.* "We'll be waiting for you tonight. Good luck."

Katie followed Dad to the car.

Sophia moved close to Mike and slid her arm around his waist. "You look worried."

"Of course, I'm worried. Dad's never acted like this before. Befuddled. Nervous. Sophia, she's a showgirl, for God's sake."

"Didn't you tell me your dad hasn't been this interested in the business and family life for a long time? It seems to me that Destiny is good for him."

"Yes. But for how long?"

"Forever, if that's what it takes to make him happy. Give him a chance."

"Easy for you to say. You won't be here to pick up the pieces if he falls apart again."

"I'm sorry, Mike. I wish I could stay around to help."

He watched her silently for a moment, then threw all caution to the wind. "Did you think about my offer?"

"Which offer?"

"You know. My proposal." The worst she could do was to say no. And maybe, if he charmed her enough or made her laugh, she'd agree to the impossible. He dropped to one knee in an exaggerated move. "Marry me, Sophie. Forget your past, throw aside your name, and marry me."

She giggled. "Mike, get up. And be serious. You're murdering Shakespeare down there. For your information, my life may be scripted, but I'm not about to turn it into a tragedy, Romeo."

Mike popped back up and gave her a hug. "You can't blame me for trying. I like having you around. I mean that. Think about staying." He tightened the embrace, hoping it would tell her what he couldn't put into words. "I'm serious. Marry me, Tiger, and I promise I'll make you happy."

She wiggled away, leaving an empty space in his arms and his heart. She had her duty. His father had his Destiny. What was left for Mike Maguire?

For the first time, the idea of a hot story and a big paycheck didn't satisfy him. It didn't satisfy him a'tall.

Later that night, Sophia made her rounds within the chili tent, chatting with returning customers and starting conversations with new ones. The popularity of their tent had picked up over the course of the festival as fairgoers passed word of the event from one to another.

Also—a factor she hadn't foreseen—the chili they offered gave hungry parents and children a chance to eat something more nutritious than corn dogs and anything else served on a stick. After her first days of tasting festival food, Sophia appreciated the appeal of sitting down to a steaming bowl of chili.

Better still, the donation boxes were stuffed with cash. Even with two and a half more days to go, the event was an unqualified success, raising enough to begin plans for the rec center as soon as the festival closed. Only one thing marred her evening.

Sophia threaded her way through the crowds to the back of the tent and slipped outside. Mike paced in the shadow of some bare trees, lost in his thoughts.

"Need some company?" she asked as she walked toward him.

He took her hand and continued to pace, although slower. Eventually he stopped. "What would you do, Sophie, if it was someone you loved?"

"Do you mean, how would I feel about someone I loved dating again? Like a widowed parent?"

He nodded.

"I don't know what to say, Mike. Everyone I've ever known until I came to Morgan's Outpost married for influence and power. Not love." She dug a toe of her boot into the ground swirling the packed dirt around a bit. "Actually, that's not quite true. The king married for love."

"That's a good thing, isn't it? Otherwise you'd have been forced to marry him, and leaving aside questions of his character, you didn't love him."

She agreed, but it wasn't quite as simple as Mike made it sound. "I'm happy he could find love and acceptance by the people. Constantine was like an older brother to me in some ways. Mostly he ignored me, but he tried to be kind. That's just the way our lives were." She shrugged. "Looking back, I have no doubt he'd have been a good husband, but for most of my life I was afraid of him."

"Why?" Mike's hand tightened on hers, and he turned to face her. "What were you afraid of?"

She held herself still, listening to the chirp of crickets and letting the cool air surround her for a moment as she let her thoughts wander. "I guess, in some ways, I projected my uncle's behavior on to him. Constantine is much older than I, and I rarely interacted with him—even before he was thrust into the role of crown-prince. But I always knew I was to marry him. Having no choice in the matter made it worse."

"What did your cousin, Helena, think? After her husband became king, couldn't she have stopped your uncle's plots?"

"Helena never supported the idea of the marriage. Neither did King Alexander during his reign. I'm grateful to both of them for that. But I think Constantine would have followed along with what he thought was his duty and married me despite their wishes." She smiled up at Mike. "Until he fell in love."

"What will you do with your life when you return?"

"If I'm lucky, I'll fall in love with someone acceptable."

"And if you fall in love with someone who isn't acceptable?" He leaned closer. "Someone like me?"

"That would be very unlucky, indeed," she whispered as she looped her arms around his neck. "Because I couldn't have you."

She sealed his lips with a kiss, not able to bear any protest he might make. She wanted him, desperately, she thought as she pressed closer, taking her arms from his neck and winding them around his middle beneath his sweater. But their time together now was numbered in hours—maybe days—but not weeks.

"Mike," she said as she broke the kiss, "don't stay in the pub office tonight. Stay with me. It may be our only chance to be together."

"Sophie, I—"

A rustle of the tent flap and a heavy tread stopped him. One of the volunteers called out to them. "Maguire, someone's looking for you."

"Thanks."

Mike looked at his watch and squeezed her hand. "Must be Dad and Destiny."

He smiled, but it was the kind of smile that could frighten children, and his grip on her hand was bone-crushing.

"It will be okay, Mike, I'll help you get through this."

Together they walked into the tent. The volunteer pointed to a young blonde dressed in a tank top with a push-up bra that pushed a little too much, and skintight jeans. She sported a dragon tattoo crawling up one arm.

Beside her, Sophia felt Mike go rigid. But he kept his smile in place and stuck out a hand. "I'm Mike Maguire. Pleased to meet you. You must be," he struggled as if he couldn't get the words out, "Destiny."

The girl laughed—giggled actually—as she shook Mike's hand. "You're so funny. Mr. Maguire told me you'd act like this. I'm Angi. I'm babysitting for the girls tonight."

Mike eyed her tattoo dubiously and relaxed just a bit. "Nice to meet you, Angi."

She laughed again. "I can see you're worried about the tat. Don't be. This one is just temporary—for Halloween." She rolled her eyes. "As if I could afford anything this detailed. Besides, I'm more of a hearts and flowers girl the rest of the year. I won't let your nieces get any ideas about piercings or tattoos from me."

She slipped into her denim jacket. "Anyway, your dad says to get moving so he can drop me off and pick Katie up."

"Let's go then." Mike gathered his things and Sophia did the same. Although she heard relief in his voice, she didn't see it in his eyes.

She braced herself for a long evening.

Mike sipped his wine and let the tension drain from his body. After taking a ribbing from his dad about his reaction to Angi, things had thawed a bit.

Now, two hours later the family enjoyed a leisurely dinner at the Hitching Post Hotel. The restaurant—despite being named the Saloon—was the fanciest place in Morgan's Outpost. Prom night packed the house. And the saloon's walls were filled with framed photos of people popping the question.

Tonight, the five of them relaxed in the nearly empty dining room. Katie sat next to dad and Mike was beside Destiny, with Sophia on his other side. She kept the conversation going during the awkward lulls, which, fortunately, were few.

He studied Destiny as she engaged in conversation with Katie. She was nearly as tall as his dad, with an athletic slenderness and a hint of curves. Her mahogany hair coiled into a neat French twist, and the royal blue of her turtleneck sweater brought out the creamy paleness of her skin. He even detected a few freckles.

He guessed, more from her conversation than from the faint smile lines that bracketed her lips, that she was in her mid to upper fifties.

As if she sensed his inspection, she turned. "Well, Mike, are you convinced I'm not a washed-up show girl looking for a sugar daddy?" Despite the bite in her words her tone and smile were teasing.

"Actually, I was thinking that, except for your name, you could pass for a good old-fashioned Irish girl."

"I am Irish, and proud of it." She smiled at him. "Let me save you the speculations. I was born Moira Lynn Murphy, of Boston. Not a grand family, but a steady one. My late husband was Adam Kinderschone, which roughly translated from the German, means—"

"Beautiful child," said Sophia. "Or Fairchild. That's a lovely way to honor him with your stage name."

"I wish you'd tell my boys that." Destiny reached for a roll and buttered it absently. "My sons—I have four of them, all grown—are still a bit skeptical of my stage career."

"But isn't it exciting, leaving your whole world behind to explore something new?" Katie leaned into the conversation, eyes bright.

"Katie, darlin', there's a difference between exploring and being irresponsible." Dad patted her hand.

"I'm not talking about myself, Dad. I've discovered a career I'm passionate about. One that will always let me take care of my girls. I have you and Mike to thank for that." She raised her wine glass. "To family."

Mike joined the toast, noting how hesitantly Sophia raised her glass. He clasped her hand in his free one and stroked her knuckles. The shadowed look in her eyes disappeared.

"Family is a blessing, except when it's not." Destiny smiled, but her voice was soft. She looked around the table. "I would give anything to be able to talk to my parents again, God rest their souls. And when Adam was killed, I wanted to die along with him. Only the thought of my boys kept me sane. But as much as I love them, they're grown now."

She stopped when a waiter approached. After he'd served the entrees, she continued. "Adam Jr. is in residency to be a cardiologist, like his father. Joel and Thomas are both in medical school too. Liam—my youngest—is already building his reputation as an investment banker. All sensible boys with their lives mapped out. Just like their father."

"It's a family to be proud of." James smiled at her, eyes filled with warmth. "My bunch, well, not an investment banker among them, but they're the salt of the earth."

He raised his glass in another toast.

They ate in silence for a while until Mike voiced the question uppermost in his mind. "So, Destiny, how did you and Dad meet?"

"Didn't James tell you that story?"

"To be honest, he told us next to nothing about you until a few weeks ago."

"James!" She swatted him on the arm. "Shame on you. No wonder your poor son worried you'd gotten yourself in a load of trouble."

James mumbled something and kissed her on the cheek before pointing a finger at Mike. "He gave me so much grief about the internet dating sites, that I quit talking to him about it."

"You met on an internet dating site?" Katie pounced on that bit of information. "Next time I want to meet someone, I'm trying it."

"There's plenty of nice young men right here in Morgan's Outpost for you, young lady. I'm not letting you out among the wolves again."

Before Katie could respond, Destiny laughed. "Don't worry, it wasn't anything as risky as that, although I did consider internet dating. The boys had a fit. The first of many."

She chuckled, and her eyes softened as she spoke of her children. "I should start at the beginning. In my day, you finished school, got married, and settled down to raise a family. In that order.

"My dad insisted I get an education first—until I told him I wanted to major in music and be a famous singer. He drew the line at that. At eighteen, I couldn't imagine why. I was the soloist in the church choir and sang in every school musical."

She took a bite of her steak and savored it, chewing slowly. Everyone waited while she spun the story out in the best tradition of Irish tales.

"In time, Dad agreed I could major in music if I had a second career major to fall back on. Like most young women of that day, I decided to become a teacher. Eventually, I met and married Adam, and while he was in medical school, I supported us by teaching and giving occasional piano lessons. I still sang in the church choir, but other than that, my musical dreams were at an end."

"What changed?" asked Sophia. "When did you stop being Moira and become Destiny?"

"I guess my whole life was building to it in one way or another. Like most children, I hated my name." She shuddered. "Moira seemed so old fashioned and stilted. But one day in reading mythology I learned The Fates—the ones who control mankind's destinies—were called the Moirae in Greek."

Sophia nodded. "Clotho spun the thread of life, Lachesis measured it, and Atropos snipped it at the end." Her shoulders trembled as if a chill had chased down her spine.

"You're a clever one." Destiny laughed. "I only read far enough to decide that Moirae and Moira were enough alike that one day I'd change my name to Destiny. But that was a child's fantasy. The real transformation took much longer."

She shifted in her chair, studying a small ring on her right hand for a moment before facing Sophia. "I stopped teaching when the children came along and dedicated myself to being the ideal wife and mother. I did everything by the book."

Although Mike listened to Destiny's words, he kept his gaze on Sophia's face. Hunger and longing transformed her features and he watched, fascinated, as her normal calm cracked and she fidgeted with her flatware during the story.

"One day," Destiny continued, "I realized that I'd lived my whole life following someone else's plan. And all the people who'd laid out those plans for me were gone. I was the one to make decisions from now on. That was when I gathered my courage, created a vocal demo and started looking for what I'd always wanted."

She took a sip of wine. "I wouldn't trade a minute of my life, but I also will be forever grateful that I stepped off the safe path."

"And that, my children," said James, his eyes twinkling, "was how we met. She started speaking and writing about how it's never too late to pursue your dreams. Her story appeared in the AARP and other 'old folks' magazines' and she even got an online discussion group going. We started chatting every day.

"When the restaurant show in Reno corresponded with one of her singing gigs, well, we decided it was time to meet in person."

"Dad, that's so romantic. Like an old-fashioned courtship through the mail, only updated." Katie dabbed at her eyes.

"Somehow, I never thought of myself as a mail-order, well, a mail-order anything. I'm sure Liam and the others will consider that another strike against their crazy mom."

James grabbed Destiny's hand and brushed a gallant kiss across her knuckles. "You may be crazy to fall for a guy like me, but then, I'm crazy for you too. I hope once your boys meet me, they'll decide I'm not some old codger after your trust fund."

"Dad, are you and Destiny getting serious about one another?"

"Katie, for the love of God, don't push them." Mike shook his head at her. "They're friends."

"Well, Michael, there's friends and there's friends, as my dad used to say. It's fine for you young folks to take forever and a day to decide you're falling in love with each other," he looked pointedly at Mike and Sophia, "but by our age, you learn that you don't have forever. Grab life when it comes, son."

Mike sat, stunned. He swallowed once. Twice. Then he felt Sophia's hand on his arm. "So, Dad, does that mean you… you're…" He lost his voice again.

"It means," answered James, looking around the table "that we'll tell you as soon as we figure it out. Meanwhile, you and Sophie need to do some figuring of your own."

Chapter 22

Sophia accepted the mug of coffee Mike slid across the pub table to her and studied him, taking in the dark reddish shadow of his unshaven beard, the bleary look to his eyes and his general lack of energy.

"I take it you didn't find the office couch very conducive to sleep last night."

"That would be the high-brow way of putting it." He grunted and took a slug of coffee. "It felt like sleeping on a bed of rocks." He shifted his shoulders and groaned.

Sophia abandoned her coffee and moved behind him. She placed her hands on his shoulders and tried to massage the tension from them. His muscles were iron-hard but her once-insignificant grip had strengthened over the weeks of waiting tables at the pub.

She pushed her thumb into a tight spot and traced the line of his muscle, feeling its rigid edge and the taut strength. With long, slow strokes she outlined it, adding pressure until he groaned and leaned forward, bracing his elbows on the table and laying his head in his palms.

"Sophie, you don't know how good that feels."

She repeated the strokes on his other shoulder. "Beginners luck, I guess. I've never done this before."

"You could have fooled me." His voice grew heavy, syrupy, releasing weariness and tension with each word and sigh as she worked. "That's heaven. Oh, yes. Right there. More." Another sigh and he fell silent.

"It's the least I can do, since you sacrificed your bed to me last night."

"No, I didn't. The apartment is yours for as long as you like. It became off limits to me the day you moved in."

"Even so, you'll remember I did invite you to share it last night." She stilled her hands, resting them on his shoulders, feeling his movement as he heaved in a breath.

Mike covered one of her hands with his own and guided her to a chair next to his. "What you offered was generous. I'm not sure you realize how generous."

His hazel eyes gleamed, greener than gold in the morning light. Full of questions. She met his gaze with her own level one. "I knew what I was offering."

His look sharpened, and he raised his free hand to caress her cheek. He trailed his fingers down her jaw, her throat. She swallowed, nervous, knowing his fingers felt the movement. "Did you really?" he whispered. "Did you know what you were proposing?"

She swallowed again, watching his gaze gleam hotter as he traced the movement with both eyes and hands. "I was raised to be the virgin bride of a prince, but I want to give myself to you instead."

"For how long?"

The regret in his eyes wouldn't allow her to gloss over his question as if she misunderstood. "Not nearly as long as I want."

Mike captured her other hand with his. He glanced at their clasped hands, then raised his eyes to hers. "I'm not a one-night stand kind of guy, Sophia. I gave that sort of thing up a long time ago."

"Isn't a single night better than nothing at all?" She couldn't quite hide the catch in her voice. "If I could make it last longer, I would but I—"

"Don't tell me you can't. It's a lie. The truth is you won't. You may come here and pretend to be a free woman, but you're not. You're tied to your duty. And you're the only one who can cut that tie. Until you do, you'll never be free."

He stood and pulled her to her feet, yanking her into a kiss that was as rough and desperate as it was passionate. No gentleness softened it. No humor lightened the edges. His beard stubble scraped her chin as his tongue thrust into her mouth.

One hand held her head immobile while the other pressed into the small of her back, forcing her closer. His body heat, always so pleasant before, burned like the Caribbean sun at noon, scorching her.

He ignored her protests as the feeble, insincere attempts they were. Her entire body grew moist, clinging, and vulnerable, but his kiss didn't soften. She'd wanted tenderness, but she'd take this wild assault if that was all he could give.

She tore her mouth away. "Mike, I—"

He claimed it again, cutting off her words, until she uttered a sharp cry as his whiskers brushed against her tender, swollen lips.

Immediately, his hold gentled, and he cradled her against his shoulder, his breath ragged. "I'm sorry, sweetheart. I didn't mean to hurt you." He touched her cheek, her temple, her hair with tenderness now.

Tears stung her eyes. She craved this sweetness, this tenderness. She craved, but could never have, this emotional intimacy with a common man.

"I'm a selfish bastard, Sophia. I don't want a taste of your passion. I want all of it. Not just passion in bed, although that would be a great start." His laugh sounded forced. "I want your passion in life. I want your passion for a life we could build together. For the children we could bring into our family. I want you. All of you. And I'm willing to give up whatever it takes to have you. But I won't unless you're equally willing."

He pulled back far enough for her to see his eyes. The combination of pain, passion, and determination weakened her knees and her resolve.

"What are you willing to give me, Sophia? Will you come out of hiding? Marry me? Take me to your home and tell the world that I'm the man you want?" He paused. "Or am I just another adventure to check off of your list before you return to Melesia?"

She blinked against the stinging tears that threatened to fall, not caring that a few escaped her attempts to contain them. "You're not a check mark on a list, Mike. At least believe that."

"But I'm not enough to risk losing your status and the life you claim is so empty for you in Melesia."

Her heart did an odd skip, then thundered in her chest as a rush of hot energy—anger, excitement, fear, and dismay—sizzled through her veins leaving her dizzy and chilled in its wake. She clung to Mike to keep her balance. For the first time in her life she faced an irrevocable choice—Mike or the ordered world she'd always inhabited.

She didn't know if she could have both. But if she could have only one, which would it be? A lifetime of training warred with her heart, and rational thought superimposed itself over passion.

She'd been raised to be a political wife and diplomat, to exist for the sake of her king and her country. But was that what her country really needed? What did it require from her now? What was she still willing to give? And what about her own needs? Confusion swirled in her mind, raising questions, but yielding no answers.

The sadness in his eyes was growing, dimming their light, and she had to speak before all of it was gone. "I want you," she said, her voice parched as the sandy coves of home. "I want you, but I don't know how to give up everything. I have to think. I need time. Just a little time."

He stilled, then stepped away from her, his weariness causing his shoulders to slump and his jaw to slacken.

"You said it yourself, Sophia. We don't have much time."

Mike stared at himself in the mirror, wondering how the hell the last week had gotten so far off track. The gray concrete block walls of the staff locker room reflected his mood. He'd wanted to show Sophia some fun. But between planning Halloween costumes for the girls, working at and touring the festival, and meeting dad's new…meeting Destiny, his simple plans had twisted and looped over each other until the tangled skein knotted into an untenable mess.

He rinsed his face in warm water and lathered on shaving cream, uncomfortable as he thought back to last night's dinner conversation. The Greek Fates, spinners, measurers, and cutters of the thread of life, would surely snip his knotted plans into oblivion if they had their way.

And they should. Because although everyone thought he and Sophia were a happy couple, he had about a snowball's chance in Melesia of winning her in real life. And he'd pretty much blown that.

Mike raised his hand to shave and realized it was shaking. Too much coffee and too little sleep. Or something. He put the razor down and sat heavily on a bare bench. Sophia, who started out as a story, then a curiosity and a project, had wormed her way into his heart. Something he should have been man enough to keep to himself.

But no—when she'd offered to share her bed with him, the blood and rational thought that didn't rush to his groin had lodged in a stubborn corner of his heart and mind. Stubborn enough to push her away in favor of the cold lumpy office couch. Stubborn enough to insist that if he couldn't have all of her, he wouldn't have any of her.

Damn his hard-headed Irish pride. He could have had a warm and memorable night or two for himself if he'd just followed her lead.

He returned to the sink and raised the razor again. His hand was steady enough to wield a safety razor, for heaven's sake. He swiped away the lather, skin stinging under his heavy-handed stroke.

Sophia had started the morning sweet and full of smiles until he'd pushed too hard for what he wanted. What he shouldn't want, didn't deserve, and likely couldn't have anyway. Like the poor slobs in the Irish tales, he'd been shown a treasure beyond measure. But when he stretched out his hand to take hold of it, instead of gold, he held icy mist and heard the chill of Leprechaun laughter.

Too late, as he'd watched her leave the pub mumbling about fresh air, he knew he'd misplayed his hand. Where was the glib charm that had netted him confidences from all and sundry? The cheap smiles that mimicked trustworthiness? Instead he'd taken what he'd wanted, grabbed it, and pushed for a declaration of love on her part. What a fool. How could he be sure she'd know the difference between love and gratitude? Why did he care?

He rinsed his face, showered, and jerked on a fresh set of clothing. As he grabbed his wallet, he paused and opened it. Inside lay the small ring from the antique shop. He grinned in spite of himself. Regular guys kept a spare condom or two in the wallet. He kept an antique engagement ring.

Fool indeed.

Shoving the wallet in his pocket, he focused on more important things first. Like winning Sophia over again. Proving he wasn't the controlling jerk who'd handled her roughly and demanded what she couldn't give. Getting another chance.

By the time he'd collected himself and headed to the kitchen in search of breakfast, she was back. She dropped a stack of papers on the table and started to read.

He lingered in the pass window, watching her, remembering the first day she'd awakened on his couch, rumpled, dazed and surrounded by three little girls and one not-by-any-stretch-of-the-imagination-little dog. Even in unfamiliar surroundings, wakened from a Benadryl-induced sleep, she'd maintained her poise and charmed him within minutes.

More than charmed him. He'd been tongue-tied for the first time in longer than he could remember. His first coherent thoughts were of how to keep her around for a while. Now, after weeks together, the longing was even stronger.

He headed to her table, fresh mug of coffee in hand, and grabbed a chair, flipping it around to straddle it and rest his arms on the back. He pushed the coffee over to her.

"I hope plain black coffee is all right, miss," he said softly.

She looked up from the papers, brow furled in confusion. "Of course, it is."

"Can I get you anything else? Breakfast? This is a full-service restaurant, you know. We've got bacon, eggs, anything you like. Although we recently took mushrooms off the menu. Someone very important to… Someone important can't eat them."

"Mike, what's gotten into you?" She folded the papers and pushed them aside.

"It's you. I'm not usually such an overbearing jerk, but this morning, I behaved badly. I'm sorry. I—"

"Don't be." She reached across the table and placed a hand—still cool from her morning walk—on his arm. "You were right. I can't continue to live in two worlds. An old Melesian proverb says that even a good captain can't pilot two ships."

He captured her hand, caressing her fingers—her naked fingers—with his thumb. "Maybe these days with GPS and cell phones he could."

"A cell phone isn't going to solve our problems."

"It can't hurt." He curled his fingers around hers and looked into her wide, still eyes. "I haven't changed my mind about what I want. I still want all of you. But I was wrong to push you for a quick answer. Wrong to think there's no room for compromise. I can wait long enough for us to find our way through this if you want to."

He stopped, before a torrent of blarney ruined his simple appeal. Waiting was the hardest thing he'd ever done.

Eventually, she nodded. "We'll navigate this together. If The Fates are with us, maybe we can chart a strong course before the storms hit."

"Or maybe there won't be the kind of storms you fear. After all, your king married an American. Why can't you?"

"Now that you mention it," she gave him an unexpected smile, "my marriage is probably the farthest thing from his mind, now." She slid one of the sleazier tabloids across the table.

"Melesian Queen Pregnant with Alien Twins." Mike burst out laughing. "Even for this rag, it's a stretch. So what else do your weekly tabloids say?"

She scanned them, passing each to him after a quick read. "It looks like all of them are focusing on the most bizarre Halloween stories they can find. Mummies. Curses. Hauntings. Except for the alien baby theory, Melesia is getting a break this week."

Mike's gut eased as he glanced at the *Stir* and saw that even Frank Kincaid had jumped on the Halloween bandwagon.

Mack the Pen would remain in retirement for at least another week.

"So," he said striving to keep the sense of ease between them, "what are your plans for today? It's trick-or-treat night tonight. I told Katie we'd arrive at her place by five so she can take the girls out early. I'll come upstairs for you at four thirty. Can you have your costume ready by then?"

"Ready and waiting." She winked. "Pardner."

Mike winced. "You need to work on that drawl a bit if you want to pass for an American cowgirl." He stood and started to the kitchen. "Meanwhile, I'll find you something to eat while you finish looking over the papers."

"Mike?" Her voice stopped him, and he turned.

"What's your costume?"

"That, Tiger, is something you'll find out tonight. But don't worry. If you don't like it, I'm sure you can find a way to make me take it off." He shot her a wink of his own and watched as a flush crept across her cheeks. The night couldn't come soon enough.

Chapter 23

Sophia pivoted in front of the mirror, still not sure about the push-up bra she'd allowed Destiny to talk her into. But when Destiny and James had stopped by the pub to visit, she'd been unable to resist the temptation to spend time with another woman. And Destiny, who'd dropped into her life like a message from Mt. Olympus, had offered her an uncomplicated affection and acceptance that she desperately needed.

"Hera and Aphrodite," she muttered. She needed someone to confide in, someone to help her navigate the waters of heart and home, but she'd had so few close friends and confidants in her life that she hadn't known where to begin. And how could she tell the whole story to anyone without risk? Thank the gods, Mike was trustworthy. No one else needed to know.

Impulsively Sophia turned from the mirror and dug in the back of a drawer for her jewelry case. Inside, lay a strand of six pearls on a platinum chain. Sophia's father had given her mother the first pearl when Sophia was born. He added one pearl to the strand every year, marking his daughter's growth. She treasured it more than the rest of the de Lyons jewels combined.

Sophia clasped it around her neck. It didn't go with the tightly fitted western shirt with its sassy snap buttons, but it made her feel like her parents were close. Close and telling her that love should always come before duty. The duke—damn him—had tried to teach her love was for fools, but even as she'd bitten her tongue to keep from contradicting him, she'd never believed him.

To Embrace Fate is Folly; to Ignore her, Disaster. Fate had brought her to Morgan's Outpost, introduced her to Mike and sent Destiny to give her the push she needed. If The Fates truly granted favors to the bold rather than the deserving, than she'd be bold tonight. She'd declare her love to Mike and start down the path with him—wherever it led.

Her cell phone rang, and she glanced at the clock. He must be coming by early. She picked up by the second ring. "Hi, handsome."

"You must have been expecting someone else," said a feminine voice.

Belatedly, Sophia recognized it was Grace Bradley. Excitement sizzled through her as she sensed the hands of The Fates weaving new strands into her life. "I'm glad you called, Grace. I've got so much to tell you. But first I have to thank you from the bottom of my heart for helping me to find out what life is really like."

Sophia pivoted in front of the mirror while she talked, grateful for Grace's friendly ear. Her confidence soared. The star badge and low-slung six shooter guns drew attention to her chest and hips while the short vest and suede skirt made the most of her waist.

"You won't believe all that's happened to me. I have a job waiting tables in a pub, and it's fun. I'm living in an apartment on my own, people actually like me and, oh, Grace, I've met someone. Someone special."

"I'm glad you're doing well," Grace said when Sophia paused for breath.

Something in Grace's voice wasn't right. Apprehension slithered up Sophia's spine, as she filled the silence, hoping that she'd heard wrong.

"Listen," Grace continued, worry creeping into her voice, "I'm sorry to interrupt, but I think there might be trouble here."

"There isn't trouble," Sophia answered injecting confidence into her voice. "And even if there is, what can I do about it?" She remembered, too late, how Grace had hidden from public attention and jumped at shadows.

"You have a duty to your country," Grace insisted stubbornly. "Besides, you're part of the trouble. I overheard Dorinda Mikolas say something about you and—"

Sophia stifled a groan. Her cousin, Dorinda, had been raised on tales of how the de Lyons had been cheated out of their right to rule Melesia. As a long-time supporter of the duke's warped political agenda, Dorinda stirred up trouble the way a speed boat churned calm waters.

Sophia had to stop Grace's chaotic thoughts before Grace inadvertently fed Dorinda's delusions. And Sophia had to reassure Grace that nothing would come of the Dorinda's meddling if they remained calm. Firmness first.

"Grace, you're imagining plots where there aren't any. Constantine stopped all of that. What you heard was probably nothing more than Dorinda grumbling about how they failed to marry me off. She likes to complain about that bloodline purity crap." She softened her voice. "Trust me, my being there would just make matters worse."

"Crap? When did you start using words like crap?"

Sophia laughed. At least she'd gotten Grace's mind off conspiracy theories involving Sophia's loony relatives. "About the same time you started using phrases like 'a duty to your country,'" she said lightly. She glanced at the clock. Mike would be here any minute now. "Look, I've got to go. I have a date."

"Are you sure?"

"About my date?" Sophia teased, deliberately using humor to distract Grace from her imaginary worries. "Very sure. Mike's a great guy. I'm also sure that there's nothing for you to worry about. Melesia can withstand anything Dorinda can dish out. And believe me, as much as I love it here, I'd be home on the next flight if I thought you were in trouble."

She meant that to the bottom of her soul. She'd never let her friend suffer for helping her. "You've given me a great gift, Grace," she added. "If I can return the favor, I will."

She meant that too.

The sound of Mike's footsteps on the stairs and his knock on the door demanded her attention. Her heart pounded as she took one last look in the mirror and headed to the living room.

"You already have, in a way," Sophia heard Grace say, but the pounding of her heart and the rush of excitement in her veins made it hard to concentrate on the problems of a tiny island half a world away. "I've started seeing—"

Mike rapped on the door again, harder this time.

"Hey, sorry to cut you off," Sophia said hastily to Grace, "but Mike's here. I'll talk to you later. I promise." She switched off the call.

Tomorrow, she vowed. Tomorrow she'd listen to Grace's news and make sure she wasn't still in a panic over the Mikolas clan. Things were changing. Melesia, Grace, and Sophia were changing with them.

Tonight was about her. About Mike. About the traditions of her soon-to-be new homeland—America. She playfully drew her six shooter, ready for anything. Until she opened the door.

And screamed.

Her shriek held just the right amount of terror, Mike thought, as he raised his hands high, causing the crimson-lined black vampire cape to fan around him. He swooped in and grabbed her, bending her back to expose her neck and nibble in his best vampire fashion.

His plastic fangs scraped her delicate skin then jarred loose. Just as well. He couldn't kiss worth a damn in them, and they tasted foul. He worked them free with his tongue, spit them out, and returned to focusing on her neck.

"Help." Giggles marred her weak protests. "No. Stop."

"Or what?" he managed between licks and nibbles as he worked his way across her warm, sweet-smelling skin. "You'll shoot?"

"Can't." She gasped when he sucked on her earlobe. "Dropped my gun."

Mike chuckled between nips. He held her back firmly and released his other hand so he could push aside her vest. He cupped her breast through the thin material of her shirt, gratified to hear her gasps turn to moans. Her nipple responded instantly to his caress.

He captured her lips with his own, delving deep into the recesses of her mouth, kissing and exploring as he backed them into the room. When they bumped against the couch, he tumbled them onto it, letting her fall on top of him. Now both of his hands were free to roam the lush softness of her skin.

A quick flick and the snaps on her western shirt popped open. He traced the plunging line of her bra blindly as he continued to kiss her until he found the fragile bit of plastic holding it together. Bless the saints, he was glad she'd chosen a style that clasped in front. A twist of his fingers and heaven was in his grasp.

Her breast filled his palm with enough left for his searching fingers and thumb to explore. Her skin, warm and smooth, teased him with its softness. Then, to his delight, his thumb felt the ridged, pebbled texture of her areola and brushed against the tight nipple. He twisted, moving her beneath him and releasing her mouth.

He trailed a few kisses down her throat then gave in to temptation, kissing her breast as hunger began to rage in him. A little lick, a tiny nibble, then he sucked, hard, on the nipple, outlining it with his tongue and pulling it deep into his mouth.

She gasped and went still beneath him. Reluctantly he pulled away and raised his head so he could look at her. "I'm sorry. Did I hurt you?"

The glazed look in her eyes faded as she focused on him. She shook her head slightly. "I never…that's…I…" She wet her lips.

Lust slammed into him, turning everything as hard as iron. Damn. He should have gone with a monk costume instead of the vampire. A hair shirt might—might—have kept his lust in check. He fought to catch a breath as he sat up, leaving the heat of her body. Now her eyes looked teary, wet.

"Sophia, are you all right?"

She tugged at his cape, stopping his retreat. "No one has ever done that before," she said, her voice husky and breathless. "I've never felt like that."

"Was it too much? Too fast?"

"Not with you. I wouldn't have wanted that with anyone but you."

Her admission hit him hard. Saints! He'd known she was a virgin, but he'd not expected her to be this untouched. Lust still sizzled and raged in his veins, but something else, far more dangerous, tightened his throat. He'd been wrong to think he was as hard as iron from head to toe. That was only his body.

Deep inside, beyond his tensed biceps and rigid shoulders, lurked a dangerous softness, an emotional quicksand that pulled everything into its trap. His heart was softening, sucking reason, logic and willpower into the void.

He loved her.

Of course, he did. What idiot hoped to marry a girl he didn't love? But he'd kept the word locked away, not even whispering it until this moment. Now, he couldn't forget it. Couldn't shove it back into the tight, controlled corner of his mind where he'd stored it all these weeks.

He loved her. And it changed everything.

"Mike? Are you all right?"

Saints! Even the hesitant question in her voice hurt like a knife now that he loved her. He couldn't leave her in doubt. "Sweetheart, I've never been happier." He cupped her jaw, then drew his hand down her neck, across her shoulder and down to the soft skin of her breast, watching a light glow in her eyes as he did so. "And you couldn't be more perfect."

He gently pulled the material of her bra together and clasped it again, then started on her shirt buttons. "Next time, we'll take it more slowly. First times shouldn't be rushed." A smile curved on his lips.

Mike pulled her to her feet and gave her a light, quick kiss. "Let's get our costumes straightened and get to Katie's place before the girls get too impatient. I promised we'd be there to take pictures before they left the house."

Ten minutes and several kisses later, she headed to the bedroom to do whatever females did while they regained composure. And he went in search of his fangs. He'd wash them off in cold water and hope it quelled the raging combination of love and lust that hovered on the hungry edge of fulfillment. He owed her that much.

"Me and Miss Sophie, next." Pipsqueak grabbed her hand and pulled her to the side of the room where Mike snapped photos of the girls.

"No, me."

"Me too."

Surrounded by a shy chef, a grinning witch, and a princess fit for a fairy tale, Sophia smiled for the camera. One by one she took photos with each of the girls, complimenting them on their costumes and basking in their enjoyment.

When Katie came out dressed as a rag doll, the girls flocked to her, ready to go begging for candy. Sophia slipped to the side and dug into her tote bag.

"Your Highness, Princess Mary Katherine," she called, trying to sound serious, "I believe your costume needs just one more thing."

When Pipsqueak raced over, Sophia pulled out the rhinestone studded tiara Mayor Aimsley had given her at the festival. "My 'Chili Queen' crown is the perfect addition to your costume." She solemnly placed it on the girl's head.

"Now I look like a real princess." Astonishment colored her voice.

"Just remember," Sophia said as she hugged her, "a real princess is always gracious and tries to make others feel comfortable. She smiles, even when her feet hurt, or her crown slips, or she gets a piece of candy she doesn't like. Can you do that for me?"

Mary Katherine nodded, her eyes wide. "I promise." Then she grinned and turned aside. "Mommy, look. Miss Sophie gave me her crown."

"Next," Sophia called, "I have something for our scary little witch, Miss Mary Frances." When the girl came to her, Sophia leaned down and whispered in her ear. "I know a secret about you. Underneath this scary costume is a loving and giving heart. Because I know, I want you to have this."

Sophia pulled a gold chain with a heart shaped locket from her bag and, after carefully removing the pointed black hat, she slipped it over Mary Frances' fiery nimbus of hair. She tucked it under the collar of the costume, making sure it rested beneath the heavy layers of warm clothing that lay hidden there.

Once she put the hat back on, Sophia touched the carefully made up wart someone had created for Mary Frances' nose. "Now we both know you have a heart of gold."

By the time she'd crossed the room, the girl had the heart out for her mother and sisters to inspect.

Finally, Sophia motioned for Mary Margaret to come over. She hugged her, remembering how easily the girl had slipped into her life, tempting her to stay at the pub when she didn't know anyone else.

"I have something very special for you." She pulled a charm bracelet out of the bag. On it was a charm shaped like a cookie. A second charm—a tiny heart—dangled close by it. She fastened it around Mary Margaret's wrist as she talked. "This is to help you remember the fun we had baking cookies together. I put a little piece of my heart on it for you. You can add charms as other special memories come your way."

"I love it." Mary Margaret looked at her with the solemn eyes she'd come to expect, then smiled suddenly. "I'm glad you came to live at the pub. I hope you stay forever and ever."

"Me too," Sophia whispered.

Then in a flurry of activity, everyone grabbed baskets, bags and stray costume bits and hurried out of the house. Sophia waved.

"What's up with the gifts?" Mike asked as he came behind her and wrapped his arms around her waist. He pulled her against him, his embrace tightening. "This isn't your way of saying good-bye, is it?"

His tension radiated through her, and she struggled to turn in his arms. When she did, she raised her hand to run it along his jaw. He'd slicked his hair back, taming the hint of curl with something black and heavy, she realized. And his eyebrows had been painted a similarly menacing black.

But the vampire costume wasn't what caused her heart to speed up, her pulse to beat in her throat or her breathing to hitch. Only the man was responsible for that. She looked into his eyes, studied the hazel mix of colors showing his every emotion and knew he feared her answer. He needn't.

"Mike, I promise you, from this point on, all of our good-byes will only be temporary. I want to share my life with you. To have you share yours with me. And the consequences—"

He cut off her words with a kiss. "I'll hold you to that promise," he whispered when he pulled his lips slightly from hers. I'll—"

She cut him off too. No need to talk when the melding of their lips said so much more than words. She pressed close, not caring if she rumpled the formal tuxedo he wore under the cape. She slipped her hands under his cummerbund, annoyed to find crisp cotton instead of warm skin.

She tugged on the shirt.

He tugged on her bottom lip with his teeth.

The doorbell rang and a handful of shrill voices interrupted them. "Trick-or-treat." The words echoed meaninglessly out-side the door, repeating in first one voice then another as the doorbell rang again.

Mike released her and stepped away. He reached into a pocket and pulled out his plastic fangs as he made his way to the door and yanked it open. "Who dares disturb me?" he asked in a voice full of gruff menace.

Giggles and refrains of "trick-or-treat" greeted him again. He reached for a huge bowl and dropped miniature candy bars into the outstretched bags of half a dozen costumed children. One by one, they thanked him and strode off the porch to a group of parents who waited on the sidewalk.

He shut the door. "Back to you, my lovely," he said in a fake eastern-European accent that made her giggle, even as the gleam in his eyes made her blush. He wrapped one arm around her and reached to remove the fangs with the other when the doorbell rang again.

"Trick-or-treat."

Sophia recognized the command in the refrain and opened the door herself this time. She complimented the children on their costumes as she put candy into the bags. Her heart warmed with each shyly mumbled, "Thank you."

Before she closed the door, another set of children started up the stairs. Mike appeared at her shoulder and helped to pass out the candy, his plastic fangs glowing in the twilight. "It'll be like this for the rest of the night," he said softly as they closed the door. "Barely time for a nibble, let alone time to bite you properly." He pulled off the fangs and nipped at her neck. "But later, tonight—"

Ding-dong. "Trick-or-treat."

"Later. Tonight," she repeated as she opened the door. The excitement that sizzled through her veins had nothing to do with colorful costumes, candy, or games of make believe. It had everything to do with the tingle that chased down her spine in the wake of his nipping teeth. And everything to do with the soft, heavy sensual promise that shivered across her damp skin on his whispered words.

Chapter 24

Sophia paced across the small apartment, her uncertainty increasing as she listened to the sound of the shower. All night, while children rang the bell and they passed out candy, Mike had teased her, keeping her senses on a low simmer of constant awareness.

A kiss here. A nibble there. A racy double entendre and a wink over the heads of the children clamoring at the door. A look. A touch. By the time they'd left Katie's place and headed back to the apartment, her nerves were strung tight with excitement.

Mike had carried her to the bed and left her with a sizzling kiss and a promise before slipping off to change. Instead of closing her eyes and imagining him naked, as he'd suggested, Sophia succumbed to a fit of nerves.

What did a woman wear for her first time with a man? She didn't have a silk nightgown in Morgan's Outpost, and the idea seemed a bit silly and antiquated anyway. But surely a cowgirl costume and guns weren't appropriate—were they? In any case they wouldn't be comfortable.

She pulled off the gun belt and draped it across a kitchen chair. The vest and hat followed. And the boots. She didn't want to make love in boots. Not for the first time. She headed to the windows in the apartment living area.

She ran her fingers through her hair. Oh Zeus! She should have kept it long instead of cutting it. Didn't men like long hair? But then, Mike had never seen her in long hair.

What else did she need? *Zeus and Io!* She wished she knew more about this. Classical mythology had the gods cavorting at every turn, but the stories were frustratingly lacking in detail.

She turned and paced back to the kitchen. What the myths lacked, her gynecologist had told her. Sort of. The basics of procreating. But, surely, she didn't just lie there naked and wait. Or should she? Why hadn't she asked Helena?

Easy. She'd wanted to push the thoughts out of her mind. She shuddered. If all had gone according to plan, she'd have gone to the king's bed, shut her eyes and let him take care of the details. She pulled aside the curtains and looked down on the street, vaguely aware that she'd paced across the room again.

Maybe that's what she should do now. Go back to the bed where Mike had left her. Lie down. Wait.

She took a step in that direction.

It didn't seem right, somehow.

Too cold. Too sterile. Too much like what she'd expected out of a duty-induced coupling with a man she didn't love. She moved away from the bedroom, dimly aware that the shower had stopped.

Oh gods.

She dropped into a kitchen chair and buried her face in her hands, confusion and despair whirling in her mind.

"Sorry to take so long in the shower. That black stuff wouldn't come out—Hey, what's the matter, sweetheart?"

Mike's hand was warm on her back, his voice concerned and gentle in her ear. She heard the scrape of a chair and felt him sit next to her. Heat burned in her cheeks. Whatever the right formula for making love was, it was not this.

"It's okay, Sophie." He brushed her hair behind her ear and traced the line of her cheek, tempting her to look up. "I promise, nothing will happen here tonight unless you want it to. You can trust me."

She nodded, ashamed of her childlike confusion and waffling. "I know that." She looked up keeping her eyes straight ahead, not ready to meet his yet. "I want to make love to you, but I don't know how to start, or continue, or finish, or anything. I—"

She looked at him, and the next words evaporated in her mouth. His hair, damp and back to its natural color curled slightly around his ears. A towel was slung across his shoulders. His naked shoulders. She dropped her gaze, following a trail of droplets that clung to his chest glistening in the smattering of curly ginger hair that dusted it. The broad muscles and planes of his chest tightened and narrowed to his rippling taut stomach.

Water glistened there, too, drawing her gaze to it, tempting her to follow the trail of droplets to the point where they disappeared into the low-slung band of his jeans.

He was beautiful. Like a classical statue, only pulsing and warm with life. She reached out and traced her hands along the smooth muscle, working her way from his narrow waist upward. Warm, smooth, hard underneath but soft to the touch— she drank in the pleasure of touching him.

"For someone who doesn't know what she's doing, you're making a good start." He sucked in a breath as she brushed his nipple with her thumb. "A very, very good start."

Her heart sped up at the rough, strangled quality of his voice, so different from the concerned whisper of a moment ago. She'd brought about the change. Just from looking at him. Touching him.

"Teach me what to do next," she whispered, leaning close so he could hear her words.

"I think you already know," he answered. Their lips were so close, she could feel the whisper of his breath across hers, taste the words, almost.

She closed the gap and kissed him, softly at first but with increasing hunger. Awareness flared again, burning away her earlier doubts. This wasn't procreating. This was making love. With someone she loved. The difference changed everything.

When he pulled her into the V of his legs and sat her on one knee, she didn't protest. When he ran his palm up her bare thigh, caressing beneath the hem of her short skirt, she didn't resist. She just kept kissing him, telling him without words that she wanted his touch.

He ran his hand back down to her knee, resting his palm there, searing her. Answering heat flared, and she placed her hands on his shoulders.

"Tell me what you like," he said, brushing a kiss across her temple. "And tell me what you don't like. Tell me everything you feel."

"I'm hot. And tight—like a harp string about to break—but it's almost as if I want to break. Does that make sense?" She pulled back to look at him.

"Perfect sense." He scooped her in his arms, all of his muscles rippling with the effort. Yet he stood easily and moved with grace toward the bedroom. He laid her on the bed and followed her down, covering her with his body. "I want to touch you. To see you. All of you."

The dark gleam in his eyes sent a shaft of something through her. Something that felt like fear—but wasn't. Something arousing and pleasant, as exciting as danger but so enticing she'd willingly embrace it. Embrace him.

But Mike had other ideas. He unwound her arms from around his neck and spread them out on the covers, sweeping along their length.

Sophia gave him a lazy smile and the gleam in his eyes flared. "Touch me."

Instead, he kissed her. Lips to lips, holding himself above her on steady arms, not touching anywhere else. She accepted his kiss, teasing him with her tongue, longing for him to deepen it. Burning in places where their bodies were close but not touching.

The bed dipped as he rolled to one side, leaning an elbow into the mattress and resting his head in his hand. The other hand slowly traced a line from her jaw to her throat. Her pulse jumped at his touch.

"Do you like that?" His soft question barely disturbed the sensual haze.

"Yes."

"And this?" Now one finger ran along the edge of her collar, slipping beneath to follow the line of her bra.

"Yes." She choked on the word as a sizzle followed in the wake of his touch. She arched toward him.

He chuckled. "Your body tells me so much more than your words." He bent his head and touched his tongue to the spot where his finger had been.

"Ooh." The ticklish, warm pleasure swirled from her breast toward her toes touching all kinds of pleasant places in between. She squirmed at the unfamiliar tingles and sighed with contentment when Mike's big warm hand pressed into her hipbone, anchoring her in the midst of the sensual storm.

He moved to the other breast, maddening in his slowness. She wanted more. She wanted him to place his lips on her the way he had before, when she'd been bare and open to him.

As if he heard her, he brushed his palm up the curve of her hip, pausing momentarily at her waist before moving to cup her breast. But only for a moment.

She almost cried at the loss of warmth, until he snapped open a button on her shirt. Then another. Cool air washed over the places his lips and tongue had been, making her shiver. Her nipples puckered in response to the coolness.

Then he flicked open her bra and covered one breast with the palm of his hand. The cool turned to fire. "Oh, that feels good."

"Mmm." His lips were too busy kissing the exposed skin to answer her.

A flick of his thumb across her nipple sent a flicker of lightning arcing through from her breast to…to there—in the cradle of her hips where no one had touched her before. To where she needed to be touched.

His lips replaced his thumb, sucking on her nipple with an almost painful tug. The almost-pain was a pleasure she'd never experienced. One that increased her need to be touched elsewhere. She raised her hips and swore she heard him chuckle again.

"I wonder what it is you want?" His lazy question was punctuated with another kiss and more sucking, but his palm swept across the suede of her skirt and pressed briefly into the juncture of her thighs. "This maybe?"

"Oh, yes," she muttered. "I want everything."

"Soon," he answered, but his palm left the aching spot to move to her knee. His slow stroke up the inside of her thigh was madness. Almost tickling. Tingling. And each time she squirmed, longing for more, he stopped and pressed his palm into her skin, stilling the movement, but building the fire.

Now even his lips and tongue on her breast weren't enough. She wanted something else. Something more. Something—*oh Zeus*! He'd swept his hand as high as it could go and brushed his finger across her panties. Wet heat scorched her, and she squirmed again, this time relieved when he pressed his palm against the throbbing ache.

"Time for me to see what's been giving me so much pleasure." With a last kiss on her breast, Mike left the bed and flicked on the bedside lamps. Light infiltrated the scene where darkness had reigned before.

She instinctively covered herself with her hands.

"Please, don't." He brushed her hands aside and pushed her bra and shirt off her shoulders. "You're more than beautiful. You're breathtaking. Let me look at you."

Mike pressed a kiss into her collar bone. "Let me look at all of you."

She melted under his words. Followed the mute directions of his hands as he helped her sit up and remove her shirt while he kissed every exposed inch. When he pressed her into the mattress and brought himself down, warm chest to naked breast she instinctively opened her legs to make room for him. To accept the press of his heavy body blanketing her with heat.

She opened her mouth under his, and urged him closer, stroking the lines of his back with her hands. He was hard, smooth, and warm. Everything her life was missing.

When his hips sank into hers, she pressed upward, moving slightly, trying to fit her newly throbbing ache against the hard ridge bulging in his jeans.

He ground against her in response, a frustrating move that didn't bring the relief she'd hoped for.

"How do you feel now?" His voice sizzled along her nerve endings. He nipped her earlobe and licked the outer edge of her ear. A shudder rippled from neck to thigh as he blew on the wet surface. "Still tight as a harp string?"

"More," she muttered. "Like a dozen harp strings pulling in different directions. Like I'm ready to break."

His tongue and breath on her ear stole the reason from her mind. Words formed, broke apart and reformed, but nothing described the way her skin quivered and shuddered at his touch. The way she craved his touch even as it woke more cravings rather than satisfying.

"I want to break," she whispered, not knowing what else to say.

He sat up on his knees, depriving her of the skin-to-skin contact that fueled her desires. The tension released, her expectations sagged. Until he moved again, his hands cupping her thighs and sliding up, bringing the skirt with them. It bunched in his hands. She wiggled to make room.

His thumbs touched the crotch of her panties again, a caress far too brief to satisfy until he lowered his body and rocked against her.

The sound that came from her mouth wasn't a word. It couldn't be. She sighed again, the mindless noise expressing her desire. Then he moved away again, and she almost whimpered.

"Roll over," he said his hand on her hip urging her to do so. "Trust me."

She followed his directions. The hiss of her zipper penetrated her consciousness. Mike swept the skirt and her panties from her body, letting his hands linger on her bottom. The foreign caress flooded her face with heat. She drew in a sharp breath and tensed when he traced the lower curve where leg met hip.

"Are you okay?" His voice held a hint of concern.

"I'm fine." She gritted her teeth against his next touch.

"You're fine," he said as he pressed a gentle kiss into the skin of her butt, "but you don't like this." His kisses moved up her spine and she relaxed a bit as he headed toward her shoulders. "Better now?"

"Yes."

With one last kiss on the shoulder, he moved her onto her back and focused his attentions on her collar bone for a while, nibbling up and down her neck, brushing a lazy hand across her breast until a heavy languor seeped into her body.

"Much better," she murmured.

"I won't ask you to do anything you don't like." Tenderness laced his words. "Just tell me to stop."

"What if you don't want to?"

"I'll want to. I want to please you, not hurt you. Not make you sorry. Let me show you what pleasure is all about."

He kissed her breast again, tugging on the nipple until she wiggled beneath him. He gentled the kiss and moved his hand back to her thigh. "You liked this, didn't you?"

She nodded.

"Let's see what else you like." Mike slid down her body, leaving a tingling trail of kisses from her breast to belly. The harp string tightening began again, tension pulling at her breasts, her belly, and lower.

She wanted his thumbs brushing against her again. At least that. As if he read her mind, he cupped her between the legs with his palm, then slid his fingers into the soft folds of flesh where she throbbed most urgently. She swallowed a cry of surprise at the slick sweep of his fingers, then bit back another when he touched higher.

Hot, wet throbbing swamped her. *Clitoris,* she thought as her anatomy lessons flashed through her mind. *A strange name for the source of liquid lightning that flashed through her.* She grimaced, mentally spitting out the inadequate word.

"Should I stop?" Mike sounded pained.

"No," she shook her head. "Don't stop."

Another flick of his fingers and the lightning flashed again. Then his mouth replaced his fingers and the liquid rush intensified. Lava erupted in her body, chasing through her veins in hot, molten streams all headed to the point where he suckled against her, drinking it in.

Images of Greek gods fled her mind, replaced with more primal, island gods. Ones that pulsed in harmony with nature, surged and ebbed with the tides, rode the flow of lava from the heart of the earth to the edge of the sea.

Like lava in the sea, the heat that poured from her to Mike formed something new. Something never before seen. Something that they owned and no one else could claim.

His tongue flicked her core in a ceaseless rhythm like waves pounding the shore, unstoppable. Lightning ignited lava with each stroke until both burned white-hot, searing her in the crackle and whip-snap of heat that incinerated her veins and nerves leaving only trails of fire.

The volcano pulsed, and she paused, ever so slightly, on the precipice before hurtling, headlong into the inferno, a willing virgin sacrifice. Her lingering cry shattered her ears as her body burned away and her spirit flew to regions beyond imagination.

And with her last conscious thought, she knew he flew beside her.

Chapter 25

ike grinned to himself as he pulled Sophia against his shoulder and wrapped her in a blanket. She snuggled close and his grin deepened. For once, he didn't care that his cock strained against his zipper begging for release. There were plenty of other days in the year, he told the wayward part of himself firmly. Today had been about her.

The memory of her thrashing under the movements of his mouth and fingers caused pleasure to zip through him too. A deeper, less immediate pleasure than that of sexual release, but more lasting. He'd have his day once he put a ring on her finger.

Until then, he had his hopes and his own two hands. She moved in her sleep and brushed against him, her hand landing on the painful bulge of his erection. Correction, he thought. He had his two hands, and if he was lucky and she was willing, he'd have her hands too.

If not, well, it didn't matter. He'd had his share of women in the past, sweaty and naked next to his own sweaty naked, satisfied body. Not one made him think of a future the way Sophia did. He'd sacrifice a dozen bouts of emotionally meaningless intercourse for a single night of lovemaking with her.

Idly, his thoughts wandered to the confessional box at church. He'd always imagined the priests shared a private wink and a nod whenever one of the parishioners confessed to the sin of sexual congress. He didn't know what they'd think about the confessions of a man who passed up the opportunity for sex and settled for less.

A few holy ones might still cringe, but he'd bet the rest of them hid a kernel of disappointment. Oh well. It wasn't as if he planned on revealing anything about his time with Sophia to them anyway. These moments were theirs. They belonged to no one else.

She stirred beside him. "Mike?" Her voice was sleepy and thick with the aftermath of pleasure.

"Hmm?"

"That was wonderful. But—" She ran her hand along his erection, causing him to grit his teeth in frustration. "I know there's more."

He grabbed her wrist and moved it away from his groin. He pressed a kiss into her palm instead, drawing her attention to his lips. "There's more," he admitted. "But I'm not easy, you know. You'll have to accept my proposal to get from here to more."

She pouted but he kissed the pout away.

"You're not like any man I've ever met," she said softly.

"That's the point." He pulled her close and ran a hand down the warm curves of her body. She didn't flinch when he rested it on the swell of her bottom. "I'm right for you because I'm not like any other man. And you know it too."

Beside him, she shivered.

"Hey, let's get under the covers and stay warm. That is unless you're going to kick me out now that you've had your way with me." He reluctantly moved away from her and pulled back the covers.

She wiggled under. He turned out the lights and slid in beside her.

"Aren't you going to take off your jeans?" she asked when he pulled her close.

"It's safer not to."

"I don't want to be safe."

He smiled in the dark and let his hand drift down to fondle her bottom again. "It is not all about you, young lady."

She stiffened.

"Hey." Mike brushed a kiss across her temple. "I'm only teasing you. What's wrong?"

He felt her shrug, but the nonchalance didn't reach her voice. "It's nothing. Just bad memories."

"Bad memories aren't welcome in our bed, sweetheart." He stroked her back in long, easy sweeps. "Want to talk about it so we can kick them out?"

He held her for a while, listening as her breathing grew soft and even. Just when he thought she'd fallen asleep, she spoke.

"Uncle Julian always called me young lady when he was displeased. I was a willful child when I came to live with him. He was displeased a lot."

He waited, prompting her when she didn't continue.

"One day, he'd had enough." Her voice whispered across his skin, the intimacy of her confidence touching him in ways even the intimacy of her body had not.

"And?"

"He called me into his office, told me I'd earned a spanking and sent me to fetch the paddle from his desk drawer."

"He hit you?" Rage coiled in Mike and he squeezed her tightly in a misguided effort to protect her.

"It's okay." She ran her palm down his chest. "It was a long time ago."

"No one has the right to abuse a child."

"Melesians—especially royal ones—don't always agree with that, Mike. And it wasn't about punishing me physically. It was about making a point. The first time," her voice trailed off, and he sensed she was choosing her worlds carefully. "I dragged my feet, like any child would. I remember feeling angry, scared, and most of all, small. I don't remember the actual punishment.

"After, I bit my lip and blinked as fast as I could to hold the tears back. My face burned with shame, and more than anything, I wanted to leave that room. I'd almost made it to the door when he called me back."

She swallowed and Mike's heart lurched, but he lay still, waiting for her next words.

"He told me being slow to accept my punishment had earned me another. My fingers shook so hard, I could barely open the desk drawer, but I hurried. I must have tried to apologize or something, because when I reached the office door after my second punishment, he called me back a third time.

"'*A lady*,' he said, '*does not complain or excuse herself.*' After the third time, he let me go, but I left the room a different child than I'd been when I came in. I knew then I was powerless in the face of his wishes. From that day forward, I never defied him."

"That bastard. I'll kill him." Anger whiplashed through him, knotting his muscles with rage. With nothing nearby to snap or bend, he couldn't blunt it. And with Sophia curled, trusting, in his arms all he could do was let the rage shriek in his mind while he fisted his free hand in hopes of containing it.

"He didn't hurt me. And he never hit me again. He didn't need to. The memory of being vulnerable and helpless was enough."

"Of course, you were helpless. You were a child."

"I'm not a child now, but the memory came back so suddenly." She shook her head against his shoulder. "I don't understand."

"I do." He unclenched his fist and returned to stroking her body. "Lovemaking is about being vulnerable too. Not in the same way, but it could trigger a memory."

"I never believed you'd hurt or embarrass me."

"No, but your body remembered hurt and embarrassment all the same." He paused, thinking. "Have you ever told anyone else this story?"

"Never."

"Then maybe you needed to tell someone. Someone who loved you enough to chase away the ghosts." This time when he slid his hand past the curve of her lower back to cup her bottom she didn't flinch. "See, you're already relaxing and letting go of the past."

He didn't linger but moved his hands to a neutral spot instead. "Any other memories you want to share? I'd be glad to chase away the other ghosts."

Slowly, she began to talk, telling him stories of her first five, wild years and the difficult adjustment she'd made from tomboy to proper lady while in the house of the duke.

He listened, soaking up the stories and filing them away in his memory. He asked questions to keep her talking but mostly, he let her lead the conversation. If he'd been fishing for a treasure trove of *Stir* articles, he'd found it. But not a single word she said was anything he'd let Frank Kincaid or the *Stir* readers ever see.

Maybe one day, with her blessing, he'd offer to write her biography, but for now, he was content to let her write the words on his heart.

"My daddy used to carry me to bed every night," she murmured against his shoulder in a sleepy voice hours later. "Then he died, and I came to live with the duke where I didn't know anyone. The house was big, and it was easy to get lost. Not many people paid attention to a six-year-old.

"One night, I was so lonely and tired I…I asked Uncle Julian if he would carry me to bed. I thought, maybe, if he would tuck me in, it would prove that he loved me. He looked stunned. He was speechless for at least a minute, while I waited and hoped. Then he pointed to the stairs and told me I had two feet and an army of servants."

Her voice was fading even as his heart twisted at her tale.

"That's when I knew that I could never go home again." Her last words slurred into sleep.

You're home now, he thought, pulling her into the curve of his body and protecting her in his arms. *And no one, Melesian or otherwise, will ever take you from me.*

Chapter 26

Like sat on the hard bench, his dad and Destiny to one side, Katie and the girls further down the row, and marveled at Sophia. She was a natural mimic, following the Mass as if she'd been born into the Catholic Church rather than the Melesian one. He reached for her hand, gratified when she didn't pull away.

He'd woken beside her in the morning more rested and refreshed than he'd been in weeks, despite his body's thwarted urges. And nothing had weakened the closeness. Not breakfast. Not the awkward juggling of showers and tooth brushing for two. Not his dad's call urging them to meet him at Mass. Nothing.

Not even Father Cabbott's long homily and the three Marys wiggling in their seats. Sophia whispered something to Mary Katherine, and she immediately sat straight and quiet. Mike's jaw dropped.

Soon enough the congregation was released into the sunshine, and they headed back to the pub where Mike had gathered food for a family brunch.

Everyone pitched in, chopping, sautéing, setting the tables and generally working together with an easy camaraderie. Destiny and Sophia moved as if they were part of the Maguire family machine, smooth and in harmony with the chaos around them.

As they headed to one of the large round tables, Mike noticed his dad slip into the kitchen again. When he returned, everyone was seated. James lifted the bottle in his hand. "Something traditional to go along with our orange juice this morning."

Mike eyed him curiously. "Champagne, Dad? Since when did we have a mimosa tradition?"

His dad grinned while he worked the cork loose. "It's not a mimosa tradition, exactly, it's more like a traditional toast. Glasses, everyone," he said as the wine fizzed out of the bottle. After a brief scramble, everyone held out assorted juice and water glasses while he filled them. Even the girls had a tiny splash in their orange juice.

James raised his glass and cleared his throat. "This toast, for those of you who haven't guessed," he looked around the table and winked at Mike, "is in honor of the lovely woman who agreed last night to become my wife. Destiny, welcome to the family."

Glasses clinked, women squealed and words of congratulations flowed in a rapid-fire cacophony. Mike eyed his father over the rim of his glass. The old man hadn't looked so full of life since, well, since before Mike had left for the west coast in an attempt at a journalism career.

"How are you doing?" Sophia's quiet words pulled him out of his thoughts.

"I'm okay, actually." He reached for her hand. "Thank you for everything."

She blushed. "I didn't do anything."

"No?" He cocked an eyebrow. "You did one or two special things last night. But I meant thank you for helping me to look for the truth about Destiny instead of jumping to conclusions. It's a bad habit of mine."

A bad habit that had thrown her life into disarray more than once, if she only knew. He wondered how many other lives he'd damaged. How many people crumpled under his scrutiny, rather than rose above it as she had?

The champagne soured in his stomach, churning uncomfortably alongside his guilt. He was a fraud, a liar. He looked at Sophia laughing with Destiny over something. Her innocence shamed him. He'd lied his way into her heart and her bed. How could he come clean with her now?

How could he not?

Sophia deserved the truth. And he'd tell her. When they were alone. As soon as he found a loophole in his confidentiality clause with the *Stir*. There had to be a way.

She'd leave. Which was exactly what he deserved. And seeing her now, laughing and chatting with his family, he knew that letting her go would be like cutting his arm off.

His dad's hand settled on his shoulder. "Can I have a word with you, son?"

Mike nodded and followed his dad into a quiet corner of the room.

"I know you think this is kind of sudden—"

"No, Dad. I was wrong. You and Destiny seem like a good match. I should have trusted you rather than assuming the worst."

"I should have told you more too. But Jesus, Mary, and Joseph! Mike, I didn't know where to begin. You were always so busy. You were trying to save the world. First the pub, then Katie, and me. You even picked Sophie up off the street and saved her. The world isn't your stray puppy, Mike. Sometimes we have to do things on our own."

If only his dad knew what a lousy job he'd done at saving anyone or anything. He shrugged, trying to put his own worries aside and smile for his dad. "You were right. About a lot of things. I'm happy for you, Dad."

"The thing is," his dad looked away and shoved his hands in his pockets. "I couldn't be prouder of you if you'd won a Pulitzer prize instead of writing whatever-it-was at that newspaper in California. You're a good person. A good family man. That's all I ever wanted my children to be. Happy. Good to each other and the world."

Mike shifted, uncomfortable with the direction of the conversation, and with his dad's references to the string of lies he'd told his family over the years. "So, Dad, when's the wedding?"

"That's what I wanted to talk to you about. We're planning to marry in Reno over Thanksgiving weekend."

"That soon?"

His dad nodded. "Destiny has a lot of friends there. And one of them is a priest willing to marry us. As soon as I meet her boys—and hopefully get their blessing—we'll set the plans in motion."

He jerked his head toward the women who were crowded around the table. "Most of the planning is women's stuff anyway. Men wear what we're told and show up when we're told. They get all the fun, and we get a wife. The only thing I have to do is ask you if you'd stand beside me as best man."

"Dad, I," Mike swallowed, the emotion that he usually hid under banter close to the surface, "I'd be honored."

"Good. It's settled then. I think Destiny's going to ask your girl to stand up with her. Some thought about you needing the moral support and her not wanting to pick from among your sisters or some such nonsense. Like I said. Women's stuff."

Ohhs and ahhs erupted from across the room. Mike looked over to see Sophia planting a kiss on Destiny's cheek. It looked like she'd agreed to the plan.

Which meant that, even if he knew how to do it, he couldn't come clean with her now and risk losing her without upsetting the entire family. He felt his dad's hand on his shoulder again.

Dad had a second chance at love. Mike wouldn't deny him that. And he wouldn't deny his sisters the joy of seeing Dad wed again.

So what if he added another dozen lies to the ones he'd already told Sophia? What was another week—or year—of suffering in purgatory compared to his dad's happiness? And if it gave him another few weeks to try to convince Sophia that he deserved her eventual forgiveness, it might be worth the pain.

He plastered on his best smile, shoved the guilt aside, and pretended to be the happiest man in the world.

Lies. All lies.

Sophia hummed to herself as she fussed about the kitchen of her tiny apartment. After a lingering morning kiss, Mike had slipped from the apartment to buy her newspapers and she'd headed to the kitchen to give him a surprise of her own.

Her body still tingled from their morning lovemaking. It was a sensation she'd come to crave. Every night in the weeks since Halloween, Mike had stayed with her, kissing her senseless, awaking her body to new pleasures with his hands and mouth and holding her in his arms while she drifted to sleep.

And while he'd accepted her kisses in return, he'd stoically refused to let her explore his body the way she longed to. Anything "below the belt" as he put it, remained off limits.

Not that she accepted his limits. Yet, he skillfully deflected her tentative advances, turning the tables on her until she was limp with satisfaction and he could scuttle off for a long shower.

Maybe tomorrow she'd crawl out of bed and slip into the shower with him. Until then, she'd find other ways to tempt him.

She checked the slip of paper Joe—the pub's cook—had given her. French toast looked like something even she could make with her limited cooking skills.

She grabbed three eggs from the refrigerator and cracked them into a bowl. Too bad Mike's thick pride wouldn't crack as easily beneath her hands. When it came to her virginity, he was as mired in tradition as the stupid aristocracy. No one seemed to care what she wanted. They only thought about what they wanted for her. Or from her.

She crushed the eggshells, grinding them to bits between her fingers, wishing she could grind away the barriers between herself and Mike. Instead, she grabbed a whisk and attacked the eggs.

Tradition. Purity. Bullshit. She flogged the eggs. *Arranged marriages. Saving herself for a political contender. Bullshit, bullshit, bullshit.* Egg foam surged to the top of the mixing bowl and she slowed her strokes.

She checked the recipe and mulled over her current situation as she added vanilla, cinnamon, a bit of sugar and milk to the eggs.

She whisked the mixture together carefully, thinking. An arranged political marriage wasn't her problem. At least not now. Her problem was Mike's stubborn refusal to let her fully consummate their relationship until she agreed to marry him.

Impossible.

She couldn't marry him. Or anyone. Not without the blessing of the King and the Church of Melesia. Unless she wanted to break with her heritage completely. Marrying on her own was akin to renouncing her citizenship and declaring herself dead to her country and family.

Not that she had any real ties left, she thought bitterly. Her parents were dead, her imprisoned, disgraced uncle as good as dead. And the rest of the de Lyons clan hadn't ever bothered with her.

She'd miss her cousin Helena, Prince Stephan, and a few of the other members of the royal family. They'd been kinder to her than her own family. Yet, what was losing a king and a few distant relationships compared to gaining a life?

She slapped butter in a skillet and watched it melt, the edges turning liquid and the middle softening. How easily it changed from a cold, hard lump to something hot and sizzling under the gentle heat from the stove. Just like she'd changed.

At her core, she was still a Melesian royal. But her edges were softer, different. Real. What would it be like to let go of that core of duty and melt into something new? Could she do it?

At the sound of Mike's footsteps on the stairs, she shoved the thoughts aside and slid a piece of egg drenched bread into the skillet. She had two weeks with him before Destiny and James married. It was a lifetime. The only one they might ever have.

"Hey, sweetie."

Mike's voice sounded heavy, and she turned in concern. He dropped a bag on the coffee table and headed toward her. Fine lines bracketed his lips, and his jaw was rigid. Sophia tensed.

"I picked up the bridal magazines you wanted as well as the newspapers."

"Is something wrong?" she asked.

"No. Nothing." He shrugged and kissed her on the cheek. "What's going on here? It smells wonderful."

"In case you couldn't tell, I'm making you breakfast. French toast."

He glanced at the skillet. "It'll be burned French toast if I don't stop distracting you." He moved across the kitchen and opened a cupboard, pulling down dishes and setting the table. "To what do I owe this spurt of domestic activity?"

Sophia grinned. "I just wanted to try something new." She divided the golden-brown bread slices between the plates and sat next to him. "I hope it's okay."

"It's great," he mumbled around a mouthful.

She took a bite and discovered that her cooking skills weren't so bad after all. "I should get the papers, and we can scan them over breakfast. Let's get that chore out of the way."

Mike placed his hand on hers, stopping her. "Let's wait. I'd rather have you all to myself for a few more minutes."

She settled back into her seat with a nod but watched him carefully. Something wasn't right. His lips smiled, but his eyes didn't. She took another nibble of breakfast. The sweet syrup and gooey bread formed a lump in her mouth, and she forced herself to swallow. To wait. And she prayed that whatever was wrong, he'd share it with her.

After breakfast, she moved to the couch and pulled a paper from the bag he'd dropped there. She heard him follow her into the room. Then, as she glanced down, everything—Mike, the apartment, her sense of happiness—faded into the background.

The *Weekly World Stir* headline, typed in six-inch high letters, burned its way into her mind.

MACK IS BACK

Underneath, another bold headline thrust Melesia, its royal family, and her uncle's scandal back into the center of public awareness.

Dimly she was aware of Mike's arms around her, cradling her against his rock-hard body. Of his words, whispered into her ear. "It'll be okay, sweetheart. We'll get through this together. Trust me."

She clung to his reassurances, even though he couldn't possibly know the power Mack the Pen and his devious stories once held over her. The power he still held.

"My worst nightmare has returned," she whispered against the comforting warmth of Mike's cotton shirt. She clung to him so tightly she could feel her own shudder of revulsion ripple across his muscles. "The gods help me now."

Her worst nightmare? Mike tightened his hold on Sophia as he digested the words. Sweet saints! Her *worst* nightmare? He accepted that—in the past—his headlines and stories had likely been a royal pain-in-the-ass to her, but surely *worst nightmare* was overstating things.

Besides, she'd barely glanced at the headline. She couldn't have read the article. If she had, she'd know it was nothing more than a teaser, whetting the public appetite for the series of articles he'd proposed to his editor.

Smoke and mirrors—that's all his writing had ever been. Smoke and mirrors with a little twist of truth. Once Sophia calmed down, he'd teach her how to look past the illusion so that nothing in print could ever harm her again.

The tremor that passed through her body wasn't an illusion. Nor was her dry, lifeless whisper. He actually felt her pulling away from him, stiffening one tiny muscle at a time. Retreating into the poised shell where she'd spent most of her life.

"Sophie." He shook her just enough to get her attention. "Hey. It's all right. You're safe here."

The drawn look on her face telegraphed tension, but at least it was a real emotion, not the frozen placid look she wore for the cameras.

"Safe, Mike?" Her bitter laugh, something he'd never heard from her, momentarily shook his confidence. "Nowhere is safe when it comes to these guys. I'm sure they've got cameras spying on every Melesian consulate in the country. They'll watch all the major airports. The smarter ones will have the train stations staked out too. Anywhere I go, they can find me."

"I'm sure you're right, but weren't they watching yesterday? Last week? You took it in stride then. What's changed?"

Sophia sank onto the sofa and pointed to the *Stir* byline. "It's him. The claims of the other reporters are too outrageous for anyone with sense to credit them. But him? He mixes in just enough fact to give him credibility and the rest of us be damned. Literally. He's damned me in the eyes of the public too many times to count."

The accusation in her voice hit him hard. Self-loathing hit him harder, because she spoke the truth. He sat beside her and put an arm around her shoulders, wishing he could exhaust his self-directed anger in a bout with a heavy bag at the gym, a series of sprints at the high school track, or by bending every damn spoon in the pub downstairs. But he couldn't. To be honest, he didn't deserve his own forgiveness, much less hers.

"Maybe the reporter's changed," he offered.

"Do rats evolve?"

"At least read the article. Knowledge is power in this situation."

Sophia gave him a strange look. "My cousin Helena told me the same thing. She said the royal family studied the tabloids as seriously as they studied the news outlets. Their tactic was to ignore most and refute the rest by showing the world a positive front. No matter what the news, they always supported one another."

"That's what family does. They stick together." He paused. "At least they're supposed to. I let my family down for years." Another reason for guilt.

"You're not letting anyone down now. I know you gave up a comfortable job to come home and run the pub. It couldn't have been easy. But look at what you've accomplished. The girls light up when you walk into the room. Your sister's about to graduate. And you've made your dad very happy by accepting Destiny."

Mike shrugged, uncomfortable with her praise when he knew he deserved her condemnation. "I wish—"

He stopped. Wishing didn't do a body any good. He swallowed and tried again. "You're like family to me, too, Sophie. I'll do everything in my power to help you."

It wasn't in his power to tell her the truth. After scouring his contracts for some loophole that would let him come clean with her, he'd finally admitted there was none. There never had been, thanks to Frank Kincaid and the *Stir*'s chiseled-in-stone confidentiality clauses. They were structured to mire the unwary deeper and deeper with each new contract.

Because the fine print spelled out that it wasn't just the advance money for this series of articles he'd sacrifice if he revealed his identity. He could only ease his conscience at the risk of paying back a decade's worth of earnings.

The amount would bankrupt him—which was no more than he deserved—but his foolish, loving family would jump in headfirst trying to save him. And whatever else he might sacrifice, he wouldn't risk their happiness. Not even for a chance at his own.

"So," he said, reaching for the paper, "let's see what the bastard has to say and figure out what we have to do to keep one step ahead of him."

Sophia's soft kiss on his cheek burned like the hell fire he deserved as she snuggled next to him and helped him dig his own grave.

Chapter 27

Mike stole a glance at Sophia, peacefully curled up in the passenger side of his Jeep. The late afternoon sun highlighted threads of rich auburn twined with the gold in her hair. It fascinated him, just as she fascinated him.

In all the years he'd studied her and reported on her stories, he'd been too blind—or blinded by ambition—to notice what a wonderful woman she was. No more. And now he was making it up to her, word by word in the new series of articles.

Instead of using his old tricks of placing a grain of truth amidst a wealth of entertaining speculation, he'd switched to using a dash of entertainment to sweeten the hard-to-swallow truth of power turning to corruption.

After each release of the *Weekly World Stir*, Sophia and he had sat together, deconstructing the Mack the Pen stories. She'd stopped tensing at the sight of each new headline and had grudgingly accepted that the so-called entertainment might serve a greater purpose.

Even so, she took pleasure in devising retribution against his alter-ego, crafting punishments worthy of a medieval torture chamber. Her bloodthirsty revenge sounded just—and more merciful than the glacial disdain she'd likely give him once the truth was out.

One day—as soon as he could engineer it—she'd guess his secret identity. His contracts stipulated that *he* couldn't reveal the identity of Mack the Pen, but they'd said nothing about *her* guessing it. When she did, he'd lose her and all the happiness she'd awakened in him.

Mike sighed and looked at the gas gauge. Loathe as he was to disturb Sophia, they needed to stop soon. He pulled off the freeway and into a truck stop.

"Sophie, sweetie, time to wake up."

She stretched, but her eyes remained closed. "Are we there, yet?" she mumbled as she raked her fingers through her hair.

"No, this is just a gas stop. We're about halfway between Salt Lake City and Reno. Maybe another four hours or so with stops."

"Do you want me to take over for a few hours? You've been driving since before dawn."

"If I'd gotten around to teaching you how to drive, I might chance it, but not now."

"Come on, Mike." She flashed him a grin. "I dare you to let me drive. I double-dog dare you." She punctuated the sentence with a yawn.

"Even I'm not fool enough to take that dare. I'll gas her up and grab another dose of caffeine. That'll be enough to get us to the hotel in Reno."

"Whatever you say. I'll get some drinks and food from the sandwich shop inside and be ready to get back on the road as soon as you are."

She stretched, drawing her sweater tight in ways that had his body on alert and his brain in overdrive within seconds. Suddenly, those four hours to Reno seemed like an eternity.

Sophia splashed cool water on her face, then dragged a comb through her sleep-tousled hair. Excitement—and something else—pooled in her stomach. Reno had been the start of her grand adventure. Would returning there be the end of it? Or the beginning of something even more grand? Only time would tell.

She glanced in the mirror, idly wondering what she'd look like in twenty or fifty years. Wondering where, and how, she'd live out those years. Eventually, she'd chose either Melesia or Morgan's Outpost. But not today. Today, she had other things on her mind.

She pulled a handful of quarters from her pocket and headed to the vending machine by the door. Should she choose *pleasure pack one*? Or *two*? Or *three*? She shrugged and filled the machine with enough quarters to get one of each. After all, they'd be in Reno for almost a week. And she'd already made the one significant choice regarding her future.

No matter what else happened, she refused to leave Reno a virgin.

Five minutes later, she paid for sandwiches, soft drinks, and a fistful of tabloid papers and hurried to the jeep. Five minutes after that, they were on the road again. She shifted in her seat and prepared to entertain Mike. If she couldn't drive, at least she could help him stay alert.

"Let's see what kind of trouble the *Weekly World Stir* is creating." The plastic bag crinkled as she pulled out a paper and smoothed away the creases. "After all, I can't let a week pass without checking up on my favorite reporter."

"Favorite reporter? Now that's a switch." A hint of a smile tugged at his lips. "Is that Mack the Pen character starting to grow on you?"

"I wouldn't go that far. But since he's come out of retirement, I have seen a different side of him." She glanced at the paper in her lap. "Or maybe not."

"Why? What's the latest headline?"

"It seems he's back to his old tricks," she murmured. "Look at this. *Is the Royal Romance Over?* There's a photo of Queen Jillian boarding a plane while the king looks on."

"What the hell is that about?" Mike grabbed the paper and scanned it. "I didn't—"

"Mike!"

A horn blared and he swerved back into their lane.

"Give me that." Sophia grabbed the paper from him. "You keep your eyes on the road, and I'll do the reading."

"Sorry. I didn't expect that. I thought his articles were focusing on your uncle and possible treason surrounding King Alexander's abdication."

"Last week they were. This week it's like the old, cynical side of him couldn't resist poking fun of us again. Listen to the rest of the story.

"'The teary-eyed Melesian queen heads home for the holidays as her husband, King Constantine, looks on, apparently unmoved by her departure. The queen took only two small bags and a modest entourage rather than traveling in royal style, leading some to wonder if she's planning to escape the royal life for a week or forever.'"

She paused and took a sip of her drink. "The rest of it continues in the same vein. Not all that interesting, really." She scanned it quickly, squinting against the fading light. "Actually, the rest of it doesn't sound like it's from him. It sounds more like something I'd expect from *The Royal Rambler*, or *Global Gossip Weekly*. No one would believe this for longer than it took to turn the page to the next story."

Mike nodded, an abrupt jerk of his head. Tension radiated from his frozen shoulders and clenched jaw. Poor man. He'd been driving since early in the day, and the last traffic incident must have rattled him.

She tossed the paper aside. "Here's a bit of trivia. Did you know the *Stir* doesn't reveal the real names of its reporters? All of them are false."

"Everyone knows that."

"But here's the part I'll bet you didn't know." She sent him a smug smile. "The paper actually owns the pen names of all its contributors. So this Mack the Pen author and the one who wrote last week's articles may not even be the same person."

"Then how do you know the articles we've been reading are from the same guy that used to cover the royal family?"

"When you've had your life turned upside down by someone for years, you get to know him." She looked ahead, her eyes focused on the freeway, her mind miles away.

"No wonder you have it in for this guy." Mike's voice had her turning to stare at his profile again. "What would happen if you did discover his identity? Would you really boil him in oil?"

She giggled. "Actually my favorite punishment was letting the sharks and piranhas slowly nibble on him. But seriously, even if he broke Melesian laws while on our soil, there's almost nothing we would do.

"Most likely he'd simply be prohibited from entering Melesia again. We wouldn't jeopardize our relationship with the United States. Unless he attacked a member of the royal family. Then I don't know what would happen, but it would probably involve diplomats and law enforcement from both countries."

"That doesn't sound like a very satisfying revenge."

"I don't need revenge anymore, Mike. Thanks to you, I can see that I behaved like a victim, waiting to be hurt. You've shown me how to take life into my own hands. *Hermes and Hades!* If I can turn twenty tables in a night, I can conquer anything."

Mike reached over and squeezed her knee. "That's my girl." A smile warmed his voice, and she saw some of the tension seep from his rigid frame. "Now all I have to do is teach you to swear like a proper Irish woman, instead of like some Greek in exile."

"Sweet Saint Patrick!" she mimicked, breaking into a laugh.

When Mike's hand left her knee, and he entwined his fingers in hers, everything was well in her world.

Mike spent the next days attending tux fittings, meeting Destiny's family, keeping his dad calm, and avoiding ever more personal questions from his sisters.

He spent his nights equally aggravated. Since arriving in Reno, Sophia's campaign to seduce him had reached shock-and-awe proportions. She'd kept him in a constant, raging state of lust, but every time he reached in his wallet for a condom, he found the antique wedding ring instead.

His determination to either marry her or send her home—virginity intact—drove him to more cold showers than he'd had in his entire life. Cold showers with the bathroom door locked, ever since the morning she'd tried to join him.

It was killing him.

He was near the breaking point when Mary Angela—the sister everyone called Angel—cornered him in the hotel arcade. Across the room at least half a dozen children—he'd lost count—swarmed Sophia, dragging her from one shrieking, clanging, banging, ear-splitting game to the next.

"Don't worry about her. She's fine." Mary Angela gave him a bear hug and steered him to a table littered with the remains of cheese fries, corn dogs and half-finished cups of soda. "Mary Margaret and I want to catch up with you."

The gods help him!—he smiled at his use of Sophia's favorite phrase—he was no match for his two older sisters.

"Tell us how you and Sophie met," began Mary Angela.

"And tell us what your intensions are." Leave it to Maggie to get to the heart of things.

"Give me a break. She's just someone I met."

"You're a liar, Michael." Maggie shook a soggy, cheese soaked french fry at him. "I know that look. You've fallen for her."

Right on both counts. "Maybe so, but I don't need you two—or Katie either—meddling in my affairs."

Uh-oh. Tactical mistake. His words opened the floodgates of the inquisition. An hour later he escaped, his mind filled with dozens of suggestions about when, where and how to pop the question. None of which he needed. It wasn't as if he hadn't asked her to marry him. She'd just refused.

As his sisters herded Sophia and the children to some pre-planned event or other, Mike went in search of a stiff drink and some male company. He found Destiny's family in the bar. Hell, Adam Jr., Joel, Thomas, and Liam Kinderschone were practically his brothers now—which was a refreshing change given his status as the single son in a clan dominated by women.

And after a few drinks, none of them would care that they were doctors and investment bankers while he was nothing more than a bar owner.

"It looks like you could use a drink." Adam signaled for a waiter. "Your family has more kids than a pediatrician's waiting room."

"Yep. We've kept a lot of OB/GYNs in new cars over the years." He ordered a beer and leaned back in his chair. "I wouldn't have it any other way. But even I wish they came with a mute button once in a while."

"We're expecting our first." Liam fiddled with his drink. "My wife's a little nervous. I don't know if seeing your family is easing her fears or making them worse."

Mike accepted his beer from the waiter and took a swallow. "I can guarantee you it'll make her glad they come one at a time." A ripple of laugher snaked its way around the table.

By the third round, they'd discussed everything from families to sports and were trying to understand women's fascination with weddings. Thank God not a single one of them gave a damn about his love life.

He ordered another round of drinks. Adam loosened his tie and unbuttoned his collar. Liam and Thomas leaned back in their chairs. Joel snagged a handful of bar mix.

For the first time in days, Mike relaxed.

Chapter 28

A shiver of awareness passed over Sophia as she entered the Three Fates Lounge. Part dread and part anticipation, the cool wash of air lifted the hairs on her neck as if The Fates themselves, not the house fans, had breathed on her.

Mike's hand at the small of her back only intensified the feeling. She glanced up at him and her breath caught in her throat. Over her weeks in Morgan's Outpost, she'd come to trust him as a friend, then a lover, and finally someone she'd consider spending her life with. But tonight—tonight it was as if she'd never seen him before.

Stories of the gods, hiding among mortals until they chose to reveal themselves in all their glory, danced in her head.

The tuxedo emphasized the width of Mike's shoulders. Its formal cut seemed to add inches to his frame. Gone was the comfortable, easy-going slouch that had made him so approachable. Even in her heels, she felt small beside him.

The handsome, near stranger beside her wasn't the Mike she'd come to know. This man had secrets, mysteries, power. Then he turned to her and winked, the illusion fleeing. He was just Mike, after all. A devastatingly handsome, debonair, and polished Mike, but not a stranger.

She reached up to adjust his tie—not that it needed any-thing—just as an excuse to touch him. She smoothed his shirt, feeling his warmth beneath the starched fabric.

Tonight, when they were alone, she'd unbutton each pearl button and taste the skin beneath, working her way downward with a slowness designed to drive him to the edge. And she didn't plan to stop when she reached the trouser buttons, ei-ther.

She'd taste every inch of him before the night was over and no distractions, misdirection, or protests on his part would de-ter her. Her face grew warm at the thought.

"A penny for your thoughts," he said quietly.

She gave him a seductive smile and a slow shake of her head. "My thoughts are worth much more than that. Here's a hint." She threaded her arms around his neck and kissed him, deeply, searching for the surrender she hoped to seduce from him.

He rewarded her by pressing her hips into his body, sear-ing her behind with his palms and imprinting his hard length through the thin fabric of her gown. "You're playing with fire," he whispered.

"Then burn me." She pulled from his arms, already feeling the flames licking at her belly, melting her insides, tormenting her private parts. "Burn me tonight."

Before he could reply the door to the Three Fates Lounge opened and others burst in. Angel, Maggie, Katie, and all the children came inside in a rush. Excited voices bounced off the ceilings and faded into awed whispers as they turned to the far side of the room.

A lace canopy floated above the raised dais, the poles sup-porting it covered in flowers of every hue. Beside her the other women were dressed in similar hues. Her own gown, a deep lilac sprinkled with silver spangles didn't match any of the oth-ers.

Over the past days, Destiny had taken the girls shopping, advising each of them on the various dresses they tried on and making suggestions. Sophia remembered sighing in relief when Destiny approved her sleek, halter-style choice.

She'd spent her life forced into frilly pastel gowns and while she would have worn whatever Destiny wanted for the wedding, she'd been pleased with the flattering, vibrant evening dress.

Looking at the others, she saw everyone glowing in gowns—no two alike—that brought out pink cheeks and radiant smiles. Destiny's oldest son, Adam, approached the knot of women.

"Mom's asking for you. She wants to see all of her bridesmaids in the dressing room. My wife is already there. While you ladies take care of business, Liam will get the men in place. Thomas and Joel are seating the guests now." He ushered them down a narrow hallway toward the dressing rooms. "I'll come and get you when everything is ready."

Inside the dressing room, Destiny, gowned in a beautiful dove-gray silk that fell to a fashionable tea length, looked at them and smiled. "Oh, girls! You're beautiful. You're my rainbow. And the love I feel for James is worth more than a pot of gold. I'm the luckiest woman in the world."

Sophia watched as Destiny handed each of the women a single white calla lily and kissed them on the cheek. She knew from last night's rehearsal that the families, husbands and children included, would surround the couple after Adam walked his mother to the front of the dais. Only she and Mike would stand next to them as they took their vows.

As the others filed out, a wave of longing hit Sophia. She'd miss this family. Miss watching parents wrap their children in hugs or dry their tears. Miss seeing the silly, sloppy grins between husbands and wives. It was everything she'd ever wanted and never had.

"Sophie?" Destiny took Sophia's face between her hands. "No one can change your past. But you can change your future. Don't wait for happiness. Grab it with both hands and don't let go."

"How did you know?"

Destiny smiled. "I've seen the haunted look you get when the others talk about their childhood. You're hiding a lot of pain. It doesn't take a fortune teller to see the longing in your eyes. Anyone with a lick of sense can tell you're in love with Mike and that he hangs on your every word."

She moved across the room and plucked the final calla lily from its vase. "Think about this," Destiny said as she offered the flower to Sophia. "You can't grab your future until you let go of your past."

Sophia pondered the words as she moved through the motions of the ceremony. Watching Destiny and James take their vows and seal the union with a kiss melted her heart. When the small crowd of friends and the large crowd of family cheered the new couple and took to the dance floor in a whirl of color, Sophia's spirits lifted.

Hours later, Mike swept her into a slow dance. As they glided across the floor, ancient wisdom and Destiny's advice tumbled through her head in time to the music.

The Fates grant their favors to the bold, rather than to the deserving.

Grab happiness with both hands and don't let go.

To Embrace Fate is Folly; to Ignore her, Disaster.

You can't grab your future until you let go of your past.

Sophia made her choice.

As the music moved into the final bars, she leaned close. "James Michael Maguire, I love you."

"I love you too, Sophie. I shouldn't, but God help me, I do."

"In that case, Michael Maguire, will you marry me?"

Half an hour later, the same priest who had married James and Destiny quietly sealed Mike and Sophia's vows while sleepy family members looked on. The former bride and groom stood up with them, smiles bright and eyes shining.

When Mike produced an antique wedding ring, Sophia's eyes filled with tears. She'd wondered whether, in all those times he'd proposed, he'd really meant it. Now, he proved beyond her deepest doubts that he'd only been waiting on her. Giving her the final choice. No wonder she loved him.

After a lingering kiss, the priest cleared his throat and demanded their attention again. "Now, my young friends, I must remind you that while the good Lord above recognizes your union from this day forth, I'm afraid the State of Nevada requires a marriage license."

He gave them a sly wink. "I've bent the rules a wee bit for your sakes. Tomorrow, I'll meet you at your hotel at one o'clock. We'll get the paperwork filed to make everything nice and legal. Meanwhile, I wish you all a pleasant good night."

Mike unlocked the hotel room door then swung Sophia in his arms and carried her over the threshold. He slammed the door behind them. "Sweetheart, if you lock the door, I won't have to put you down."

"Anything to help." Sophia uncurled her arms from around his neck and complied.

Mike carried her to the bed and tossed her onto it, following her down and covering her with his body. "Did you mean it?" he asked as he braced himself on his elbows and feathered kisses across her jaw.

"Did I mean what?"

"You said you loved me. Did you mean it? Or did you just marry me so you could share my bed?"

"Does it matter?"

Mike froze mid-kiss. Her careless words sliced through his cocky self-confidence, ramming into a tender spot he hadn't known he had. He pulled far enough away to look into the shimmering green of her eyes. "It matters."

She returned his gaze, then lifted a hand. The cool stroke of her fingers soothed his stubble covered cheek. "I've loved you for a long time. I wouldn't want you in my bed if I didn't."

"Do you love me enough to risk everything? Because if you don't, we can leave town without filling in those legal documents and pretend tonight never happened."

Her fingers moved from his cheek to thread in his hair. "The risk doesn't matter. You matter. You and I together matter. No king or proclamation in the world can keep us apart now. I love you."

He kissed her. He couldn't help it. She tasted sweet, like Irish cream. Like honey. Like chocolate. Each kiss brought a new flavor, a new texture, a deeper connection. Mike stroked the inside of her mouth, savoring the warmth and the soft sounds of her surrender.

His cock throbbed, only this time pleasure, not frustration, flowed through his veins. He shifted to one side and stroked the swell of her breast, stopping when his calloused hands snagged on the glittering fabric of her dress.

"You're wearing too many clothes," he grumbled. "Let's get you out of them." He tried to roll to the edge of the bed, but she followed him, refusing to release her hold on him. Together they stood, tangled in the fabric of their formal wear.

She kicked off her shoes.

Mike found her zipper and slid it open, caressing the bare skin of her back in a smooth, long sweep. He buried his fingers beneath the lace of her panties, savoring the sleek curve of her behind.

Sophia loosened his tie, unbuttoned his collar, and tugged at his cummerbund, unfastening the hooks and letting it fall to the floor. When she pulled his shirt free and burrowed beneath it, Mike smiled against her lips.

Sweet, predictable Sophia. He'd grown used to the feel of her cool fingers stroking his bare back whenever they kissed. He anticipated her next move: she always pulled him closer, snuggling against him like a puppy seeking warmth.

She surprised him. Instead of resting her cheek on his chest, she kissed the hollow of his throat, licking and tasting, working her way up to his Adam's apple, finally nipping the underside of his chin. Nibbling his jaw. Devouring him.

Sweet Saints! She teased his neck with her kisses and sucked his earlobe into her hot, wet mouth. He ground his hips into hers, aching for the feel of her bare skin against his rock-hard body, but she pushed him away.

Only for a moment. A cool wash of air hit his bare legs as his tuxedo trousers slid down. She'd managed to undress him while distracting him with kisses. He kicked off his shoes and shimmied out of the trousers. One layer of clothing down. Too many more to go.

Mike focused on his own stealth attack. He kissed her neck while working the catch on her halter top loose. Then he peeled the fabric back, slowly licking the delicate hollow where collar bone met shoulder, kissing exposed skin as he moved, millimeter by millimeter toward her breast.

He nuzzled his way beneath the material, shoving it aside with his tongue, searching for the tight little nipple he knew waited for him. When he tugged it into his mouth, she moaned and arched against him. He pulled harder, sucking her deeper into his mouth, bunching her skirts in his hand as he did.

He pulled away and whisked the dress over her head, smiling briefly at her cry of frustration before he covered her other breast with his mouth.

Sophia struggled, wiggling to free her arms from the folds of the dress. He took advantage of the wiggle and pressed his hips into hers, rotating, gyrating until she moaned and grabbed his backside in a futile effort to control his movements.

"Eager for a taste of the unknown, sweetheart?"

She swept her palms up his back, tugging at his shirt. "Does this answer your question?"

He released her and pulled the shirt and jacket off, dropping them in the heap of clothing at their feet while she ran her fingers over his chest. His own nipples tightened, and he sucked in a breath when she scrapped her teeth over them.

Fire raced through his body, fueling his arousal. He buried his hands in her hair, holding her in place, greedily accepting her attentions until he felt ready to burst.

"Sophie, slow down." He tilted her head up so he could gaze into her eyes. Those beautiful green eyes nearly glowed with desire. "I've wanted you for so long. This night should be perfect. Just like you are perfect."

"I'm sick of perfect." She licked her lips sending another jolt of desire through him. "My whole life has been about perfect. I want honest. Messy, noisy, all-or-nothing, passionate loving."

She pressed her hips into his and moved slowly until he nearly lost control. He thrust her away, almost brutally. "Keep that up and you'll get messy but unsatisfied. Trust me. It isn't what you want."

"I know what I want," she insisted stubbornly. "You've already taught me about pleasure."

"You don't have any idea." He kissed her lips to remove any sting his words might have carried. "But you will."

He stepped away and stripped out of his boxers, biting back a groan as the brush of soft cotton threatened his control. Sophia followed his movements. He took pleasure in the way her eyes widened at the sight of his erect penis.

"*Zeus and Io,*" she whispered. Her cheeks turned pale.

Mike chuckled at the reference to the Greek god and his nymph lover. "While I'm pleased that you think my proportions are Olympian, I promise you I'm not just scratching a lustful itch."

He cupped her jaw in his hand, gently running his thumb along her cheekbone. "I love you. Enough to give you everything my heart, my soul, my body. I could lose myself to you, in you, and count it a blessing."

Her eyes darkened, and her skin lost its pallor. She reached out to brush her fingertips along his length. The tingling stroke felt like ice, or fire, or both. He throbbed, little shock-wave pulses begging for release.

It was torment. It was bliss.

It was almost too much.

He grabbed her hand and pressed a kiss into the palm. "No more teasing," he murmured.

"But teasing you is so much fun." She stroked him with her other hand.

He captured it too. "You've kept me one stroke away from fulfillment for weeks while I've done nothing but pleasure you." He threaded his fingers through hers and squeezed gently. "It's payback time."

Mike swept her onto the bed and removed her panties. Her whole body blushed in the dim light. He covered her with kisses. In their weeks together, he'd uncovered every one of her sensitive zones, and he ruthlessly exploited each in turn, working her to the brink of satisfaction before pulling away.

She writhed beneath him, instinctively reaching to touch or stroke or rub against him.

He moved out of reach and slipped on a condom.

"Please." A breathy sigh escaped. "Please, I'm so close."

"This," he said as he stroked the tender, ticklish skin of her neck, "is what it's like to linger on the knife edge of desire. To want and not be able to have."

He kissed the corner of her mouth, then stroked his fingertips lightly over her breasts, briefly caressing her taut nipples. Slowly, intentionally, he used his fingers and his lips to work her to a fever pitch of passion again, sensing when she was on the brink of release. And pulling back to leave her hanging.

"Gods above, I want you. I'm begging you, don't make me wait." Her body flushed with desire, heat pouring from it in waves that threatened to scorch him.

He pressed a kiss into her navel and chuckled again, watching her skin quiver at the touch of his breath. "You made me wait, Tiger. Every time I asked you to marry me, you made me wait. And suffer. How does it feel?"

"I want you." Her other words were garbled, nonsense.

Mike swallowed and focused. He was nearly ready to burst, himself. He slid down to give her a last series of caresses, using his tongue to lick the sweetness from her core, to tease her into a frenzy again.

She was wet. Wet enough to ease his entrance and near enough to orgasm to accept him without pain. He inhaled her scent, letting it envelop him, losing himself in it.

She whimpered, and he relented, working his way up her body with kisses until his lips rested on hers and the tip of his penis nudged at her entrance.

"Mike, I want—" She panted. "I want—"

"I know, love. I know." He eased his way inside, watching her reactions, careful, lest he cause her pain. "I want it too."

He felt her stretch, slowly adjusting to him. The slippery, tight warmth threatened to undo him. He pulled back, then thrust again, closer to burying himself in her.

Her eyes glazed over, darkening to nearly black, and he knew she was close. He pushed in, pulled out, then thrust, fully embedding himself in her as she cried out.

The waves of her orgasm caused her to tighten and pulse around him, clenching and releasing in a rhythm as unbearable as it was pleasant. He thrust once, then twice. The tingling, pulsing burn at the head of his penis intensified. Her body contracted around his shaft, and the burn exploded into a thousand sparks, engulfing him in fire.

He collapsed and gathered her in his arms. "I love you," he murmured into the warm, damp curve of her throat. "I always have."

Sophia lay quietly, listening to Mike's soft breathing. He still filled her, a foreign delight. The gentle throbs of her body squeezed against his shaft, reminding her of the shattering pleasure of reaching her peak with him inside.

No wonder people risked kingdoms and riches for this.

She ran her hand along his back and snuggled deeper into his warmth. Sex was fantastic. She'd known that since he first took her to his bed.

But something more had happened tonight. Something special. This, the lingering feeling that lodged in her heart and warmed its way to her soul, didn't fade the way the pleasure in her body faded. While her body's tremors ebbed, the feeling in her heart grew. Engulfing her. Surrounding her. Claiming her.

Love. It couldn't be anything else.

And while people risked power and wealth for sex, she knew in her soul that she would risk much more—everything she had, was, or ever would be—for love.

Chapter 29

In the morning, they filed their legal documents in Reno. Sophia suppressed a twinge of guilt when she presented Grace Bradley's driver's license as identification and filled in the false information.

Beside her Mike stiffened and pursed his lips but remained silent. She passed her information across the counter to the clerk and stood on tiptoe to kiss Mike's cheek. "Sorry," she murmured, "it's all I have with me." His look softened.

In her heart and mind, she'd always be his wife. If the priest was to be believed, she'd be his wife in the eyes of God too. At least after last night. So what if there was a legal snarl to unravel with the U.S. government? Her stomach knotted. They would find a way to make it right. They were married. In love. No matter what the documents said.

She refused to contemplate a future in which they would be anything else. Sure, she still had to break the news to the royal family. And to petition to have her marriage recognized by the Church of Melesia and blessed by the king.

But while Melesia might force her to choose between her marriage and her country, no one could tear her marriage apart. That was built on a rock-solid foundation of trust.

After waving James and Destiny off to their honeymoon and saying a tearful farewell to Mike's sisters, she and Mike had slipped back to their hotel room for one more blissful night of nonstop lovemaking. Then they'd taken their time returning home, meandering through tourist stops and generally acting like a couple in love. Which they were.

Back in Morgan's Outpost, life settled into a happy routine—lovemaking, working at the pub, devising plans for her children's foundation, more lovemaking—what else could a woman want? The days slipped by in a contented blur.

Sophia settled in at a table near the pub kitchen on Monday morning to scan the newspapers while Mike went for donuts. She tossed aside the weekly tabloids—nothing in them could hurt her now—and focused on the major newspapers. World events were predictable. No political upheavals. No new wars. Nothing of import.

She flipped to the society pages.

Shit. Trouble greeted her with a capital T. Make that a capital G. *Grace Smith, an American student studying at the Melesian Royal Academy, strolls with Price Stephan of Melesia at a student event. Shit, shit, shit.*

Grace wasn't strolling with Stephan, she was looking at him with stars in her eyes. Looking as if her world revolved around him.

Sophia searched her mind for the last time she'd spoken with Grace. There had been Halloween night, and then— Surely, she'd spoken with her after that night. Hadn't she? She'd intended to.

Grace had been rattled by something one of Sophia's crazy aunts or cousins had said about bloodlines. Typical de Lyons bluster. Only Grace hadn't known that. And Sophia had left her floundering in doubt.

Zeus! This was a twisted knot. If Grace had turned to Stephan for help, it could ruin everything. Today's picture in an obscure society page could easily become the public's next hot gossip item. Nothing would raise the collective de Lyons ire faster than another American consorting with a Melesian prince.

They'd pick apart their strategies and failure to marry her to King Constantine, then cast about for a new angle. An angle that most likely involved throwing her at Stephan. Which meant they'd finally show an interest in where she was.

They would discover that she wasn't where she should have been. Stephan's cover up of her disappearance—at least she assumed he was the one covering up for her—would be for naught. The entire royal family, and perhaps the entire country, would be thrown into chaos.

And the gods knew what else could happen if the press discovered Sophia had married using Grace's identity. Worse, she'd surrendered Grace's driver's license in order to get her own—under the name of Sophia Maguire. *Hades and Persephone!* Suddenly what she'd written off as a minor paperwork mix-up loomed like an international disaster.

Both the internal chaos and the international disaster could have been prevented if she'd followed some semblance of royal protocol. If she'd asked for the king's blessing before marrying Mike; if she'd listened to her head first and her heart second; if she'd gathered her courage instead of hiding in the happy little cocoon she'd woven for herself in Morgan's Outpost…

Wishing is for the masses. The royal class doesn't wish for things to happen. We make them happen. Uncle Julian's lessons chided her, but for once, she didn't flinch or resist. Wishing was futile. She had to act.

She'd go to the king. In person. With or without Mike. She'd apologize for her absence and ask for the royal blessing and either accept it or renounce her citizenship. Publicly. Her presence could avert disaster.

First, she needed to buy herself some time. She scanned the article again. The photo had been taken only a few days ago.

All she had to do was convince Grace to lie low for a little while longer until Sophia could set things straight.

She took a deep breath and pulled out her phone. Anger simmered as she waited for the call to connect. Anger at her family and their stupid obsessions. Anger at herself, her cowardice. When Grace answered the call, the anger boiled over before she could control it.

"I thought you were going to stay low and avoid the press, Grace. Photos of you and Stephan were all over yesterday's news."

"What?" Grace sounded panicked.

Zeus, she was messing this up. She wasn't angry with Grace. Sophia softened her tone.

"They were picked up by the Associated Press. Most of them are buried in the human-interest sections of the papers, but you need to be more careful."

"It was an official school function. Stephan is Chancellor of the Royal Academy, after all."

"He's also an eligible bachelor prince, and that's news. He's not the kind of person you want to be seen with if you value your anonymity. Or mine."

He's also not the kind of person you want to be with if you value your heart. It was too easy for a starry-eyed American to fall for a title and a bit of royal courtesy.

"Listen, we need to talk about that." Grace sounded worried. Sophia steeled herself for what would come next. "It's time for you to come home. You were never supposed to be gone for more than a few days, anyway. Everyone in the family is worried about you, especially Stephan. I've heard he's in charge of finding you."

"All the more reason to for you to stay away from him."

"I can't, Sophia. I won't. I—"

Oh Zeus and Aphrodite. Grace had already fallen for Stephan's charm. The gods help her, she had to stop this infatuation. Now. Sophia forced a hint of royal hauteur into her voice.

"Don't tell me you think you're in love with him. It takes more than a walk at a school function to fall in love. He's not some fairy tale hero that's yours for the taking."

"You're right," Grace insisted stubbornly. "He's much more than a story book hero. He's a wonderful man. A man I love. And I won't lie to him anymore. I'll give you one hour to call and tell him where you are. Then I'm going to come clean with him. I won't keep your secrets anymore."

Sophia needed to buy some time until she could get home and straighten things out. No telling how many ways Grace could get herself into trouble if she raced headlong into an ill-advised confession. Sophia crossed her fingers behind her back in a gesture she'd seen Mike's nieces do a hundred times.

"What about your own secrets? Do you really believe a man like Stephan is going to overlook all of the laws you've broken by helping me?"

"You've broken laws too."

"Yes, but I'll claim ignorance." At least she could claim not to understand American law. "And I'll also be covered by diplomatic immunity. Neither of those things will help you. In Melesia, it's a crime to conspire against a member of the nobility. Treason is defined differently than in your country."

"I didn't conspire against anyone. You wanted to disappear."

"A Melesian court may not see it that way."

"But Stephan—"

"You may fancy yourself in love with him, but he'll uphold the law, no matter what the cost. He will always put the needs of his country, and the royal family, above everything and everyone else." That much was true. The D'Malia family placed country and duty above all.

"That's not true. He loves me."

"Has he told you so?"

The silence on the other end of the phone tore at Sophia's heart. She'd crushed Grace's dreams. The girl was such an innocent. *Damn it to Hades.* Why did putting things right have to be so painful? She softened her tone. "I didn't think so. Don't risk losing everything. Don't tell him."

"But I," Grace's voice wavered as if she were fighting tears.

"He might not want to hurt you," Sophia added, "but he's bound by an oath of duty. All of them are. Even your sister. Just keep my secret for a little while longer, and I'll see that no harm comes to you. Trust me."

Trust me for two days. In two days, she'd be home mending political fences and comforting Grace. Only two short days.

"But—"

"Trust me, Grace. Good-bye." Sophia ended the call before she could break into tears herself. *Hades!* Her selfish web of deceit was so sticky it had trapped everyone.

Even Mike. Especially Mike. The chime above the pub door jangled as he walked in carrying a box of her favorite donuts. The minute he saw her face, he put the box down and gathered her in his arms.

"Whatever it is, we can get through it. I'm here for you."

His whispered words comforted her, and she buried her head in his shirt for a minute. Then, before she lost her resolve, she stepped away and faced him. "Mike, there's trouble at home. At least there will be if I don't return. I need to go back as soon as possible."

"I'll come with you." He closed the distance between them and clung to her—a tad too tightly—as if he, too, were afraid of what was to come. "Whatever it is, we'll face it together."

Together. Sophia had never heard a more beautiful word. She kissed him fiercely, putting all her love, fear, and faith into the kiss. "Together would be lovely. But either way—together or alone—I'm coming back to Morgan's Outpost. They'd have to lock me up to keep us apart."

"You're my wife," he said roughly. "I'd storm any prison, risk any hardship to keep you by my side. Together."

She leaned toward him, taking comfort in his words, before breaking away to busy herself with their morning routine. Making coffee. Eating donuts. *Committing every action to memory in case this was their final morning together.* Until she couldn't pretend anymore. She abandoned the pretense of normal and snuggled into Mike's arms again, using him as a buffer against the inevitable.

The ringing phone interrupted them. Sophia snatched it up, hoping Grace had come to her senses. But the voice on the other end didn't belong to Grace Bradley.

"Hello, Stephan," she said weakly. Her knees collapsed and she sank into a chair.

That bastard! Mike paced across the room his fists balled, tight and dangerous. Two hours ago, Sophia had lain in his arms, happy and content. One hour ago, he'd returned to find her tense and pale.

Her fingers shook even though her voice remained steady while she took an unexpected call from home. Ten minutes ago, another call—make that two calls in rapid succession— had come for her. Now she was a wreck. All thanks to Prince Stephan son-of-a-bitch D'Malia.

He'd never paid Stephan much attention before, but now the man stood between Sophia and her happiness. Far from the harmless buried-in-a-book prince he'd been a year ago, now Stephan was a bloodhound, intent on finding Sophia. Intent on destroying the happiness she'd created for herself.

Mike wouldn't let that happen. One way or another, he'd teach Stephan not to interfere in Sophia's life.

Mike grabbed a pair of ice tongs from the bar and ripped them apart before bending one of the halves back and forth, forcing his tension to burn itself off on the metal rather than by slamming his fists into the bar.

How had they learned where to find Sophia? Had they discovered his secrets? Revealed them to her? He dismissed the idea. She wouldn't have turned to him for solace if she knew. So, what was the problem? Why did she have to hurry home? And if he accompanied her, would anyone believe that he did it out of love and not for a damn news story?

Unless the trouble wasn't about his identity. Maybe it was about their marriage. Damn all of them to hell. The metal arm of the tong snapped in his fists. He started on the other piece. Bending. Working out the rage. Controlling his reactions. She might leave him one day, but he'd be damned forever if he let someone take her away.

The second piece of metal snapped, draining away the bulk of Mike's tension. He moved to stand behind Sophia and knead her tense shoulders. She leaned into him with a sigh of relief.

"Do you really think a press release is sufficient?" she asked into the phone. Her voice was softer, more controlled. More relaxed. "I understand," she said after listening for a minute. "The official story is that I left the tour for an extended holiday and to visit distant relatives. Please request the press to respect my privacy."

She paused again her lips set in a firm line. "I know. I said the same thing when I left after the king's wedding. I'm prepared for the tabloids to torment me. I'll keep my location secret as long as possible. No, Stephan, I'm not telling you, either.

And do me a favor. Stay away from Grace Bradley. Don't break her heart."

Sophia's face twisted in a grimace as she listened to the reply. "No, I don't believe you. You're talking nonsense. When has anything ever been more important to you than your duty? You're just like all of them… Yes, I know my duty too. I'll be in touch."

She shut off the phone call. "I guess there's no need for a trip after all. The royal family has me on call, but otherwise, I'm free to enjoy my so-called extended holiday in America."

"Is that right?" Mike slid his hands from her shoulders and planted a kiss next to her ear. "Does this press release say how long you'll be in America?"

"No." She shifted in her chair to face him. "It does mean I'll be headline news in the tabloids soon. Should we, that is, should I go away for a while? I'd hate to attract unwanted attention and bring your family under scrutiny."

Mike pulled her to her feet. "Aren't you forgetting something?" He kissed her left hand, near her wedding ring. "First, it's *our* family, not just mine. Second, if anyone goes into hiding, it will be *us* not *you*. That's what for better or worse means in those vows we took. Got it?"

Her fingers tightened on his. "Got it. Thank you."

"Anyway, it's best to hide in plain sight. Everyone in Morgan's Outpost knows you as Sophie Maguire—their friend, not Sophia de Lyons—royal runaway. They'll only raise questions if you leave suddenly."

"Are you sure?"

"Trust me." He wrapped her in his arms. "I've done it more than you know," he added under his breath, not sure if he wanted her to hear his whispered confession or not.

Either way their peaceful days were numbered.

Chapter 30

The minute Sophia stepped into the shower, Mike raced downstairs and locked himself in the pub's office, a special edition of the *Weekly World Stir* clutched in his fist. *Damn Frank Kincaid to hell.* He jabbed in the numbers to the corporate offices of the tabloid.

"*Weekly World Stir*, how may I direct—"

"Get me Kincaid. It's Mack Maguire."

He paced the office, one ear cocked for sounds of Sophia and the other filled with the sappy crap they always played while you were on hold. He didn't even bother trying to control his anger, just let it build with each minute that passed.

"Mack, sorry to keep you waiting—"

"What the hell were you thinking, Kincaid? *Intended Bride Ousted as American Sister Steps In?*" He slapped the latest edition of the paper on his desk. "That's my photo you ran, but it isn't my story. What happened to the copy I sent you?"

"Easy there, Mack. Yes, I ran your photo. It's great. Shows the missing duke's daughter and the royal bride's sister looking as alike as two peas in a pod. Fits like a charm with the catchy new headline. Very nice work. Work that the *Stir* owns, by the way."

"Yeah, yeah. Bought and paid for over a year ago. I get it. But you're using my byline to print a bunch of hogwash. Where's your journalistic integrity?"

Kincaid laughed. "Mack, since when did I have journalistic integrity? We provide entertainment, the juicier the better. Don't take me wrong. I'm not complaining about the stuff you're sending me. Pure gold, that bit about secret plots to topple the Melesian government. That kind of dirt always sells. But it's last year's news. Mack, what did you expect me to do? While you're playing barkeep in that pub of yours, Melesia is making waves again."

"I've got a source—"

"Sure, you do. But the minute the new kid read the press release from the de Lyons girl, he was on a plane to Melesia trying to ferret out the rest of the story. You know the drill. A celebrity goes into hiding and we cross our fingers, hoping for a detox or secret baby angle. Time was when you'd have been on that plane. Tell me, did you even know about the press release?"

"Of course, I did. I'm not an idiot."

"You knew? But you didn't report on it?" Kincaid spit out a string of expletives. "You're too mired in your so-called legitimate angles. You've gone soft, Mack. The readers don't want soft. Never did. Face it. You've lost your fire, your passion."

"A minute ago, I was pure gold, and now I've got no fire? That's bullshit, and you know it."

"Come on, kid, what was I supposed to do?" Kincaid let out a heavy sigh. "Look at the competition's headlines: *Secret American Plot to Overthrow Melesian Government. A Fool for Love: Is the King Fit to Rule? Is Prince Charming in Over His Head?* I have to compete. Even an in-depth expose on political corruption takes a back seat to this kind of stuff."

Overhead, Mike heard footsteps. An upstairs door slammed shut. He only had a few minutes before Sophia found him. He stared at the paper, frustrated hopelessness replacing his anger. "Did you have to use my byline?"

"Mack, don't take it personal. The new kid doesn't have a tenth of your talent, but he's here, and he's full of passion. You told me yourself this series was the last you'd ever do for the *Stir*. If you want your job back, say the word. I'll reassign him. If you don't, I'll accept that too. But either way, the owners have decided that the 'Mack the Pen' byline is here to stay."

"What if I leak—"

"Don't even think about it. The *Stir*'s parent company just got bought out and the new owners play hardball, Maguire. They'll hold you to the letter of the contract if they even think you've compromised their pen name." Something in Kincaid's voice told him this wasn't the usual bluster. "Take my advice. Decide what you want out of life. Don't try to have it both ways. It'll never work, Mike. We both know that."

Mike crushed the tabloid into a ball and threw it across the room. "I'll finish the series and be done with it."

"Good choice, kid, good choice." Frank Kincaid disconnected the call.

Kincaid's article had raised the stakes, but Mike had made a career of turning innocent facts into damning lies. He could just as easily turn today's salacious lies into an attack on an innocent target.

He still had a literary trick or two that could turn Sophia into a hero. He dredged up a smile to show Sophia when she came down. No matter what else happened, he vowed he'd protect her.

The smell of evergreen filled the air, mingling with the scent of mulled apple cider and fresh sugar cookies as the family gathered in the Maguire homestead.

Sophia accepted a cup of the warm cider and propped her slipper-clad feet on the love seat. After hours of tromping through the snow in search of a perfect Christmas tree, she appreciated being warm and dry. Mike settled in next to her.

Max lumbered over to them, turned around in a circle or two then plopped down with a contented woof.

Across the room, James and Destiny were seated together on the couch looking as happy as she felt. Katie's voice wafted through the house singing Christmas carols as she mixed up a fresh batch of cookie dough.

Mike and James had strung the tree with lights earlier and now the girls scrutinized the array of ornaments spread out on the floor. Mary Katherine—Pipsqueak—sat wearing the Chili Queen crown Sophia had given her at Halloween, dividing her attention between the tree ornaments, a plate of cookies, and Sophia's cell phone.

"Do you think he'll call again, Aunt Sophie?"

Sophia glanced at her watch. A Melesian press conference was scheduled to air in about fifteen minutes. "I don't think he'll call now, sweetie. But keep the phone just in case."

Over the past days, papers worldwide capitalized on her absence. Some displayed photos of Grace and Stephan together, speculating about another royal romance. Others linked the alleged romance to an American plot to destabilize the Melesian government. She could probably blame the de Lyons political activists for those headlines.

She'd taken it in stride, except for Stephan's daily—sometimes hourly—updates. Eventually she'd told him not to call except for emergencies. Then she'd given the phone to Mary Katherine and told her it was a magic phone which only rang when a real prince was on the line. The girl's eyes had grown wide, and she'd guarded the phone like a rare gem.

Sophia grinned at her perfect revenge. Stephan's love for children was well known in Melesia. So when Mary Katherine, not Sophia, answered his next call, she knew she'd backed him into a corner. The awe in Mary Katherine's voice and her shy responses no doubt charmed Stephan as much as he charmed the child. All while gritting his teeth because he couldn't talk to Sophia.

She'd occasionally returned his calls, but only after she made it clear he was no longer in charge of the situation.

Katie had chided Sophia about the elaborate lengths she went to in order to fuel Mary Katherine's princess fantasy but hadn't otherwise seemed concerned about the ruse. Sophia pushed her guilt about using the child aside. It was harmless. Sort of.

"Put your magic phone away, Pipsqueak. Let's get started on that tree." James hefted her in his arms and carried her over to the boxes of ornaments. "You coming, Sophie? Mike? It's our first Christmas together as a family, after all."

"I'll be there in a bit, James," she said. "There's a news story I want to catch up on first."

James shook his head. "You're too serious for your own good, Sophie. The girls and I will check the attic to make sure we didn't overlook any Christmas boxes, but when we get back, the TV has to be turned off, and you have to start having fun."

"It's a deal." She smiled at James and indicated Mike should join them, then she turned her attention to the press conference. The royal family calmly posed for photos, issued their statements and answered questions. Grace seated beside her sister, the obviously pregnant Queen Jillian, looked tense and worried.

When the press turned their carefully worded questions on her, a confused Grace fell into their trap—and agreed the king was a fool for falling in love with Queen Jillian. Then she tried to explain her faux pas.

Pandemonium broke out as Grace fumbled until—finally—she stopped talking. King Constantine and Prince Stephan glossed over the incident and smoothly redirected the questions, after a stricken Grace left the room on her sister's arm.

Sophia sighed and turned the TV off. Poor Grace. She was as unprepared for a royal press conference as Sophia had been for waiting tables. She only hoped Grace's story ended half as happily as her own.

She pushed the thoughts aside and joined the others in decorating the tree. Small and fragile ornaments went up high while unbreakable bulbs clustered at the bottom of the tree. Soon she was laughing and enjoying the family. Christmas music boomed from the stereo, drowning out her worries.

Until the phone rang.

"It's him. It's him!" Pipsqueak bounded around, searching for the phone and shouting with glee when she answered it. "Merry Christmas, Prince. We're decorating our tree. What are you doing?"

Someone turned down the music. Pipsqueak's voice carried through the room. "You want to talk to Sophia? Do you mean Miss—I mean Aunt—Sophie?"

Mary Margaret—aka Miss Manners—snatched the phone from her. "I don't care if you are a prince. You can't talk to *Aunt* Sophie. She doesn't need a prince to rescue her. She's married. To my Uncle Mike."

"Oh, *Zeus*. Sweetie, give me the phone." Sophia hurried to Mary Margaret and snatched the phone from her. "Stephan, I am so sorry."

His laughter drifted over the connection. "Well, if it isn't Aunt Sophie. Married to Uncle Mike. When did you plan to tell me? Or did you think you could keep it a secret forever?"

"I honestly don't know." She slipped out the back door and onto the quiet patio. Instantly she regretted it as she shivered in the dark. "You've had a lot on your mind, and I, well, I've wanted my privacy."

"Privacy is a rare luxury, Sophia." A hint of steel and tightly contained disapproval crept into his voice. "I'd say you've had more than your share lately. Enough to get into some trouble by the sound of it."

Mike slipped out the door and wrapped her coat around her shoulders. She smiled at him in thanks and took his hand.

"There isn't trouble, Stephan. I love Mike, and he loves me. I'm begging you, don't interfere."

At the other end of the line, halfway across the world, he sighed. "I don't want to steal your happiness. Believe me, I'll do everything in my power to help you live the life you want."

"I know that," she answered softly. "I'm sorry I accused you of anything."

"At least you could have invited me to the wedding. I would have been happy to be there with you."

"Sure, you and the Melesian Press Corps and the rest of the world's news outlets." She would have liked to have had Stephan present, if only the cameras didn't follow his every move when he traveled. She turned from Mike and took a few steps across the patio.

"I suppose you saw the press conference," Stephan said.

"Yes. I'm sorry about that too."

"We'll manage. We always do. I'm worried about Gracie, but I think she'll be okay after some sleep. I was wondering, would you be willing to do an interview with the Melesian press? You wouldn't have to leave your new family. I could set it up so you can call in—no traces on the line, no attempt to find you. Just a chat to ease some of the tensions that are mounting."

"Of course, I'll do it. I'll do whatever you need. Even if you need me to come home. Just, please, don't ask me to choose between my husband and my country."

"I would never do that. You deserve some happiness. If I may, I'll call you later to set it up."

"Yes. I'll be waiting. And Stephan? I'll keep the phone with *me*."

He laughed, but the sound was filled with weariness. "As long as you promise say good-bye to Mary Katherine for me. She and I have become friends lately."

"I promise. Good night, Stephan."

Sophia closed the phone, troubled by something in Stephan's voice. He'd been like a brother to her all her life, and she knew when something was wrong. She just didn't know how—or if—she could fix it. Instead, she went inside with Mike and joined the family celebration, hoping their love could wash away her concerns.

"Problems at home?" Mike murmured. He fisted his hands in the coat and slipped it off Sophia's shoulders, wishing he held Stephan's neck in a death grip rather than the folds of down-filled polyester. He forced himself to be gentle as he brushed a kiss across Sophia's temple and waited for her answer.

"Nothing much. I agreed to do a phone interview to convince the world that I'm alive and well. Stephan will set it up so that my location won't be revealed."

"Wherever it is, I'll be with you. And if you have to go to Melesia—"

"I don't." She turned and gave him a quick kiss and a smile. "At least not now. When I do, I want you with me."

Mike nodded. "Sophie, remember, I—"

The girls interrupted, pulling them apart before she could hear his words. "I love you," he added under his breath. He tossed the coat on the couch and headed to the kitchen, needing a moment alone before rejoining the party.

He jerked open a drawer and grabbed a spoon while he fought for control. Stephan D'Malia. The scholarly brother, Mike remembered from his research. Stephan had never been a good source of stories. The *Stir* readers weren't interested in the high-brow intellectual pursuits that he favored.

His love life rarely yielded anything of interest, either. Enough women to give him the title of eligible prince, but too few to label him a playboy. He'd been harmless. Until recently.

Since Thanksgiving, he'd plagued Sophia with calls like the one Mike had overheard tonight. *I'm sorry.* Sophia's voice echoed in his memory. If she'd apologized to the prince once, she'd done it a hundred times over the last weeks. He was damned tired of hearing her apologize to that f-ing prince and beg him for...for whatever it was she'd asked of him. She didn't need his forgiveness. Or his support.

Mike couldn't stand to see Sophia beaten down just because Stephan was a prince and Sophia was some lesser noblewoman. The rules of her world made no sense to a hard-headed barman like him.

Mike grabbed the spoon in both hands, wrenching on it, letting his anger intensify instead of dissipate. It snapped. He grabbed another and focused on it. The damn trick didn't work anymore. He'd owe his dad a drawer full of cutlery if he didn't get his rage under control.

The next time Sophia talked to Stephan, he'd grab the phone from her and give that bastard-of-a-prince a piece of his mind. Or he'd hop on a plane and storm the palace and confront the man in person. Settle things the old school way: man-to-man. Or… The second spoon broke. Mike sagged against the counter.

He wouldn't do any of those things. Sophia had asked him to let her handle the situation with her country. Any action he took could throw fuel on an international fire that would rage out of control and burn them both. But, by God, one day…one day he'd confront the man who'd made her life such living hell and make him apologize to her.

"Uncle Mike, hurry. It's time to put the star on." A chorus of young voices urged him to return to the festivities.

"Coming." He threw the broken spoon away and pasted a smile on his face. For the sake of the family. For Sophia. Because he loved them. And God help anyone who hurt the ones he loved—commoner or king.

Chapter 31

Mike hunched over his computer, banging out another story for the *Stir*, hating every word he typed. The faint sounds of Christmas music filtered into the office from the restaurant, but the memory of Kincaid's words drowned out the cheerful lyrics. *A detox or secret baby angle. Detox. Secret baby.* If Mike didn't cough up a story on Sophia soon, that was exactly the kind of claptrap the *Stir* would run.

With her scheduled to give a telephone interview and speech to the Melesian public tomorrow night—Christmas Eve—interest in her would peak over the remainder of the holiday season. After the *Stir* ran the obligatory Christmas and New Year's issues, a story on her would be next in line.

His distraction methods had failed. The *Stir* had run several weeks' worth of his stories on the D'Malia/de Lyons feud. He'd blasted the duke for his high-handed treatment of commoner and royal alike.

Finally, he'd titillated the public with a series of articles on *The Politics of Sex* where he'd exposed the duke's tactics of manipulating royal marriages for over two generations.

He'd realized his mistake the minute he hit the send button. Having set the duke up to be the character everyone loved to hate, he now had to make Sophia the poor victimized underdog who everyone cheered to succeed.

And he had to do it before Kincaid—and his cub reporter on the prowl in Melesia—decided to print a detox or secret baby story, turning Sophia into another icon who fell from grace.

Like it or not the best way to protect Sophia from a vicious article was to expose her in a true one—*Reclusive Royal Reveals All,* the article he'd pitched to Kincaid before he'd gotten to know her. Before he'd fallen in love with her. *Shit.* Who was he kidding? None of that mattered. He'd known from the beginning that it was wrong to exploit her. And now to save her, he'd have to betray her trust.

And when the copy hit the newsstands, he'd no longer worry about the ethics of revealing his identity as Mack the Pen to her. She'd know. And hate him for it.

Christmas passed in a blur of happiness for Sophia yet, somehow, as the Christmas cheer and New Year fervor faded into January, a chill crept into her soul. One that even Mike couldn't chase away.

She climbed out of bed and threw on a robe before padding to the window. She scratched the layer of frost until she could look out on a snow-covered landscape. Only a few weeks ago, when the snow fell on Christmas Eve, she'd thought it beautiful. Then, her life had been charmed.

Now she stared at dirty piles of slush thrown against the white snow and shivered as she wondered where things had gone wrong. Was it when Stephan first called that Mike had begun to look at her with worried eyes? Or did the tension creep into his embrace after her Christmas Eve interview with the Melesian press?

Either way, the man who'd promised—for better or for worse—to go into hiding with her if necessary, now recoiled at the mention of a trip to Melesia.

To his credit, he'd agreed that she should go and he'd made it clear that he'd go with her, but the grim set of his jaw and the way he avoided her gaze told her something was wrong.

She didn't doubt his love, but the gods help her she was beginning to doubt his ability to cope with her aristocratic status in the country of her birth.

Behind her, the sound of the shower stopped. Soon, Mike would come out, press a kiss to her cheek and leave. By noon he'd be buried in paperwork or running errands for the pub. At night, he'd fall into bed exhausted.

In the morning, for a few precious moments when he'd kiss her awake and make love to her with slow, sweet movements, she'd dream that everything was okay. Yet each day he left her bed before she could snuggle in the warmth of his arms, exchanging confidences like they had so many times before. He loved her with his body, but his soul, that innate warmth that had first drawn her, retreated further each day.

She suppressed another shiver and pasted a smile on her face as the bathroom door opened. "Good morning, husband." She twined her arms around his neck before he could give her his usual perfunctory kiss.

Mike stiffened and wrapped his arms around her in an awkward embrace, but his lips softened beneath her onslaught. When she pulled back, his eyes were soft too.

"Sophia." He stopped to clear away the rasp in his voice. "I love you more than I can say. I don't want to see you hurt. Whatever else you believe, please believe that."

"I believe you. But I also know something's bothering you. Is it my family? Are you worried about how Melesia will react to our marriage? About meeting the king?"

He stopped her with a gentle finger to her lips. "Nothing like that." Mike gathered her in his arms. For an instant, she felt the warmth she'd been missing. "It's not you, sweetheart," he whispered into her hair. "I'm wrestling some old demons. God willing, I'll slay them for good this time."

"Let me help you." She cupped his jaw in her palm. "I love you. No matter what happens, we're in this together. For better or for worse—remember?"

"Generous as your offer is," he gave her a lingering kiss, "this is a battle I have to fight on my own."

He turned and left, taking the fragile warmth and connection with him. A shiver racked Sophia's body, and a tingle of foreboding raced down her spine. Gods above, had The Fates given her a taste of love only to snatch it away so soon?

She drew herself up and stared at the empty room. *Bullshit.* She'd cowered before her uncle and the demands of *Duty to King and Country* for too many years.

Her days of freedom had changed that, for the better. And now, having tasted love, she would fight to keep it. Even if she fought The Fates themselves.

Sophia headed toward a private booth, paperwork for the Hercules Labors of Love Foundation clutched in her hand, but her thoughts focused on her fight for her marriage. She hurried past the kitchen where Mike's dad, Destiny, and Katie huddled together, talking and laughing.

"Sophie, can you give me a hand?" Katie waved her over. "Everyone's helping me plan for my final class project."

"Mike mentioned you're working on something for school."

Katie gave her an impish grin. "I'm surprised he didn't tell you it was some half-thought-out scheme. He's been reluctant to introduce new menu items. So I decided to create a separate restaurant within the pub as a way around his objections. Dad moved some tables into the back room for me and Destiny's helping me decorate."

"How can I help?" Sophia asked.

"You can get Mike out of our hair for a while." James winked at her. "Take him off on a honeymoon. We need a couple of weeks to get *Katie's Corner* up and running."

"I'm afraid it isn't that easy." Sophia sighed. "I've tried to talk him into a trip, but his heart isn't in it."

James frowned. "Mike used to love travel. Went all kinds of places with his job before he settled down to work at the pub."

"What did he do?" Mike had never been specific about any of the jobs he'd held before she'd met him.

"Mike didn't talk much about his job. He worked for a small newspaper doing fact checking or something. I do know he was on the road a lot. He lived in Los Angeles, New York, even spent some time abroad. Once, he let it slip that they'd assigned him to the society and entertainment columns. They probably liked the fact that he was a photographer as well as a journalist.

"I think he was ashamed of doing celebrity news. That's the real reason he never talked about it. Mike always hoped to be a reporter. If I hadn't called him home to take over the pub, maybe he'd have made it." James's voice trailed off, and Sophia could see the sadness in his eyes.

"It's never too late to follow your dreams." Destiny put her hand on his shoulder and gave him a smile.

"You're a living example of that." James returned her smile then faced Sophia again. "I wish Mike had been more open with me. Maybe he was embarrassed about not climbing the ladder faster. Or he worried that I would rib him about his work. But more likely, he thought I was disappointed when he didn't want to take over the pub.

"Either way, I missed dozens of chances to tell him how proud I was of him. His mom, bless her soul, didn't miss anything. She knew he had other ambitions. She—" He paused, his words trailing off into memories.

Sophia watched as Destiny gave his hand a squeeze.

"James and Mary Katherine imagined growing old together, like most happy couples. Adam and I had the same dream. When death steals it from you, the grief can be unbearable."

James nodded. "After Mary Kate's funeral, I took some time off. But a week became a month and after a while, it just took too much energy to handle things at the pub. That's when Sam stepped in." His face darkened with anger.

"Sam was my ex-husband." Katie pushed aside the stack of menu ideas she'd been working on and joined them. "He swept me off my feet during my first year of college."

"Your first and last year of college," James grumbled. "She dropped out to marry that no good, miserable excuse for a man."

"You didn't think he was such a miserable guy when Mary Margaret was born." Katie dropped a kiss on her dad's cheek. "Sam gave me three beautiful girls, and I'll never regret them, no matter how much I wish he'd been different."

"Those girls were the only good that ever came from the likes of Sam. The bastard lied his way into our lives and stole his way out. For years, I treated him like a son. Then he embezzled from me, nearly bankrupting the pub. Worse, he broke Katie's heart when he left. Good riddance to him."

Sophia swallowed, her own misery growing as she looked at the three of them. She'd lied her way into their lives too. The sooner she told them about her real identity, the better, because she wanted to stay and become a part of this family, not just an outsider, pretending.

"Don't look so distressed, Sophie." Katie gave her a smile. "Things were rocky, but it all worked out in the end. We hobbled along for a while then dad asked Mike to come home. Because of him, I was able to go back to school and find a career I love. Dad found the new love of his life, and Mike found you."

"I'm happy to be a part of this family," Sophia began.

"Yes, and we're happy you're here, but that's not the point." James pulled her into a one-armed embrace. "The point is that you and Mike are young newlyweds. You need time alone together. Time to have fun, not to spend working. Destiny has this vacation club that's been in her family for years. If you could lure Mike away from the pub, then we could…"

James and Destiny steered her out of the kitchen and toward the office, outlining their plans as they went. Plans for the pub. Plans for her honeymoon with Mike. Plans that she just might be able to use to convince Mike to extend their vacation by visiting Melesia and asking the king's blessing on her marriage.

For the first time in her life, everything she wanted seemed to be within her grasp.

Chapter 32

Two days later, Mike boarded the first-class airline cabin and settled in next to Sophia. As he relaxed against the leather seats and accepted a drink from the flight attendant, he tried to shut out the whirlwind pace of the last days.

His dad and Destiny had done everything but pack for them after gifting them with airfare and accommodations for two weeks at the Disney World Resort. He'd put up a fight, but it was clearly a losing one. In the end, he and Sophia had accepted the generous gift.

He might as well make the best for these two weeks with the woman he loved, because God alone knew if they'd be his last. One way or another, he'd come clean with her during this trip and admit to his deception. By the end of their honeymoon, she'd know he was *Mack the Pen* and either love him still or leave him the way he deserved.

He thanked God for the phony credentials that prevented their hasty marriage from being legal. When she'd signed their marriage certificate as "Grace Bradley" his heart had twisted, but now he knew that technicality would save her a world of trouble when she returned home.

If she returned home.

Hope rooted in his heart with all the stubbornness of a dandelion; every time he ripped it away, it sprang back, refusing to die. *She might forgive you*, it whispered. *She loves you.*

He took a swig of his whiskey and Coke, ignoring the voice of hope. Instead, he reached for the stack of papers he'd shoved in the seat pocket in front of him. In researching their vacation spot, two things caught his eye.

First, Epcot announced the opening of its new Melesia exhibit in the World Showcase. Second, the government of Melesia was gifting the center—as well as universities and aquariums throughout the United States—with a marine wildlife exhibit, to promote education and conservation.

He'd covered enough international gift giving ceremonies to know they always included smiling government officials posing for the cameras. So he was confident that someone from Melesia would present this gift. Someone Sophia could turn to when he broke her heart. Someone who would see her safely home.

"Mike?"

Sophia's soft question interrupted his thoughts. He shoved the papers back in the seat pocket and turned to her.

"Is something wrong? You look like you're in pain. You're not afraid to fly, are you?"

He smiled at her. "No, nothing like that. I was just reading up on our destination. So," he said, trying to change the subject, "what's going on in the world?" He nodded to her stack of newspapers.

"Not much. World events are pretty quiet this week. Even the tabloids are too preoccupied with a story about some psychic in India to pay attention to Melesia."

Mike breathed a sigh of relief. He had a week, maybe two, to make his confession. If his apologies—and the gift he'd put his heart and soul into—earned her forgiveness that was all he'd need. If they didn't, no amount of time would be enough.

"Just one more picture," Mike called. "One more, in front of Cinderella's castle. Everyone needs that picture."

"Okay." Sophia laughed and posed for Mike in front of the castle while he snapped off a rapid-fire series of shots. She'd hated having her photograph taken since she was fourteen when her first photo appeared in a tabloid.

She'd hated the posing, the smiling and the pretending that were a part of her everyday life. But today, with Mike, she didn't hate it. Having someone she loved and trusted behind the camera lens made all the difference.

So she'd posed with Mickey, Minnie, a handful of dwarfs, and every princess in the Disney collection while Mike snapped photos and made memories. And tonight, she planned to do something even more daring.

Tonight she'd ask him to take some photos of her in seductive poses. In her negligee. In a towel. In nothing at all. She'd seen such photos before in art galleries. The black and white renderings, shadowed and romantic, were evocative rather than exploitive. The ones she and Mike took would be for their private viewing only. And the act of posing nude for him would free her of her fear of photos forever.

"Perfect," Mike said. He stashed the camera back in its bag. "In those last few shots you had a wonderful, dreamy look on your face."

"Like a woman in love?"

"Exactly."

"Then let's head back to our suite so I can show you how much in love I am."

"That's the most tempting offer I've had all day." He brushed a quick kiss across her lips. "Tonight is your night, sweetheart. Anything your heart desires is yours."

"And if I wished for the moon?"

"I'd find a way. Or die trying."

"I don't want the moon," she whispered. "I only want you."

Sophia twined her fingers in his and they strolled to the park entrance. In their days away from work, Mike had relaxed, his earlier tension disappearing. She still caught his occasional, worried looks, but they were less frequent than before.

At other times, his gaze held such tenderness that her breath caught in her throat. When they made love, his attentions to her were sweeter, more open, and somehow tinged with a poignancy that tugged at her heart. But the minute she remarked on any of these things, he disappeared behind a mask of gaiety and teased her about her overactive imagination.

Today, however, he was the relaxed, open man she'd first fallen for. Once the door to their villa closed behind them, he turned to her, eyes twinkling. "Now, didn't you say you had something to show me?"

"Here's a sample." She kissed him, lingering over his lips before slowly moving a fraction of an inch away. "There'll be more after I get out of the shower."

He leaned forward. "How about I help you with that shower?" He captured her lips, preventing a response. She took a step backward. He followed, never breaking the kiss. Step by step, they crossed the room until her progress was blocked by the cool glass door to the walk-in shower. "So," he murmured, pulling away from her lips, "what do you say?"

"Want to join me?"

"I thought you'd never ask."

She fumbled with his shirt buttons while he worked her tank top out of her waistband. They kicked off their shoes, pushing them aside into the space beneath the sink and counter. Clothing flew everywhere until they stumbled into the tiled enclosure still locked in an embrace.

Mike pulled away long enough to turn on the water and adjust the temperature then, with a twist of his wrist, the overhead shower jets came to life, drenching them in water as warm as spring rain.

He claimed her lips again, kissing her with slow thoroughness while the water trickled down her back, off her shoulders, splashing onto the tile floor.

Sophia curled her arms around his back, following the path of the coursing water past his hips to his thighs where she kneaded the tight muscles.

He groaned and pulled away. "You're killing me, sweetheart." He reached blindly for the soap, never taking his eyes off her face. "Keep it up."

"You're doing a good job of that without my help." She reached for him, grasping his erection between her fingers and squeezed.

"Believe me, it's all because of you."

Mike closed his eyes for a minute then gently removed her hand and threaded his fingers through hers. "Let's see if I can return the favor." He slid the soap over her water-slick body, caressing her breasts with the smooth bar, his eyes darkening when she moaned and arched toward him.

He angled her away from the direct stream of water and continued to lather her body, circling the fullness of her breasts first with the soap, then with his thumb. He swept the soap across the undersides, slowly lifting and teasing her before sliding it in long, languid strokes across her stomach.

Disentangling their fingers, he toyed with her nipples with one hand while the other dipped lower until she felt the slide of the soap along her cleft. She cried out as the tip of it nudged her, tweaking her already sensitive flesh.

The soap dropped to the floor with a thud, and he captured the cry with his mouth. Mike ran his soapy hands over her butt, pulling her close, sliding his wet chest across her slick one. The delicious friction of his chest hairs stimulated her hot flesh, and she thrust her tongue into his mouth rewarding his every move.

He responded in kind, then dragged her under the water spray. When he gripped her hips and lifted her against him, she instinctively wrapped her legs around his waist, opening herself wide, inviting his invasion.

He took the invitation, his swift, smooth strokes adding a new friction against her sensitive nub. Cascading water and the sound of her own heartbeat filled her ears. The floral scent of soap mixed with their own musk surrounded them.

Her lover's taste filled her mouth. With each stroke, he stretched and filled her, ratcheting her desire into ever tighter coils. Her body answered, clenching him tightly, slowing his escape, welcoming his return.

When at last her heart beat in rhythm with his strokes, she knew it wasn't just her body but her soul and her heart that strove to capture and hold him. The realization was followed by a flash of pleasure so sharp and clear it bordered on pain.

She closed her eyes and accepted it, relaxing into his embrace, feeling her body pulse in time to his. And as she drifted in the space where body and soul were one, there was only Mike, the warm waterfall, and the passion they shared.

Mike slipped behind Sophia as she stood wrapped in a towel, working a comb through her hair. He planted a kiss on her shoulder and licked the drops of water that lingered there, nibbling his way up to her ear. He watched her expression in the mirror and felt a ridiculous sense of pleasure when her eyes clouded with passion, switching from emerald to stormy jade.

"Why don't I call for room service? We can stay in the rest of the evening." He pressed his hips into her butt, feeling his growing reaction under the towel he'd slung around his waist.

She cupped his cheek in one hand, never taking her eyes off their mirrored reflections. "That would be lovely. But have them deliver it in a couple of hours. I have plans."

"Anything you desire, love."

Mike made his way into the other room and fumbled through the room service directory, his mind more on Sophia than on food. A restless energy edged aside the lovely, sated lethargy he'd felt after the bout of shower sex.

His cock stirred as he imagined peeling the towel from her body and revealing every perfect inch. The moist dusky pink of her mouth teased his imagination, reminding him of the taste of her kisses. He'd start by kissing her slowly, savoring her mouth before—

Before nothing. He slammed the door on his imagination and yanked on a pair of jeans. He didn't deserve her. And he wouldn't touch her again until he'd told her the truth. The stains on his soul couldn't be washed away with a simple shower. They had to be scrubbed with painful truth, purged with confession and acts of contrition.

Behind him, he heard Sophia fussing with the blow dryer. He didn't have much time. He hurriedly ordered the best offerings on the menu from room service then went to the closet and dug through his suitcase.

There, in the bottom, lay a small gift-wrapped box. He pulled it out and put it on the bed. Inside were a couple of flash drives loaded with all the stories he'd ever filed on her.

All the photos he'd ever taken during his years as a journalist. Even the photos he'd taken of her at Morgan's Outpost, laughing in a shower of autumn leaves, or clowning around at the chili cook-off were there. Every byte, every pixel, existed only on those devices. He'd wiped the memory of his computer, erasing her permanently from its drives.

The only place he couldn't erase was his heart. Her smile was engraved there, the lilt of her voice was as much a part of him as his own blood surging in his veins.

The flash drives were a weak offering, a mere pittance against the enormity of his crimes against her, but there was nothing else he could offer. He only hoped she'd forgive him.

He stared at the package, dimly aware that the sounds from the bathroom had stopped. His gut tightened as he heard her soft tread behind him. He clenched his jaw and turned.

God, she was beautiful. Her hair floated in soft waves around her face, accenting the tinge of pink on her elegant cheekbones. Her lips glistened, as if begging to be kissed. The towel, still knotted between her breasts skimmed her luscious body, hinting at its delights even as it hid them.

His mouth went dry.

"Mike? I wanted to ask you for something."

"Anything. I swear. But first I have a confession. I—" He swallowed, trying to ease his parched throat and raspy voice. It didn't work. He closed his eyes and swallowed again. "That is, before I came home to Morgan's Outpost I worked as a journalist. No, that's whitewashing it. I wasn't an actual journalist. I worked digging up—"

Her fingers covered his lips, stilling his confession. "It's all right, Mike. I already know."

"You do?" How could she, when her eyes shone with generosity and love? How could she caress him when she should slap him instead? "How?" he whispered. "How did you find out?"

"Your father told me."

The surprises just kept coming. Dad had known too? He reeled like a drunk in a bar fight, dazed from the haymaker, punch-to-the-gut combo she'd just dished out. He stumbled back a step and sat on the bed, stunned. "I didn't tell him. How did he find out about the *St*—"

"He knew."

Sophia wrapped her arms around his shoulders and cradled his head against her breasts, stroking his hair tenderly. "Your father figured it out a long time ago," she said, her voice soothing his raw conscience. "He knew you were ashamed of your work. But it didn't matter to him. He was proud of you, even when you weren't proud of yourself."

"But the things I did, the lies I told—" His voice was muffled against the towel she wore. "I swear it was supposed to be a temporary job until I could write about real news. I got sucked into the glamour of it all and lost my way. Believe me, I never meant to tell so many lies, to hurt so many people." He looked up. "I never meant to hurt you."

"It's all right. Your father loves you. And I love you. You did what you had to."

He stilled. Somehow, despite everything, the impossible had happened. She knew, and still loved him. Could it really be that easy?

"I'm sorry," he whispered again.

When she simply tightened her hold on him, he soaked in her scent, her warmth, her touch. He was as unworthy of her love as he was of her forgiveness. Yet she gave both, humbling him and filling him with awe at the same time. He vowed he'd earn her love if it took a lifetime of trying. And no matter what, he'd never again betray her trust.

Sophia stretched out on her side, enjoying the feel of the cool bed sheets beneath her naked skin. Mike helped her drape one arm strategically over her breasts and carefully positioned a throw pillow at the junction of her thighs.

"Ready?" he asked, a hint of hesitation in his voice.

"I trust you." It wasn't the direct answer to his question, but it was the answer he'd needed.

As Mike moved around her snapping photos, arranging her in new poses, fiddling with the lighting, props, and camera settings, she marveled at the new closeness between them.

Odd as it sounded, the source of his tension had all been related to his past work at the newspapers. He had been ashamed of the nature of his job. Had he thought she'd hate him because he'd wanted to be a journalist? That she'd judge his efforts and find them wanting?

He'd hesitantly offered her copies of his work, seeming almost embarrassed. Sophia had tucked the box of flash drives away in her luggage with care, treasuring his vulnerability even more than his work.

Then she'd shown him her faith and trust by asking him to take the nude photos.

At first, he'd balked. He'd argued that they could fall into the wrong hands, that she shouldn't trust anyone—not even him—withh such potentially explosive material. But she'd argued that the photos would be private, that she wanted to share them only with him.

He hadn't relented until she shared a story from her past.

After her first public appearances at fourteen, the duke had forced her to sit with him and analyze the newspapers' photos of her. Uncle Julian had scrutinized her posture, the way she held her mouth, her hand gestures, even her hair and dress styles—although he'd selected both.

Over the years, his tutoring made her painfully aware of every nuance or potential imperfection. She practiced her expressions and poses in the mirror until, in the end, she'd felt like nothing more than a plastic doll displayed for public admiration.

"Sophie?" Mike's voice drifted to her from behind the camera. "You're tensing. Don't think about the camera."

She tried to relax, but he'd posed her in an uncomfortable sitting position, draping her in ways that felt unnatural. She suddenly wondered if her hair was out of place. Had her chin dropped? Were her eyes too wide?

"Sophie, sweetheart, look at me." He put the camera down and smiled at her. "You are the most beautiful woman in the world, but your true beauty is inside. Here." He came close and touched her chest, right over her heart.

Mike leaned forward and kissed her, slowly, letting his lips linger over hers until thoughts of the photo session drifted away. She closed her eyes. His breath tickled her lips and she licked them in anticipation.

"Now," he whispered, "just keep thinking of that."

Before she knew it, the camera snapped again, clicking off a series of photos. Mike kept up a light banter, distracting her from the shots.

"When we're done, I'm going to kiss you again. I'll start at your lips and not stop until I reach your toes." Snap. Click. "Of course, I plan to linger in one or two of my favorite spots. Behind your ear. Your throat. Your breasts."

Sophia grew warm, thinking of his lips wandering over her body, pressing moist kisses into her naked flesh. She tingled at the thought and shifted slightly.

Mike chuckled in approval and continued his monologue. She focused on his words, barely aware of the camera, letting her imagination run wild, until his voice became as arousing as his touch. Enticing words swirled around her in a thick baritone, seducing, awakening, tempting, but not satisfying.

She collapsed on the bed with a moan, consumed by feeling, no longer caring what she looked like. When he joined her, matching his actions to the promises in his words, she surrendered to the magic, letting the love in her heart and the passion in her body meld with his until no barriers separated them and no force could tear them apart.

Chapter 33

Mike woke with the late morning sun in his eyes and Sophia's warm body tangled with his. She slept soundly, her head pillowed on his shoulder. For the first time in weeks, his heart was light.

He eased from the bed and started the coffee brewing before he shaved. He quietly gathered up his camera and supplies, careful to remove the SD card with the private photos and store it safely away. He replaced it with a fresh card. Then he gathered the coffee and the papers left outside their door and headed back to the bed. Sophia stirred as he slid back in beside her.

"Good morning, sleepy. I brought you coffee and the daily news."

"Yes, to the coffee. The news can wait. I'm on vacation."

Mike watched as she stretched, the sheet slipping off her breasts, baring them to the morning sun. Life didn't get much better than this. Until she crept out from under the covers and headed to the bathroom, giving him a full view of every delightful inch.

Speaking of inches, he was gaining them by the second as he watched the swish of her butt. Maybe he could convince her to forgo exploring the theme parks and explore him instead. With a sigh of contentment, he leaned against the pillows and scanned the news. Melesia wasn't even on the radar screen for the national press.

The resort press, however, featured the country—and its aristocracy—prominently. It was a reminder of all that lay before them.

Sophia had expressed her desire to petition the king for permission to marry, thus obtaining the blessing of her country. While she'd been willing to renounce her citizenship if need be, Mike had no intension of asking her to do so.

Now that she'd accepted him, past sins included, he knew it was time to make their marriage legal. According to both United States and Melesian law. He looked forward to leaving the specter of Sophie Bradley behind them and to be wed to Sophia de Lyons instead.

When Sophia slipped back into bed, he turned to her with a smile. "If you're homesick, there's a grand opening and reception at the World Showcase Melesian exhibit this afternoon. Some royal dude named Apollo Mikolas is dedicating an aquarium full of exotic fish donated by Melesia."

"Apollo's here?" She wrinkled her brow. "That's odd. He's more into nightclubs than aquariums. I would have thought Stephan would make a presentation like that."

She took a sip of coffee. "Of course, Stephan's too busy badgering me and trying to find his lost girlfriend to worry about his official duties these days."

"What do you mean badgering you? I thought he'd decided to give it a rest after your Christmas Eve interview."

She sighed. "I thought so too, but apparently I was wrong. About a lot of things. It turns out that Stephan's fallen head over heels for Grace Bradley. You know, the girl whose ID I used in the U.S."

"I remember. But what's wrong with Stephan falling in love? I'd think that would be a good thing. Falling in love's done miracles for me."

"You, my love, mellowed." She kissed him. "Stephan, on the other hand, turned into a raging maniac. I've never seen him like this. Around New Year's he started calling again."

Mike's gut tightened at the look of distaste on Sophia's face. Damn, but he hated the way the royal family took advantage of her. He took a breath, trying to calm his instinctive reaction. "What did he want this time?"

"He kept asking me where Grace was. He was fixated on the fact that she and I had communicated over the past year. Somehow he jumped to the conclusion that I was still in touch with her."

"Why didn't you tell me about his calls?"

"Mike, I'm not blind," she said. "You'd been tense and distant. It always seemed to get worse when I mentioned the royal family. I thought," she paused and shrugged. "I thought my status as a Melesian peer bothered you, and I didn't want to rub it in your face."

He sat up and gathered her in his arms. "Nothing about you bothers me. It never has." He placed a kiss on her hair then let her go. "But you're right about the royal family and my reaction to them. I hate the demands they place on you."

"I don't mind most of their demands. Supporting my country and its goals is my job; just like running the pub is yours. But since I met you, I've learned to stand up for my own needs too. I used to dream of falling in love like King Constantine and Jill. I wondered what she had that I lacked."

"You don't lack anything," he insisted.

"But I did." She rose and began dressing. "Until I met you and started working at the pub, I lacked confidence. I'd never stood up for myself and made my needs known, even once, before I left Melesia. And I didn't know that I could stand on my own two feet. Now that I do know, I'll never go back to being a puppet again."

Mike's heart swelled with pride at her hard-won confidence. She'd grown so much in their time together. She'd—Sweet Saint Patrick, she was shimmying into her clothes in a way that made his baser instincts swamp out his noble thoughts.

He watched her slip into a pair of khaki shorts and a deep blue, sleeveless blouse. As her pink lacy thong and matching bra disappeared behind the buttons and zipper, he fantasized about undressing her later tonight.

"The thing I don't understand," he said, forcing his mind back to their conversation, "is why you didn't use some of that newfound confidence of yours to tell Stephan to take a hike."

"I did. More than once. But he was insistent. I got in the habit of cutting him off as soon as I realized it wasn't a matter of national importance."

"Next time he calls, let me talk to him." Mike jumped out of bed, grabbed a pair of jeans and a shirt, and started dressing. "I want to make sure he understands you have a new family now. One who's willing to protect you."

"I doubt he'll call again soon."

Mike snorted.

"Seriously," she said, "after the fight we had when he came to visit, I—"

"He what?" Mike whirled to face Sophia. "He's given up calling only to bother you in person? When did this happen? Why didn't you tell me?"

"Mike, slow down. Yes, Stephan came to the pub. It was a week or so ago. You were out picking up supplies." Sophia put her hands on her hips and glared at him. "In case you're interested, I handled the situation on my own just fine. I told you, I'm my own person now."

"So much so that you had to hide his visit from me?"

"I wasn't aware I had to report my every move to you."

The frosty edge in her voice set off warning bells in his head. Ones he ignored. "Reporting your every move and trusting me with your problems are two very different things."

"My problems with Stephan weren't likely to get resolved by the two of you beating your chests and roaring at one another. As it happens, he brought me some of the family jewels I'd pawned and asked me to give him Grace Bradley's driver's license. He went ballistic when I told him I'd surrendered it when we married."

"I'm surprised he didn't call our marriage into question."

"He did that and more."

Mike sank to the bed, shirt clenched in his fist. "The bastard." His gut churned with suppressed anger, and his muscles twitched, itching for a fight. But it wasn't a fight with Sophia that he needed.

He gritted his teeth and strove for a gentle tone. "I know our marriage isn't really legal. Yet. But it's binding in my heart, and I'll do whatever it takes to make it binding in the law too. Even deal with your cursed royal family."

She laughed. "And you wonder why I hesitate to discuss them with you."

"At times like these, I envy the guys that only have to deal with a mother-in-law. I have a whole royal-family-in-law to please." He grimaced. "Look, why don't you go use the computer in the business center and see about booking us tickets to Melesia? I need to go for a run and burn off some energy. We'll meet back here for lunch, then go to the Melesia Exhibit opening. I promise, I'll play nice with this Apollo guy."

"And in return I'll show you my heartfelt appreciation." She gave him a secret smile.

"Deal."

While Sophia went to slather on sunscreen, Mike hid his camera and gear in a gym bag. He'd ditch the gym bag once Sophia was out of sight and put his plan into action.

He dug in the camera bag until he came up with the press pass Kincaid had supplied for him and put it in his wallet. Then he grabbed the resort flier and scanned it. Prince Stephan D'Malia of Melesia was scheduled for a publicity stunt on the stage at Cinderella's castle at noon.

With luck, there would be press coverage and Mike could use his credentials to get close to the prince. Anger surged in his gut. Mike glanced at the coffee station. Its surface was littered with plastic straws and spoons, nothing that would take the edge off his wild emotions. He tamped them down and prayed for control. Sophia was right about one thing. Fighting Stephan wasn't the way to get what he wanted.

It was time they met face-to-face, however, and settled matters between them. With words. Although he doubted his identity as a *Weekly World Stir* reporter would endear him to the prince. Still…something about the idea of confronting the prince while in the guise of Mack the Pen nagged in his brain.

What had Sophia told him about the royal family's policy toward the press? She'd stressed that they ignored reporters and always would, unless a reporter attacked a member of the royal family. Even then, she'd worried about diplomatic repercussions.

What if… Plans churned as his mind, spinning like the ball in a roulette wheel, bouncing from one idea to another until the chaos settled into a semblance of order. He could, just possibly, kill the two proverbial birds with one stone.

If he were careful, a public confrontation—make that a shouting match—with the prince could wreak enough havoc to make the *Stir* back off Melesian stories for a while. And afterward, with luck, he'd be able to talk to Stephan, man-to-man, about Sophia.

He could do this. Even if it meant public embarrassment. Or swallowing his anger till it burned a hole in his gut. Whatever he had to do, he'd ensure that Sophia was free to live the life she wanted.

Because when it came to protecting the woman he loved, Mike wasn't backing down. Not to the prince, the king, or the entire Melesian army. He wasn't backing down at all.

Sophia paced the room, a knot of worry forming in her gut. Mike should have returned from his run an hour ago. Her stomach rumbled, but she ignored it. Where was he? She'd tried his cell phone once only to learn he'd left it in the room with her.

She paced to the window. Outside, the day was clear and bright, perfect except for the unease that plagued her. When someone knocked on the door she almost sighed with relief.

She cracked the door open. "Hello?"

A uniformed man stood there. "Mrs. Maguire? Hotel records said you and your husband Mike checked in several days ago."

Her heart sank to her toes, but she maintained her poise. "Yes, officer, that's true. Is my husband all right?"

"He's fine, Mrs. Maguire, but I'd like to ask you to come with us."

"Yes, of course." Sophia gathered her things and followed the officer. He led her from the hotel to the parks, taking her through a series of special entrances and passageways until they ended up in a surveillance room beneath Cinderella's castle.

"What is this all about?" Despite her best efforts, her voice shook slightly.

"There's been an incident. The park fears international re-percussions." He flipped a switch and a monitor sprang to life showing Stephan, dressed in full regalia, onstage greeting costumed Disney princesses. In the background a few photographers, sporting cameras with network logos, photographed the event. She spotted a familiar figure among them.

"Oh dear gods, Mike, what have you done?"

She watched in horror as Mike jumped toward Stephan, shouting and swinging his fists. He landed a blow to Stephan's jaw, knocking him into a piece of the set.

Before Stephan could react, a costumed princess grabbed Mike's camera and slapped him. The girl—*oh Zeus!* It wasn't just any girl, Sophia realized. The costumed princess was Grace Bradley. Grace stumbled, then bent and snatched up her shoe, hurling it at Mike.

A swarm of security guards descended, some Melesian, some park guards, and escorted Mike, Grace, and Stephan off stage as a series of colored sparklers erupted from the front of the stage, obscuring the view. Other princesses returned, dancing with partners decked in royal Melesian uniforms, distracting the audience with gaiety and fun.

The officer beside her shut the tape off and turned to her. "As you can see, your husband caused quite an incident. Were you aware of his intentions?"

She shook her head.

"The park generally does not allow news photographers, but as a favor to the Melesian government, they made an exception for this event. Certain members of the press were invited, Mrs. Maguire, however, I can assure you the *Weekly World Stir* was not among those invited."

"The what?" Her heart stopped, and her breathing hitched. It couldn't be. Not Mike.

"The *Weekly World Stir*, Mrs. Maguire. It's one of the sleazier tabloids. They issued your husband's press pass. He's been employed with them since last September according to his most recent contract."

Sophia sucked in a gasp of air, too little to fill her starved lungs. Images of Mike's confessions last night rushed back at her. That's what he'd been trying to tell her? That he worked for the *Stir?* Or had he been hiding that truth, and confessing to a lesser crime? She struggled to find her voice. "Did you say his most recent contract?"

"Yes. According to our search, he's worked for the press on and off for a number of years."

Years. The word stung like a slap. Mike Maguire had worked for the *Stir* for years. Mike. Something clicked in her brain. *Hey, Mack, can you set me up with another drink?* How many times had she overheard that refrain from the bar? Mike, whose friends called him Mack, had worked at the *Stir* for years. As Mack the Pen.

She stared at the officer, her jaw slack, her mind numb. From the first, he'd known who she was. Maguire had led her into a trap. A trap that ended last night with a disk filled with naked photos of her. *Holy Mount Olympus.* She was in over her head.

Beside her, the officer's cell phone rang, and he turned to answer it. After a short conversation, her faced her again.

"You and your husband are very lucky, Mrs. Maguire. The prince has decided not to press charges. However, we will be escorting your husband off premises as soon as he is released. You are welcome to stay."

Sophia stood. She worked her wedding ring loose, tugging at the tight band, feeling as if it were choking her. "No, I won't be staying long. Before you release my hus—" She couldn't say it. She swallowed and called on years of training to hold her composure together. "Before you release Mr. Maguire, I'd like to speak to Prince Stephan."

The officer's eyes widened. "Surely, you don't think the prince would grant an audience to you? He's unavailable, and—"

"If Prince Stephan is unavailable, then summon Lord Apollo Mikolas." She inched her chin higher and fixed him with her most regal gaze. "Tell him Lady Sophia de Lyons requests the honor of his presence."

Mike knew the minute he opened the hotel room door that she was gone. Cool, sterile air swirled around him, as desolate as deepest winter.

When he'd left hours ago, he'd had a plan, a way to confront Stephan about Sophia. But when he finally saw Prince Stephan, plying the crowds with his smiles and false charm, something in Mike had snapped.

His emotions had poured forth in more than words. He'd bounded onto the main stage, punching the air in a flurry of violence. Until Stephan took a step toward him. Then his fist contacted Stephan's jaw and everything changed.

He hated himself for throwing the punch. Hated Stephan for stepping into it.

He'd created a media uproar that dwarfed anything Frank Kincaid and the *Weekly World Stir* could cook up. On the other hand, the media interest was now on him, and perhaps on Prince Stephan, but not on Sophia.

So maybe he'd done something right, after all.

The other reporters at the scene would connect the dots between the *Stir*, Mack the Pen, and Michael Maguire. His rash actions had effectively killed the pen name that had caused Sophia so much pain in the past.

And because one of their reporters—make that a former re-porter—had attacked a Melesian prince on a diplomatic mission, the *Stir* would bend over backwards to ingratiate itself to the Melesian government. No salacious stories on Sophia, or any of them, would appear in its pages for years to come.

He'd accomplished his mission of freeing her forever from the tabloid. His broken heart and shattered soul were a small price to pay for her freedom.

"Mr. Maguire, please pack your things." The uniformed officer's steely voice cut through Mike's ruminations. The security team behind him fanned out around the room, eyes trained on Mike, anxious to finish their job.

He moved woodenly, following their orders without thought. Housekeeping had cleaned the room, taking away even the faint traces of her scent that might have clung to the bed sheets. Everything, every last trace of her, was gone.

He headed to the bathroom to gather his shaving kit. There, lying next to his toothbrush, was the ring. The one he'd given her on their wedding day. He tried to slip it on his pinkie finger, but it didn't go past the first knuckle. Instead, he opened his wallet and put it back in the place where he'd carried it for so long.

He tossed the rest of his things into the suitcase and zipped it closed.

He followed the security team out, loaded his bags into a cab and headed to the airport.

There was nothing left for him here.

For the first time, he wondered if there was anything left for him anywhere.

Chapter 34

The Island Kingdom of Melesia

Sophia slowed her steps and smoothed the hem of her suit jacket. The cobalt blue hue favored her coloring and the severe cut, she hoped, projected seriousness. Confident she looked her best, she turned the corner and headed toward the ornate door where two pages were stationed, like medieval guards.

When she'd arrived home and petitioned the king for an audience, she'd imagined seeing him in his office. Instead, she'd been summoned to the king and queen's private apartments. Unease rippled across her frame, but she dismissed it. She'd always been uneasy around King Constantine. No doubt today, she deserved to be.

As she approached, a page opened the door. Sophia entered the room, and the door closed with a quiet click behind her. Across the room the king helped a pregnant Queen Jillian to her feet before turning to Sophia.

She dropped into a curtsey. "Your Majesties."

They greeted her formally.

Sophia turned toward the king, her posture brittle and erect. She fixed her gaze on the knot of his tie rather than meet his eyes. "Thank you for granting me this audience." She thanked the gods her voice was steady. "I owe you, and all of Melesia, an apology. My reckless behavior has been a disgrace to the country. I am fully aware I have failed in my duty to you, and I bear the responsibility of—"

"Sophia."

The king's voice cut her off. She waited in silence as she studied the gold embroidery in his tie.

"Sophia, look at me." King Constantine stepped closer and placed a hand under her chin, drawing her gaze up. The aqua-blue of his eyes held an unexpected warmth. "*Mi'cochida-ba*, it is I who have failed you. For that, I am truly sorry."

Tears shimmered in her eyes at the gentleness of his voice and the endearment. *Mi'cochida-ba*, a Melesian term for beloved little sister, implied uncommon affection when bestowed upon distant relatives. More affection than her uncle had shown her in all her years with him.

"It was wrong of us—all of us—to allow the duke to isolate you. I thought keeping my distance would lessen your uncle's ambitions, not fuel them. You never should have grown up believing that you were valued solely for your bloodlines and marriage potential."

"Thank you, Your Majesty." This time her voice did waver.

The king wrapped his arm around her shoulders and gave her a smile. "Sophia, we were almost engaged for over half of your life. You needn't be so formal with me."

"Yes, sir," she replied, still uncomfortable using his given name. He led her to the couch where Queen Jillian had returned to her seat. Gods above, this was not what she'd expected from today's interview. Instead of censure, he offered kindness and understanding. She sat, knotting her fingers tightly, hoping she wouldn't break down and cry like a child.

The king sat in a wing chair opposite them and looked thoughtfully at her. "You must know that we were all very worried when you disappeared."

"Yes, sir. I regret causing you concern."

He held up a hand to stop her. "I know what it's like to want to see the world. If you had come to me, I like to think I would have helped you." He leaned forward, elbows balanced on his knees. "I hope in the future you'll give me a chance to help. No one has to shoulder every burden alone."

"I do need your help, sir." She took a deep breath. The worst was to come. "I'm afraid I allowed, that is, there were compromising photos taken that are now in the hands of a journalist."

He was silent for a long while, brow furrowed, lips pressed tightly together. Sophia's stomach lurched as she waited for him to speak. Instead, she felt the queen cover her clenched hands with her palm and give her a little squeeze.

"I think there's more to the story. He wasn't just a journalist, was he, Sophia?"

"No, madam."

"Sweetie, I'd like it very much if you would call me Jill. It wasn't so long ago that I was just like you, a young woman in love with a man I thought I could never have."

At that, the king stirred. He sent his wife a smile full of so much love that it took Sophia's breath away.

"When it comes to matters of the heart, we both had a lot to learn, didn't we, *Ba'hona-mei*?" He turned back to Sophia. "Were you in love with this journalist?"

"I thought so." Pain sliced through her as she thought of the illusion Mike Maguire had created for her to fall in love with, and she wondered if she'd ever seen the real man.

"Did he love you?"

"He used me."

"Are you referring to this?" King Constantine handed her a copy of the *Weekly World Stir* with a prominent headline. *Reclusive Royal Reveals All.*

"Oh my God." Sophia moaned and buried her face in her hands. Her heart shifted like wet sand dragged to the sea by the pounding waves, helpless against the undertow of emotion. She dropped her hands and faced the king, dreading the answer to her next question. "Does it show the photos?"

"The only photos were at least a year old," said Jill. "Nothing in them could hurt you."

"The piece itself is rather benign for the *Stir*," remarked the king. "It does mention that you have a passion for helping children and single parent families as well as a weakness for maple frosted donuts. Neither of which I knew, by the way."

Sophia didn't know how to answer his unspoken question, so she focused on the obvious. "I suppose I should brace myself for the photos to run next week."

"We should plan to retrieve the photos, but I doubt you are in immediate danger of having them exposed." The king handed her a competing tabloid, this one showing Mike in handcuffs. *Secret Reporter's Identity Revealed: Mack the Pen is Dead.*

She turned away and swallowed, hard. Even the grainy black and white photo couldn't vilify his handsome features or stop her instinctive reaction to him.

"Clearly, there are many pieces missing in this puzzle." King Constantine stood and came to help Jill to her feet. Sophia scrambled to join them.

"I think it best," he said "if we start at the beginning. Jill and I would be pleased if you would dine with us. Since we no longer have the luxury of going incognito," he winked at his wife, "we'll have to enjoy your adventures."

For the rest of the evening, Sophia told them the details of her time in Morgan's Outpost, keeping to the facts until the king excused himself. Then, at Jill's urging, she shared the emotional turmoil that she'd suffered.

As the two women talked late into the night, Sophia's burdens lifted. When she returned to her rooms, she locked the past away and determined that she would focus on the future. A future spent alone.

Morgan's Outpost, Colorado

Mike headed to the pub office only to find Destiny seated at the desk looking over the accounts.

"Need any help?"

She shook her head. "Everything's up to date. I'm just transferring some of the older files to electronic versions."

"Oh. Great. Do you need me to pick up any supplies?"

"They've already been delivered. Your dad is at the liquor supplier tasting some wines that Katie and I found yesterday. She wanted his opinion before putting in an order."

Mike digested that. "It looks like *Katie's Corner* is doing a good business."

"Katie's excited about her success." Destiny gave him a thoughtful look. "She's grateful to you for believing in her when she wanted to go back to school. She feels like you put your dreams on hold for her sake. We all do. That's why we're working hard to keep things running here. So you can have a second shot at your journalism career."

"I'm pretty sure that option's gone for good."

Destiny let out an exasperated huff. "Mike, one setback can't kill a career. The only reason to stop chasing your dream is if something else becomes more important. We'll support your decisions. But you have to figure out what you want in life."

"I will. Eventually." He shrugged. "Right now, I'm going for a run to clear my head."

Ten minutes later he was on the road, for the third time today. His feet pounded the pavement, crunching bits of rock salt under his soles. He welcomed the burn of frigid air rushing to his lungs and the labored puffs of steam forcing its way out. His fingers tingled with the cold, and his legs burned with exertion.

Physical pain pushed aside thoughts of the *Stir*'s lawyers with their threats to bankrupt him for breach of contract, slander, and a host of other crimes. He'd be lucky to get out with a dollar to his name.

His family's pity was even worse than the legal scandal. After their initial shock of learning the truth, they had all rallied. Their support was a bitter chaser to an already bad taste in his mouth. He was supposed to be the reliable one. The one who sacrificed to pull them back from the brink of disaster. Sweet Mother Mary! Now his baby sister managed the pub while *his* life spiraled into the sewer.

He picked up the pace, trying to drown out everything except the sound of his feet on the pavement. Eventually, his burning muscles and starved lungs forced him to stop. He gasped for air, sides heaving, then straightened.

Shit. Ahead loomed the site of the new children's recreation center. The one Sophia had championed.

God, he missed her. He missed her laugh, the way she always lit up when he came into a room, the sound of her voice. He even missed the horrible coffee he'd forced down each morning just because she'd made it.

He'd missed her enough to send a stumbling letter of apology trying to explain his side of things to her. When the letter garnered no response, he'd tried again. And again. Until he accepted the inevitable. His apologies weren't enough. He wasn't enough.

He wondered if she found anything about her life with him worth remembering.

Mike headed back to his apartment, moving more slowly now, planning for the future. He needed a decent job—soon. Even so, he refused to sell off another piece of his soul. He'd turned down several lucrative offers to write an unauthorized biography of Lady Sophia de Lyons. Everything he knew of her would stay locked in his mind, and his heart, forever.

When he reached the pub, he ripped off his gloves and grabbed the mail. Katie waved to him when he passed the kitchen. In the dining room, the girls looked up from their homework, regarding him with sad eyes.

"We miss Aunt Sophie," said Miss Manners.

"Yeah. When is she coming back? I want her to come back!" All three expressed their discontent in a jumble of voices.

"I miss her, too, but I can't make her come back."

"Did you even ask her to?" Mary Margaret pinned him with a stare.

"It's not that simple," he began.

"That's what I thought. You didn't ask her." She turned back to her homework.

He had sent letters, he thought resentfully. But what if they'd been tossed by some royal aide? How did he know they'd even reached her? Mike shook his head. He should have tried harder.

His niece was right. At least one person in his family knew exactly where to lay the blame. Mike sighed and headed to his apartment, shuffling through the mail as he climbed the stairs.

A letter from his lawyer with news he wouldn't like.

Letters from publishing houses with offers he didn't want.

A thick, official looking envelop from— Melesia.

His heart sped up and the other letters tumbled to the ground. Maybe she'd written to him after all. Forgiven him.

Decided to give him another chance. He tore at the seal and pulled out the single typed sheet.

Dear Mr. Maguire,

We have been informed that you are in possession of private photographs that are the property of Her Grace, Sophia, Duchess de Lyons. The crown is prepared to offer you the sum of 1.5 million U.S. dollars for the return of the original photos and the destruction of all copies.

Please travel to Melesia at your earliest convenience. We will arrange for your accommodations and the timely transfer of the aforementioned photos.

Mike scanned the rest of the official language, pausing at the royal family crest that stood in place of a signature. He crumpled the letter in his fist.

So, they'd made her a duchess, had they? What other ways were they going to use her to further their own political agenda? Clearly, they'd forced her to reveal intimate details of her life—like the existence of the photos. Did they think it added to their leverage over her? And what made them think they could bribe him into compliance with their wishes?

He'd head to Melesia all right. But he wasn't going to surrender the photos for a mere 1.5 million dollars. He had another price in mind. One that would leave the royal family of Melesia at his mercy.

Chapter 35

ike shouldered his duffel bag, presented his documents to the Melesian passport control officer and walked straight into the custody of a security detail. With polite efficiency they escorted him to Royal Island and left him waiting in a luxurious suite of rooms.

With guards at the door.

For three days.

He paced the rooms. This comfortable confinement chaffed, rubbing his patience raw. He wanted the coming confrontation over with. So he could go home to the pitiful remains of his life.

It was a relief to be summoned to an audience with the king. Mike took his time dressing, deliberately slowing his movements to avoid looking anxious. He slipped on a suit jacket and pocketed both the media cards and his list of demands. He'd been tempted to wear jeans and a tee shirt to the appointment but decided he'd have a better chance of getting what he wanted if he played by the unspoken rules.

He accompanied the plain-clothes guards through the private living areas of the palace. The wide corridors could easily allow a troop of soldiers to pass should they be needed to defend the occupants. Occasionally they passed a student worker making up rooms or running errands.

In the public areas of the palace warm, plastered walls gave way to cool marble. They passed the grand entrance with its floor-to-ceiling aquarium, the rotunda with the queen's shopping gallery, and some fifteen minutes after they left his rooms, arrived at the door to the king's office.

A liveried doorman opened the door and indicated Mike should enter. The guards remained outside. Inside, ancient stone walls were whitewashed, reflecting the sunlight that poured through the narrow-mullioned glass windows that lined the seaward wall of the office.

King Constantine sat with his back to the windows regarding Mike with a quiet interest. Mike had seen him before, even photographed him dozens of times. Up close the king exuded a controlled power and leashed energy. A wise man wouldn't make an enemy of him.

But when it came to Sophia, Mike wasn't wise. He'd been a fool when he'd lured her into his life and a besotted fool when he let her into his heart. And he couldn't regret any of it. Not even proposing his story to the *Stir* in the first place. Because if he hadn't, he'd have bundled her off to the train station without ever having known her.

He'd already lost his career, his reputation, and his family's respect because of her. But whatever else he might lose today, he couldn't lose the negotiation with this man. Not if he wanted to assure Sophia's future.

With her firmly fixed in his mind, he approached the desk.

"Mr. Maguire. Please, be seated." The king motioned to a chair. "I hope you've been treated well during your visit."

"Better than most prisoners, I imagine," Mike said, striving to match the king's bland tone.

"That's a bit of an exaggeration. You've been free to move about the island as you liked."

"With my jailor trailing behind?" In fact, he hadn't even considered he'd be allowed to leave the rooms. But having started the verbal sparring he saw no need to back pedal.

"Bodyguards are a way of life for many of us, Mr. Maguire. How you choose to view them is, of course, entirely your decision."

"And I thought I was a master at twisting words," Mike replied dryly.

Constantine regarded him in silence for a moment. Mike instinctively counted to ten, then fifteen before realizing he'd met his match. Five more seconds ticked by.

The king broke the silence. "Did you bring the photos?"

"I have them right here." Mike pulled the media out of his pocket. He smirked slightly. "You'll have to trust me when I tell you there are no copies."

The king nodded. "If you'll give me the media and your bank account number, I'll see that the funds we discussed are transferred immediately."

"Not good enough." Mike slipped the case back into his pocket and pulled out an envelope. "What I want, everything I want, is in here. Sign this agreement in return for the photos." He tossed it onto the desk.

The king took the document and read, brow furrowing in concentration. Silence blanketed the room, broken only by the distant pounding of the surf on the beach.

The sound of scurrying feet and childish laughter echoed in the hallway, growing close then fading away again. Just as his nieces' laughter had faded away when Sophia left. He shoved the memory away and watched the king.

Eventually Constantine put down the documents and pinned Mike with a stare. "Let me get this straight. You want me to agree not to force Sophia into a political marriage or other arrangement without her consent?"

"Yes."

"In other words, you want to assure she's free to marry for love?"

"Right again."

"To you?"

Mike flinched then set his jaw. "I think we already know that option ended in disaster."

Constantine nodded, still searching Mike's face. The silence descended again. "That's a bold demand for someone who just made 1.5 million dollars on a few photos."

"You really don't get it, do you? I don't want your money." Mike stood. "The pictures are not for sale. Agreeing to that contract is the only way to get them." He turned to the door.

"Maguire. Sit."

Mike turned back to the king but remained standing. He watched as the king signed the document with a flourish and stamped it with the royal seal.

Constantine stood and handed the papers to Mike. "You do realize that document isn't legally binding. You'll have to trust me." The smile he flashed was cold. "Now, give me the pictures."

This time Mike didn't flinch. "I'll hand the pictures personally to Sophia. Then we'll be done."

"She doesn't want to see you."

"She'll see me, or there's no deal." Mike waited a moment, then turned to the door again. He'd almost reached it when the king's voice stopped him.

"The guards outside could forcibly take the photos from you. You are in my country now. On top of that, you assaulted a member of the royal family. So far, we've been lenient with you. And yet you continue to make demands as if you had every right to do so. What I want to know is why." He rounded the desk and moved a few steps to the door.

Mike met him halfway. Tension crackled between the two men and Mike fought to keep his fingers from curling into fists.

"Those photos are the private property of Sophia. The only way I can be sure no one else sees them is to hand them directly to her. For what it's worth, I haven't looked at them, either. I don't care if you believe me or not."

"Why go to all this trouble? Why risk coming here at all?"

"Because I'm a fool. A fool who's in love with a woman he can't have and doesn't deserve. I've hurt her. And the least I can do before I go is to make sure that no one else ever hurts her again." He held the king's gaze for a long moment.

"Better to be a fool in love than a complete idiot who lets it slip thorough his fingers," the king said, a genuine smile lighting his face now. "I'll send word once she agrees to see you."

With those enigmatic words, Mike found himself dismissed and in the hands of the guards once again.

Though the royal palace was many times larger than the de Lyons estate, Sophia felt at home there. Perhaps her memories of a rigidly choreographed childhood haunted the estate's halls. Or perhaps its vast emptiness kept her away.

In any case, she'd gratefully accepted when the king had offered her rooms and offices at the palace. Here, she'd been swept into the family, debating with Jill over the décor for the nursery, helping Gracie plan for her royal wedding to Stephan, and getting to know Constantine.

Just as she'd been swept into Mike's family. Her heart twisted at the loss of them. She forced herself to concentrate on the documents of incorporation for the Hercules foundation.

Instead, her mind wandered to the strange change in her relationship with the king. She pushed the paperwork aside and moved to the settee, thoughtfully sorting through fabric and wallpaper swatches that covered the surface.

For years, Constantine had been an unavoidable, unwanted duty looming over her future. But now he was a trusted advisor, supporter, and friend, leading her through the maze of duties required of a new duchess. Had she changed or had he?

Almost as if her thoughts had summoned him, the guard at her door announced the king. She shoved aside the book of fabric samples in her lap and rose from the settee as he strode into the office. "Your Majesty."

"Your Grace," he answered, a hint of laughter simmering beneath his serious tone.

Although he'd invited her to use his given name on several occasions, Sophia had been slow to shake the formality and deference her uncle had drilled into her. By the time she'd assumed the title of Duchess de Lyons, Constantine had found the means to crack her resistance. Every deferent *Your Majesty* was returned with a grave, polite *Your Grace*, until she'd finally relented.

Today, she simply smiled at him and cleared fabric from a chair before inviting him to sit. "It's an unexpected pleasure to see you this afternoon, Constantine."

He plucked a swatch from a pile on the low table in front of the settee. "I take it from the pattern of tiny ducks in raincoats that you are still helping Jill pick nursery decorations?"

"Actually, no. These are for some of the playrooms in the Hercules House."

"Ah. The newest project in the Labors of Love Foundation charter? Don't you think you should incorporate, set up a board of directors and plan a budget before picking out wallpaper?"

"Of course, I should. I just needed a break from the paperwork. The swatches were already here, and— None of this pertains to why you're visiting me today."

"Gods, no. If you'd asked me to help with this kind of task, I'd have called an emergency meeting of the Council of Nobles just to avoid it."

"And I used to think such meetings were only for important matters of state." When he didn't laugh or respond, she looked more closely. Frown lines bracketed his eyes, turning him serious.

"Are there urgent matters of state? Or family problems? Is Jill all right?"

That roused him. "Everything is fine with both the state and my family. I came to see you about another matter."

She waited.

"Maguire is here."

Sophia's stomach lurched, cramping as a rush of tension whipped through her body. "Did he bring the photos?"

Constantine nodded. "He did, but he refused to leave them with me. He insists on giving them to you in person."

"Give him more money to convince him otherwise. I'm sure he has his price." She busied herself stacking fabric swatches and closing the pattern books. Anything to avoid thinking about Mike.

"He certainly ought to. My sources indicate he's up to his neck in lawsuits and attorney fees."

Alarm shot through her. "Is his family or their business in trouble?"

"No, not the business or his family. Just him. He's being sued by the *Weekly World Stir* for damages. It's ironic."

"So what are his terms?"

"That, *mi-cochida*, is where things get interesting. He refused to give up the photos unless I signed a document promising never to make you marry for political reasons. He wants to assure any marriage you make is one of your choosing."

"And what else? He gets the exclusive right to cover the love story?"

"Nothing else. Just a contract promising you'll be free to choose your own future. With the caveat that he hand you the photos in person, so that there is no doubt they have been returned to you unviewed."

She pondered that. A traitorous warmth tugged at her heart. This was how the man she'd once trusted should behave.

"Sophia, let me tell you something. Not as an advisor or king but as a man. We do stupid things. The most stupid of all are the things we do around the women we love. I nearly lost Jill because I thought love and duty were mutually exclusive. Even when I'd decided she was the only one for me, I waited until too late to tell her."

He rose and paced the length of the room, mussing his hair as he dragged his fingers through it. "Two years ago, I nearly proposed to you out of a sense of duty and honor. You would have accepted for the same reasons. Back then, I was an arrogant ass, and you were a frightened mouse. It would have been a disaster."

"You were a good man. I just couldn't see it."

He shook his head. "I was a good prince. I became a good man when I fell in love. There's a difference. You were a dutiful child. You've grown into a competent woman."

"Not because I fell in love."

"Maybe, maybe not." He shrugged and returned to his chair. "My point is I did stupid things for good, or at least logical, reasons. I almost lost my chance at happiness because of it. All men do stupid things, especially men in love.

"I pushed Maguire, today. Pushed him hard. He stood up to me, even when I made it clear he was at my mercy. The one reason—the only reason—he did it, was for you. The man's in love with you." Constantine took her hands in his. "You owe it to yourself to hear him out. When you do, listen—and respond—with your heart."

It was too much to hear, too fast. She pulled her hands away. "Is that an order, Your Majesty?"

A ghost of a smile lit his face. "It's the voice of experience. And as one whose name means wisdom, I suggest you learn from it, Sophia." He rose to leave.

"I'll send for Mr. Maguire tomorrow morning," she said to his retreating back. "I want to hear his side of the story."

Chapter 36

At nine o'clock the next morning, Sophia sat at her desk, outwardly calm, but with a racing heart. She'd finished the documents of incorporation for the Hercules Foundation and cleared away the accounts for the de Lyons estates. Now she stared blankly at a contract—for what, she couldn't say. But it gave her something to do while she waited.

She put on her most impassive face, the one she'd always used when dealing with the press. She didn't want him to be able to read the vulnerability in her expression. Not today.

The sound of guards moving outside her door alerted her to his arrival. "Her Grace will see you now," she heard them say. Then they opened the door and announced him.

Mike walked into the room, steps sure as always, but she sensed a hesitancy. His suit hung loosely on his frame, unfitted, as if he'd lost weight. Even from a distance, she could see the haggard look to his perfectly groomed appearance. He bowed, an awkward movement for an American.

"It's good to see you, Sophia. I mean, Your Grace." He walked as far as the chair in front of her desk, but instead of sitting he stood behind it, hands resting on the curved leather back.

"It's ironic," he said. "When I first met you, I thought your name was Grace. It fit." The softness in his eyes was at war with the stiffness in his voice.

"We both know you weren't under that impression for long, Mr. Maguire." He recoiled at her formality. "When exactly did you realize my true identity?"

He didn't answer. He just stood there, one hand gripping the chair until his knuckles turned white, the fingertips of his other hand running along the brass studs imbedded in the leather. "Do you know why I gave up my job as a reporter for the *Weekly World Stir?*"

"Because you assaulted Prince Stephan and nearly ended up in prison?" Her lips twitched, but she compressed them tightly.

"No." He shook his head, his own lips curving ever so slightly in response to her slip. "I meant why I quit the first time. I left the job because I'd grown tired of twisting the truth. Because I'd come to respect your royal family over the years. When I stopped seeing them as icons and began seeing them as human. I saw people with integrity. People who were more like the man I wanted to be."

"That's hard to believe, given how easily you decided to manipulate me."

He let go of the chair back and moved to sit in it instead.

It was only inches closer than he'd been before, but it struck her like a physical blow, taking her breath away. She dropped her eyes to the contract in front of her, ignoring him until her breathing returned to normal.

"You were always so perfect," he said, his voice soft and tempting.

She looked up before she could stop herself.

"You floated above everything, never showing any emotion. It was as if you were carved from ice, or marble. It was easy to mistake that aloofness for condescension."

He leaned forward, obliterating another few inches of her breathing room, chipping away at the emotional distance she'd worked so hard to establish.

"My family was in trouble, Sophia. We were one late payment away from losing the business. When the *Stir* called and asked for a piece, all I could see were the girls, Katie, and the people who depended on the pub staying in business so they could feed their families."

"So, exploiting me was the noble choice? Pardon me if I don't believe that."

He leaned back, whether from the aristocratic frostiness of her tone or his own conscience, she didn't know.

"It wasn't you, Sophia. It was never you. It was the icon that you created. And no, I don't expect you to believe it was noble. It was self-serving from the start. But I thought I could control things and create a story that wasn't an exaggerated lie. I tried as hard as I could to be fair. Not to hurt you. Clearly, I failed."

"Yes. *Reclusive Royal Reveals All.* That title put me front and center on the world stage again. You had to know how I felt, especially given the intimate photos you had in your possession."

"Would you have rather seen the headline *Lady de Lyons' Secret Love Child Revealed?*"

"That's low, Mike. Even for you."

Mike felt a stab of guilt as he watched the blood drain from her face in response to his harsh tone. Yet he also felt hope. She'd dropped the icy manner for a second, allowing him to see the Sophia he loved.

In that second, his goals shifted. He still knew there was no future for them, but he couldn't leave letting her think it was all a scam. He had to leave her with the knowledge that what they'd shared—the important parts least—was real.

"I'm sorry," he said, hoping she could hear the sincerity in his voice. "But surely you know how these things work. No one had seen Sophia de Lyons for weeks. And when your radio interview asked that you be left in private, every tabloid on earth was desperate for a glimpse of you. If I hadn't filed my story, that was exactly the headline they'd have run. It was already queued up for production."

"Dear God." Her face became even paler, almost as pale as when she'd passed out in his arms after their first kiss.

"I'm sorry," he whispered again. He leaned close, closing the distance between them. "I know it hurts. And I don't expect your forgiveness." How could he, when all his story had done was try to put a bandage on a wound too deep to heal? "But I want you to know, I stopped thinking of you as an icon a long time ago."

He stood and put the media cards of photos on her desk, his gaze locked on her eyes. "None of our time together was about the story. Not really. I," he swallowed, the movement of his Adam's apple painful, "I liked being with you. I wanted you to stay because I…cared…about you. Unfortunately, I'd already made my deal with the devil. I'm just sorry that you had to pay part of the price."

He wanted to shove her desk aside and pull her out of the chair into his arms. He wanted to tell her he loved her. He wanted to erase the recent past and return to the bubble of happiness they'd shared. But he had no right to do any of that. Instead, he let the image of her sear his mind, burning it into his memory before dropping his gaze.

"If there's nothing further, Your Grace, I believe there's a plane waiting to take me stateside." He headed to the door, every step heavy. He reached for the handle, feeling the cold brass under his fingers.

"There is just one more thing, Mr. Maguire."

Her voice was close behind him, as if she'd followed him. He turned, not knowing what to expect and came face-to-face with her. "One more thing?"

She nodded. "I still love you."

The words slammed into him, releasing a torrent of dammed-up emotion that thundered through his body and soul. "I've never stopped loving you," he replied.

And then she was in his arms, though who moved first he couldn't say. She tasted like honey, washing away the salty taste of regret in his own mouth as she kissed him deeply. And—blessed Saint Mary some things never changed—she worked her cold hands beneath his shirt, skin-to-skin, and pulled him close.

He tore his lips from hers and kissed his way up her neck to her ear. "I don't deserve you," he whispered between kisses. "I'm a penniless writer without a single prospect. A former tabloid reporter without scruples. But I can be more. I want to be more. Will you give me a chance?"

"Lucky for you I'm a rich duchess with a need for a biographer. And a knack for seeing the best of people in the worst of circumstances."

"Then will you marry me? For real, this time?"

"For real and forever."

And then there were no more words, no more need. Only two lost people who found themselves in each other. And the best was yet to come...

Read My Lips

Riches & Royals
Excerpt

Chapter 1

Clayton Arthur McClaine glanced out the darkened limousine window one last time. No one was watching. He turned to his driver. "O'Shea, you'd better be right about the disguise. If the paparazzi get wind of this, they'll have a field day."

"I've watched your back since third grade, boss. You'd think after the first twenty years or so, you'd start to trust me."

"If I didn't, Jimmy, you wouldn't be here."

Jimmy shifted in the seat, stripping off his sunglasses and looking him in the eye. "Clay, you don't have to do this. We've managed just fine until now."

"I can't keep counting on you to cover for me. Unless you want to give up your role as silent investor and move into the executive suite, I have to do this."

"I told you before, I like driving the cars, not sitting in the back. You've always been the public face of the corporation. I don't like the limelight. But that don't mean you have to risk being seen. We've done fine. No one suspects anything."

"Right. Nobody suspects anything. Yet. But someday they might. It's a risk I'm no longer willing to take. I don't like putting our business in jeopardy, Jimmy. This deal could triple our distribution network and open the European markets, but if I blow it, Milford Johnson will have the opportunity to bleed the corporation dry. He goes after weakness like a shark after blood."

"So do you. What's the problem?"

Clayton rubbed his temples, wishing he could find another way around the dilemma. "Johnson senses something. He's insisted on closed-door negotiations. Just the two of us."

"He doesn't expect you to sign a contract without your lawyer reviewing it."

"No, but a last-minute addendum could change everything. I won't have the luxury of funneling that paper through you or my secretary." Milford Johnson was sharp. There would be last-minute alterations to the contract.

"I guess even a photographic memory has limitations."

"Phonographic, Jimmy. In my case, it's phonographic. I remember everything I hear."

"Whatever." Jimmy turned from him and flipped open a thin newspaper.

"What's that? The masthead looks like the Huntersville Daily Press."

Jimmy grunted. "Unlike you, I try to keep up with what's going on in the hometown."

"Since when?"

"Since now. A man's got to have something to do besides chauffeur his best friend around and help him sneak into places he should be walking into, head held high. Besides, neither of us knows how long you'll be gone. I'll sit tight and wait till you're finished."

Clayton hesitated, wondering if the rewards justified the risk.

"Don't you have an appointment to keep, boss?"

Clayton grimaced from the edge in Jimmy's voice then focused his attention on the matters at hand. He slipped from his warm limousine into the dank chill of the parking deck. Giving Jimmy a last cocky grin, he huddled into the frayed, plaid wool coat and pulled his ball cap lower over his eyes. "Wish me luck."

He jogged down the stairs of the garage and headed to the street. A gust of wind pierced his thin trousers and flimsy tennis shoes. *Damn. April in Chicago is just as cold and rainy as it is in Huntersville.*

But he'd grown from a scrawny kid going to work at the poultry farms and slaughterhouse into a man who had beaten the odds more times than he could count. He neared the small store-front office at the end of the block and steeled himself to meet the next challenge. And win.

A muted chime sounded when he pushed open the door. He glanced around the room, taking in the comfortable armchairs, mismatched couches, and scattered tables. Brightly colored toys spilling from a basket in a haphazard heap dominated one corner. Books and magazines littered almost every horizontal surface.

Across the room, two women sat side by side at a small round table. The younger woman excused herself and walked toward him, brushing a strand of light brown hair behind her ear as she crossed the room. The gentle sway of her hips and the hint of soft curves beneath her lightweight sweater almost made him forget why he'd come here.

It had been a long time since he'd been attracted to a woman. It had been even longer since he'd been in the company of a simple, unassuming one. Someone who wasn't trying to snag the title of Mrs. McClaine like it was a prize at the county fair.

A rush of nervous anticipation, the kind he hadn't felt since his high school days, flooded his senses. He didn't like the nervousness or the memories it evoked.

"Hi," she said, extending her hand. "I'm Claire Lennox. Welcome to the McClaine Literacy Clinic."

He forced his gaze away from her body and focused on her mouth, studying her small, perfectly white teeth and her pink, slightly chapped lips, rather than meeting her eyes. He shook her hand, swallowing his fear like a man downs a shot of whiskey, letting it burn into oblivion in his clenched stomach.

He raised his eyes. So help him, if he saw an ounce of pity or a flicker of recognition on her face, he'd be out the door before she could blink.

All he saw were innocent, brown eyes and her little, welcoming smile. He shifted his weight onto the balls of his feet and tensed, locking his gaze on her. No sense sugarcoating his condition with a fancy label. He was a bottom-line man. "I can't read. Much." He threw the words at her like a gauntlet and braced to meet her response.

"That's why the clinic is here. I'm glad you trust us to work with you. Unfortunately, my assistant is out for the day," she said, still smiling and looking as pleasant as if he'd said nothing more surprising than good afternoon.

"I'm working with Mrs. Jablonski right now, but if you could wait a few minutes, I'd be happy to give you my full attention. There's a video about the clinic if you'd like to watch." She motioned to a small TV near a well-worn couch. "Have a seat, Mr. …"

"Artie," he muttered, the urge to fight draining from him. "Artie McC— Michaels. Artie Michaels."

She nodded. "I'll be with you soon, Mr. Michaels."

He slumped in a chair. Only ten minutes into the venture and he'd almost blown it.

"Clayton Arthur McClaine." He tensed at the sound of his name, spoken in a soft, hesitant Polish accent.

"Wait. You're not planning to read that article from *People* magazine today, are you, Mrs. Jablonski?"

Even though his back was to the women, he could picture Claire Lennox moistening her lips and leaning toward the older woman as she spoke, that troublesome lock of honey-brown hair falling across her cheek.

The knot in his gut eased slightly for the first time since he'd come up with the plan. Jimmy's suggestions about how to avoid the press just might work.

"Have you seen, Miss Lennox? You must be up with the birds to get the early copy. By noon, the newsstand, she was already sold out. I can not blame you for wanting to get your hands on 'America's Ten Most Wanted Bachelors.' Especially since Mr. Clayton Arthur McClaine of Chicago is bachelor number one."

Excitement caused her accent to thicken and blur. "Look at this picture of him. He looks like such a nice, young man with beautiful, thick hair, and a good strong jaw. Handsome like, like... evil."

"Do you mean 'handsome as sin'?"

"Yes. Sin. Handsome like sin. Look at his office—bigger than this whole clinic. Wasteful. What that man needs is..."

"Let's skip the photos and focus on the words for today, Mrs. J."

He heard the scrape of a chair and the rustle of magazine pages punctuated by the older woman's sigh. Clayton forced his tight body to relax. *People see what they want to see.*

He concentrated on keeping his shoulders slumped and his cap low over his eyes. *Behave like a factory worker, and that's what she'll see.* He strained to hear Mrs. J's monologue, but kept his gaze focused on the dirty tennis shoes of his disguise.

Clayton weighed his reasons to stay against his desire to go. Too much was at stake. The deal with Johnson opened the European markets. But with knowledge of his private struggle with dyslexia, a manipulator like Johnson could make him look like a fool, embarrass and, perhaps, even discredit him in the eyes of the business community. He had to do this now, before someone discovered his secret and exposed him as a fraud.

But there was more to it than just that. Even his reason for being here was a fraud. He reached inside his thin coat, feeling for the letter he'd carried with him since the day he'd settled his mother's estate last fall. This was the real reason that drove him to the clinic.

The negotiations were a smoke screen. Handling his investors, including Johnson—and even the public—would be tricky, but not impossible. He'd handled scores of business deals on his way to the top.

He caressed the battered envelope, the wrinkles and creases of the once-crisp paper, a silent testimony to the times he'd tried to read his mother's last thoughts. He had no doubt that she'd poured her heart onto these pages. She'd been a lover of books and letters. She'd want her last message to him to be more permanent than a phone call. So she'd put it into words. Words he couldn't read. Words he didn't want anyone else to read for him.

Words.

The one thing he couldn't conquer.

"'Clayton Arthur McClaine knows what it takes to make a woman happy.'" The soft Polish voice spoke in a careful cadence, pulling him back to the present. "'Chocolate. McClaine, founder of the Fantasy Fudge Gourmet Chocolate Company, tooted...'"

"Touted," corrected Claire quietly.

"'...touted as *the stuff dreams are made of* is himself the stuff of dreams. The thirty-four-year-old, self-made billionaire transformed a simple chocolate recipe into the McClaine Industries empire. In the process, he transformed himself from a Huntersville, Iowa,'" she paused. "What's this word, Miss Lennox?"

"Pauper. It means a poor man."

"Paw-per. Paw-per." Mrs. J mouthed the word several times. Clayton tensed with each syllable as if she were peeling away his disguise and exposing him.

"Very good, Mrs. J. Can you read a bit more?" Claire's voice broke the spell, and Clayton breathed a sigh of relief.

"'In the process, he transformed himself from a Huntersville, Iowa, paw-per into a sought-after prince of industry. McClaine credits his… his… phe-nom-en-al,'" she paused.

"That's great work. Sounding out the letters almost always works with new words. Go on."

"'…phenomenal success to hard work, honesty, and integrity, but we think there's more to it than that. Chocolate, to be sure. But there's also those darkly handsome good looks, the James Bond sense of style, an easy smile, and those mysterious eyes. As we said earlier—he knows what it takes to make a woman happy.

"'So, what kind of woman does this perfect-ten fantasy man dream of? That secret is as closely guarded as the recipe for his famous fudge sauce. Still, something about the way his eyes twinkle when he smiles makes you believe, just for a moment, you may be the one.'" Mrs. J. stopped and sighed. "Does that not make you just want to melt, Miss Lennox? Deep down, every woman wants a man like that."

"I'm sure lots of women fantasize about their dream man, but I prefer watching the pleasure you get from reading."

"I know, that's your way of telling me to finish reading my piece. All right, then."

Clayton fought the urge to turn around as he listened to the crinkle of magazine pages followed by Mrs. J's soft voice.

"'The combination of money, chocolate, and toe-curling sex appeal make Clayton Arthur McClaine our ir-re-sis-ti-ble… irresistible,'" she repeated with motherly warmth, "'top pick for bachelor of the year. Heck, we'd probably love him even without the billions.'"

"Very good."

"So what you think, Miss Lennox?"

"Your reading is really improving. I'm proud of the progress you're making."

"No, no, no. What you think of Mr. McClaine?"

Claire laughed, a musical, lilting sound. Clayton smiled in spite of himself.

"I don't think about Mr. McClaine one way or the other."

Clayton's smile turned into a frown. He squared his shoulders and started to rise, only remembering at the last second that he was supposed to be an invisible factory worker. He slumped back in the chair and looked over his shoulder. They hadn't noticed.

"But you work for him, don't you, Miss Lennox? This is Mr. McClaine's clinic, no?"

"McClaine Industries sponsors the clinic, but I've never met him personally. It's a large company and the executives in the main office keep to themselves." Claire and Mrs. Jablonski rustled past him and headed to the door.

"You still have chance," the older woman said, "to meet him. See, here is the list telling where to meet the bachelors. Mr. McClaine, he throws big party every June to raise money for clinic. You should get invitation. You run clinic.

"Such a shame, man like Mr. McClaine and no wife. And you, Miss Lennox. You should be home, teaching babies to read. You make wonderful mother. Here," she shoved the magazine toward Claire. "Look good at those pictures. Get yourself invitation to big, wonderful party. You be surprised what can happen."

Claire shook her head. "Mrs. Jablonski, why don't you keep the magazine. Every client today has read me that article. Believe me, I've got Mr. McClaine's biography and vital statistics memorized."

"Well… You are sure?" Mrs. J. shoved the magazine into her overstuffed canvas handbag and checked her watch. "Late, late, late. As usual, you spend more time with me than you should. I must hurry to catch next bus or Mr. Jablonski, he will faint from hunger while he waits for his supper. I will see you next week. Good-bye, Miss Lennox. Think about McClaine party in June," she called as she walked away.

Claire sagged against the door. "Save me from matchmaking clients," she muttered.

Clayton cleared his throat.

"Oh, my goodness." Claire spun around, her cheeks flushing a tantalizing shade of pink. "Mr. Michaels, I didn't mean for you to hear that."

"Don't worry, Miss Lennox." He smiled for the second time since he stepped through the door. She looked adorable when she was flustered. "I don't intend to play matchmaker." *Unless I'm playing for myself.*

"Thank goodness. One more word about Mr. Clayton Arthur McClaine and I think I'll scream. That's all anyone's talked about all day. I've had his picture shoved under my nose so many times, I'll probably imagine his face on everyone I meet for the next week."

He deliberately pushed the ball cap back on his head and stared at her, tempting fate, but despite her words, no flicker of recognition lit her eyes.

"Let's just go over here and I'll tell you a bit more about the clinic." She directed him toward a table and opened a glossy picture book as she chattered about the clinic's mission. Her eyes sparkled and her hands practically danced, punctuating her dialogue with graceful gestures.

Words might be a jumble to him, but he could read people. Claire, with her unpretentious enthusiasm, was no challenge at all. He'd also perfected the art of sending messages to people with his own carefully scripted body language. Once, he'd been a nobody, pretending to be a successful businessman. Now, he was a success, pretending to be a nobody.

Except in Claire's company, the unexpected happened. It was written all over her face, in her eyes, and in the way she leaned toward him and cocked her head when she spoke. To her, he was anonymous, but he wasn't a nobody. His smile deepened. Learning to read from Miss Claire Lennox might not be painful after all. In fact, it might even be pleasant. For the first time in months, he relaxed.

AUTHOR'S NOTE

Simply put, I think of *Counterfeit Commoner* as a mash up of the old movies *It Happened One Night* and *Roman Holiday*. Yes, I'm dating myself with the references, but an entertaining story is an entertaining story, even if it is an old black & white film.

But as I crafted *Counterfeit Commoner*, it grew into so much more.

One of the most powerful aspects of fiction (in my mind, at least) is its ability to transport the reader into the very skin of another person, letting them see the world through someone else's eyes. I love interconnected stories that show the world from different points of view. (As an aside, author Gregory Maguire is a master at taking a story you thought you knew and turning it on its ear. From classic fairy tales to works that inspired the Broadway play *Wicked*, he challenges the reader/viewer to see the world through the eyes of someone unexpected.)

Back to Sophia's story. When you first meet her in *Royally Scandalized*, she's nothing more than a pawn, without substance. In *Reluctantly Royal*, she begins to find herself, but if I'm being honest, she comes off as a bit of a…well, a bully. At least when you view her from the outside. When you understand her motivations, however, she is much more sympathetic.

As I plotted her story, I challenged myself to use the same timeline as the events in *Reluctantly Royal*, including several identical scenes. If you compare scenes that appear in both books, they should have *exactly* the same words and settings, but very different emotions. It was a challenge as a writer to keep this consistency yet allow you, the reader, to immerse yourself in a completely different story.

I hope you enjoy Sophia's journey and come to see her as a heroine, just as I did. And maybe the next time you run into a real-life bully, you'll want to dig in and see what their backstory is. Afterall, readers understand that what looks like a villain at first glance, just might be/become a hero!

For those of you wondering if more installments will be available in the *Riches & Royals* series, I can answer with an affirmative YES! Look for stories from Apollo Mikolas (first see in *Reluctantly Royal*) and Jimmy O'Shea (first seen in *Read My Lips*).

While you are waiting for the next installment, can I ask for your help?

Reviews and word-of-mouth are critical for authors when it comes to finding new readers. Please consider leaving a review or even just a rating of the book at on-line retailers (you know who they are!), Good Reads, Book Bub, or wherever you go to find new books. Then tell two friends about the book and ask them to do the same!

Thank you from the bottom of my heart!

ABOUT THE AUTHOR

Photo Credit: RJRICE Photography
http://www.rjricephotography.com/

Kelle Z. Riley, writer, speaker, global traveler, Ph.D. chemist, and safety/martial arts expert has been featured in public forums that range from local Newspapers to National television. In addition to her works of fiction, a personal story was included in "Chicken Soup for the Soul: Living with Alzheimer's and Other Dementias."

Her fiction publications include cozy mysteries and contemporary romance.

In the Undercover Cat Mysteries a cupcake baking scientist turns sleuth—an much more. *The Cupcake Caper, Shaken, Not Purred, The Tiger's Tale,* and *Studying Scarlett the Grey,* as well as free short stories set in the Undercover Cat world are available on Amazon or wherever books are sold.

In the *Riches and Royals* series, modern career women fall for princes-in-disguise, only to discover that *"happily ever after"* isn't guaranteed. Can love turn their cautionary tale into a glittering fairy tale, or will their hearts shatter like glass slippers?

A former Golden Heart Finalist, Kelle resides in Chattanooga, TN. She is the past program chair and popular speaker for the Chattanooga Writer's Guild, a member of Sisters in Crime, Romance Writers' of America and various local chapters. When not writing, she can be found pursuing passions such as being a self-defense instructor, a Master Gardener, and a full time chemist with numerous professional publications and U.S. patents.

To learn more about the Riches & Royals world, as well as Kelle's other works, visit www.kellezriley.net or scan the code below.

Book one of Riches & Royals: Read My Lips
Book two of Riches & Royals: Royally Scandalized
Book three of Riches & Royals: Reluctantly Royal
Book four of Riches & Royals: Counterfeit Commoner

Join Kelle's newsletter list to get announcements for FREE short stories, upcoming releases, deleted scenes, and inside information on how the Kingdom of Melesia was born!

 www.kellezriley.net

 www.facebook.com/kellezriley

 www.twitter.com/kellezriley